THE UNION QUILTERS

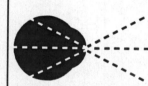

This Large Print Book carries the
Seal of Approval of N.A.V.H.

AN ELM CREEK QUILTS NOVEL

THE UNION QUILTERS

JENNIFER CHIAVERINI

LARGE PRINT PRESS
A part of Gale, Cengage Learning

GALE
CENGAGE Learning·

Detroit • New York • San Francisco • New Haven, Conn • Waterville, Maine • London

GALE
CENGAGE Learning·

LIBRARY OF CONGRESS CATALOGING-IN-PUBLICATION DATA

Chiaverini, Jennifer.
    The Union quilters : an Elm Creek quilts novel / by Jennifer Chiaverini.
        p. cm. — (Thorndike Press large print core)
    "An Elm Creek quilts novel."
    ISBN-13: 978-1-4104-3332-9 (hardcover)
    ISBN-10: 1-4104-3332-3 (hardcover)
    1. Quiltmakers—Fiction. 2. Quilting—Fiction. 3. Pennsylvania—
History—Civil War, 1861–1865—Fiction. 4. City and town life—
Pennsylvania—History—19th century—Fiction. 5. Domestic fiction.
6. Large type books. I. Title.
PS3553.H473U65 2011
813'.54—dc22   2010046040

ISBN 13: 978-1-59413-512-5 (pbk. : alk. paper)
ISBN 10: 1-59413-512-6 (pbk. : alk. paper)

Published in 2012 by arrangement with Dutton, a member of Penguin Group (USA) Inc.

Printed in the United States of America
2 3 4 5 6   16 15 14 13 12

FD142

To Jody Ewing, in gratitude

ACKNOWLEDGMENTS

I am deeply grateful to Denise Roy, Maria Massie, and everyone at Dutton for their contributions to *The Union Quilters* and the Elm Creek Quilts series.

I am indebted to the Wisconsin Historical Society and their librarians and staff for providing excellent research resources for this book, and to Dr. Paul A. Cimbala of Fordham University for his insightful responses to my questions about African American soldiers and the United States Veterans Reserve Corps.

Many thanks to Geraldine Neidenbach, Heather Neidenbach, Marty Chiaverini, and Brian Grover, whose careful readings and thoughtful questions offered essential help throughout the writing of this book, and to Nic Neidenbach, who never failed to assist me with computer problems at crucial moments. Thanks also to my teammates from Just For Kicks, Ignition, and Oh-Thirty —

especially Marty Gustafson, Laura Wolf, and Jean Mescher — for offering camaraderie, friendship, stress relief, encouragement, insomnia remedies, and the occasional bag of homegrown tomatoes. My sons, Nicholas and Michael, enrich my life with laughter, joy, and love every day, and I am forever thankful.

Finally, the following works proved invaluable during my research: Samuel P. Bates, *History of the Pennsylvania Volunteers, 1861–5; Prepared in Compliance with Acts of the Legislature.* Volumes II and X (Harrisburg, PA: B. Singerly, 1871); William Blair and William Pencak, eds., *Making and Remaking Pennsylvania's Civil War* (University Park, PA: The Pennsylvania State University Press, 2001); F. F. Cavada, *Libby Life: Experiences of a Prisoner of War in Richmond, Va., 1863–64, by Lieut.-Colonel F. F. Cavada, U. S. V.* (Philadelphia: J. B. Lippincott & Co., 1865); Paul A. Cimbala and Randall M. Miller, eds., *An Uncommon Time: The Civil War and the Northern Home Front* (New York: Fordham University Press, 2002); Paul A. Cimbala and Randall M. Miller, eds., *Union Soldiers and the Northern Home Front: Wartime Experiences, Postwar Adjustments* (New York: Fordham University Press, 2002); Michael A. Dreese, *The Hospi-*

tal on Seminary Ridge at the Battle of Gettysburg (Jefferson, NC: McFarland & Company, 2005); J. Franklin Dyer, *The Journal of a Civil War Surgeon* (Lincoln, NE: University of Nebraska Press, 2003); Tom Huntington, *Pennsylvania Civil War Trails: The Guide to Battle Sites, Monuments, Museums and Towns* (Mechanicsburg, PA: Stackpole Books, 2007); Diane Ragan, *Grand Army of the Republic Department of Pennsylvania. Personal War Sketches of the African American Members of Col. Robert G. Shaw Post No. 206* (Pittsburgh, PA: Western Pennsylvania Genealogical Society, 2003); John F. Schmutz, *The Battle of the Crater: A Complete History* (Jefferson, NC: McFarland & Company, 2009); Keith Wilson, ed., *Honor in Command: Lt. Freeman S. Bowley's Civil War Service in the 30th United States Colored Infantry* (Gainesville, FL: University Press of Florida, 2006). Jinny Beyer's outstanding and comprehensive encyclopedia of pieced blocks, *The Quilter's Album of Patchwork Patterns* (Elmhurst, IL: Breckling Press, 2009) inspired several of the designs used in Melanie Marder Parks's beautiful endpapers, and I believe no quilter's library is complete without it.

"In this extraordinary war, extraordinary developments have manifested themselves, such as have not been seen in former wars; and amongst these manifestations nothing has been more remarkable than these fairs for relief of suffering soldiers and their families. And the chief agents in these fairs are the women of America.

"I am not accustomed to the use of language of eulogy; I have never studied the art of paying compliments to women; but I must say, that if all that has been said by orators and poets since the creation of the world in the praise of women were applied to the women of America, it would not do them justice for their conduct during this war. I will close by saying God Bless the women of America."

President Abraham Lincoln
Remarks at the closing of the
U.S. Sanitary Commission Fair
Washington, D.C., March 18, 1864

CHAPTER ONE

1861

Dorothea tied up the sack of salt pork and hard bread — enough for a week if Thomas didn't find some poor soul in greater need to share with — and pressed the back of her hand to her forehead, taking a deep breath, fighting to still the whirl of thoughts. She knew she had forgotten something, something essential, something her husband would suffer without on the long marches through hostile lands, on the cold, lonely nights away from home. If she remembered what it was after he left the Elm Creek Valley, after he crossed the pass through Dutch Mountain with the other brave and patriotic men who had decided to answer Mr. Lincoln's call to arms, it would do him no good whatsoever. Though he was the love of her life and her most cherished friend, she could not follow him into war.

From behind her came the sound of a

muffled sob, and Mrs. Hennessey emerged from the pantry, wiping her eyes with the corner of her apron. At the sight of the housekeeper's tears, Dorothea pressed her lips together and inhaled sharply, briskly tightening the knot on the sack of provisions. She would not weep; she must not weep. Thomas had asked her for only that as he held her after they had made love the night before, that she not mourn him until he was truly gone. "I have every intention of returning to you," he had said, kissing her cheeks, her lips, her forehead, brushing her long brown locks gently off her face. "You must believe it too. Your hopes will sustain us both." In the semidarkness she had nodded, not trusting herself to speak. Thomas was not a superstitious man; he knew very well that men died in war, and the prayerful wishes of a devoted wife would offer him no protection from a Rebel minié ball. But neither would worry, and with baby Abigail to care for and many friends and neighbors looking to her in their worry and distress, she must choose confidence, hope, and determination. She could not, on the eve of his departure, distract Thomas with worries that she could not manage without him.

Mrs. Hennessey did not need to disguise

her true feelings. "A man like Mr. Nelson's got no business marching off to war," she said, her ruddy cheeks flushed with indignation, frenzied strands of curly gray-streaked auburn hair escaping the bun at the nape of her neck. A longtime employee of Thomas's parents, she had cared for Thomas since he was a boy in Philadelphia and had accompanied him when he came to Water's Ford to take over Two Bears Farm and run the town primary school twelve years before. "A man like him ought to be in Washington City running things, not risking his life scrapping with the rabble. Don't he have a farm to look after, and his book to write, and a family that needs his protection?"

"All the other soldiers have families and livelihoods too," Dorothea pointed out, as she had the first dozen times the proud and protective housekeeper had expressed that opinion. "They can't all stay home. Nor could Mr. Nelson both advise the president on matters of state and look after things around here."

Mrs. Hennessey dismissed that with a wave of her hand, as if to say a smart man like Thomas Nelson could figure a way around the impossibility of being in two places at once. "All I know is, you don't want him to go any more than I do, and he

15

wouldn't, if only you'd tell him about your condition."

Dorothea nearly dropped the bundle of food she had packed so carefully. "How did you —" But of course. Every Tuesday, Mrs. Hennessey did the washing. She would know that Dorothea was late. "You must not tell him. Promise me. It's much too early."

"Of course I won't breathe a word. It's not my place." Mrs. Hennessy gave her apron a vigorous tug, then hesitated, brushing off imaginary crumbs. "But if telling him would change his mind —"

"He might go anyway." Thomas believed the Union cause was just and noble, and he was not a man to sit safely at home while other men risked their lives for principles he held sacred. "Would you have him go into battle worried and distracted?"

"I wouldn't have him go at all, and neither would you." Mrs. Hennessey regarded her sharply, her blue eyes red and puffy from tears. "You and your parents, and all them folk from Drowned Farm —"

"Thrift Farm," Dorothea amended mildly, out of habit. As a child, she had lived with her parents and brother in a community of Transcendentalist Christians who had been enlightened ethicists and philosophers but

16

poor farmers. Though the farm had been lost to a flood years before, obliging Dorothea's family to move in with her cantankerous uncle Jacob, even newcomers to the Elm Creek Valley, like Mrs. Hennessey, considered it a fine subject for jokes.

"Pacifists, each and every one of you," Mrs. Hennessey declared. "Pacifists and abolitionists. You might as well be Quakers."

"Might as well," Dorothea agreed, setting the bundle of food beside the rest of the gear Thomas had left near the front door, wishing she could remember what she had forgotten to pack for his long and dangerous journey away from Two Bears Farm.

She found her husband in Abigail's room, standing silently beside her crib, stroking her soft, downy hair with a touch as light as a feather. She watched him from the doorway, his slim, wiry frame as familiar to her as her own limbs, his sandy hair boyishly thick, his beard neatly trimmed, bearing only a few threads of gray. His round spectacles caught a narrow shaft of sunlight that slipped between the drawn curtains. Blinking back tears, Dorothea came up behind him, wrapped her arms around his waist, and pressed her cheek to his back between his shoulder blades.

"I'm tempted to wake her," he murmured, clasping Dorothea's arms with one hand, resting the other upon Abigail's head, as pretty and fine as a porcelain doll's. "To say a proper good-bye, to hear her laugh one last time —"

"It won't be the last time you hear her laugh."

"I know, but my little baby will be gone by the time I return. She'll be walking, talking, a proper little girl rather than a babe in arms."

Dorothea almost blurted out her precious secret, but she had lost a baby early once before, and she was thirty-one, rather mature to be carrying only her second child. She could not stuff one last heavy burden of worry into his pack just before he set out. "The sooner you win this war for Mr. Lincoln," she said instead, "the younger she'll be when you come home."

"I'll get right to it, then."

Dorothea tightened her embrace. "There's no hurry."

He laughed softly, amused by her quick contradiction. "We can't miss the festivities. You and your friends worked too hard to make sure we had a rousing send-off."

"It was mostly Gerda's doing," said Dorothea. "Anneke too." Anneke Bergstrom was one of Dorothea's few friends with cause to celebrate that morning. Her husband, Hans, had no plans to enlist, and since he had never become a naturalized citizen after immigrating to the United States from Germany, he could not be drafted if the state failed to meet its recruitment quotas with volunteers. Gerda Bergstrom's emotions, however, were surely conflicted. Though she was likely relieved that her brother would be safe, she was thoroughly and irrevocably in love with Dorothea's brother, Jonathan, who intended to enlist as a regimental surgeon. The grand farewell in front of the courthouse in Water's Ford was intended to rally the men's spirits before they set off for Harrisburg to enlist, but perhaps it would also serve to stoke the women's courage. Preparations for the men's departure had occupied their time and thoughts for two weeks, but after the last notes of fife and drum faded and the banners and bunting were taken down and put away, many long, lonely, empty days would stretch ahead of those left behind.

"My modest beloved," said Thomas dryly, turning to embrace her. "Always giving the credit to others."

"The rally was Gerda's idea."

"Yes, but you organized the ladies of the

town, assigned tasks according to their abilities, kept everyone on schedule, and negotiated more than one truce between squabbling parties. I think Mrs. Hennessy perhaps chose the wrong Nelson to send to Washington City."

Dorothea smiled, wistfully, at the often-discussed suggestion, wishing once again that Thomas could go to Washington rather than to war. "I organized the ladies of my sewing circle," she acknowledged. "They organized their own neighbors and sisters and friends. I didn't do everything on my own."

"The ladies of this town would accomplish little outside their own homes without you to lead them." Thomas laced his fingers through hers and kissed the back of her hand. She loved his hands, their strength and tenderness, the farmer's calloused palms and the scholar's ink-stained fingertips. "You have a gift, my dear. Use it well. With their men gone, many of your friends will be at loose ends. You could encourage them, help them to be industrious —"

"Yes, I certainly will," she choked out, fighting back tears, forcing a smile. "I'll be as stern a taskmistress as I was once a teacher. I won't allow any of my friends a single idle moment to waste in worry. When you men return, you'll see how well we women managed in your absence, free at last of the yoke of male dominion."

His eyebrows rose. "You make me afraid to leave you."

"You may not recognize our town when you return, so marvelously will we transform it in your absence into a feminine utopia. When the war is over and you tally our accomplishments, you will no longer deny us the vote."

"You know very well that I could deny you nothing."

Then don't go, she almost asked, but she knew her arguments would not persuade him now where they had failed before. Though he considered himself a humanist, he did not share her philosophy of non-violence. He was willing to fight and sacrifice his own life if necessary to defend those he loved and to protect the noble principles he held most dear. Dorothea was prepared to give her own life on those same grounds, but she would not take another's life, and that was where their opinions diverged. What she dreaded most of all was that Thomas would not survive the war, but after that, what she feared most was that he would return to her entirely changed by the violence he had seen — seen, and inflicted.

21

Sighing, Thomas bent to kiss Abigail's cheek and led Dorothea from the bedroom, leaving the door ajar. Mrs. Hennessey met them at the foot of the stairs, red-eyed, and gave Thomas a fierce hug. "I'll say the rosary for you every night," she vowed. "God bless and keep you safe from harm." He thanked her quietly and asked her to take care of his family while he was away. She pressed her lips together and nodded before fleeing for the kitchen.

With a heavy heart, Dorothea helped Thomas gather his pack and provisions. She followed him to the barn, and as he hitched up the horses, she suddenly remembered. How could she have forgotten something so treasured, so essential to his comfort?

"I'll be right back," she gasped, hurrying back to the house. She startled Mrs. Hennessey, who sat at the kitchen table with her head in her hands, weeping openly, and raced upstairs, her heeled boots clattering on the wooden staircase. At the foot of their bed, she threw open the lid to the steamer trunk Uncle Jacob had bequeathed her and withdrew a quilt she had packed away for the summer. She draped it over the bed, sparing only a glance for the painstakingly arranged triangles and squares of Turkey red and Prussian blue and sun-bleached

muslin, some scraps
her household sewing
dressmaker friend and
sewing circle. She folde
lengthwise, quickly rolled
bundle, and tied it off with
ribbon she had been savin
When she returned outsid
the horses ready and waitin
silent and perplexed, as she p
into the back of the wagon
and provisions.

"It's the Dove in the Window
climbing onto the seat beside
gathered the reins. "I know it's y
ite."

"It's yours as well. I shouldn't tak
"It's hardly my favorite. I prefer o
ding quilt and the Delectable Moun
made for my uncle. But even if it w
ould rather you had it."
He shook his head. "It's too fine to
he road. It could be soiled or torn
Likely the army will issue us stur
s with our uniforms."
f they don't, or if those blankets are
Dorothea countered. "You'll be
r this quilt when winter comes,
an't appreciate it now."
iate it, all the more so becaus

I recall
of the c
"I am
face."
fought
quilt.
comfo
warm
He
"Ver
"You
later
U
nod
the
on
th
an
h
s

how hard you worked on it. Think
conditions we'll face —"

thinking of the conditions you'll
she felt wretched, helpless, but she
to keep her voice even. "Take the
It's not much to carry, and it'll
rt me to know that it's keeping you
when I can't."

fell silent, his eyes searching her face.
y well." He chirruped to the horses.
're right. If I don't take it, I'll regret it
."

nwilling to trust herself to speak, she
ded and pressed herself against him on
wagon seat, heartsick, resting her head
his shoulder, imagining she could feel
e warmth of his skin upon hers, his arm
ound her. She longed to lay her hea
s chest, pull the quilt over them h
leep, sleep until the war passed
ike a thundercloud, holding th
torrent until it cleared the m

After her sons fi
stance sent them ba
to scrub their faces
their ears before the
Sunday suits. She nev
town unless they were a
nd dressed in their best.

w
on t
lost.
blanke
"And
delayed?
grateful fo
if you

a respectable family, decent and hardworking, and if they needed to dress twice as fine as every white family in the valley to prove that point, she would do it. She wouldn't give anyone cause to look down on her boys, not when ignorant folk could invent plenty of fictitious reasons on their own.

She paced from the kitchen to the front room, calling up the stairs to the attic bedroom George and Joseph shared, to urge them to hurry, picking up darning and setting it down again, restless, keeping busy so she wouldn't have time to sit and think. She checked Abel's pack again, though of course nothing had fallen out or otherwise changed since the first five times she had checked it that morning. She wrung her hands, closed her eyes, and took a deep breath. Abel wanted to fight and would be restless and unhappy to stay at home while the battle raged on, and she knew better than anyone in the Elm Creek Valley that the cause was just.

At the sound of the boys' shoes on the attic stairs, her eyes flew open. She forced a smile as she turned to face them. "Why, don't you look fine," she said, straightening George's collar, smoothing a wrinkle on Joseph's suit coat. Usually the boys basked in her praise, but now they merely nodded and murmured, "Yes, ma'am," their voices subdued, their dark eyes solemn. Suddenly, Joseph blinked furiously as if he were fighting back tears. His elder brother, all of eleven years old, nudged him and shot him a look of warning. Joseph swallowed hard and looked at the floor, clutching the banister.

"It's gonna be all right," Constance assured them with more confidence than she felt. "He won't be gone long. You know what a crack shot your father is, especially with that powerful new rifle. He'll take out any Rebels in firing range before they have time to load their powder."

"They really gonna let him fight, Mama?" asked George.

"Course they will," said Joseph with a nine-year-old's confidence and innocence. "Didn't the newspaper say Pennsylvania has to send ninety thousand men? He's not too old."

Though Abel was fifteen years older than Constance, he was strong and vigorous and sharp-eyed, and while at forty-seven he would likely be one of the older men to enlist that day, he was certainly not too old to fight.

"They wouldn't turn him away because of

his age," George informed his brother, "but because he's colored."

Joseph's brow furrowed as he glanced from his brother to Constance and back. "But those colored men from Pittsburgh signed up. Father said so."

"They guarded a railroad," George retorted. "In the North. They didn't shoot at anyone."

"Hey, now," Constance admonished. "Don't you mock their service. That railroad moved soldiers and supplies and a lot more besides, and you'd better believe the Rebels would have been very happy to blow it up. Losing those railroads would cripple the North. Any service to the Union is honorable, whether it's guarding a railroad or firing a gun or patching up folks like Dr. Granger's gonna do."

"Yes, ma'am," said George, chastened, but uncertainty clouded his dark eyes. He surely remembered the two colored regiments that had formed in Philadelphia earlier in the spring — formed and dispersed when the Union refused to muster them in. Constance wished she could assure him that his father would be allowed to enlist alongside the other men of the Elm Creek Valley, but she couldn't. Until Abel wrote to her from the soldiers' camp and described the drills, the marching, the uniforms, she wouldn't believe that the Union would encourage a colored man to shoot at a white man, even a Rebel.

She placed her hands on her sons' shoulders and turned them toward the front room. "Check your father's pack one more time. Make sure his rifle's ready to go and he didn't forget his powder and bullets."

They nodded and obeyed. Gnawing on her lower lip, Constance balled her skirts in her fists and went to the bedroom she and Abel shared, but hesitated before entering. "Abel, you ready?" she asked as she opened the door. He had finished dressing in his best suit and stood motionless in front of the mirror above the bureau. It was old and cloudy, and offered a wavy, distorted image no matter what angle they regarded it from. Constance had learned to bob and weave and tilt her head and assemble the different glimpses in her mind, but she had long ago decided that her husband's admiring glances were a far more accurate measure of her appearance.

He quickly turned to smile at her as if embarrassed to be caught staring at himself in the mirror. "Just imagining what I might look like in a blue Union uniform."

She pictured a blue cap trimmed in gold

28

covering his short, graying black curls, his shoulders square and straight in a smart blue coat with a stiff collar and brass buttons up the front. "You'd look mighty fine." Catching her mistake, she said, more forcefully, "You *will* look fine."

He regarded her ruefully, understanding her doubts. "When the Twelfth Pennsylvania Volunteers organized in Allegheny County back in April, they took men of color."

"I know. I read the papers too."

"Company I, the Zouave Cadets under Captain George W. Tanner. They guarded the Northern Central Railroad from the Mason-Dixon Line all the way to Baltimore." He turned back to the mirror, adjusting his suit and squaring his shoulders. "They need men, Connie. Not just white men. When they see I'm a sharpshooter, they won't waste me on guarding some railroad depot or frying up corn cakes in a cookhouse away from the front lines."

"I'd rather they did." Constance sat down heavily on the edge of the bed, stroking the string-pieced star quilt she had brought with her out of Virginia, wrapped around her few worldly possessions. The piecing of it, begun after Abel had proposed and promised to buy her freedom, had given her hope in hard times, but the soft cottons and muted colors offered her little comfort now. "I don't want those white folks shooting at you, nor do I want them to capture you. What do you suppose they'd do with a colored man they catch down South in Union blue? If they don't kill you outright, they'll sell you so far south you'll never know freedom again. After a year as a slave, you might find yourself wishing they'd killed you."

He didn't know what slavery was like, not really. She had told him, and he had seen the nature of it on his visits south, but he didn't truly know the horror, the fear, the constant strain upon the spirit, because he had not lived it. Freeborn in a Northern city, he had bought land in central Pennsylvania and set himself up as a dairy farmer when she was still a girl. He traveled south to Virginia every few months to sell his cheeses, and Constance's mistress had been one of his best customers. Constance had not known what to think when the cheese man, freeborn and fifteen years her senior, began seeking her out in the tobacco fields or the curing barn to tell her about life in the North. He had brought her cheese, of course, and other gifts, and after a year of this odd courtship, he had begun to talk to her about running away. He had helped other slaves, he confided, and his home in the North was a station on the Underground Railroad. He knew the best routes and manners of deception to see her safely to the North. Fearful of capture and punishment, she had refused to hide in his wagon and escape with him, even after she had accepted his offer of marriage. It took years for Abel to save up the two thousand dollars her resentful master demanded, but eventually he had purchased her freedom and brought her to the Elm Creek Valley. He hated slavery as a Christian, as a colored man, and as a loving husband, but it was not only to end slavery that he wanted to fight.

Abel took her hands and gently pulled her to her feet. "If I lay down my life for my country, if hundreds or thousands of colored men do, our deaths will serve a greater purpose."

She wrenched her hands from his grasp. "You ask the wives and children of all those hundreds and thousands of colored men what they think, and I bet they'd say they'd rather have their menfolk alive and safe at home, and hang your greater purpose."

"Constance," he reproached her gently. "I don't want to die any more than the next fellow, but I do want to fight. Our people,

31

enslaved and free, North and South, need colored men like me to fight."

"I know." The Nelsons and the Grangers and the Bergstroms all said the same: If colored men fought for the United States, the nation would have no choice but to recognize them as full citizens of the land of their birth, to grant them all the rights and privileges established in the Constitution. Constance was proud of her husband and knew how he chafed at being treated as less of a man than their neighbors, but she had come to love him dearly since that long-ago day she had married him for security rather than affection, and she would not choose to sacrifice him to any cause, however noble.

"I know," she said again, and took his hand. "You'll make us all proud. Let's go or we'll be late. I don't want the boys to miss seeing the whole town cheering their father as you march off with the other soldiers. They'll never forget this day, not even when they're gray-haired old men, the war's long over, and slavery's just a memory."

She would let him go and cheer him on as loudly as any proud wife, but all the while she would pray the Union Army saw fit to waste his sharpshooter's eye on some safe, dull duty miles to the north of the nearest Confederate cannon.

■ ■ ■ ■

Gerda heard the cheerful strains of a Scottish march as she leaned out the second-story window of the courthouse, hanging on to the sill with one hand and the end of the last rolled banner with the other. "I'll toss it to you on three," she called to Prudence Nadelfrau, who nodded from the window above the far side of the portico. Unseen within, Gerda's sister-in-law, Anneke, held Prudence by the waist to keep her from tumbling into the street three stories below.

"Eins, zwei, drei!" Gerda threw the rolled end of the banner to Prudence, unfurling it as it flew through the air. Too late, Prudence made a startled grab for the free end, but grasped only empty air. Muttering under her breath, Gerda rolled up the banner as it blew gaily in the wind. With their luck, it would snag on the roof of the portico and tear.

"You said 'on three,' " Prudence protested. The faster they raced to finish their preparations, the more mistakes Prudence made, and the more frustrated Gerda became with her. " 'Dry' isn't 'three.' "

"I assumed that with a name like Nadelfrau, you'd know the German." The truth was, Gerda often slipped into her native tongue when distracted, upset, or fatigued, and at the moment, she was all three. In her foul mood, she was unwilling to admit that the fault was hers rather than her friend's. "Let's try again, one last time. One, two, three."

This time, Prudence anticipated the throw and caught the other end of the banner between her palms. Quickly they pulled it smooth and tied it securely to the drapery hooks with sturdy twine. A few impudent boys who had been watching from below and jeering the ladies' first half dozen failed attempts cheered and applauded before wandering off down the street in search of some other entertainment. For the adults, the banner and the rousing music signaled that it was almost time to begin, and they pressed forward into a semicircle at the base of the courthouse steps, where the mayor's assistant was setting up a podium. Somewhere in the courthouse, Gerda knew, the mayor himself was rehearsing his remarks, and elsewhere, throughout the town, mothers, daughters, wives, and sweethearts were preparing themselves for a bittersweet parting.

Carrying the spool of twine and her

second-best shears, Gerda met Anneke and Prudence in the hallway, her frustrations forgotten in her anticipation of the moment. They hurried downstairs to the foyer, where thirty-four of the most beautiful young women of the valley wore sashes of red, white, and blue embroidered with a name of one of the states. There had been some debate about whether only the twenty-three loyal states should be represented and not the eleven in rebellion, but Dorothea had decided that since the object of the war was a unified nation, the pageant should depict all of the United States. Near the doorway to the prison, Mary Schultz Currier was sorting out a disagreement between two young ladies who both wanted to portray Pennsylvania, and along the opposite wall, Mrs. Claverton was distributing baskets of late summer flowers to a dozen young girls while instructing them on the proper time and manner to toss them in the path of the departing soldiers. Mrs. Claverton's daughter, Charlotte, was by her side, holding fast to her young son's hand as she straightened one girl's bonnet and knelt to coax another to hold her basket so the blossoms didn't spill upon the floor. Her glossy black hair hung in glorious ringlets down her back, and although she hadn't announced her news to the rest of their sewing circle, Gerda suspected she was again with child — unless she was simply getting fat.

Except for those who, like Dorothea, were still occupied saying private farewells to their menfolk who intended to enlist, the ladies of the sewing circle bustled about, in and outside the courthouse, putting final touches on the rally now only moments away. Gerda wished she could steal a private moment alone with Jonathan to bid him a proper good-bye, but she knew it was unlikely. He knew her heart, she told herself resolutely, and she knew his, and no words they could exchange in the minutes before he set out could make their feelings any clearer to one other. They had promised to write as often as they could, although Gerda had prepared herself to send three letters for each one she received from the battlefield. A few days before, she had given Jonathan the gift of an ingenious writing case with a hard surface suitable to serve as a lap desk and compartments for paper, pens, nibs, and two small bottles of ink. She had doubted that he would be able to find them in the soldiers' camps or field hospitals and wanted to remove any potential impediment to their continued intercourse. He had thanked her profusely, and assured her that he could transport the writing case with his medical supplies by wagon and would not have to carry it on his back. "My first letter will be to you, to describe our camp," he had promised, knowing how she longed to share his experience, to witness the war through his eyes, the good and the bad, the mundane and the harrowing. She hoped in turn to offer him as much comfort and encouragement as the written word could provide.

They had both long believed that war was inevitable, their certainty going as far back as the previous December when South Carolina had seceded from the Union. In those days, most of their neighbors had believed that the standing national army could quickly and decisively quell any minor skirmishes that might erupt, and some northern newspapers pleaded for negotiations and appeasement.

Gerda felt as if she had held her breath all through that Christmas season and into the New Year, waiting for President Buchanan to declare war, although he had seemed inclined to sit out the rest of his term without taking action and to pass along the crisis to Mr. Lincoln once he took office. At times she marveled that life in Water's Ford went on as it always had. Neighbors called, and worked, and gossiped, and feuded, and made merry. Gerda took pride and pleasure in cooking three meals a day for herself, Hans, and Anneke, glad to be spared the tedious work of the household sewing, which thankfully Anneke enjoyed. She helped Anneke keep house and care for two-year-old David and Stephen, a pair of charming and delightful boys who got into everything their weary parents and distracted aunt forgot to put out of reach. And at least once a week, there was Jonathan.

Unless he was busy tending to an ailing neighbor, Jonathan came for supper every Saturday afternoon, as he had almost without interruption for years. He and Gerda would linger at the table hours after Anneke had cleared the dishes away, poring over the latest newspapers from Philadelphia and Baltimore and New York as well as the Copperhead rag out of Bellefonte, dissecting and debating every last detail until Hans cleared his throat and pointed out that unless Jonathan intended to stay the night, he should leave for home while his horse still had enough light to see by. But for all their talk and worry and waiting, day after day had passed with only increasingly agitated newspaper stories to suggest that South Carolina's secession had changed anything for the residents of their rural Pennsylvania valley. So Gerda had planned her spring garden by the warmth of the fireside and waited for winter to end, pondering the Union blockade of Charleston Harbor and wondering how much longer Major Robert Anderson's men would be able to hold out at Fort Sumter, their supplies and hopes for reinforcements dwindling after the *Star of the West* was turned back from Charleston Harbor.

Whenever the sewing circle had gathered at Two Bears Farm for a quilting bee, their conversation had quickly turned to the latest news from beyond the Elm Creek Valley. While many women of their acquaintance were content to think of Water's Ford as their entire world, the women of the sewing circle — the most well read and well informed of Gerda's acquaintance — knew their shelter was illusory. Surrounded by the rolling Appalachians, with the nearest train station a difficult half day's ride through the southern pass, they had often felt isolated from the outside world, but the threat against their nation had filled them with apprehension, for they had known that even if war did not find them in their homes, their men would go forth to meet it.

By the end of February, Mississippi,

Florida, Alabama, Georgia, Louisiana, and Texas had seceded from the Union and joined with South Carolina to form the Confederate States of America, giving the sewing circle much to speculate about and worry over. Letters from friends and family in those far-flung states had been passed around the circle and analyzed line by line. "To think, my cousin now lives in a foreign land," Charlotte had marveled as she handed Dorothea a letter recently arrived from North Carolina.

"It depends whether you consider their secession legitimate," Gerda had replied. "I would argue that secession is illegal and that therefore North Carolina remains a part of the United States."

Charlotte, who acquiesced too easily when challenged in debate and often agreed simply to be agreeable, merely shrugged, tossing her glossy black curls and frowning prettily. Beautiful Charlotte — complacent wife, happy mother, the object of Gerda's envy — exasperated Gerda most when she refused to engage her in argument.

In March, the women of the sewing circle had welcomed Mr. Lincoln's inauguration with relief and hope tempered by concern for how he would resolve the enormous challenges bequeathed to him by his predecessor. They were staunch Republicans one and all, and they would have voted for Mr. Lincoln in the last election had they been permitted. Dorothea, in fact, had tried, but had been turned away at the polls by the exasperated mayor, who had been warned of her intentions the day before.

Dorothea had told no one but her family and friends of her determination to cast her vote, which had convinced Gerda that a weak-willed member of their circle must have unwisely confided in her husband, whose loyalty to his sex had driven him to warn Mayor Bauer. Gerda had proposed that they question their friends subtly until the guilty party was compelled to confess, but Dorothea, not surprisingly, had objected. "One of our friends trusted her husband with my secret, and he betrayed her," Dorothea had said. "I can't fault any of our friends for mistakenly believing her husband to be trustworthy. How could any rebuke from me sting more than her sad discovery that he isn't?"

Gerda, who knew what it was to be betrayed by someone she loved, could not pursue the matter. The women of the sewing circle had stood by her in difficult times when less courageous women would have withdrawn their friendship.

Gerda, Hans, and Anneke had come to the Elm Creek Valley in 1856 after Hans had won title to a farm in a horse race. Dorothea and Thomas, their nearest neighbors, had become their first and most treasured friends. Anneke, a gifted seamstress, had admired Dorothea's quilt making so much that she copied one of her designs. Only after an unexpected arrival of a fugitive slave at their front door did the Bergstroms discover that the quilt hanging on the clothesline was a secret signal marking their home as a station on the Underground Railroad. Joanna — feverish from an untreated burn inflicted by her master with a flatiron, pregnant with his child — had become lost in a snowstorm on her way from Constance and Abel Wright's farm to Dorothea and Thomas Nelson's. Until Joanna stumbled into their care, the Bergstroms had been completely unaware of their friends' roles as stationmasters. Throughout the long, hazardous winter, the Bergstroms had sheltered Joanna, awaited the birth of her child, and devised a plan to spirit away mother and child to Canada when they were well and strong. As the months passed, Gerda had taught Joanna to read and they became friends. But just when freedom seemed imminent, Anneke, fearful for her own family's safety, was deceived into betraying their secret. Slave catchers stormed their home, dragged Joanna from her hiding place, bound her wrists, and led her stumbling after their horses as they rode off toward the southern pass, toward Virginia and slavery.

As Joanna was taken away, Gerda, Hans, the Nelsons, and the Wrights — including their two young sons — were arrested for defying the Fugitive Slave Law, a law mostly ignored in the free North. Only after their release a few days later did Gerda and Hans discover that in the confusion, the slave catchers had missed Joanna's infant son.

In the months that followed, the Bergstroms cared for Joanna's baby, passing off the light-skinned boy as the twin to Anneke's own son, born only a few weeks before him. To foster the illusion, Gerda led people to believe that the boy was her own illegitimate son by Jonathan — and since Jonathan never expressly denied it, for he had delivered the child and was as determined as the Bergstroms to protect him, that was as good as an admission of guilt for most people. The rumor spread swiftly, as rumors of a woman's shame always did, and although Jonathan never suffered for it, Gerda's reputation was destroyed forever. It did not help her that the arrests brought the town unexpected notoriety. As newspapers across the Northeast repeated the story of how local police had allowed Southern slave catchers to invade citizens' private homes, Creek's Crossing became synonymous with ignorance and mob rule. Civic leaders endeavored to correct the record by pointing out that all charges had been promptly dismissed as soon as the investigation concluded they had done no wrong, but their rebuttals never captured the imagination the way the scandal had, and Creek's Crossing's reputation never recovered. Only two months before South Carolina seceded from the Union, the hapless civic leaders ruled to change the town's name to Water's Ford, retaining the original sense of Creek's Crossing while setting aside the taint it had acquired. It remained to be seen whether their efforts would be rewarded, or even if the new name would be adapted into popular use. Elderly residents stubbornly insisted upon calling their town by the name it had borne all their lives; distant friends still mailed letters to Creek's Crossing and the letters still reached the post office on First Street as reliably as before.

Gerda, of course, could not change her name and quash the memory of the story she had concocted to conceal the truth about Joanna's son. Except for Dorothea and Anneke, even her friends in the sewing circle believed the lie she had devised to conceal another lie. They could have cast her out or quit the quilting circle rather than risk damaging their own reputations, but they had not. No one ever discussed the rumors about Gerda's secret shame in her presence, nor spoke of the boy as anything but Anneke's own son — not even Charlotte, who determinedly pretended to be unaware of the rumors that would forever bind Gerda and Jonathan as illicit lovers. As for the children, by the time they were old enough to understand the townspeople's thoughtless whispers, Gerda prayed Joanna would be free and reunited with her son, so she could explain the truth to him herself.

Finding Joanna had become the ruling passion of Gerda's life. For more than two years, she had written at least once a week to Joanna's owner, Josiah Chester at Greenfields Plantation in Wentworth County, Virginia, to inquire about her captive friend. More recently, after she had saved up enough money, she had also offered to purchase Joanna's freedom. She had yet to receive a single word in reply. Her brother and most of her friends urged her to give up her fruitless quest, but she could not accept Joanna as lost forever.

War might thwart Gerda's attempts to find Joanna and purchase her freedom, but a Union victory would hasten the abolition of slavery. Perhaps for the immediate future, Josiah Chester could refuse to ransom a single slave, but he would be powerless to prevent Joanna from returning to Elm Creek Farm if slavery were destroyed altogether. Knowing that the war would hasten the demise of slavery made it easier to accept Jonathan's enlistment — that, and her confidence that he would be relatively safe, a mile or more behind the front lines in a field hospital.

A sudden flurry of activity as Mayor Bauer emerged from his office roused Gerda from her reverie. "Help Charlotte and her mother get the girls in place," she instructed Anneke and Prudence, wishing she possessed half of Dorothea's calm authority. All would be in order if Dorothea were there. "I'll help Mary sort out this nonsense between Pennsylvania and New Jersey."

Not five minutes later, the pretty young women in their appropriate sashes took their places on the courthouse steps and recited their lines with patriotic passion. High above them, the banner Gerda and

Prudence had hung declared, "Pennsylvania for the Union Forever." Red, white, and blue bunting graced every window up and down High Street, and the entire block was filled with people, young and old, waving flags and cheering. By Gerda's estimation, a good fifth of the men were dressed for travel. Scanning the crowd, she spotted her friend Eliza Stokey making her way through the crowd to join her husband, Charley. He was entertaining his friends with some story or joke or another, the fine line of a faded scar running from temple to jaw, the remnant of a harvesting accident with a scythe, barely visible in his thick blond beard. Mary Schultz Currier had also left the courthouse and had joined her husband, Abner, a few feet from the podium, where they would enjoy an excellent view of the pageant. Gerda wondered if Mary's father intended to come out of retirement and resume control of Schultz's Printers during Abner's absence. If Mr. Schultz did not, what would become of the newspaper? Surely they needed the *Water's Ford Register* at wartime more than ever. Across the street, Constance stood soberly with her husband and sons near the back of the crowd. Abel rocked back and forth on his heels and threw back his shoulders as if he couldn't wait to depart, while his boys eagerly took in the spectacle without straying more than a few paces from their father's side. Alone amidst the celebration, Gerda's brother Hans leaned against a post at the end of the block, his arms folded over his chest, his expression one of resigned bemusement. When his eyes met Gerda's, he grinned, doffed his hat, and offered her an elegant, sweeping bow. She frowned and shook her head in disapproval before returning his grin. He was incorrigible and irreverent, but she couldn't help adoring him.

Gerda estimated that nearly every citizen of Water's Ford and many from surrounding towns had turned out for the occasion, and she quickly found herself swept up in their patriotic fervor. After the pageant concluded, the band struck up "Hail Columbia," and the mayor was introduced to enthusiastic applause. He spoke for a half hour about the importance of preserving the Union, and of heeding the call to arms to fight for liberty and freedom, and of the noble courage of Pennsylvania's brave youth, who would gladly offer up their lives for their country. It was a stirring speech, or at least the crowd seemed to appreciate it, but Gerda, searching for Dorothea and Jonathan, could not have recited back a single phrase. As her friends and neighbors and strangers from throughout the valley cheered and waved flags and tossed hats in the air and clapped in time with the band, her heart pounded with the realization that war was no longer merely a foreboding subject for lively debate around the dinner table and sewing circle. War had come, and Jonathan was leaving, and she might never see him again.

Her throat constricted as the Lutheran and Methodist ministers took the podium together to offer a joint benediction for the brave men who would soon depart the Elm Creek Valley, some perhaps forever. As the young girls showered the volunteers with late summer blossoms, the men formed ranks in the street in front of the courthouse, rucksacks on their backs or bags slung over their shoulders, the crowd parting before them. Abner fell in, as did Abel, as did one man after another, some perhaps who had not intended to enlist that day but had succumbed to the fevered nationalism of the moment. Gerda searched the men's faces, praying for one last glimpse of Jonathan before he marched off to war, but she despaired of finding him in time.

A hand closed around her elbow. "Gerda." With a gasp she spun to face him, her beloved Jonathan, and without thinking she flung her arms around him. "I thought you had gone," she murmured, her lips brushing his neck. She smelled rainwater and shaving soap, and the new wool of his long overcoat.

"Without saying good-bye?" He held her for the briefest of moments, then released her and gave her a look of mock reproach. "You'd never let me hear the end of it."

A cheer went up from the crowd as the men began to march away. "Shouldn't you —" Gerda broke off, unwilling to prompt him to go.

Jonathan grinned and spoke close to her ear so that she would hear him above the din. "This is mostly for show," he confided. "Those of us with horses are riding to Lewistown. Mine's tied up on Church Street with Thomas's, out of the way of this throng. Hans offered to accompany us as far as the camp, and he'll bring the horses home."

Hans had not mentioned this to Gerda, or, she suspected, to Anneke. But riding or walking, Jonathan would be leaving soon. Boldly she reached for his hand, not caring who in the weeping, shouting, cheering throng might observe them. "Take good care of yourself," she implored. "Stay out of

50

harm's way as best you can."

"No one would fire upon a hospital," he assured her. "Rebels or not, they're still civilized men, and they'll respect the rules of war."

She nodded, but her heart sank. "Come back sound and soon." She meant *Come home safe to me,* and when he held her gaze and nodded, she knew he understood.

Suddenly a sweet cry pierced the din. "Papa!"

Gerda and Jonathan turned toward the courthouse just as a dark-haired boy jumped the bottom two steps and plowed into Jonathan, wrapping his arms around his legs. "Robert," Jonathan cried joyfully, laughing as he pried the boy loose and swung him into the air. "I thought you'd marched off with the soldiers."

With a pang, Gerda watched as Robert placed his hands on his father's cheeks and regarded him solemnly. "Are you going to shoot the bad Rebels, Papa?"

"No, I'm going to stitch people up and give them medicine and bandages just as I do here at home." Jonathan caught Gerda's eye and shook his head, amused, but Gerda found no merriment in the scene and could not manage even a halfhearted smile. Glancing past the father and son, Gerda caught

51

sight of Charlotte descending the court-house steps, her lips set in a line of displeasure, her porcelain skin flushed pink, her ebony ringlets spilling down her back from beneath her best bonnet. Gerda stepped back, putting a discreet distance between herself and Jonathan, her heart sinking as she realized the time for their private farewell had come and gone.

Charlotte tucked her small, gloved hand into the crook of her husband's elbow. "My brother found the other bottle of morphine just where you said it would be," she said, acknowledging Gerda with a nod and laying a hand upon the almost imperceptible swell of her belly. Painful realization seared Gerda: Charlotte *was* with child again. "He wrapped it in cloth and packed it in your saddlebag. It should be safe until you can move it to your satchel."

"Good man," said Jonathan, patting her hand in approval and tousling their son's thick hair, as black as Charlotte's own.

He spared Gerda one last glance over his shoulder as Charlotte led him off to where the rest of their family waited to say one last good-bye. Alone and bereft at the foot of the stairs, insensible to the shouts and tearful farewells all around her, Gerda watched until the crowd closed around them.

Caught up in the zeal of the assembly, Anneke waved her flag and cheered as the men marched off down High Street, tears of pride and apprehension in her eyes. The shouts of friends and neighbors and strangers carried on until the enlistees rounded the corner and disappeared. Before long, even the sound of their footfalls on the hardpacked dirt road faded. Only then did the women and old men and children left behind lower their flags and voices, collect themselves, gather up children who had wandered off, and disperse. Some chatted as they departed for houses or farms, others seemed vaguely perplexed, as if they had not considered that they would need to make any other plans for the rest of the day. Eventually, except for the usual traffic of townsfolk with errands at the post office or market, the streets were quiet, littered with trampled flower petals and discarded handbills. The ladies of the sewing circle and their children old enough to assist remained behind to take down the bunting, roll up the banners, and collect the assorted flags, gloves, and other articles dropped in the press of the crowd and forgotten.

Anneke spotted Dorothea on the courthouse steps, thanking the mayor for his speech, which Anneke had found particularly stirring. Often she had been tempted to glance over her shoulder to the lamppost where Hans stood, to see if he had been moved by the impassioned call to arms, but she did not want to draw attention to him. Instead she kept her gaze resolutely fixed on the mayor.

"Perhaps I should pack a rucksack for you just in case you change your mind at the rally," she had suggested after breakfast earlier that morning. Amused, Hans had assured her that he would not change his mind, not at the rally, not ever, and he was heartily sorry that the thought of his continued presence around the house vexed her so. Stung, she had not spoken another word to him before she departed to prepare for the rally, had not even smiled at his sweet, cajoling attempts to soothe her temper. How could he pretend to misunderstand her on such a serious occasion? Of course she didn't want him to go, especially in her delicate condition, nor did she doubt his courage. But when all the other men were off fighting for their country, how could he remain safe at home and not worry that their neighbors would consider him a Copperhead — against the Union and willing to concede anything and everything to make peace with the South — or even worse, a coward?

Spotting a pile of cloth near the court-house door, Anneke lifted her skirts and climbed the stairs to investigate, only to discover several of the sashes she had embroidered so painstakingly, all bearing the names of Southern states. Their wearers had probably discarded them with loyal disgust immediately following the pageant. As Anneke folded the sashes, she spied Charlotte on the grassy corner below, weeping in the arms of her mother, who patted her on the back and murmured words of comfort. Her conversation with the mayor finished, Dorothea hurried over to console her sister-in-law. Poor Dorothea, who had bade farewell to a brother as well as a husband, and yet still attended to another's comfort before her own. Anneke's heart went out to her friends, but she felt helpless to offer them condolences when she was not suffering as they were.

"Look at her, sobbing like a child, as if she were the only woman to see a loved one off today," said Gerda in an undertone, joining Anneke on the portico. Gathering up her skirts in one hand, she stooped down to pick up the last three discarded sashes —

Alabama, Texas, and Florida — and briskly folded them. Her long, brown hair, her only beauty, was parted neatly in the middle and gathered in a wide bun at the nape of her neck. The jewel neckline and wide sleeves of her brown wool dress improved her thin, lanky figure — Anneke had sewn it herself — but nothing could ameliorate Gerda's sharp, narrow features, especially when she was reminded that the man she loved was happily married to someone else. In those moments her eyes, usually bright with intelligence and wit, grew hard, her mouth pinched into a thin, bitter line, and she looked every bit the vinegary spinster Anneke had prayed she would not become. Why Gerda had thrown her youth away on a man who had courted her while secretly engaged to another, and why Jonathan continued to call on Gerda and dine weekly with the Bergstroms as if he were an eligible bachelor, Anneke would never understand. Why Charlotte tolerated such carrying on was another mystery. If Hans paid such attention to another woman — but of course he never would. Hans had adored her from the moment he spotted her fresh off the boat in the immigration depot at Castle Garden in lower Manhattan, just as Anneke had come to adore him.

How foolish her spat with Hans seemed when she considered what a true and steadfast husband he had been to her for so many years. She wished she could go to him that very minute, humbled and contrite, and apologize for implying he should act contrary to his principles merely so the neighbors would not think less of them. But her apologies would have to wait until Hans returned from Lewistown with his friends' horses. Anneke would have her husband at home tonight, unlike so many of her acquaintance, and he would be home to see the birth of their child, unlike Jonathan when Charlotte delivered.

"Leave Charlotte alone," she rebuked Gerda quietly. "I would be sobbing twice as hard if I were in her place."

Gerda opened her mouth to speak but thought better of it and frowned, busying herself with folding the last of the abandoned sashes. Anneke knew that her sister-in-law had almost declared that she *was* in Charlotte's place, and *she* wasn't making a spectacle of herself with childish tears. The bitter truth was that although Gerda loved Jonathan, she wasn't in Charlotte's place and never could be, and that was the defining tragedy of her life.

Or rather, one of two defining tragedies.

"What time does Mrs. Craigmile expect us to collect the children?" asked Gerda, glancing up and down the block as if estimating the amount of work remaining. "I wanted to mail a letter."

"We have time to stop at the post office," Anneke assured her, adding her folded sashes to those in Gerda's basket. Hans had long ago grown exasperated with his sister's futile quest to find Joanna, and even Dorothea worried that her persistent fixation would damage her health. Anneke alone never discouraged her. How could she, when it was her fault Joanna had been recaptured? The guilt and shame would never leave her, although blessedly, Gerda never rebuked her for her betrayal, not since the day Gerda was released from prison and Anneke had begged forgiveness. Now all Anneke could do to atone for her terrible mistake was to love Joanna's son and raise him as her own, a blessed obligation that grew easier each day, as it seemed less and less likely that he would someday be taken from her by his real mother. Unlike Gerda, she no longer believed Joanna would return to claim her son. Hans and Anneke were his only parents now.

When the trappings of the rally were cleared away, Dorothea gathered the ladies of her sewing circle at the foot of the courthouse stairs, praised them for their hard work, and declared the rally an unqualified success. "Take heart," she encouraged them as they parted. "We have much to do to support our men and all those who serve our country. We must not give in to loneliness and grief."

"We won't all be lonely," someone muttered. Anneke stiffened but refrained from turning her head to see who had spoken. Who had it been? Eliza, a recent bride? Mrs. Barrows, whose husband had astonishingly shaken off his usual lethargy to enlist with his two eldest sons?

She felt a hand squeeze hers and assumed it was Gerda offering her support, until Constance said in an undertone, "Don't you mind her. That's her sorrow talking."

Anneke nodded. She had expected criticism and envy as word of Hans's refusal to enlist spread, but not so soon, and not among friends.

Gerda's errand at the post office took only a moment — no letter from Josiah Chester's Virginia plantation awaited her, but three out-of-town newspapers did — so Gerda suggested that they stop at Schultz's Printers to inquire about the fate of their own local paper. Mary, Dorothea's childhood friend and a founding member of Dorothea's sewing circle, assured them that her father would not allow the *Water's Ford Register* to founder while Abner was away. She managed a wan smile as she caught sight of their nearest competitor's journal folded in Gerda's basket beside *The New York Times* and the *Philadelphia Evening Herald.* "You won't like what the Bellefonte *Democratic Watchman* has to say about Mr. Lincoln," she warned.

"Gerda never likes anything that paper says," Anneke replied. "And yet she insists upon reading it, even though it only upsets her."

"It's important to know the opposition's arguments," said Gerda. "How else will I refute them?"

"Rest assured our newspaper will remain staunchly in favor of the Union," said Mary. "I also intend to print letters from the soldiers, so if you receive any you wouldn't mind sharing — not from your husbands, of course, since Hans didn't go and Gerda doesn't have one, and both of your sons are too young — I mean, Anneke, *your* sons are *both* too young —" She clasped a hand to her forehead, distressed. "I'm sorry. I don't know what I'm saying. Forgive me. With Abner gone —"

"We understand." Anneke took Gerda's arm and nudged her toward the door. "There's nothing to forgive. We'll see you at Dorothea's on Tuesday."

Mary nodded distractedly as they quickly left the printers. "No one knows quite what to say to us anymore, do they?" mused Gerda. "You, the wife of a wartime pacifist, and me, the spinster adulteress." Inspired, she dug into her basket and riffled through the sashes. "Perhaps I should wear an embroidered red *A* upon my bosom. Ah! Alabama will do nicely, if I pick out the other stitches."

"I don't see how you can find this amusing," said Anneke, hastening to the vacant lot behind the church, where they had left the team and wagon. With her longer legs and vigorous constitution, Gerda quickly caught up to her. "You shouldn't speak of Hans as a 'wartime pacifist,' as if he adopted his convictions recently for mere convenience."

"I've known Hans all his life, and he never mentioned these convictions before."

"Well, when would the subject have come up, except at wartime?" Anneke climbed onto the wagon seat, leaving the care of the horses to Gerda. "Didn't Our Creator tell the people of Moses, 'Thou shalt not kill'?

61

Didn't our Lord Jesus tell us, 'Turn the other cheek?' We shouldn't wonder why Hans isn't going to war but rather question why any true Christian would."

"I never considered Hans particularly devout." Gerda seated herself beside Anneke and took up the reins. "I also recall quite clearly several occasions when your peaceful Christian came home with bloody knuckles and black eyes."

"A boy's scraps with other boys," Anneke countered. "Since then, he's put aside childish things."

"That may be, but I've never heard my brother cite a devotion to the peace of Christ as his reason for refusing to enlist."

Anneke hadn't either, if only because Hans had never given her any reason for his choice. "I'm sorry that the thought of his continued presence around the house vexes you so."

Gerda sighed and chirruped to the horses. "Don't be petulant. I'm thankful he'll be safe, and you know it."

Anneke did know it, and wished that the words had sounded as bitingly witty as when Hans had spoken them.

Soon they were on their way to pick up the children from the kind neighbor who had offered to watch them during the rally, and then onward to home. The horses, a beautifully matched chestnut stallion and mare, knew the route well and needed little direction from Gerda as they followed the road south from Water's Ford along Elm Creek.

Gerda frowned thoughtfully as they passed Two Bears Farm. The recently harvested fields had been shorn bare of all but broken stalks of corn and barley, giving the white clapboard house at the top of the hill a forlorn look of barren midwinter. Near the barn, one of the Nelsons' hired hands was watering a horse, suggesting that Dorothea had already returned and was inside the house, alone except for baby Abigail and the housekeeper.

"Dorothea doesn't want me to offer to buy Joanna's freedom from Josiah Chester," said Gerda suddenly.

"Why ever not?"

"She believes that putting money into a slaveholder's hands rewards him for his evil deeds and endorses the South's 'peculiar institution.' "

"And what do you believe?"

"I believe that in the absence of simple human decency, avarice can be an effective motivator." As they rode on, the Nelson house disappeared behind a thick stand of oaks divided by the abrupt zigzag of a worm fence marking the boundary between their land and the Bergstroms'. "However, I told her I'd be willing to debate the issue all she liked once Joanna was safe in the North. She smiled — you know that smile of hers — and reminded me that the best time for debate and discussion is before one takes action. How else will rational people know whether they've made the right decision?"

Anneke shrugged. "By the result, of course."

"That's what I told her," said Gerda, "which prompted her to remind me that there are many paths to the same destination, and not all are fit to travel."

Anneke knew Dorothea had once been a schoolteacher, but did every conversation have to become a lesson? "I think you had it right. Get Joanna free and safe however you must, and debate philosophy later. Josiah Chester will own slaves with or without your money in his pocket. Why shouldn't you buy Joanna from him, if that's the best and swiftest way to make her free?"

"But what if Josiah Chester uses my money to buy rifles for Confederate soldiers, prolonging the war and thus slavery for others?"

Suddenly, Anneke understood what was

happening, and she fixed Gerda with a level stare. "I realize you miss Jonathan, but don't think for a moment that I will endure months of acting as his surrogate. Unlike the two of you, I don't argue for sport."

Gerda burst out laughing. The mare's ears flicked in their direction, but the horses were too well trained to shy or break trot. "I'll remember that," Gerda gasped as she struggled to compose herself. "You, a replacement for Jonathan, indeed."

Anneke muffled a sigh and took in the passing scenery.

Hans had told them not to expect him back for hours, so while Anneke tended to her chores and played with the boys in the yard, Gerda fixed a simple supper of potato pancakes and stewed greens, keeping some back to serve her brother later. It was after dusk when he finally returned home. At the sound of the horses' hooves, Anneke set aside her sewing and Gerda her book and they both carried lanterns out to the barn to meet him.

He was weary from his long journey over the southern pass to Lewistown and back, so after embracing him and kissing him fondly to show that the morning's argument was forgiven, Anneke refrained from querying him too much while he tended to the horses — his own, Thomas's, and Jonathan's. Abel's was not among them, she noticed. Hans had passed the Wright farm on the way home, and had probably gone ahead and left Abel's horse there, although the arrangement had been to return the horses the following day. When Gerda did not show Anneke's restraint and began peppering him with questions, Anneke suggested rather firmly that she go inside and prepare Hans's supper. As his sister hurried off, Hans thanked Anneke wearily and fell silent, his brow furrowing as he watered and unsaddled the horses. Anneke set down the lantern and fetched the currycomb, wondering if he regretted his decision not to enlist.

Later, after he had eaten and rested, he sighed, pushed his chair back from the table, stretched his legs in front of him, and described what he had seen in Lewistown. Men from all over the county had gathered to sign their names and put on Union blue. The men of the Elm Creek Valley had been assigned to Company L of the 49th Pennsylvania Volunteers, and as a regimental surgeon had already been appointed, Jonathan had been named one of his assistants. The next day they would join up with the rest of the regiment at Camp Curtin in Harrisburg, where they would await orders and prepare for war.

"They're staying in Harrisburg?" asked Gerda, her face lighting up with hope.

"For now," said Hans. "I don't know how long."

"We could visit them," Gerda exclaimed. "Dorothea and I, Constance, Mary — all the ladies of the sewing circle. We could carry with us anything they might have left behind or didn't realize they needed. You saw the camp, Hans. You can advise us what to take." She touched Anneke on the forearm. "You wouldn't need to go, of course, not with the boys to mind and Hans here at home, and your delicate condition."

Anneke nodded, relieved to be spared the trip. "I'll do whatever else I can to help you prepare. If any of our friends need any sewing or knitting for their husbands finished, or if Constance wants her sons to stay with us while she's away — that would be all right with you, wouldn't it, Hans?"

"They'll likely move on before you could get organized." Then Hans winced, raked a hand through his thick brown hair, and rested his elbows on his knees. "In any case, Constance wouldn't need us to watch her sons because she wouldn't be traveling with you."

"Why not?" said Anneke. A glance to Gerda showed that she was equally perplexed.

"They didn't let Abel enlist," said Hans. "He argued, his friends spoke up for him, but in the end they wouldn't let him put pen to paper. I don't want war, you know that, but to turn away a sharpshooter, a brave man, a good loyal Unionist, all because of the color of his skin —" Hans shook his head. "Foolishness, utter foolishness, and it may cost the Union the war."

Anneke could picture the scene vividly, and yet it was incomprehensible. Until that moment, she had thought the Union cause just and noble, their army led by wise and courageous men, and victory certain. The officers' hubris shocked her, transformed all her confidence into doubt. How could the Union afford to turn away not only a single willing and able man, but thousands, thereby hindering the very cause they all urgently wanted to serve?

She wondered if Constance were at that very moment praising God for restoring her husband to her so unexpectedly, or if she were cursing the foolish officers who had shamed the man she loved by sending him away.

CHAPTER TWO

George and Joseph were first delighted and then puzzled to discover their father in the barn when they rose at dawn to do their chores. Constance wasn't sure how Abel explained matters to them, but when they returned inside for breakfast, their sweet faces cloudy and brows furrowed, her heart sank. Abel would not have made false excuses but would have given them the plain, hard truth: As badly as the nation needed soldiers, the Union Army had not wanted their father because he was colored. Young boys should see the whole world open to them, but almost daily she witnessed her sons' expectations shrink little by little. Their father would never appear less of a man in their eyes — to them he would always be the hero who had rescued their mama from an evil slave owner and brought her to freedom — but as they grew, how would they endure the restrictions and prohibitions that had chafed their father all his life? Already, Abel spoke to her in confidence about saving enough money to help the boys get a good start out west when they were grown. "I want them to have opportunities I didn't," he had said the last time he put a silver dollar in the iron strongbox he kept hidden beneath a loose floorboard in the kitchen.

Constance agreed that they should put money aside for their sons' future, but not that George and Joseph should leave Pennsylvania. How could Abel be sure the West would be any better for colored men than the East? The same laws of the United States and its territories would apply. The white people would be the same out west as they were in the east, some friendly to colored folks and others hostile. And what of the boys' desires? George adored his home — the goats, the cows, the fields, the forests — and she couldn't imagine him happy anywhere else. Until Abel started his talk about the West, she had assumed he intended their eldest son to take over the farm someday. As for Joseph, he was so bright and so good about tending ill or injured livestock and helping Abel deliver kids and calves that Constance thought he would make a fine doctor. She had spoken to Dorothea about apprenticing him to Dr. Granger when he was old enough, and Dorothea had agreed to ask her brother when the time came. Constance figured her plans for the boys were as likely as Abel's to ensure their future happiness — and far more likely to ensure hers. "I've seen too many families split up by slavery to consider dividing up mine by choice," she had told Abel on more than one occasion. "If the boys go west, we go with them. Our family stays together."

That usually stopped Abel's talk of the West for a while, for he loved his farm and did not want to leave it, except to sell cheese or to fight Rebels. His people were from York County and he did not want to be more than a day's ride from his brother, sisters, and their families. How he could entertain the idea of sending the boys away "for their own good" when he didn't want to stray too far from his own home and kin mystified her.

At breakfast, Abel said little except to undo all the instructions he had left the boys for taking care of the farm in his absence. Constance suppressed a smile to see her sons' barely concealed relief; for all their staunch assurances that they were ready to be the men of the house with their father away, they were thankful that the whole burden of farming and dairying wouldn't fall on their shoulders.

The rest of the day went on like any other: seeing her boys off to school, cleaning, cooking, milking, ringing the triangle to call Abel in for lunch, tidying the house, greeting her sons when they returned home and sending them back outside again to help their father with the herd. Only as she and Abel climbed into bed that evening, weary from the day's labors and still unsettled by the jarring return to normalcy after so much preparation for their lives to change utterly, did she tell him the truth: "I'm not sorry those white officers sent you away." All across the valley, women were pulling back quilts and climbing into bed alone, reaching out to touch the hollows in the mattresses that once cupped their husbands' sleeping forms. Mothers lay awake, wondering if they would ever see their precious sons alive again. Constance was one of the blessed few who had her husband and her children close and safe. "I'm only sorry about why."

Abel managed a smile before he blew out the lamp. "I thought maybe you were looking forward to some time without me underfoot."

As he lay down, she snuggled up beside

him and rested her head on his shoulder. "Don't talk foolishness."

He stroked her hair and was silent for a long moment. "I wish I'd joined the Zouave Cadets when I had the chance."

"You never did have a chance. The Twelfth Pennsylvania had organized and set out before anyone around here knew they had let colored men in that Company I."

"Even so . . ." He sighed heavily in the darkness. "Joe and I have been talking — us and our sisters' husbands and some other Centre and York County colored men. We thought we might form our own company, see if some of the mustered-out Zouave Cadets would join us, find a sergeant and officers to take charge and train us. Colored businessmen from Williamsport to Mercersburg have pledged enough money to completely outfit a company with uniforms, rifles, and supplies."

When had all this talk been going on? Constance sat up on her elbows and stared at him in the semidarkness. "Where you going to find a colored sergeant and officers?"

"Not colored, white. With white officers, supplies, and proper training, we won't be easily dismissed."

Constance fell back against the pillow and flung an arm over her eyes, muffling a groan. Just when she thought her husband was safe — but she should have known he would persist. When he grabbed hold of something, he held on like a bulldog — growling, relentless, and determined. "You really think they'd muster you in?"

"They mustered in the Zouave Cadets."

"But what about those Hannibal Guards? What if the Union Army treats you the same way?"

Abel fell silent, and Constance knew he was reflecting upon the company of colored men that had formed in Pittsburgh back in April, at a time when one by one the Southern states were voting to secede and President Lincoln had issued a call for seventy-five thousand militia to put down the insurrection. "We consider ourselves American citizens and interested in the Commonwealth of our white fellow citizens," the captain of the Hannibal Guards, Samuel Sanders, had declared. "Although deprived of all political rights, we yet wish the government of the United States to be sustained against the tyranny of slavery, and are willing to assist in any honorable way or manner to sustain the present administration." His fine words had sent a thrill of pride and apprehension down her spine when Abel had read them aloud from the newspaper,

74

but the Union Army had apparently remained unmoved, for the Hannibal Guards had never been mustered into service.

"Captain Sanders is colored," said Abel. "We'll have a white officer."

"If you can find one." Constance rolled over onto her side, her back to him. "One who isn't already leading a white company and is willing to lose a lot of white friends by agreeing to lead colored men into battle."

"There must be a veteran from the Mexican War who would put love of country above all else, who would see only soldiers in blue Union wool and not black or white skin."

"A man with so much love of country is probably already volunteering," Constance countered. "But say you do find such a man, and say they let your company muster in. What if they put you to digging ditches or guarding trains?"

Abel ran a hand over his jaw. "It would be a start. If we have to prove ourselves before they let us fight, then so be it."

Constance was too weary to prolong the argument, and after a time, she fell into fitful sleep. The next day, Abel said nothing about his plans to form a colored company with his brother and brothers-in-law, but the next week, he made an overnight trip to

Mercersburg to meet with them and other potential volunteers. He returned, energized and optimistic, bursting with news of names enrolled and money raised. They had not found a white officer, but a corporal from the disbanded Company I of the Pennsylvania 12th had agreed to train them while they continued to search.

Throughout October, the men of the Susquehanna Militia, African Descent met on an open field outside of Mercersburg every Saturday to drill and march, in uniforms sewn by their wives and mothers. Constance felt her resistance ebbing when she saw Abel's pride reflected in their children's eyes every time he put on the blue frock coat and trousers she had reluctantly but faithfully sewn. Wasn't it their country too, even as Abel said? If the fight belonged to anyone, it belonged to the colored.

She did not want Abel to risk his life, but it was his to risk, and the cause was just.

November came, and still they had not found a white officer willing to assume command of the company. For a time, Abel and his comrades were heartened by reports from the South of "contraband," escaped slaves who had crossed federal lines and wanted to serve the Union. Some Union officers had already used contraband on fortifications and were anxious to continue, so they asked Washington to clarify its official policy. Eventually, the secretary of war had concluded that the Fugitive Slave Law must be respected in loyal states, but in those states in insurrection, runaway slaves clearly could not be returned to their rebellious owners. For more than a year, the Union Navy had been paying contraband laborers a full day's ration and ten dollars a month, while the Union Army offered eight dollars a month for men and four dollars for women at Fort Monroe. It was not soldiering, but it was a start, and rich with the hope of more to come.

But more did not come, not for the contraband and not for the men of the Susquehanna Militia, African Descent. One officer after another declined their invitation to lead them, and seeing their opportunity slipping away, the men named the corporal from the Zouave Guards who had trained them their commander, and made plans to report to Camp Curtin and enlist.

A second time, Constance prepared Abel's supplies and packed his haversack with as much as it could hold. Again, Abel prepared the farm for his absence and instructed George and Joseph on their duties. Again, Constance steeled herself for a painful leave-taking, but she sent Abel off proudly, with silent prayers for God to protect him.

The next day, he returned home. The Susquehanna Militia had presented themselves to the commander in charge and had persuaded him to watch them march and drill. Abel had earned grudging praise as a fine marksman, and a few onlookers remarked that they carried themselves better than most new recruits, but in the end their appeal to be mustered in was rejected. A few of the men, Abel included, were offered work at Camp Curtin cooking and building and otherwise laboring, but the men had farms and businesses and jobs back home, and while they were willing to give them up for a time to become soldiers, they would not merely to cook and clean and carry if they could not also officially join the army.

Abel's explanation was abrupt and angry, and after that first day, he said no more about his second rejection from Camp Curtin. The Susquehanna Militia, African Descent disbanded, and Abel's fine uniform was put away, carefully folded and stored in a trunk, as proud and neat as the day he had first donned it.

But Constance knew from the cold fire in Abel's eye that he had not given up.

■ ■ ■ ■

Autumn faded, golden and glorious, and winter set in. Letters from Thomas arrived almost weekly, an unexpected blessing Dorothea attributed to his regiment's posting in Washington City. If the 49th Pennsylvania were on the march instead of defending the capital, she doubted he would have the time to write letters or the ability to post them.

His letters always opened with reminders of his affectionate devotion and thanks for the necessary items she and her friends had sent to Company L. When Thomas's first letter had described the primitive conditions at Camp Curtin — the inadequate and uncomfortable lodgings, the troubling lack of provisions and supplies — Dorothea had resolved to do all she could to improve his situation. At the next meeting of her sewing circle, she had read his letter aloud and had seen her own dismay reflected in her friends' faces. Mary too had received a letter from her husband, which described the men's circumstances in nearly identical phrases.

"Jonathan says the men have no fresh vegetables, either," Gerda said, frowning in concern. "It's been weeks since they've had so much as a potato, and the men are falling ill from it."

"They can't fight if they're ill," Mrs. Barrows said, turning to Charlotte. "What did your husband say afflicts them?"

Charlotte made no reply, her expression one of stark confusion. "No, no, I have it here," Gerda said, taking a letter from her pocket. She murmured to herself as she scanned the first few lines, oblivious to the frowns and knowing looks some of the other women exchanged when they realized Jonathan had shared that news with Gerda rather than his own wife. "Ah. Here it is. 'The men have received a ration of potatoes but once in the past month, and vinegar only a trifle more often. I have discovered a half dozen cases of scurvy in our brigade in the last fortnight. I have written to headquarters again and again to requisition fresh vegetables, but they are not to be had, and when I describe the men's condition I am informed by men with no medical experience whatsoever that I must be mistaken. Scurvy, you see, comes from a want of fresh vegetables, so therefore our soldiers could not possibly be afflicted with it, because they receive plentiful quantities of nourishing food. Therefore my misdiagnosis and not the men's pitiful diet is the cause of their trouble. I tell you, my dear, if my diagnosis had the power to create symptoms, I would gladly declare them the healthiest men in the army. We shall see if that course of treatment has them quickly leaping from their sickbeds. Unfortunately it is the only remedy army headquarters will provide.' " Gerda folded the letter, shaking her head. "Jonathan can hardly rely upon army headquarters to provide what the men need if they refuse to admit there's a problem."

Despite his usual comic turn of phrase, not even Charley Stokey could disguise his dissatisfaction. As the weather had turned colder, he wrote, the men had taken to constructing makeshift furnaces in their tents by digging trenches from the fireside in front, beneath their tents, and out the other side. They covered the trenches with stones, made chimneys of gun barrels at the far end, and thus drew the heat along, warming the ground they slept upon and keeping themselves warm and dry. "Eliza my dear we are so comfortable that I think I would move us into a tent when I return home except you would have no place for your pretty things," he joked. In the same letter he told of how several hungry men had slaughtered some pigs they had found on the march and had been obliged to pay

81

twenty dollars to their commander to re-imburse the Rebel owner. Charley would not have minded so much, he said, if they could have used worthless Confederate dollars instead of good Federal greenbacks. "I guess we had the last laugh on our commander," Charley had written, "because soon after we left, Jackson passed through the town and had the benefit of all the pigs we had not taken, at which time I figure our commander wished we had slaughtered a few more rather than leaving them to feed the Rebs."

The women were shocked to discover that their soldiers had not been better provided for. "We must make a list of everything our men need," Mrs. Claverton declared as Eliza put away Charley's letter, "and see that they receive it, even if we must take it to them ourselves."

Dorothea quickly fetched pen and ink and paper, and the list swiftly grew as the circle of friends called out suggestions inspired by letters from their own husbands, brothers, and sons. Before long, Dorothea had filled half a page, and after a brief debate, the ladies decided to make quilts, clothing, bandages, and food their priority. No longer would they sit and worry and wait as they went about their daily lives as best they could with their loved ones far away. They could take action; they could contribute.

After the quilting bee, the friends departed, feeling cheered, invigorated, and eager to begin their assigned tasks. Only Charlotte lingered after the others left, and as she helped Dorothea tidy the front room, Dorothea thought her sister-in-law seemed somewhat puzzled. "Jonathan has said nothing to me of shortages or discomfort," she confided after Dorothea gently prompted her. "He describes the camaraderie of the physicians and the devotion of the nurses, but his only complaint is about the quality of the food — which I think he says only out of a wish to compliment me and my cooking rather than any real dissatisfaction."

"His letter to Gerda was about little more than the quality of food," said Dorothea, but she felt disingenuous and ashamed, since of course Gerda had not read the entire letter aloud. Dorothea also had seen Charlotte wince to hear her husband call Gerda "my dear," and she wished Gerda had had the good sense or the discretion to omit the endearment.

That same pained expression marred Charlotte's pretty features as she considered Dorothea's words. "There was more . . . substance to his letter to her, even on the same topic. Don't you agree?"

"Perhaps conditions are better for surgeons than for soldiers," Dorothea replied. "Or perhaps Jonathan doesn't wish to upset you in your condition."

Instinctively, Charlotte rested her hands upon her abdomen. Though she was not as far along as Anneke, her waist had thickened, and the fullness of her petticoats did little to conceal her pregnancy from any but the most oblivious onlookers. "I'd rather have him upset me with the truth than pretend all is well when it isn't."

"All must be well," Dorothea assured her. "Jonathan wouldn't deceive you."

Charlotte fixed her with a level stare. "Indeed."

"Perhaps I should have said that Jonathan has never been particularly good at deceiving you," Dorothea amended. "If he's holding back some details out of concern that they'll hurt you, you'll discover the truth on your own in time."

Charlotte had pondered Dorothea's words for a moment before nodding and thanking her for her honesty.

Though sympathetic, Dorothea had almost forgotten the conversation until reminded of it a few days later, when Gerda showed her the first page of a letter she had received from Jonathan. For Gerda he had described his conflict with the regimental surgeon, whose outdated methods threatened to do more harm than good; his frustration with ongoing supply shortages; his concern about the rapid spread of the flux through camp due to unsanitary conditions; and his fears that his experience and resources would be inadequate if the men of the 49th faced more desperate action than they had seen thus far guarding Washington City. Dorothea did not ask to see the second page of the letter, which she assumed offered more of the same grim reports, as well as expressions of fond longing between her married brother and her friend. She did not wish to know how intimate they truly were, or had once been. She was troubled, but not surprised, that Jonathan had been more frank with Gerda than with his wife. Dorothea was one of the few who knew the truth about Joanna and her son, but she also knew that Jonathan and Gerda shared an intense and passionate friendship. Although Jonathan had not fathered a child with Gerda, Dorothea often suspected that he could have.

If nothing else, Jonathan's conflicting letters underscored the dire conditions the men of the 49th faced, spurring Dorothea on to encourage her friends to work harder and faster to provide the men with all they lacked. They sewed quilts and clothing, and collected lint for bandages. They organized a Christmas fair to raise money to buy essential medicines and instruments. After Gerda read aloud an article from *The New York Times* describing the United States Sanitary Commission, an organization that accomplished on a grand scale what they attempted to do for their own men, they agreed to transform their group from a quilting bee into a local chapter of the commission for the duration of the crisis. "For the duration of the war, we'll no longer be a simple sewing circle," Dorothea had declared, making it official. "We'll be the Water's Ford Sanitary Commission and Union of Loyal Quilters."

They soon shortened the cumbersome title to the Union Quilters in all but their official correspondence and applied for official recognition from the USCC. Their mission redefined, they redoubled their efforts, making whatever items they could, raising money to buy what they could not, knitting socks and scarves, and sending the men any books and magazines they could spare in addition to their own heartfelt, encouraging letters. The soldiers' days were dull and tedious, Thomas had reported, and after hours of drilling and marching and standing picket duty, they had few worthwhile diversions to occupy their time, and thus sank into melancholy, longing for home. They were starved for reading material, but aside from a few novels and histories that had been passed around from soldier to soldier so often that the covers were falling off, they had only religious tracts distributed by the Christian Commission and "cheap books" full of sensational stories that promised thrilling adventures but, in Thomas's words, "utterly and inexorably eroded the intellectual faculties."

Dorothea felt such sympathy for her husband that it pained her, knowing how he despised boredom and dullness, and she promptly organized a book and periodical drive. The Union Quilters knocked on neighbors' doors requesting donations of old copies of the *Atlantic Monthly* and *Harper's Weekly* and any decent books their owners could bear to give away. As Dorothea weeded the shelves of the lending library, finding few duplicates that could be sent to the front, she fought the crushing weight of despondency that always seemed to come upon her when she was alone too long with her thoughts. The Union Quilters worked tirelessly, raising money and sewing for the soldiers in addition to their usual chores and all the extra work that had fallen to them in the wake of the men's departure. And yet, for all their accomplishments, Dorothea despaired that their efforts would ever be enough to meet the enormous and perpetually increasing need of the men at the front. Their accomplishments, though essential, had been too small, their goals too limited in scope. They had to do more.

Exhausted, aching for Thomas, she sat down on the step stool and drew the back of her hand across her forehead, letting her gaze travel around the one-room library. The librarian, currently a private in the 49th, had organized a list of volunteers to manage the modest collection in his absence. Dorothea had immediately signed up for one weekly shift, and in March, when Anneke delivered a fine baby boy, Dorothea took over her shift too. She loved to read and adored the library, which she had played no small part in creating. More than a dozen years earlier, the wives of several prominent citizens had formed a library board and invited Dorothea to join. To raise money for the construction of a new building, Dorothea had proposed that they obtain the signatures of renowned authors on rectangles of bleached muslin and stitch them into an Authors' Album opportunity quilt. As word of the quilt spread, the library board sold so many chances that Mr. Schultz twice had to print additional tickets. They had raised enough money for lumber and labor and new books as well, and the winner of the drawing had donated the quilt back to the library, more out of distaste for some of the "objectionable" and "radical" authors Dorothea had included than from true generosity. The priceless quilt was proudly displayed on the wall above the circulation desk, a tribute to the library board's vision and perseverance. For Dorothea, expelled from the library board on the very night of their triumph, the quilt also served as a reminder that she could expect to suffer for her unpopular, unconventional beliefs. But gazing at it then, missing Thomas and Jonathan, longing to help and to share their burdens as best she could from so great a distance, she was suddenly inspired.

When the Union Quilters gathered at Two Bears Farm three days later, they began by sharing letters they had received from the front since their last meeting. In the more than five months since the men had marched off to war, the women had learned that letters from the regiment were more reliable and informative than the out-of-town newspapers, which exaggerated triumphs, glossed over misfortunes, and omitted the small, precious details of their men's daily lives that were admittedly not newsworthy but mattered greatly to the women who loved them. Since the letters described the experiences not only of the author but also of friends and neighbors in the company, the Union Quilters had come to think of them as community property, to be read aloud to all, except for paragraphs of the most personal nature. Mary took notes for her father, who printed the most relevant excerpts in the *Water's Ford Register* on the same page as the list of regimental casualties, which thus far had been blessedly light, and included no one from Company L.

Mary herself read first, a letter Abner had sent more than two weeks before. Next, Dorothea shared Thomas's news, which had arrived at the Water's Ford post office the same day as Abner's, though it was dated a week later. "The rest is just for me," she said, when a half page yet remained. She forced a smile and fought back tears as her friends teased her, mistakenly believing that in the passages Dorothea had not shared, Thomas's prose had taken a turn for the romantic. What they did not know, what she could not bear to tell them, was that Thomas was grieving for the child she had lost on the day of his departure. She had finally summoned up the courage to tell him how she had returned home from the rally only to be overcome with cramps and to find that her courses had come upon her, heavy and painful. She had assured him she had fully recovered, and that she was under Mrs. Hennessey's watchful care, and that they would surely be able to try again. But relief that she was well and hope for the future did not mitigate their sorrow.

"I have a letter," said Gerda as Dorothea carefully folded Thomas's and returned it to the envelope. "From Jonathan."

Charlotte drew in a sharp breath and shot Dorothea a look of outraged incredulity, but Gerda did not seem to notice. An awkward silence descended upon the circle as Gerda unfolded the pages. "My dearest friend," she began. Dorothea exchanged a quick, stricken glance with her mother, Lorena, and silently chided her friend for her insensitivity — and her brother for his indiscretion. "Thank you for your warm and witty letters, which provide me with pleasant company at the end of my exhausting days. If not for my fatigue and the noise of the camp, I could almost imagine that it is Saturday afternoon and I am seated at your kitchen table, enjoying a delicious meal and a clever argument —"

"That's very nice," Mrs. Claverton interrupted coolly. Beside her, Charlotte flushed scarlet, fists balling up her skirts in her lap. "However, if you don't have any relevant news to share, perhaps someone else —"

"I'll skip ahead," said Gerda, turning over the page. Dorothea could not tell if she was oblivious to Charlotte's consternation or enjoying it. "He continues, 'We have had some new arrivals in camp of late, and among them I discovered some companies from western states that had not yet been examined or mustered into service. I commenced with the examination, and to my consternation I discovered that a full fifth of the men were unfit and would have to be dismissed.' "

"And yet some perfectly fit men aren't even allowed to get that far," said Constance, frowning as she tightened her lap hoop around her most recently finished top. She sewed and knitted as diligently as anyone, though her creations went to neighbors or strangers rather than her own kin. For his part, Abel provided an abundance of cheeses in every shipment of goods sent to the regiment, as if he harbored no ill will over his exclusion and was content to contribute to the army in this manner instead. The Union Quilters knew otherwise. Since the company had left the valley, Abel had grown increasingly outraged and resentful that he was not allowed to fight, and the strain of Constance's utter inability to placate him was beginning to show.

"It's a grave injustice, Constance," said Gerda, frowning as she returned her gaze to the letter. "Jonathan goes on to describe some occurrences of typhoid in the camp, but apparently no one in Company L has been afflicted." A sigh of relief went up from the circle. "And now this: 'Ever since we were attached to the 1st Brigade of the Army of the Potomac, we have anticipated forthcoming orders to depart Washington City and move further into Virginia to engage the enemy. For days rumors have abounded that we will strike camp soon.' "

"Oh, dear," murmured Mary.

"It was inevitable," said Dorothea, though her heart plummeted. "They've been posted at the capital for months. With the coming of spring, the fighting has picked up, and they're needed elsewhere."

Gerda nodded, eager to continue. " 'Last night speculation reached such a fevered pitch that many of the men convinced themselves that they would see fierce fighting by the next afternoon, and they began to celebrate their impending departure, and, regrettably, to fortify themselves with liquor courage. A few of them got hold of some rum and made themselves quite merry on it. I'm sorry to say that our own Rufus Barrows overindulged, tripped over a tent peg, and managed to knock out a tooth and sprain his ankle in the fall.' "

Someone quickly choked off a laugh, and Prudence coughed into her handkerchief. "Our first casualty," said Mrs. Barrows dryly, shaking her head. "I should have known it would be my husband, and rum the weapon. Does Jonathan mention my boys? They're usually smart enough not to get caught up in their father's carousing."

"I'm sorry. He doesn't." Gerda turned to the second page. "The next few paragraphs are . . . inconsequential, but he added a postscript: 'A few lines more, written in haste: The rumors have proven true. We are striking camp and advancing to Manassas. Barrows cannot march on account of his ankle, and as he will remain behind in camp, he has promised to mail this for me. I will write more as soon as I am able.' "

The room fell silent except for the rustling

of paper as Gerda returned the letter to the envelope and slipped it into her pocket. Dorothea's heart pounded, but she took a deep breath and asked, "Did Jonathan date his letter?"

"March the ninth," said Gerda.

Dorothea felt a hand upon her shoulder and glanced up to find her mother smiling at her reassuringly. "It could be a while before we hear anything more," said Lorena. "We can't waste that time in worry. We must continue to work and pray, and hope for the best."

"You're right." Dorothea cleared her throat and inhaled deeply, and straightened her shoulders. "Our biggest challenge now will be figuring out where to send all the goods we've been collecting for the men."

"If the next letter from the company doesn't say, I'm sure the Sanitary Commission will advise us," said Lorena.

Dorothea started, remembering the second letter she had meant to share. "I'll ask when I respond to their letter," she said, retrieving it from the fireplace mantel. "Apparently our fame as skilled quilters has spread beyond the Forty-ninth Pennsylvania throughout the Army of the Potomac. The secretary of the Sanitary Commission has written to us personally to ask us to provide quilts for a new military hospital in Washington City."

Her friends brightened and a murmur of excitement filled the room. It was no small honor to be recognized for their handiwork, and they quickly agreed that they could continue to support their own regiment while also providing quilts for these other sick and wounded soldiers. Indeed, they should look beyond carrying for only their own and support all soldiers who fought for the Union.

"How many quilts do they need?" asked Prudence. A dressmaker, she was probably calculating how many bags of scraps she had on hand at her shop and how far they would stretch.

"They'd like sixty." Exclamations of astonishment went up from the circle, and Dorothea raised her voice to be heard above them. "But they'll take whatever we can give them."

"If they need sixty, we should give them sixty," said Constance. "We don't have to make them all ourselves. We're not the only women around here who sew well enough. Let's invite other ladies to join us."

"We couldn't all fit in Dorothea's front room," said Charlotte, glancing around at their chairs drawn closely together. "There's just enough room for each of us; that's why we've limited our membership all these years."

"We could hold a quilting bee at the school," said Eliza, who had served as the schoolteacher after Thomas, until her recent marriage. "Didn't you do that years ago?"

Dorothea could not have asked for a better introduction for her ambitious proposal. "We do need more space," she agreed, "and not only for this grand quilting bee. Think of what we could accomplish if we had a place of our own to host any fund-raiser we could imagine."

"A place of our own?" Mrs. Claverton echoed, with a hint of amusement. The Claverton farm was adjacent to Uncle Jacob's — now Jonathan and Charlotte's. Not only had she known Dorothea since childhood, she had also been a member of the original library board. She could recognize the signs that Dorothea had a scheme in mind.

"Imagine: no more asking the churches to let us rent their halls. No more restricting the attendance to our fairs and entertainments based upon how many people we can squeeze into the Barrows Inn." Dorothea threw an apologetic look to Mrs. Barrows, who nodded ruefully and shrugged, for she knew the hotel's dining room was too narrow for a ball and too full of echoes for lectures or musical performances. "I'm tired of working so hard to raise twenty dollars here, thirty dollars there. Aren't you? If we had our own hall — spacious, bright, comfortable, with fine acoustics — we could raise a hundred dollars or more with a single event."

Constance and Lorena looked intrigued, Mary and Mrs. Claverton, amused. The others looked uncertain, or even wary. "When you say large," queried Prudence, "what exactly did you have in mind?"

"Large enough to comfortably accommodate six hundred people," Dorothea replied, forging ahead with her argument before they had time to convince themselves that such an undertaking was too ambitious for a simple sewing circle. If they owned a suitable hall, they could sponsor fairs, concerts, balls, lectures, exhibitions, and other public events, including quilting bees. The money they earned selling tickets to these performances would far exceed everything they had raised thus far. They need consult no one before planning and scheduling an event, they need pay no rent — in fact, they could raise even more money for the soldiers by renting the hall to other

98

organizations on days when they did not need it. "We have been thinking too small," said Dorothea. "That's not a criticism; it's simply the truth. We're neither accustomed nor encouraged to think beyond our own families or close circle of friends. But just as war demands noble deeds and courageous action from our men, it also demands the same from us. Yes, there is risk involved, and a great deal of work besides, but if we want to accomplish great things, we must think on a grander scale than we have in the past."

Dorothea had risen to her feet as she spoke, her excitement mounting as she tried to make her friends see what she envisioned, and now she sat down again, studying her friends' expressions with breathless anticipation. They would either get behind her idea now and carry their accomplishments to unforeseen heights, or they would demur and her dream would founder, never to be mentioned again.

Mrs. Claverton broke the silence. "There's that vacant half acre behind the Lutheran church."

"My uncle owns that lot," said Eliza. "I could speak to him. I think he would be willing to sell it, considering our intentions."

"Land and buildings cost money," Lorena

reminded them. "As Dorothea has pointed out, our fund-raisers barely bring in enough to supply the regiment. What would become of our soldiers if we direct our efforts elsewhere?"

No one wanted the soldiers' immediate needs to be forgotten in the pursuit of long-term goals, but Dorothea had accounted for that. Their current efforts would continue as before, the soldiers remaining the beneficiaries. They would launch new endeavors to pay for the hall.

"We shall sell subscriptions," she proposed. "For twenty dollars, an individual will be permitted to attend all events at the hall in perpetuity."

"All events?" echoed Prudence.

"All events. We need sell only twenty-five such subscriptions to raise five hundred dollars, which would be sufficient to buy a half-acre lot and materials, even without a discount from Eliza's uncle."

"But no one wants to attend lectures and concerts alone," objected Charlotte, "and forty dollars may be too much for many families. Why not fifteen dollars for an individual, twenty for a couple? People will believe they're getting quite a bargain and be inclined to spend the whole twenty dollars."

Gerda raised her eyebrows as if astounded to hear such wisdom coming from the young beauty, and the others quickly chimed in their agreement. "Think too of how we raised money to purchase books for the library," Dorothea called out, smiling as she waved them to silence so she could explain the rest. "We charged five dollars for those brass plates bearing sponsors' names affixed to the bookshelves. Similarly, we could engrave bricks or stones with sponsors' names and include them in the construction. Those funds could be put toward furnishing the hall with chairs, draperies, a stage — anything else we would need."

"You can't furnish something you haven't built," cautioned Mrs. Barrows. "You'll need money to pay for labor too, not that there are many men to hire these days. My Mr. Barrows built our inn, but he's off to war and can't help us. Who's going to build this grand hall of ours? Me? You? Young Charlotte there with a baby on the way?"

Constance's voice carried proudly above the others. "My Abel will lead the construction. He's a fine carpenter and helped build the library. I'm sure Hans Bergstrom will do his part too. There are other men around who can't fight for one reason or another but can still swing a hammer, and boys like mine, too young to fight but old enough to help. We'll get our hall built, sure enough."

"Now you've bought the land, built the hall, and decorated it in fine fashion," remarked Mrs. Claverton as the circle of quilters chimed in their support of Abel's nomination as construction foreman. "And our pockets have been thoroughly emptied, with nothing left over to sponsor the entertainments. We'll need a fund-raiser to raise enough funds to hold our first fund-raiser."

Someone laughed, but Dorothea knew Mrs. Claverton was merely playing devil's advocate. "Think again of the library," she said. "We collected autographs from famous authors and other noteworthy personages, and our neighbors were eager to pay for the opportunity to win the beautiful quilt created from the authors' signatures. I propose we undertake a similar project."

Prudence's brow furrowed. "You think we should offer up the Authors' Album quilt a second time?"

"No," said Dorothea, laughing. "That quilt belongs to the library and, aside from the books, is its only adornment. We don't want to tempt our librarian to desert the regiment and come home to prevent us from taking it down."

"Then you think we should make another autograph quilt?" Constance asked, dubious.

"We don't have time to request and receive signed pieces of muslin, nor would a duplicate quilt inspire the same interest as the original did." Nor did Dorothea wish to impose upon the contributors' generosity a second time. "What I suggest is an entirely new quilt, something every quilt maker in the world would desire and pay good money to win."

Gerda abhorred sewing and had joined Dorothea's quilting bee only for the stimulating political discussions and enjoyable company, but even she believed that Dorothea's idea was sheer brilliance. When she carried the news home to Anneke, who had missed the meeting to care for six-week-old baby Albert, Anneke declared that Dorothea was a genius.

The Union Quilters would invite every woman in the Elm Creek Valley to donate a six-inch patchwork block of her own invention or a favorite traditional pattern that was not particularly well known. Each participant would also provide templates and suggestions for how to best construct her chosen block. Quilters would be encouraged to respond promptly by the restriction that only the first block made from a particular pattern would be accepted; any duplicates would be returned to their makers with regrets and encouragement to try again. The blocks would be sewn together into an exquisite sampler, quilted by the finest needleworkers in the valley, and offered up in a drawing. The fortunate winner would claim quilt, templates, and instructions, and thus win a lovely quilt as well as an extraordinary catalog of quilt patterns, enough to keep even the most industrious quilter pleasurably occupied for years to come.

Although Gerda was inclined to put off making a block until she was sure they really needed it — what was one block more or less, after all — she decided to get the unpleasant task over with when Dorothea urged the Union Quilters to submit at least one block apiece, because they could hardly ask others to do what they would not. Gerda contrived a simple block, a square of Balmoral plaid framed in narrow strips of bleached muslin and set on point by Prussian blue triangles, and titled it Cornerstone in honor of their first steps toward achieving Dorothea's grand ambition.

As spring came to the valley, Gerda threw

herself into spreading the word about the quilt project and the proposed Union Hall. Eliza's uncle agreed to sell the half-acre lot at the cost of his investment alone in exchange for a lifetime subscription to their public events and a brass plaque in the foyer commemorating his generosity. Mary and Dorothea collaborated on an article for the *Water's Ford Register* announcing the sale of subscriptions, and within the first week they had sold fifteen. Dorothea decided that those sales were sufficient to justify proceeding with the purchase of the lot, which Hans accomplished in their name.

"If Hans had gone off to war, we wouldn't have been able to proceed with Dorothea's plan," Anneke remarked one afternoon as she sketched quilt blocks while the baby and his two older brothers napped at the same time — a rare occurrence she intended to make the most of. She had already sewn two blocks for the quilt but had been inspired to make several more after the Union Quilters voted to offer one complimentary raffle ticket for each block contributed to the sampler.

Gerda refrained from noting that if Hans had been away, they could have found another man to purchase the lot for them, because Anneke seemed to need evidence that Hans had done the right thing in refusing to enlist. Gerda understood how much the disparaging remarks about suspected Copperheads in their midst disturbed her sister-in-law, even when they were not specifically directed at the Bergstroms, although they often were. She knew her brother was no Southern sympathizer and she wondered how the same townspeople who recalled every detail of her pregnancy, which had never occurred, could have forgotten how Hans had risked his own life and freedom to assist runaway slaves. Only the exposure of their station and the impossibility of continuing to shelter fugitives when the Bergstrom farm was one of the first places slave hunters investigated had prevented him from doing more. And while she looked askance at his newfound pacifist ideals, recalling too well the boy who had enjoyed a good brawl with his playmates and the young man who had once threatened to kill a slave hunter, she could not prove that his beliefs were not real.

What irked her far more than spiteful insinuations about Hans's cowardice or disloyalty were the archaic laws that prevented her or Dorothea or any of the Union Quilters from purchasing the lot themselves, requiring Hans to act as their buyer. Was it not their idea, their efforts, and their fund-raising that would bring Union Hall into existence? Most of the women simply accepted this as the way things were and couldn't waste any time brooding over it, but Gerda knew that this particular inequality bothered Dorothea as much as it bothered her.

A week after they broke ground, Gerda stopped by the construction site on her way to the post office to observe the laying of the foundation and to pass along a message to Abel from Hans. Abel had accompanied Constance to the last meeting of the Union Quilters to show them his revised drawings and to discuss their budget. When Dorothea inquired about the labor crew he had assembled, Abel had hesitated before saying that although their numbers were few, they were competent and willing, and they were aptly assisted by numerous young men not old enough to enlist. Afterward, when Abel went outside to see to the horses before departing, Constance confided to Dorothea and Gerda that her husband had barely managed to gather together the minimum number of men required for the job. "They don't want to take orders from a colored man," she had said angrily. "If he was white, he'd have twice as many carpenters and masons laying bricks and sawing boards, and the hall would be finished in half the time. Maybe we should tell everyone Hans Bergstrom's in charge of construction too."

As Gerda watched Abel calling out instructions to one group of men and supervising the placing of large blocks of limestone by another, she reflected that these men, at least, cared more about the noble purpose of their work than about who was in charge. They had taken precious hours away from their fields on a clear, sunny spring day to finish the foundation. Tomorrow these men would work in their fields, and another team, Hans among them, would man the construction site. While the men labored upon the hall, the Union Quilters sold subscriptions and collected quilt blocks, and gathered weekly to assess their progress, sew and knit for the regiment, and read aloud letters from the front.

From Manassas the 49th had gone to Alexandria and were, as far as the women could determine, currently on the Virginia Peninsula. Gerda had not heard from Jonathan since the regiment struck camp in Washington. Neither had Charlotte, but Gerda did not consider that cause for worry, not yet. Mrs. Barrows's eldest son had written a letter from Alexandria, and if Jonathan had perished, the letter would have mentioned it. Some of the men supplied vivid descriptions of the grim sights and sounds and smells of the battlefield and their own sensations, whether fear or boredom or fervor, while others offered straightforward accounts of miles marched, towns passed, and rivers traversed. The Union Quilters pieced together these scraps of information from the disparate letters as they pieced together scraps of cotton and wool, and just as they assembled quilts that were functional and beautiful, so too did they assemble a mosaic portrait of the war that was functional, if lacking in beauty.

Gerda had two letters of her own to mail that morning — one to Jonathan, the other to Josiah Chester in Virginia. Although she wouldn't admit it to anyone, as the regiment advanced, she dared to hope that someday soon, by a strange quirk of fate, the 49th might engage the enemy near Greenfields Plantation and liberate Joanna.

She had just turned away from the construction site when she spotted the mayor hurrying across the street toward her. "Miss Bergstrom," he called out, red-faced and puffing as he removed his hat. A stocky man with a fondness for his own home-brewed beer, he had shattered an ankle in a fall from a horse in childhood and the bones had not healed properly. Still, his position in the government would have precluded him from enlisting even if his pronounced limp had not made it impossible.

"How do you do, Mr. Bauer," she greeted him, shifting her basket to her other arm. Hans thought the mayor was a timid fool, too apt to follow the bidding of the town council than to think for himself, but Gerda found him amusing and harmless. His wife was an avid reader and often swapped books with Gerda, so she figured he couldn't be too bad if he had won the affections of an intelligent woman.

"Fine, fine. I hope you are well?" When she assured him she was, he smiled and nodded toward the laboring men. "The hall is coming along admirably, I see."

"Right on schedule. Thank you for your subscription."

"All the thanks should go to my wife. She insisted. She declared that she's waited too long for culture to find the Elm Creek Valley to think of missing it now." He laughed self-consciously as if realizing that it was impolitic to criticize his own electorate. "We were wondering — that is, the town council and I — if we may be of assistance to you ladies as you undertake this —" He raised his eyebrows knowingly and nodded toward the construction site. "This really quite substantial undertaking."

"We'd be very grateful," said Gerda. "Several of the councilmen have not yet purchased subscriptions. If you could encourage them to do so, we would put the money to good and immediate use. Their participation would encourage others to subscribe too. There's also the matter of publicizing the opportunity quilt. We've already collected forty charming blocks, but we were hoping for three times that. If you could perhaps pass a resolution —" Mr. Bauer was wincing uncomfortably. "Is something wrong, Mr. Mayor?"

"We can certainly do all that," he said. "However, we are most interested in offering our services in a more . . . administrative capacity."

"Whatever do you mean?"

"It's been brought to our attention that Union Hall, when complete, will be an important community asset. You ladies should be commended for taking the initiative while we men have been preoccupied with the business of war, but now we'd like to take the burden of its management from your delicate shoulders."

He smiled, but Gerda was not charmed.

111

She straightened her not so very delicate shoulders, and taking full advantage of her height, peered down at him. "It's a burden we're quite happy to carry ourselves."

"Of course you're willing, no one doubts that. It's a question of experience, my dear. Managing a facility like this one takes knowledge of business, sums, public communications, and other subjects outside the feminine realm. For the sake of the community and the soldiers we are all dedicated to assisting, we cannot allow such a noble endeavor to founder."

Gerda felt her features hardening into a tight mask of civility. "I appreciate your concern, but I assure you we ladies are more than capable of managing this enterprise ourselves. Mrs. Nelson is a former schoolteacher and apt with figures and writing. Mrs. Currier, as you no doubt recall, is the former Miss Schultz and has ample experience with public communications via the *Water's Ford Register*. For nearly three decades, Mrs. Barrows has been as responsible as her husband for running the Barrows Inn, which is not unlike managing a hall." Gerda willed her features into a tight smile. "That's quite an abundance of relevant experience, wouldn't you agree, Mr. Bauer? And that's only three of us."

"You're exemplary women," soothed Mr. Bauer. "A credit to your sex. War has demanded much of you, but this profound task, at least, need not trouble you. We would be happy to have control of the hall revert to the town council, not only happy but also prepared. Will you share our good news with your sewing circle?"

"I'll tell them about our conversation, but I doubt they'll consider it good news." Gerda nodded briskly and left, too furious to remember the message from Hans she had meant to deliver to Abel.

She was still seething when she left the post office, the absence of a letter from Jonathan adding worry to her indignation. She stormed down the block to Schultz's Printers, where she told Mary about her encounter with the mayor.

"Dorothea won't like this," Mary said, frowning worriedly as she set aside an advertisement she had been proofreading for her father. "That's what happened with the library. After it was built, the town council swooped in and assumed control of it. Dorothea had been dismissed from the library board well before then, so she was in no position to object, and most of the other ladies were all too happy to have the council take responsibility for it. Not Prudence, though. She resigned in protest when the board was given no say in the hiring of the librarian, and once Mr. Childs was appointed, he had sole discretion over acquisitions. Now the library board has no voice whatsoever, and they meet only when Mr. Childs needs them to raise money."

"We can't let that happen to Union Hall."

"Certainly not, but what can we do?"

Gerda didn't know, but she was determined to figure out something. "I've just been to the post office," she said. "Have you had any word from Abner?"

Mary shook her head and glanced into Gerda's basket, which carried only a folded copy of the Bellefonte *Democratic Watchman*. "Not you, either?"

"Nothing. Has your father had any news?" He received the most recent casualty lists by telegraph, but Gerda could not bring herself to ask for that specifically.

But Mary easily guessed. "There were two losses to the regiment, but none from Company L."

"Praise God," Gerda breathed. They'd been fortunate thus far, but how much longer would their luck hold out? "On the subject of news, I should warn you, don't read the most recent *Watchman* unless you have a high tolerance for fools. Mr. Meek is in rare form. He's hit upon a remarkable combination of sentimentality and disloyalty. I wonder how he can sell a single copy of such Copperhead trash."

Mary laughed. "You buy it. You're one of their most avid subscribers. If I were inclined to jealousy, I'd be alarmed that you seem to prefer that paper to ours."

"I don't prefer it," Gerda protested. Indeed, she didn't even enjoy reading it and only did so out of a strange fascination with Peter Gray Meek's frenzied criticism of the Lincoln administration. She marveled that anyone would believe his obvious partisan lies, so easily disproven if one cared to examine the facts, and was astounded that his blatant appeals to his readers' fears and prejudices did not insult their intelligence and prompt them to seek out more objective sources. What disturbed her most of all was that Mr. Meek seemed to be succeeding. If loyal Union papers like the *Register* were willing to resort to lies and dirty tricks, they too could whip the people of central Pennsylvania into a frenzy, but the Schultzes prided themselves on their ethical standards and journalistic principles. As Abner had joked in the months leading up to the war, when the debate over appeasement versus military action was aired in the Northern press, they were "hobbled by their scruples." Hans had joked back that the Schultzes need not fear becoming rich that way, to which Abner had replied, "That's what the print shop is for."

He could joke about such matters because everyone knew that Abner Schultz, like his father-in-law before him, cared more about the truth than the almighty dollar. As far as Gerda could tell, Meek knew only one truth, his own, and cared not a whit if he trampled the facts underfoot as he raced to spread it. During the 1860 election, his zealous rhetoric had cost him his position with the *Watchman* after his vicious attacks on Mr. Lincoln had led to a decline in subscriptions and the loss of advertisers. His firing seemed only to inflame his opposition, for two years later he purchased a half interest in the paper and named himself editor. With far more control over the paper's content than ever before, Meek indulged his fervent desire to criticize the president in one tirade after another, issue after issue.

"If only Meek's tactics weren't so persuasive," Gerda mourned, sitting down heavily on a stool at the print shop counter. "How can good, loyal, Union journalists hope to compete against that?"

"Indeed. How dare we stand against him,

when we're armed merely with the truth?" asked Mary, amused. "If you disagree with his position so intensely, why don't you write a rebuttal?"

"Meek would never run it."

"My father might."

"Do you think so?"

"If it's well written, perhaps. Nothing sells papers like controversy."

"I'll have something for your father before the week is out," Gerda declared as she snatched up her basket and left the shop, already making mental notes of her most persuasive arguments.

Anneke let Gerda worry about overbearing town council members and unpleasant newspaper editors; as soon as she felt sufficiently recovered from childbirth, she chose to devote her energies to the far more pleasant task of soliciting blocks for the Loyal Union Sampler. She was delighted when, in a unanimous decision, the Union Quilters put her in charge of the project, citing her beautiful handiwork, unequaled talent for arranging disparate blocks into a pleasing pattern, and gift for balancing contrast and color. That she had already sewn half a dozen blocks for the quilt may have swung the vote in her favor; Prudence, the only other woman to express an interest in the role, had sewn only two.

Anneke promptly asked Prudence to be her second in charge, and not only to console her for losing the top role. Organizing an opportunity quilt was too large and too important a task for one person, and Prudence, a professional seamstress, was the obvious choice to assist her. Like Anneke she owned a sewing machine, which would allow them to quickly stitch the blocks into rows, and rows into a top when the time came, and the accuracy of her piecing was exemplary.

Anneke was surprised but agreeable when Constance requested to join their committee. Constance was as good a quilter as any in their circle, but she was already a member of the wool drive, the lint collecting, and the knitting committees, and Anneke worried that she would spread herself too thin. Constance, like Abel, seemed determined to work twice as hard as anyone on the home front to provide for the soldiers, as if to compensate for Abel's absence from the battlefield. It was no secret that Abel chafed at his exclusion, nor was it a secret that while Constance was relieved Abel was safe, he was eager and determined to fight, and she wanted what he wanted. Anneke did not understand why he was so avid to endure the hardships the men of the 49th wrote home about. The color of his skin had brought him so many hardships; why could he not look upon his exclusion from war as a rare blessing? At least *he* would not be considered a Copperhead for staying out of the fight, and Constance, a Copperhead's wife.

While Hans alternated days between the Union Hall construction site and his fields and stables, and Gerda composed an epic denunciation of Peter Grey Meek, who had apparently become her sworn enemy although they had never met, Anneke cared for her darling boys, kept house, and sought blocks for the sampler. Their committee printed a letter in the *Water's Ford Register* and personally asked their neighbors and acquaintances for blocks, but they also distributed handbills at Prudence's seamstress shop, the dry goods store on First Street, and the library. Occasionally, in pairs or alone, they would visit church groups and other sewing circles to spur interest in the project, which never failed to result in generous donations of bundles of charming blocks and the occasional invitation to call on a new acquaintance at home. Anneke found the whirl of activity and the widening of her social circle so delightful that, except when someone muttered "Copperhead" in her direction at the market, or when Gerda brooded over casualty lists, or when a Union Quilter read aloud a letter from a loved one in the 49th, she could almost forget that the nation was divided by war. She had her husband, a delightful new baby, her darling twins, friends, and pleasant diversions. The farm and stables thrived. Even the work to build the hall could be imagined as an end unto itself and not the means to raise money for the soldiers. The war seemed very far away, as if it were happening in another country, and she did not wish to draw it closer, to pore over articles in the *Atlantic Monthly* as Gerda did in a vain attempt to feel what the soldiers felt. Anneke knew such thoughts were selfish and reprehensible, so she kept them to herself.

Anneke looked forward to every meeting of the Union Quilters. Most of all she enjoyed displaying each new addition to the collection of Loyal Union Sampler blocks and sharing ingenious piecing tricks she learned from reading the contributors' notes and examining their templates. On one lovely evening in early May, she also displayed blocks made by members of their own circle: one called Memory from Mrs.

Claverton, and another named Manassas from Dorothea, who seemed inclined to commemorate the adventures of the 49th in fabric. Her friends admired the new blocks and praised her and her committee for their accomplishments, and as Anneke took her seat to listen to Abel's construction report, her only disappointment was that the circle was not complete. Charlotte, who had borne a beautiful baby girl on a rainy day in early April, was still recovering from a difficult labor, and Eliza, who ordinarily attended every gathering without fail, was also inexplicably absent. Anneke decided to set the new blocks aside to show them later.

Abel's report was followed by a brief debate over what to do about Mr. Bauer and the town council, who had ignored their polite demurrals and seemed determined to badger them until they relinquished control of Union Hall out of sheer exhaustion. Dorothea, who seemed unusually troubled even for those circumstances, reported that she had exchanged several letters with a lawyer friend of Thomas's in Philadelphia. He assured her that the town council probably could not seize the hall even by invoking their power of eminent domain, but he was investigating measures they could take to protect themselves, just in case.

"In the meantime, we will go about our work and refuse to be intimidated." Dorothea took a deep breath and withdrew from her pocket an envelope, creased and soiled as if it had made a difficult journey to reach her. "I'm sure you're wondering why Eliza did not join us today."

Mary bit her lips together and dabbed her eyes with her handkerchief, which alerted Anneke that she already knew what Dorothea was about to tell them. "Is Thomas all right?" she asked, suddenly nervous.

"Oh, yes," said Dorothea quickly, indicating the letter. "I received this from him yesterday."

"Praise God he's well," murmured Lorena, although everyone knew the arrival of a letter meant only that the author had been safe at the time of its writing. Anything might have befallen her son-in-law in the interim.

"What is it?" asked Prudence, alarmed. "You look so pale."

"I can't — I think I should just read." Dorothea cleared her throat and began.

May 5, 1862

My beloved Dorothea,
    I pray you and darling Abigail are well.

Physically, I am sound, but my thoughts are so confounded I hardly trust myself to set them down on paper. I will attempt to do so, however, not only because I bear sorrowful news, but also because speaking to you always helps me to frame my thoughts.

At the beginning of April, we departed Fort Monroe and marched up the Virginia Peninsula toward Richmond only to encounter Confederate defenders at Yorktown. On April 4, our forces managed to push through their first line of defense but were thwarted at a second, more effectively reinforced line further north. The following day, after some skirmishing and reconnaissance, men from the 5th Wisconsin and the 6th Maine drove off the Confederate pickets and captured several prisoners. Their commander, an able leader called Hancock, believed he had discovered a weakness in the Rebel defenses, but inexplicably, General McClellan ordered him not to exploit it until he had the opportunity to conduct additional reconnaissance. You know I favor the gathering and thoughtful study of evidence, but such conduct is often more suited for the library than the battlefield, where opportunities must be seized and held firmly before they slip away. Rather than push forward, however, our general ordered us to dig in.

The misfortunes we experienced in the days that followed might have been humorous if the consequences had not been so tragic. Although we were confident that we boasted the superior artillery, the terrain made it difficult to determine whether we possessed superior numbers. The Confederate leader, Major General John Magruder, had been an amateur actor before the war, and although we did not realize it at the time, he paraded his men and artillery back and forth in an ostentatious manner in order to confuse us into believing that his numbers were greater and fortifications more strongly held than they were. To satisfy our General McClellan's desire for intelligence, the balloon corps sent a brigadier general aloft to observe from above, but capricious winds sent his aircraft drifting over enemy lines, causing quite a stir of alarm amongst the Union command until he was brought back to earth safely.

Whether this aerial excursion discovered something of significance I could not say, but on the 16th, several regiments were ordered to attack the same point Hancock had identified ten days earlier. However, as one might have expected, as soon as our foray had discovered those weaknesses in the enemy defenses, the Rebel commander had begun to reinforce them. Some companies from the 3rd Vermont were ordered to attack the Confederate works on the west bank of the Warwick River overlooking a dam near Lee's Mill. Although at first it seemed the Vermonters had the advantage, they were eventually forced back, suffering casualties as they withdrew under heavy fire. Some of the wounded drowned as they stumbled into the waters held back by the dam.

Thus thwarted, McClellan ordered the transportation and installation of massive artillery batteries, an arduous process that took the remainder of the month to complete. Only days before the great siege engines were to be deployed, several escaping slaves crossing over into our territory reported that Confederate supply wagons were departing the earthworks and moving north toward Richmond. For reasons I cannot fathom, McClellan disregarded these reports, refusing to believe that an army so superior in numbers (or so Magruder's antics had deceived him) would withdraw without a fight. Two evenings ago, the Rebels bombarded us briefly and then fell silent. Yesterday morning, a Union aeronaut ascended in an observation balloon and discovered that the Confederate fortifications had been abandoned.

Stunned, McClellan sent cavalry in pursuit and ordered another division to sail upriver on navy transports, but it remains to be seen whether he will succeed in cutting off the Confederate retreat. The 49th will also be on the move again soon, but without Charley Stokey, who was badly wounded in the head and the shoulder in the last bombardment. He has drifted in and out of consciousness since he was hit, and it grieves me to look upon his arm, which I doubt he will be able to keep. He is shortly to be transported to the field hospital, where I am sure Jonathan and his colleagues will do all that can be done. I cannot help thinking that if only we had exploited the Rebel defenses when Hancock first detected a weakness, we would not have been bombarded that evening, and Charley would not at this moment be suffering. I know what you would say; Charley might have been wounded on that earlier day in that place instead, or if not him, then another soldier. It does me no good to brood over what might have been, but I cannot seem to fix my thoughts otherwise. His anguished moans tear at my heart, and there is nothing I can do for him.

I finish this letter in haste so it can go out with the ambulance team, but first I wish to tell you that you were right to insist that I bring along the Dove in the Window quilt. It has brought me immeasurable comfort in these harrowing months, not only for its warmth and softness, but also for the fond remembrances it evokes of its beloved maker.

You are always in my thoughts, my darling, as I know I am in yours. I will always be

Your devoted husband,
Thomas

Dorothea blinked back tears as she folded the letter. "Forgive me for that lengthy preamble, but I didn't know how else to say it. Mary's father received the casualty list from the battle by telegraph just this morning. Charley did not survive."

Gasps and cries of distress went up from the circle. "Oh, poor, dear Eliza," exclaimed Lorena. "Married less than a year. How will she bear it?"

Dorothea shook her head, as if she could not imagine how anyone could endure such a loss.

"My father sent word to her mother and sister in Williamsport," said Mary. "They're coming to care for her. She's with her mother-in-law now, at Charley's boyhood home."

"We're her closest friends," said Gerda. "We must do something."

It was quickly agreed that they would provide food, comfort, companionship — anything Mary needed. Lorena offered to set out immediately. "I'll go with you," said Anneke, trembling as she put away her sewing. Albert slept peacefully in his basket at her feet, and Hans would be fine with the twins at home a little while longer. She was suddenly and profoundly ashamed. How could she ever have found any pleasure in the work of war? How could she have allowed herself to imagine that the conflict occurred in another country, to other people, that it was akin to a glorious adventure scribbled in broad strokes as in a cheap dime novel?

She longed to beg Eliza's forgiveness, and that of all her friends who constantly feared the devastating blow the new bride had suffered, but she knew her confession would only pain the young widow and bring her no absolution. Never again, she silently vowed as she hastened after Lorena. Never again would she forget how close to home the war raged.

CHAPTER THREE

Eliza did not return to the Union Quilters. A month after Charley's death, she sold the farm, half in cash and half on credit, to Charley's cousin, a young man of barely eighteen who had generously plowed the fields and sown the spring crops in Charley's absence. Charley's aunt was even more thankful for the opportunity than the cousin. The young man had been counting the days until he was old enough to enlist, eager to do his part for the Union, but acquiring his own land changed his mind. In mid-June, when the hills surrounding the Elm Creek Valley were green and lush and the farmers' fields sent forth shoots and stalks that promised a bountiful autumn, Eliza, clad in mourning black from head to toe, moved back to Williamsport to live with her mother and sister. Eliza's mother confided to Dorothea that although the sale of the farm would give Eliza enough to live on frugally for several years, she intended to encourage her daughter to return to teaching after a suitable interval so that she might occupy the lonely hours with productive work.

Charley Stokey was only the first of many fatalities Company L suffered. Mrs. Barrows's eldest son died of wounds suffered in the Battle of Williamsburg, and one of Dorothea's former classmates succumbed to typhoid in a field hospital not far from where Charley had fallen. More Water's Ford men perished in the pursuit of Confederate troops to the Chickahominy River. There were other casualties, men who had lost limbs or suffered blindness or were so debilitated by illness that they could not fight. As spring turned to summer, the first of these soldiers began returning home only to find themselves objects of intense curiosity or pity. They could not stir anywhere in the Elm Creek Valley without being pressed to describe their experiences, the adventures they had enjoyed, the horrors they had seen. The veterans Dorothea met bore their empty shirtsleeves or trouser legs or eye sockets as badges of honor, self-evident signs of their courage and heroism. Somber but determined, they seemed to want nothing more than to resume the lives they had left behind when they marched off to war. For the most severely wounded, this was not something easily accomplished. Some had sons old enough to help around their farms, sisters or wives who could mind shops and businesses, but others returned to their families unable to take up their former livelihoods.

"We must help them," Anneke declared, tears in her eyes after Lorena described how a bachelor neighbor who had lost both legs had asked her to sew him a padded cushion for a cart so that he might hitch it to his mule and thus get to and from his job as a bank clerk without relying upon anyone to transport him. The Union Quilters agreed that the nation's duty to wounded soldiers did not cease upon an honorable discharge, but the question remained what to do.

The wounded veterans' needs evidently weighed heavily upon Anneke's heart, for she declared that the funds raised by the Loyal Union Sampler, as she had named it, should be redirected to benefit those men. Her proposal sparked a heated debate among the Union Quilters, but in the end they decided that since they had asked for quilt-block donations to support Union Hall, they must use them for that purpose as planned. Instead of continuing to give all the money earned through their fund-raisers to the soldiers at the front, however, they would reserve thirty percent for the needs of their wounded veterans. Anneke seemed satisfied despite the defeat of her proposal, because the revised plan would allow them to begin helping the veterans immediately rather than waiting for the quilt to be finished.

The Union Quilters and the men of Abel's construction team were engaged in a friendly competition to see who would complete their grand project first. Anneke collected their eightieth block on the same day Abel drove in the nail that completed the framing. A church sewing circle dropped off the blocks that pushed their total above one hundred on the same day a one-legged veteran finished the interior staircase. Hans jokingly complained that it was not a fair competition because the women could determine that they had received enough blocks and begin assembling the top whenever they chose, whereas the men could not decide that they had run out of time and forgo adding a roof or plastering the walls. To make things more fair, and because it would be easier to plan the layout if she knew how many blocks the quilt would contain, Anneke settled upon 121 blocks, or eleven rows of eleven blocks apiece, framed by a floral appliqué border. She told the Union Quilters that she and Prudence would begin the border right away rather than wait for the central rows to be collected, arranged, and sashed, and anyone who wished to help would be welcome to join them.

Overwhelmed with other responsibilities, Dorothea gave the committee her regrets. They apparently had not expected her to assist with the quilt assembly, for they regarded her with surprise, and Constance said, "Of course not, Dorothea. Your days have only the same number of hours as anyone else's." Dorothea wished for a few extra. She felt as if she were never at rest, and she rarely completed more than half of the items on her daily to-do list. Mrs. Hennessey was a tremendous help around the house and she doted upon Abigail, but the responsibilities of running Two Bears Farm fell to Dorothea alone. She had not realized how much she and Thomas had relied on each other while making the countless daily decisions and handling the unexpected problems that confronted the farm. The hired men knew their jobs well and performed their duties ably, and Hans was only a short ride away if an emergency cropped up, but Dorothea greatly missed being able to find Thomas in the fields, barn, or study and seek his advice. Letters were too slow and too unpredictable for matters requiring an immediate decision, so Dorothea had gradually become accustomed to deciding on her own. In the first few months of the war, when confronted with an unforeseen problem or opportunity, she would consult Thomas by mail and wait to hear from him before taking action. When ten acres went up for sale along the northern boundary of their land, she proposed that they acquire it for pasture, and then waited three weeks for Thomas's reply before she went ahead with the purchase. Over time she grew impatient with such delays and would sometimes pose a question in a letter to Thomas but chose for herself before his reply arrived. Sometimes she asked herself what Thomas would prefer, but more and more often, she simply followed her own instincts. Eventually, she simply made the necessary decisions and informed Thomas after the fact. She had little choice, and she knew he would not be offended. If he had wanted a wife who could not think for herself, he wouldn't have married her.

But what of other wives whose husbands had gone off to war? Dorothea considered herself quite independent and was accustomed to speaking her mind, yet even she noticed a subtle but unmistakable increase in her confidence and self-reliance since she had been obliged to run the farm on her own. How much greater the change must be for those wives left at home who, through habit and custom, had deferred to their husbands in all matters. Of course, as a mother of a young child, she had constraints upon her freedom, but it was a new and strange sensation to discover that for the first time in her life, she need please no one but herself in matters small but consequential — when to retire for the night, what to prepare for supper. She would gladly relinquish her new independence to have Thomas home and safe, but it was not her choice to make, so she supposed she ought to take what satisfaction from the situation she could.

If women like her all across the valley — all across the North, she could well imagine — were enjoying a new and unexpected liberty, she refused to take a step backward and allow a small-town mayor to intimidate her into giving up even one tiny part of hers. Thomas's lawyer friend had advised her on a course of action, and now she was determined to embark upon it.

One afternoon, she saddled her favorite bay mare and called on the Bergstrom family. Hans spotted her first as she crossed the meadow near the young apple orchard Gerda had planted near the barn. "Gerda's Folly," her brother called it, mostly in jest, but it seemed to Dorothea that the trees thrived, although none had yet borne fruit.

Hans inspected the horse and praised Dorothea for the fine care she was giving it; it was no small matter to him, for he had bred the horse himself. He was making quite a name for himself as a horse farmer, not only in the Elm Creek Valley but also in surrounding counties.

"Still holding out?" she teased him, handing him the reins and accepting his assistance down from her horse. Since the first rumors of war had begun circulating through the valley and they discovered their mutual abhorrence of violence, they had to pretend to wager over which of them would give in to the relentless appeals to their patriotism, loyalty, and duty — and fears of insults, ostracism, or worse — and join the army. Hans insisted against all common sense that Dorothea was more likely to put on a uniform than he.

"Still holding out," he replied, "although I

137

endure the shame better than my poor wife does."

"Anneke, ashamed?" Dorothea shook her head. "I can't believe it. She adores you. I assure you she's never said a single critical word about you that I've ever heard."

"That's not her way," he said ruefully. "She doesn't criticize me. Instead she praises all the brave souls who have enlisted, and reads aloud stories of heroism from the *Atlantic Monthly,* and makes impassioned speeches about the importance of preserving the Union and freeing the slaves. What she may not understand is that I agree with her, mostly. I believe the men who enlisted are brave, though also misguided. I like stories of heroism as much as anyone, although I don't think heroism requires me to kill my fellow man."

"Holding fast to your honorable convictions, though you may earn the enmity of everyone around you, is another form of heroism."

"Tell that to Anneke. And to Gerda. She's lost patience with our Mr. Lincoln and his slow, measured steps toward abolition. She wants slavery to end now, today, by force of arms if necessary, with no compensation offered to owners who voluntarily renounce slavery."

Dorothea didn't think much of Mr. Lincoln's compensation proposals herself. "Gerda wants all slaves everywhere to be free, but especially Joanna." Dorothea understood. She too was haunted by the faces of the runaways who were recaptured in their home on the day they were betrayed. "We sheltered two that night, a husband and a wife."

"I remember," said Hans, brushing the bay's coat until it glistened like silk.

"I wish I could know what had become of them, but unlike Gerda, I don't have an owner's name or location." She hesitated. "Sometimes I wish Gerda didn't either."

Hans paused and regarded her curiously. "Why not?"

"If, like me, Gerda didn't even know where to begin, she might not waste so much time on a search that I fear is doomed to fail." Dorothea reconsidered her words. "I don't mean that the search isn't noble, but she persists against all logic and all hope, and I worry that she's exhausting herself and making herself vulnerable to melancholy."

"Gerda has good reason to continue the search."

"Yes, of course." Instinctively, Dorothea glanced out the barn door, though it was unlikely anyone who didn't already know the secret would have come upon them unnoticed. "And for Joanna's sake, I hope she succeeds. But what will this mean for your family?"

Hans resumed brushing the horse. "I love the boy as much as if he were my own son. Anneke feels the same. But how can we hope that Gerda fails? She still believes that Joanna will be found and freed, and that a Union victory will hasten that day. As for me, I think Joanna is long gone, but if it does my sister any good to hope . . ." His voice trailed off and he shrugged.

"I suppose you could be right," said Dorothea, although she was not sure how much good Gerda's relentless, fruitless search was doing her. "Who am I to say there's no chance?"

Hans shrugged in response and with a sigh, Dorthea went into the house to find Gerda and Anneke, entering through the kitchen door without knocking, as was the habit between their families. "Gerda?" she called, finding the kitchen empty. "Anneke?"

Hans had built his family a fine home, with two stories and an attic, four rooms downstairs and five above, with an innovative, efficient cookstove in the kitchen, a massive fireplace in the front room, and all

140

the modern conveniences that were available at the time. He had hauled the gray stones to the site from riverbanks and creek beds, from his own land and from the countryside for miles around. He had taken one large limestone boulder to a stonecutter, who had squared it off and engraved it with the words *Bergstrom 1858.* This cornerstone had inspired Dorothea's plan to engrave donors' names on limestone markers for Union Hall, and that same stonecutter had donated his services in exchange for a prominent stone near the front entrance bearing his own name and profession.

"We're in the front room," called Anneke. When Dorothea joined them there, she found Gerda holding baby Albert and trying to distract the energetic twins in a corner while Anneke knelt on the floor, patchwork blocks of all colors and patterns spread out around her. "One hundred and eleven blocks," she announced proudly. "Constance, Prudence, and I have already finished the borders and need only attach them to the center once we receive the last few blocks and sew them together. And the men still have to finish the roof and install the windows."

"Wonderful," praised Dorothea, amused by how much Anneke relished the competition. "I'm tempted to sew the last few blocks myself to make sure we don't lose our lead."

"I'll help you, if it comes to that," promised Anneke.

Gerda grimaced as she tried to herd the playful boys away from the center of the room. "As for me, I'll cheer you on and admire your work. Anneke, would you please pick up the blocks now? I said I'd keep the boys away from them, but I had no idea what strong little wrestlers they've become."

"Here, let me take Albert," said Dorothea, and with a grateful sigh, Gerda handed her the baby. Holding him, Dorothea helped Anneke gather up the blocks, often pausing to admire a particularly lovely pattern. One simple but attractive design reminded her of the Boy's Nonsense pattern, but longer, narrower rectangles than she was accustomed to seeing framed the central square. "Deborah Madigan calls that pattern Drummer Boy," Anneke explained. "After her son."

Dorothea nodded, remembering the boy she had taught at the Creek's Crossing school many years before. He was too young to fight, but he had been determined to accompany his older brothers, so his father acquired a drum for him and made his other sons swear to protect him as best they could.

Another striking block resembled a traditional Churn Dash, with right triangles in the corners and narrow rectangles along the four sides, but instead of a solid, light-colored square in the center, there was a Turkey red square framed with two sets of concentric triangles. To Dorothea's delight, Anneke informed her that it had been made by Joan Sheridan, the wife of the owner of the dry goods store on High Street. She had donated several bolt ends of fabric and spools of thread for the quilts they had made for the military hospital in Washington, and since she was also an intelligent, well-read woman, Dorothea had considered inviting her to join the Union Quilters after Eliza's departure had left a vacancy. Joan had named the block Union Hall in honor of their "noble enterprise."

"Show her Eliza's block," Gerda suggested, but in that moment of distraction, the boys darted around her skirts. Crowing with joy, they scrambled on their hands and knees to snatch up the nearest blocks, toss them into the air, and watch them fall to the floor.

"Two more minutes was all I would have needed," Anneke admonished her sister-in-law. Searching through the blocks as they flew through the air or slid across the smooth wooden floor, she spotted the one she wanted and managed to pry it from Stephen's grasp. "Eliza made this before Charley was killed," she said, handing a blue, red, and light tan block to Dorothea. "Her mother found it while unpacking her things in Williamsport and mailed it to us."

With a pang of regret for her absent friend's loss, Dorothea studied the block. Four identical arrangements of blue squares and triangles in the corners framed a central red square set on point. "Did Eliza give it a name?"

"Campfire," said Gerda, quickly snatching blocks off the floor before her nephews could scatter them further. "Her mother wrote that it reminded Eliza of Charley and the men of the Forty-ninth sitting around the campfire after a long march, reminiscing about loved ones back home."

Dorothea sighed, missing Eliza, mourning Charley. He had been a childhood friend and classmate, and it pained her to think that he was put to rest hundreds of miles from those who loved him.

"It was good of Eliza to think of us, and Union Hall, in the midst of her grief," said Anneke. "I think we should invite her to attend the grand opening of the hall as an honored guest."

"Not as a guest, but as one of us," Dorothea replied, shifting Albert to her hip. "Once a Union Quilter, always a Union Quilter, in my opinion." And Union Hall must always belong to them. The town council did not fear that the Union Quilters would manage the hall badly because they were proven incompetents but because they were women. They could list their skills and accomplishments and qualifications until they were hoarse; it would do them no good. The town councilmen would not be persuaded because they would not listen. They had already made up their minds that the Union Quilters were incapable of making Union Hall a success. Dorothea refused to let an extraordinary opportunity to prove them wrong pass her by.

"Gerda, Anneke," she said, handing the blocks she had gathered to Anneke, who put them on a high shelf near the window, out of the children's reach. "I have a plan to discourage the town council from continuing their ridiculous demands for us to turn over Union Hall to them."

"Good," declared Gerda. "At first they were merely persistent, but lately they've become thoroughly annoying."

"What do you think we should do?" asked Anneke.

"I think we should incorporate," said Dorothea, "and I need your help."

Gerda found Dorothea's proposal astonishing, intriguing, and delightful. By writing up a list of bylaws and declaring themselves "a body corporate," they would not ~~secure~~ themselves legal protection from the town's power of eminent domain, but they would force the council to give them full due process under the law. "They will have to deal with us on an equal footing," said Dorothea, "as rational adults, and not as dependent inferiors. If they want to seize control of Union Hall, they'll have to do it the long, difficult, messy, ugly way — through the courts. I suspect they won't do it."

Gerda lacked Dorothea's faith in the reasonableness of their neighbors. As she knew all too well, many otherwise sensible people took a certain malicious delight in slinging mud at others, realizing only after they found themselves in it up to their knees that they couldn't avoid soiling themselves in the process.

"Why don't we just put everything in Hans's name?" asked Anneke. "That's what we did to buy the property. Or, if that seems

146

too self-serving, give equal shares to all of the Union Quilters' husbands — the agreeable ones, anyway, the ones that won't give us any trouble. The council won't challenge a Union Hall board comprised of men the way they challenge us."

"That's probably true," admitted Dorothea. "But don't you see? That's precisely why we can't do it. We have to take a stand now, when it matters. We can't keep waiting for another, better opportunity, one we can afford to lose. The men aren't going to give us the vote willingly. We have to fight for that right little by little in battles such as this."

"So you've chosen this battle," said Gerda, "knowing that losing it would mean losing Union Hall as well?"

"If I'm not willing to work and fight and sacrifice to win equality for women, then I don't really deserve it, do I?"

Gerda considered. "If it's a question of what rights one deserves, I refer you to the Declaration of Independence. Mr. Jefferson and the Founding Fathers believed that the rights to life, liberty, and the pursuit of happiness were granted to us by God, not any man. I would argue that you deserve your liberty implicitly and should not have to fight man for it."

"Even our Founding Fathers had to fight for their rights."

"Gracious, Dorothea, I believe we may see you in a soldier's uniform after all," exclaimed Anneke. "Only what would you wear? Certainly not Confederate gray, but you sound like you want to pitch battle against our own government, so not Union blue, either."

"I'll wear a double-breasted frock coat in a lovely shade of pink, with gold epaulettes," Dorothea retorted, smiling. "You know very well that I'll never take up arms. My fight is intellectual — with a dash of cunning."

The Nelsons' lawyer would guide them through the necessary steps to acquire official legal status, but it was up to the Union Quilters to define themselves. They would need to compose a series of resolutions and bylaws, outline their purpose, and declare themselves a body corporate. "We shall become an official relief organization devoted to providing essential goods and services for active and veteran soldiers," said Dorothea. "The town council will have a more difficult time convincing the public that they should wrest control of Union Hall from an official relief organization than from a simple sewing circle."

Gerda thought Dorothea's plan was a

stroke of genius, but Anneke frowned and shook her head. "I don't think all these machinations should be necessary," she said. "Haven't we done quite well as a sewing circle? Think of all the clothing and food the Union Quilters have provided the 49th. Think of the relief funds we've raised for our wounded veterans. Didn't we furnish quilts to three wings of the new military hospital in Washington? Why must we pretend to be anything more than a sewing circle, when clearly a sewing circle can accomplish great things?"

Dorothea hesitated. "You make a very good point."

"She does?" asked Gerda, looking from one to the other in surprise. "If men are impressed by fancy titles, then let's give ourselves a fancy title. What's the harm?"

Anneke found a stray block on the back of an armchair and smoothed out the wrinkles with her hands. "I only wish it weren't necessary to demean sewing circles."

"I wish none of this were necessary," said Dorothea. "I wish the town council would trust us to manage Union Hall as well as we've managed the fund-raising and construction. I wish slave owners would voluntarily release their slaves and make sufficient reparations so they could make a good start in life as free people. I wish the Union could be preserved without resorting to war. I wish I would go home to find Thomas in his study with Abigail on his knee. There are many things that are not the way I wish them to be, but to save this one, important thing, I'm willing to compromise. I'm willing to publicly declare that we are more than a sewing circle, because, my dear friends, we *are* more than a sewing circle, and always have been."

As she listened to her friend speak, so brave and impassioned and true, Gerda felt a strange spell come over her. Dorothea's words made her feel as if she had tapped only a small wellspring of all the rich possibilities she contained, that she could accomplish anything she put her mind to if she believed in herself and refused to give up. "If you run for governor of Pennsylvania, I'll vote for you," Gerda declared, full of pride and amazement. "I would say president, except that I like Mr. Lincoln rather well."

Dorothea laughed. "Mr. Curtin's job is safe from me, and so is Mr. Lincoln's." She smiled and regarded her friends fondly. "Now. Will you help me?"

Gerda readily agreed, Anneke, more hesitantly. Dorothea explained that she wanted the three of them to draft a statement of purpose and bylaws, which they would present to the other Union Quilters at their next meeting. Gerda's talent for writing made her indispensible. "But English isn't even my native tongue," she protested, although Dorothea's praise flattered her vanity.

"That certainly hasn't prevented you from expressing your opinions with bold eloquence in the *Water's Ford Register,*" said Dorothea, "Mr. G. A. Bergstrom."

"I never claimed to be a mister," Gerda replied. "If people read 'G. A.' in the byline and assume the author is a man, that's none of my doing." It wasn't even her choice. Concerned about propriety, Mr. Schultz had required her to conceal her gender, unwilling to offend their more conservative readers, or even worse, have her thoughtfully written articles dismissed unread as the uninformed prattle of a naïve woman. With Dorothea's bold words fresh in her mind, Gerda wished she had insisted upon identifying herself as a woman regardless of the consequences. The fact that G. A. Bergstrom was indeed her name, and that so few Bergstroms lived in the county that anyone putting forth a modest effort could discover her identity, did not make her feel any less abashed.

"I know you didn't ask me to help because of my flair for the written word," said Anneke. Her spoken English, though heavily accented, had become quite fluent through the years, but the Bergstroms spoke German around the house, and Anneke rarely practiced writing in English.

"You'll contribute ideas, if not specific phrases," said Dorothea. "And then, when we've finished, you'll help convince the others that our plan is sound."

"I'm not so sure that it is."

"That's precisely why your opinions are necessary. Gerda and I think alike and everyone knows it. Of course she agrees with my plans and I with hers. If *you* believe in our bylaws, however, it will prove we've considered opposing points of view and accommodated them. If our proposals are sound enough to satisfy you, then they must be strong indeed."

Anneke considered that for a moment. "Very well, but although I love you both dearly, I won't stand up in front of our friends and claim to support any bylaws and resolutions that I don't truly believe in. I'm also going to make it clear that if I had my way, we would remain a sewing circle, but that this step is necessary to protect Union Hall."

Dorothea assured Anneke that she would expect nothing less. They gathered paper, pens, and ink and spread an old, faded quilt on the grass outside so they could keep watch over the boys playing nearby while they worked. Gerda thought they made good progress that first afternoon, but they continued to discuss and revise their bylaws and resolutions over the course of several days.

When they agreed upon a final draft and Dorothea took it home to copy it over in a fair hand in anticipation of the next meeting of the Union Quilters, Gerda resumed her other writing projects, letters to Jonathan and to Josiah Chester as well as opinion pieces for the *Water's Ford Register*. G. A. Bergstrom had become one of the paper's most popular authors, her thoughtful essays on the war, abolition, and the responsibilities of those on the home front as eagerly anticipated as her sharp, acerbic, but always accurate refutations of Meek's editorials in the Bellefonte *Democratic Watchman*. Naturally, Meek retaliated in his own paper with mocking rebuttals of the "ill-informed Mr. Bergstrom's feeble diatribes." As Gerda went about her errands in town, she sometimes came upon readers engrossed in one of her essays, or others discussing with a spectator's glee how soundly Bergstrom had thrashed Meek in the most recent issue. The *Register* did receive the occasional letter from an outraged reader who thought G. A. Bergstrom had crossed the lines of civility, but since most of these were postmarked from Bellefonte, Gerda didn't let them trouble her. For his part, Mr. Schultz was delighted and regularly congratulated himself for taking his daughter's advice and taking a chance on an unproven writer. Subscriptions were on the rise, and he need pay Gerda only half of what he would have paid a man in her place. Gerda never would have known this except for Mary's whispered confession, but although she was displeased, she decided not to complain, either to Mr. Schultz or to the Union Quilters. Dorothea would have insisted she demand equal pay, and Gerda was not about to put her new job at risk. Not only was she writing and publishing and being read, she was earning an income. For years she had sold her fine preserves to Lawton's Market to help contribute to the family and lessen the burden of remaining an unmarried woman in her brother's household, but that was only seasonal work and, even at half wages, not nearly as lucrative.

Nor did Gerda want to stop publishing and allow Meek to believe he had won their ongoing debate. Even when the *Watchman* printed the truth, which was rare, Meek selected pieces and slanted the language to lambaste the Lincoln administration and endorse a Copperhead point of view. A recent article, purportedly the firsthand account of a recent German immigrant tricked into enlisting, especially irked Gerda. Leonhardt Kraus (or so the article called him, if such a man existed) claimed to have arrived in Castle Garden in August of 1862, eager to begin a promising new life in the American West. On his first night in the country, when he informed his innkeeper, a German like himself, that he planned to join his brother in Wisconsin, the man offered to show him around New York before he departed. The next day, Mr. Kraus accompanied the man through the city and eventually into a basement room where a lone man sat behind a desk. Turning to his new friend, Mr. Kraus discovered that he had quietly departed and a guard leveling a bayonet at him stood in his place. Not speaking a word of English, Mr. Kraus did not understand what the man behind the desk was saying to him as he held out a pen and gestured for him to sign the papers lying on the desk, but Mr. Kraus refused and demanded to be released, his meaning perfectly clear in any language. More than an hour passed before another German entered the small, dark room and explained that the nation was divided by war and that both sides were determined to fill their ranks one way or another. In German he advised Mr. Kraus to go ahead and sign the enlistment papers. The guard would release him until they had enough recruits to muster in an entire company, and in that interval, he could flee to Wisconsin. Thus assured, Mr. Kraus signed the papers, but rather than releasing him, the guard led him to an office a few blocks away where Mr. Kraus and several other bewildered immigrants were briskly examined by a doctor and taken under armed guard to a steamer that delivered them to Rikers Island. There, over the course of a week, they were formed into a company, provided with muskets and gear, and shipped off to Annapolis, where they relieved a Pennsylvania regiment charged with guarding Confederate prisoners. Desperate to be released, Mr. Kraus wrote to his brother in Wisconsin as well as to the German Consul in New York, but nothing could be done for him, since he had signed the enlistment papers knowing full well what they said. If the translator had unwisely advised Mr. Kraus to sign the papers but flee before mustering in, it was all to the better that Mr. Kraus had been unable to follow that advice, because the penalties for desertion were severe.

Gerda wasn't sure what outraged her most: the depiction of her countryman as both gullible and duplicitous, or the suggestion that German immigrants were not eager to support their adopted country. In response, she had hoped to prove that Leonhardt Kraus's account was entirely fictional, but when her research turned up similar tales of dubious recruitment practices, she decided instead to pen a tribute to the many recent immigrants — German, Irish, English, and otherwise — who had gladly chosen military service as a way to achieve citizenship. With the help of Dorothea's Eastern relations, she had collected several inspiring anecdotes to support her thesis. She only wished her brother had a story of loyalty and patriotism she could include among them.

Spurred on by the competition with the Union Quilters, Abel's men put up Union Hall with impressive speed, and yet with an attention to the finer details of craftsmanship appropriate for a building intended to become a city landmark. Constance had never been prouder of her husband, or more worried about him, not even during those hazardous days when he had traveled into the South to sell cheeses and help desperate slaves escape to freedom in his wagon. Now he faced different dangers, as exhaustion, anger, and frustration took their toll. He wanted to fight, and each time a new call went out for soldiers and the state scrambled to meet its quota with volunteers rather than resort to a draft, he took his rifle out to the firing range he had set up on the far edge of their property and practiced his marksmanship with fierce determination, his jaw set and eyes glinting as if he contained a thunderstorm.

"They need us," Abel told her and sympathetic friends, the Grangers, the Nelsons, and the Bergstroms. "They need us to win this war. But all along they've denied men of color the vote because they say voting is a privilege reserved for those who accept the full responsibilities of citizenship. We've been clamoring for those rights as well as the responsibilities for years. We're prepared to take them on. But no matter how much they need us to shoulder those responsibilities, they'd rather lose the war than give us the privileges."

His words filled Constance with fear. She believed what he said about the Union's reluctance to enlist men of color as soldiers, but she prayed he was wrong about the Union's willingness to sacrifice the country rather than allow men like Abel to fight. She followed the war in the papers and listened intently as letters from the 49th were shared among the Union Quilters, but those sources could not confirm how closely matched the two sides truly were, how near or far one side or the other was from victory. Some battles went to the Union, others to the Confederacy. The Union seemed perpetually short of troops and supplies, but she had heard that the Rebels suffered even more severe deprivations. The colored newspapers had reported rumors that slaves were being used to support the Confederate troops as cooks and laborers. Why wouldn't the Union do at least that much, and free the white soldiers in those positions to fight? She knew better than to mention this to Abel; he wanted colored men to be allowed to enlist in any capacity for which they qualified. She just wanted to win the war. The thought of a conquered North, with slavery brought up from the South and

159

imposed upon them by cheering, malicious overseers, was more than she could bear. Perhaps at the outset the Southern states had only wanted to withdraw from the Union, but after so much violence and with such hatred on both sides, who was to say what the Rebels would do in victory, driven by vengeance and want?

She wanted to believe that Mr. Lincoln would put rifles in the hands of colored men long before he would let the nation perish, but in the meantime, she could only work with the Union Quilters to support the 49th and offer what comfort and encouragement to Abel she could. The construction of Union Hall was a source of great pride to him, and she had heard him declare more than once that he was honored to wield hammer and saw in support of his country. She wondered what he would do when the hall was complete, and found herself hoping that the construction would fall behind schedule and prolong his service to the 49th — for that's what it was, in her opinion — but Abel was too good a foreman to allow that to happen.

The quilt was also coming along beautifully, and it seemed as if the women might win the race. Throughout June, the quilters of Elm Creek Valley stole moments from their busy days tending to farms, shops, and families to piece blocks for the Loyal Union Sampler. Patchwork patterns commemorated battles the 49th had fought, places they had seen, tasks performed on the home front, and people dear to the quilters' hearts. One of their own provided the one hundred twenty-first and final block — Charlotte, recently returned to their circle after recovering from the difficult birth of her daughter. Cradling baby Jeannette in her arms while Dorothea held up her block for all the friends to admire, Charlotte explained that she called the pattern Jonathan's Satchel in tribute to the noble services her husband provided the ill and wounded men of the 49th. It was true that numerous letters read aloud at their meetings included soldiers' praise and admiration for their hometown physician. Several soldiers had declared that the men of Company L would rather trust in Providence and go without medical care than be treated by any other physician. From what she had heard about some of Dr. Granger's colleagues, Constance figured that decision had saved many a life.

As both quilt top and hall neared completion, the Union Quilters decided that they would celebrate the grand opening of Union

Hall with a Summer Fair and Quilting Bee on the Fourth of July. They would solicit donations from the bounty of their neighbors' spring gardens — herbed vinegars, pickled vegetables, fruit pies and preserves — and sell them to raise money for the Veterans' Relief Fund. Subscription sales, which they would feature prominently at the event, would pay off their last construction debts. To encourage sales, the same lovely young women who had participated in the pageant the previous fall would lead potential donors on tours of the building, ending at the observation balcony at the top story, where visitors could enjoy a bird's-eye view of the Independence Day celebrations in the streets below. At the heart of the fair would be the Loyal Union Sampler, its three layers held snug and smooth in a quilt frame in the center of the spacious performance hall. Every quilter present would be allowed to take at least a few stitches, and those with a finer hand would be encouraged to do more. Anneke anticipated that they would be able to finish the quilt, binding included, by evening, so the drawing would be held at the conclusion of the fair. The lucky winner would have to return the following afternoon to claim the prize, however, since Anneke had arranged for a photographer to come the morning after the fair to take a picture of the quilt hanging proudly from the lower balcony. Afterward, he would take an image of the Union Quilters gathered on the front stairs of the hall. Dorothea intended to display the photograph on the foyer wall beside a framed copy of their charter.

For to Constance's amazement, the Union Quilters and Soldiers' Relief Society had become a body corporate. Dorothea received the official documents from her lawyer in the middle of June, and as word spread, the town council's persistent inquiries about placing Union Hall under their authority dwindled and disappeared. For a while, there were rumors that the mayor wanted the town to construct an even grander hall of its own, but after the *Water's Ford Register* ran an editorial questioning whether this was the best use of tax dollars, considering the ongoing demands of war and the existence of an excellent new hall that could be rented for town events, the rumors faded away.

As the men of the 49th toiled in far-off Virginia, the women anxiously awaited news from the front. Casualty lists brought new heartbreak to the Elm Creek Valley almost every week, while calls for new troops came again and again. Constance was torn between relief that her husband would not be called upon to fight and distress for him, to see him rebuffed again and again when the need for men was so great. Since being sent away from Lewistown, twice more he had tried to enlist and twice more he had been rejected. Newspaper reports that in May, Union major general David Hunter at Hilton Head, South Carolina, had ordered the emancipation of all slaves in South Carolina, Georgia, and Florida and had authorized the arming of all able-bodied men of color in those states sent Abel's spirits soaring, even though Hunter's unauthorized order had never been approved by Congress and was soon disavowed by President Lincoln. "Our time is coming," Abel insisted. "Officers in the field wouldn't put rifles in the hands of colored men if they didn't believe the men capable and the need urgent. Eventually, Mr. Lincoln will believe it too."

"I hope so, Abel," she replied, and she did, although she feared for him.

The quilt top and the hall were completed within hours of each other on the first day of July, the winner's margin so narrow that both teams agreed to declare the race a tie. Proudly the men escorted the Union Quilters on a tour of the glorious building their efforts and vision had wrought, Abel in the lead pointing out features of the concert hall and distinctions between the two galleries, one that would be ideally suited for art exhibitions, the other for smaller lectures or musical performances. Passersby on the streets below waved up at them in delight as they strolled along the observation balcony, admiring the view of the gardens Mrs. Granger and Mrs. Claverton had so beautifully planted around the hall. The exterior architecture was rendered in the Greek Revival style, simple but elegant and refined, sure to stand the test of time. In the grand hall, the Union Quilters tested the plush chairs, which had arrived from Harrisburg only two days earlier, and proclaimed them the most comfortable seats they could imagine, and praised the decision to use movable chairs rather than permanent installations so that the seating could be altered to accommodate a variety of events or removed altogether to convert the space into a ballroom. Abel showed them storage closets and offices, dressing rooms and stairwells. All that remained was to hang the luxurious velvet draperies, lay rugs upon the floors, and give every piece of woodwork a final dust and polish before the grand opening.

After much planning and a flurry of eleventh-hour activity, the Union Quilters welcomed friends, neighbors, and visitors from throughout the Elm Creek Valley and beyond to the inaugural gala at Union Hall. Constance wore a new summer dress of a blue foulard print with a gathered bodice and a lace collar attached to the jewel neckline. Abel and the boys wore their best suits, as befitted the occasion. As they rode into town, Abel seemed in better spirits than he had been in months. Although Constance was glad to see him so cheerful, she worried how he would feel the next morning, when he had no construction site to report to and only the usual chores of dairying and tending crops to occupy him.

The streets of Water's Ford were at least as crowded as they had been on the day of the enlistment rally so many months before. The band played a stirring march, drawing the people to the block in front of Union Hall. While the boys ran off to join friends, Abel and Constance met the Union Quilters and the leaders of the construction crew on the portico. Charlotte and Prudence had tied a long, broad red ribbon around the two center pillars and had set a podium in front of it. Anneke carried a gleaming new pair of shears in her pocket, and she fidgeted so nervously as she fussed with last-minute details that Constance feared she would injure herself.

At last the moment came. The band's lone trumpeter, the other having gone to war, played a fanfare as Anneke took a deep breath and stepped to the podium. She had asked Dorothea to offer the opening remarks, protesting that her accent was sure to render her unintelligible to the crowd, but Dorothea insisted that Anneke accept the honor, since she had organized the creation of the Loyal Union Sampler. Hesitantly at first, but with increasing confidence, Anneke welcomed one and all to the gathering and thanked them for making the Summer Fair and Quilting Bee a success, which she was certain they would. She thanked the various businesses that had donated supplies and services to the cause, praised each founding subscriber by name (and noted that subscriptions were still available for purchase in the East Gallery, where visitors would also discover a variety of tempting refreshments), and complimented the construction crew who had built the hall, and the many quilters who had contributed blocks to the sampler. "I'm sure you will all wish to buy many, many tickets once you see the beautiful quilt you might win," she added, evoking a ripple of laughter from her listeners.

Finally, Anneke declared Union Hall officially open, and, taking the shears from her pocket, summoned Dorothea and Abel forward to cut the red ribbon. A murmur of surprise went up from the crowd, who, like Constance, had probably expected Dorothea to be summoned, but not Abel. A quick glance exchanged with her husband across the portico told her that he had not expected the honor, either. But why shouldn't he cut the ribbon? Who would have built the hall if not for him? Hans, all on his own? The other men, with no one to lead them? Abel deserved this recognition as much as Dorothea. Union Hall was a monument to his loyalty and patriotism, his contributions made all the more significant by his nation's persistent indifference to his willingness to risk his life in battle to preserve it.

Together, Abel's calloused, weathered farmer's hands on Dorothea's smooth, graceful ones, the two friends cut the ribbon, which fluttered in two red streamers to the floor of the portico. A muted cheer went up from the gathered throng, as if they still were uncertain how they felt about what they had just witnessed. From the podium,

Anneke beamed and gestured to welcome guests through the tall double doors into the marble foyer as if she could not imagine that anyone could possibly object to the sight of a colored man and a white woman honored with the distinction of opening what was sure to become a town landmark — and touching hands, no less. Still disconcerted, Constance caught Gerda's eye only to discover her friend grinning proudly at her sister-in-law. Steeling herself with a deep breath, Constance decided that likely no one would want to spoil the celebration with unpleasantness over Anneke's spontaneous invitation, so she decided, like Anneke, to pretend that nothing was amiss.

She soon forgot her worries in the whirl of excitement as crowds filled the hall, marveling at each new discovery. Many paused in the foyer to find their own names engraved upon a wall of honor, a tribute to their contributions. Several members of the band had set up their instruments in a corner of the performance hall and kept the visitors entertained with merry jigs and reels. Women filled their baskets with delicacies from the bountifully laded tables arranged along the sides of the room, while others admired the exquisite masterpiece in the quilt frame. Charlotte seemed overwhelmed by the sudden rush to purchase tickets once the people saw what they might win, so Constance quickly stepped in to help her, pausing only occasionally to check on the boys and to observe Abel from a distance, happy to see him accepting congratulations from one and all. The incident at the ribbon cutting had apparently been forgotten, if it had ever seriously concerned anyone but Constance in the first place.

Throughout the day, people came and went, admiring the grand hall, taking a few stitches on the sampler, and shopping at the fair. Hour by hour the quilt neared completion, until finally, shortly after nightfall, the last corner of the border was finished, the gears on the end of the frame loosened one last time, and the quilt removed from the frame. Then the Union Quilters, directed by Anneke, bound the quilt by stitching a narrow strip of bias-cut fabric over the exposed edges of top, batting, and lining.

At last the quilt was finished. The band played another fanfare as Gerda and Constance, the tallest of the Union Quilters, carried the sampler to the stage and held it up for all to admire. Constance had never seen a lovelier quilt, 121 different blocks in a multitude of colors and fabrics, all in harmony despite their differences, held together by an intricate pattern of quilting stitches in scrolls, feathered plumes, and flowers, framed by elegant floral swags fashioned in appliqué. Along the top border, the phrase *Union Forever* was embroidered, and along the bottom, *Water's Ford, Pa.* As the applause faded, Anneke announced that ticket sales would continue for fifteen minutes more, and in the meantime, the quilt would be draped over a long table on the stage so that everyone could judge for themselves if it was worth an additional ticket or two.

The Union Quilters would have gladly extended the interval if the line at ticket sales warranted, but eventually they squeezed the last dollar from their guests and collected all the ticket stubs in a hopper. They insisted that Dorothea draw the name of the winner, for she had been the impetus behind the entire venture, and not a stitch would have been taken or limestone block set in place without her. The winner was a woman named Faith Morlan, a beloved friend of Mrs. Stokey's since childhood, whose contribution to the quilt had been a striking block she had named Charley Stokey's Star. All agreed that it was only right and just that a woman who had sewn a tribute to a fallen hero of Company L should take home the quilt.

The Summer Fair and Quilting Bee was a triumph by any measure. Union Hall was opened to great public acclaim, and the sales from the fair alone earned over four hundred dollars for the Veterans' Relief Fund. The opportunity quilt raised enough to pay off their outstanding debts, with a healthy amount left over to invest in the bank and draw upon for operating costs.

The glow of their success burned brightly for the next two weeks, with jubilant reviews in the *Register* and a congratulatory as well as conciliatory letter from the town council echoing the praise the Union Quilters heard wherever they went. Abel resumed his usual schedule of dairying and farming, and devoted the hours he had once spent on the construction site at target practice or scrutinizing the *Liberator* and other papers. With one great success behind him, he seemed ever more certain that he would not long be denied the right to serve his country as a soldier. If such hopes, however unlikely to be fulfilled, kept him from sinking into melancholy now that the hall was finished, Constance would say nothing to discourage him.

The Union Quilters were busier than ever, even with the Loyal Union Sampler completed, photographed, and delivered to the lucky winner. In addition to conducting their own fund-raisers, they also entertained requests from other groups to rent the hall. The women found themselves in an unexpected position of authority as they chose between various organizations and events. If an event reflected their own values, such as an enlistment rally or a lecture from a renowned abolitionist orator, the organization was graciously welcomed, but if the sponsoring group's mission seemed antithetical to their own — such as a lecture by Ohio congressman Clement Vallandigham, an outspoken Copperhead — the request was cordially refused. The pages of the *Watchman* fairly sparked with outrage after the representative's visit had to be canceled, but as G. A. Bergstrom retorted in the *Register,* the Peace Democrats shouldn't have invited such an eminent guest until they had secured a venue, but failing that, they were welcome to construct a hall of their own.

Sobering letters from the 49th reminded them how essential the work of the Union Quilters was to the soldiers at the front. Jonathan's grim letters to Gerda about the wounded men in his care spurred them on to raise money for bandages, medicines, and other supplies, while his more sanguine

173

notes to Charlotte encouraged them to believe that their efforts were improving conditions in the field hospitals. But the details of the battles lingered in Constance's thoughts and haunted her nightmares. Names of distant towns and battles blurred together in her mind — Second Bull Run, Sugar Loaf Mountain, Crampton's Pass, South Mountain. The flurry of communications that followed the Battle of Antietam stood out even amidst pages and pages of descriptions of astonishing events, bloodshed, and violence. Thomas wrote first of rumors about a curious incident that he had not been able to confirm, hearsay that in mid-September, a soldier from the 27th Indiana, while crossing a campground recently vacated by the Rebels, had discovered on the ground three cigars wrapped in a piece of paper. Astoundingly, the document turned out to be a copy of General Lee's battle plan for Maryland, which the soldier promptly turned over to his superiors. Already possessing superior numbers, Union General McClellan — informed of Lee's plan to divide the Army of Northern Virginia and armed with foreknowledge of the Confederate troop movements — had been handed the opportunity to defeat the separate wings of Lee's army decisively.

Thomas had ended his letter before the consequences of the Union's providential discovery had become evident, but other letters from Company L soon followed, describing the Battle of Antietam in stark, horrifying detail that left the women dazed and shocked and sickened. Although the 49th Pennsylvania had come under fire at Antietam, they had been only partially engaged; the 3rd Brigade of the VI Corps had taken the most active role, with the 7th Maine and 20th New York suffering the most severe losses. What their men had not been spared was the grim aftermath of the battle. Thousands upon thousands killed and maimed, hillsides dotted with prostrate corpses clad in blue, sunken roads filled with bodies in butternut and gray mowed down like grain before the scythe. Men frozen in the final acts of their brief lives — a hand gripping a sword hilt as a lieutenant rallied his men, teeth clenched in a last grimace around the bitten end of a cartridge as a corporal reloaded his weapon. Brains and blood splattered on the rich green leaves of corn; bodies bloated in death, fallen alone, in pairs, in clusters amidst the rows of stalks. The men's horror and anguish poured off the pages, and the women wept as they read or listened, utterly powerless, utterly bereft, unable to comfort their sons and brothers and fathers and sweethearts, stunned by their sudden need to protect their protectors.

Silently, Constance prayed for her friends and their absent loved ones — and thanked God that her husband had been spared the nightmare that would haunt the other men for years to come, perhaps forever. She could not imagine how any man, no matter how strong or valiant, could forget such horrors, once witnessed. She also suspected, though dared not say aloud lest it grieve her friends, that the letters contained only what the men could bring themselves to write about, to share with the women back home. Surely they had seen and heard and smelled and done much more and much worse than they had wanted to sear into the imaginations of their beloved mothers, sisters, and darlings.

Despite the devastating cost, the Union considered the battle of Antietam a victory, for although the overcautious General McClellan did not destroy General Lee's army, he ended Lee's invasion of Maryland and forced him to withdraw back into Virginia. Wishing she could not so vividly imagine the scenes the men had described, Constance hoped that some good might yet come of the great sacrifice of men's lives.

Before the end of September, she had her answer.

She was on the front porch shelling peas when Abel came racing up the road, his horse in a lather. "Constance," he shouted as he sped toward the barn. Her heart froze in her chest. He had gone into town to discover what news he could of the war; she could not imagine what he had learned. She forced herself to stand, and wondered vaguely if she should call for her sons or pray that they did not overhear whatever it was that had sent Abel racing home.

Abel passed the barn and came right up to the house, where he pulled the horse to a stop and swung down from its back. "Constance," he said, taking the porch steps two at a time. When he seized her hands, she realized he was beaming. "He's done it. At last, he's done it. Mr. Lincoln's freed the slaves."

Anneke followed Gerda and Dorothea's explanations as carefully as she could, but they could not dispel her puzzlement. Mr. Lincoln had wanted to free the slaves all along, they said, despite his earlier statements that the war was being fought only to preserve the Union, nothing more and nothing less. He had begun writing his Emancipation Proclamation weeks or even months earlier and had presented it to his Cabinet at the end of July, but he had been obliged to wait until after a decisive Union victory before he could announce the proclamation to the American people. Antietam was that victory.

"But why wait?" Anneke queried them. "He's the president, isn't he? If he wanted to end slavery, why not just do it?"

"To make such an announcement after a series of defeats would appear an act of desperation," said Gerda, but Dorothea said there was more to it than that. Mr. Lincoln had needed to determine whether freeing the slaves was constitutional, and he had come to believe that it was indeed legal for him, by virtue of his war powers as commander in chief, to declare the slaves in areas under rebellion henceforward and forever free.

Dorothea added that Mr. Lincoln had also confronted a delicate situation regarding the slaveholding border states that had remained loyal to the Union. If he had acted too soon, declaring an end to slavery when their loyalties had not yet settled, those states might have been compelled to join the Confederacy. The president instead had encouraged slaveholders in those states to voluntarily emancipate their slaves, promising them government compensation to offset their losses.

"He had to keep them in the Union or all might have been lost," Dorothea explained. "He knew that winning the war and preserving the Union would lead to the end of slavery. He had no choice but to wait until he thought the people would accept the proclamation. He and his party will still suffer for it in the fall elections, I fear, but not enough to throw the nation off this noble course."

That all made sense, more or less, but her friends' joy still perplexed Anneke. She had read a copy of the Emancipation Proclamation posted outside the Water's Ford courthouse, and it seemed full of ambiguity and uncertainty. What would become of the men, women, and children enslaved in the loyal Union border states of Delaware, Kentucky, Maryland, and Missouri? Why were Tennessee and entire counties within Louisiana exempted simply because they had returned to Union control? What practical good did it do to declare slaves free in areas where the people didn't even consider Mr. Lincoln to be their president and therefore were highly unlikely to obey his laws? Anneke acknowledged that she might have missed something as she read the English words and translated them into German in her head, but it seemed to her that Mr. Lincoln had emancipated slaves where the Union could not free them and kept them enslaved in places where the Union did enjoy the power to give them liberty. She failed to see how that was cause for celebration.

Two weeks later, even Gerda and Dorothea had their elation sharply cut short at alarming news from the southern part of the state. On October 10, Confederate general Jeb Stuart led eighteen hundred cavalry across the border into southern Pennsylvania on a mission to capture horses, take hostages to hold for ransom, and burn a railroad bridge over Conococheague Creek at Scotland, five miles north of Chambersburg and about one hundred miles south of Water's Ford, in order to cut off Union General McClellan's supply lines. In Mercersburg, the raiders looted stores of boots and shoes, seized horses, captured several hostages, and terrified the people. In St. Thomas, a small band of defenders scattered when fired upon, but two fled to warn the citizens of nearby Chambersburg. That evening, Stuart set up his cannons on a hill above the town, demanded its surrender, and occupied Chambersburg without incident. His men cut telegraph wires and captured wounded Union soldiers recovering in local hospitals, though Stuart promptly paroled them. When Stuart sent out a party to burn the Cumberland Valley Railroad bridge, the men returned with the disappointing report that the bridge, made of iron, would not burn. Fortunately for the Union, Stuart's men did not bother to confirm the clever townspeople's story, for the bridge was actually made of wood, and quite flammable. The Rebel rearguard found other resources to burn as General Stuart led his men out of Chambersburg — the railroad depot, railroad cars, warehouses storing military supplies, machine shops, business — and they managed to avoid Union troops led by General Stuart's own father-in-law as they made off with goods, several hostages, and more than twelve hundred horses.

Word of the daring raid did not reach the Elm Creek Valley until after General Stuart and his men had already left Pennsylvania and crossed White's Ford into Virginia, but it left them badly shaken. Until then the war had seemed far away, their homes and farms never truly in danger. Their men had marched off to enlist little more than a year before, but never had the women and children and elderly left behind felt their absence more keenly.

The war did not pause to give them time to catch their breath and allow their fears to subside, and neither did politics. On the same day General Stuart left Pennsylvania, the congressional elections were held. Dorothea's prediction came true, for the Democrats made gains in Pennsylvania as well as several other states. For the first time too, Pennsylvania had not met its federal enlistment quota and had begun enrollment for a draft. Recruiters urged men to volunteer while they could, because if they were drafted, they could be stuck in any regiment anywhere rather than with men they knew and trusted. Although Hans dismissed such talk as scare tactics, other men were thus compelled to enlist. But not everywhere. Not long after the election, resistance to the unpopular militia draft erupted in several Pennsylvania counties, the most severe occurring about 125 miles to the east in Luzerne County, where troops were called in to put down opposition. Further dismaying Anneke was talk of a growing Copperhead movement in the state, especially among the German population. Dissent amongst their

182

countrymen would only cast additional suspicion upon Hans. Another man might decide to enlist to prove his loyalty, but not Hans. He was stubborn, and he didn't care that their neighbors believed him to be a coward or glared jealously at Anneke in the market or around the sewing circle because her husband was safe at home.

Anneke was determined to give no one any reason to question her loyalty. She worked at quilting bees and fairs and entertainments at Union Hall to raise money for the soldiers, baby Albert in her arms. She served on the committee for the Harvest Dance, an annual Water's Ford celebration that the Union Quilters took over from the town and turned into a fund-raiser for the Veterans' Relief Fund. After President Lincoln delivered his annual address to Congress on the first of December, a month before the Emancipation Proclamation would take effect, Anneke arranged for a distinguished professor from the University of Pennsylvania to present a lecture on the subject. Despite the snow falling outside, a curious and eager crowd filled Union Hall to hear the scholar's interpretation of the address, his analysis of the president's proposed constitutional amendments, and his predictions for the future. At twenty-five cents apiece, the admission charges paid for the professor's fee and travel expenses, with a healthy sum left over to purchase enough supplies to knit two pairs of warm wool socks for each soldier in Company L.

In addition to raising money, the professor's lecture prompted other questions for Anneke, especially regarding President Lincoln's proposed constitutional amendment that Congress provide federal funds for the voluntary colonization of free persons of color abroad. "Would you want to go?" she asked Constance, the only colored person she knew well enough to feel comfortable asking.

Constance seemed taken aback by the very idea. "I was born in this country. My husband and children were born free in this country. What are we going to do, sell our farm, load Abel's cattle and goats on a boat, and start dairying somewhere in Africa? I'm sorry, but unless Mr. Lincoln plans to change that 'voluntary colonization' to 'forced,' he's stuck with us colored folks for the long haul."

Anneke knew Constance was far more concerned about a certain provision of the Emancipation Proclamation that would definitely take effect on the first day of January than a proposed amendment that might not go anywhere: the statement that all emancipated slaves "of suitable condition, will be received into the armed service of the United States to garrison forts, positions, stations, and other places, and to man vessels of all sorts in said service." If freed slaves could serve in that manner, wouldn't freeborn men of color in the North be permitted to as well? Anneke almost envied Constance, who might soon be the proud wife of a Union soldier — sooner than Anneke would, at any rate.

The Union Quilters hosted a lucrative Christmas Fair at the hall, made another five dozen quilts for a second new military hospital in Washington, and sewed a banner for the men of Company L to carry into battle. Anneke participated in every cause, thinking that surely any reasonable person would conclude that Hans was no Copperhead, or he would not permit his wife to engage in such activities.

The New Year began with prayers for a better year than the one before. The men of the 49th Pennsylvania wrote home about the ill-fated Mud March under General Burnside and their encampment at White Oak Church in Virginia. At the end of February, Congress passed a new conscription bill declaring that all able-bodied male citizens and men of foreign birth between the ages of twenty and forty-five who had declared their intention to become citizens were liable to perform military duty in service to the United States. Some exceptions were made for the infirm, officials within the highest levels of government, the only son of widows, the only son of aged parents dependent upon his labor, and felons, among others, but the remainder would be subject to the draft. Quotas for each district would be established based upon the population and the number of residents already engaged in the service. Once drafted, a man could hire a substitute or buy his way out of the service for three hundred dollars. Dorothea found this provision appalling. "It is bad enough that any man should go to war," she said, "but now rich men will avoid service while poor men fight in their stead."

Hans thought the threat of the draft alone would increase volunteering, but Anneke wasn't so sure. "Perhaps you should pay the exception fee," she suggested.

"What for?" Hans replied. "I never declared my intention to become a citizen, I've never voted in this state, and I'm in no danger of being drafted."

"But this would be an honorable way out."

186

Hans's expression became stormy. "Standing by my convictions is my honorable way out. If you want me to give three hundred dollars to the cause, I'll sell a horse and send the money to Jonathan. The army is desperate for horses, and God knows Jonathan has great need of cash to improve those tents in the mud that pass for field hospitals."

So they did, and Jonathan wrote a lengthy letter thanking them and describing in detail every good purpose to which he had put their donation. Even so, Anneke found Hans's alternative unsatisfying, because only Jonathan and the Bergstroms knew about it. What good was conclusive evidence of Hans's patriotism if it were not made public? How unlike Abel he was, Abel who followed the news of colored Union regiments forming in Southern states and eagerly awaited his opportunity to carry his rifle into battle.

Spring came to the valley, cool and rainy. The farmers returned to their fields, the women to their gardens. News came of bread riots in Richmond, naval attacks on Charleston, and the death of Stonewall Jackson, who had succumbed to pneumonia after the amputation of his arm. The 49th Pennsylvania saw action at Chancellorsville,

Franklin's Crossing, Bernard House, and other distant towns that Anneke had never heard of and would surely never see. In Boston, the 54th Massachusetts Volunteers set out for Hilton Head, South Carolina, the first colored regiment to be sent from the North. Constance reported that Abel was fairly bursting with anticipation, sure that he would soon find a way to go forth and meet the enemy.

But then, defying all expectations, it seemed that the enemy would come to him.

General Lee's Army of Northern Virginia was marching steadily toward Pennsylvania.

CHAPTER FOUR

The Virginia countryside was almost deserted, the heat oppressive. On the way to Aquia, the 49th Pennsylvania passed only a few ramshackle houses, occupied by poor whites and some Negroes who watched them march by without surprise or rancor. They had seen armies come and go before and were resigned to them.

"We should go into the Rebel states, take all we can, use it up and destroy the rest," Abner was saying. "If we don't, the war will never end. What good do we do ourselves to set guards upon secesh property along the line of our march? After we pass through, the Rebels come back, and they use all those carefully protected goods for their own sustenance. We should leave them nothing to eat, no place to rest, no succor, no comfort."

It was an old argument, and although Thomas saw some logic in it, he was too parched to spare the breath for rebuttal. Aside from the immorality of stealing or destroying the scarce provisions of women and children, the moment a soldier left the ranks to sack and despoil private homes, he was ruined, unfit for duty. That the Rebels might benefit from what the Union left for those poor innocents was a risk Thomas was willing to take, and he was glad his superiors apparently agreed. Besides, from what he could see, there wasn't much left in that country to sustain the VI Corps anyway.

They passed through a town, or the remnants of one — a courthouse, a jail, a church, and two other buildings, one of which was on fire. It was past noon when they were called to a halt, to give stragglers a chance to catch up before Rebel snipers picked them off and to allow the ambulance crews to attend to the men who had collapsed from sunstroke. Three had died, Thomas heard as he stumbled to the thin shade offered by a pair of beech trees, a scant coolness he shared with eight other men.

Drinking sparingly from his canteen, he took measure of his surroundings and found that they had come to a stop a few yards from an old farmhouse. A man not ten years his elder watched them from the doorway, silent and dour. A curtain whispered away from a lower window; Thomas glimpsed a woman's thin cheek and a thick tangle of brown hair on a young girl before the white linen drifted back into place.

The man squinted as he studied the soldiers sprawled out before his home, scowling around the mouthpiece of his pipe, the bowl cold and empty. Even in Virginia, tobacco was scarce, and when it could be found, it was ridiculously overpriced. In the yard, stiff weeds and grass grew where a garden had once been, and among them were tree roots, though there were no trees left nearby, curiously curved and shaped and bleached white by the sun —

"You there," Thomas called to the man angrily. "Why haven't you given those men a proper burial?"

"Probably buried them where they fell," muttered David Barrows. "Why go to the effort to move blasted Yankees?"

"If they *are* Yankees," another soldier said. "But I guess if they were Rebels, he would have carried them to the churchyard."

"He could have covered them up, whoever they are," said Abner, indignant. "It doesn't look like he threw a single shovelful of earth over them."

"I buried a heap of them," the man called

191

back, gesturing with his empty pipe to the east and west. "Rain carried the dirt away."

Wearily, Thomas pushed himself to his feet, leaving his gear in the shade. "Fetch me a shovel," he ordered the man, who grumbled and obeyed. As the call sounded to resume the march, Thomas swiftly covered the men's remains — two had fallen in the man's yard, he counted two rib cages, two skulls — and patted the earth flat over their graves with the back of the shovel. There was no time to fashion a marker, barely time for a hastily murmured prayer. The corps was moving again. Thomas threw the shovel toward the house, snatched up his gear, and fell into place in the ranks. The whole country was one vast graveyard. They marched over battlefields where they had fought months before, treading on the fallen.

They marched until late afternoon and bivouacked near a creek, where Thomas and many others washed off the heat and dirt and fatigue of the day. It had been a terrible march, made in haste. Anticipating an attack on the rear or flank, their commanders had ordered them to destroy any broken-down teams, wagons, and equipment if they could not be easily brought along. Nothing could be left behind for the Rebels. The stench of burning had filled Thomas's nostrils for hours and he seemed to smell it still, even after he scrubbed the dirt and smoke from his hair.

The next day they broke their fast with hard bread and coffee — Thomas pictured Jonathan in the field hospital grumbling about the lack of potatoes and fresh vegetables — and scrambled to write letters or mend clothing or seek respite in the Bible before resuming the march. They had barely set out when news spread along the lines that the Army of Northern Virginia was marching in force into Pennsylvania.

"Fifteen thousand crossed at Shepherdstown yesterday," a man from Company A reported. "Near the old field of Antietam."

"The Southern army is now north of us," said another, shaking his head in disbelief.

Thomas knew well where Shepherdstown was — less than a hundred miles from Water's Ford, from Two Bears Farm, from Dorothea and Abigail. Not since Jeb Stuart's raid had the war come so close to those he loved most dearly. "They'll set fire to property, destroy railroads, and take all the provisions they can find, but they'll soon turn toward Washington or Baltimore," he said, more to convince himself than his fellows.

Abner nodded. "They won't head into the Elm Creek Valley, not with the southern pass so difficult to cross and far more appealing targets closer to hand."

"They won't get past Harrisburg," said Rufus Barrows. "I hear Governor Curtin called upon the citizens of our fair state to defend their homes and firesides."

"If they respond with the same courage they showed at Chambersburg when Jeb Stuart paid 'em a call," another fellow chimed in, "then the city is surely doomed."

A ripple of low laughter passed through the ranks, but Thomas felt a pang of alarm. "They'll do some damage, as in Chambersburg, and perhaps they'll even strike Harrisburg, but Washington or Baltimore must be Lee's intended target," he insisted. "That's where we'll cut them off. We can reach Leesburg and cross at Edward's Ferry in short order. I'm sure that's what General Hooker is planning right now."

Someone snorted. "Hooker's preoccupied with his battle of wills with Mr. Lincoln."

Thomas hoped not, and prayed not. If Lee's army was indeed pushing deeper into Pennsylvania, he wanted the general to concentrate on casting him out.

The Army of the Potomac did indeed reach Edward's Ferry and cross the river on

June 25, with the last of brigades following the next day. They encamped around Frederick while Hooker set out for Harpers Ferry, which the Union held and the Confederates had bypassed on their way to Pennsylvania. Everyone knew that Hooker believed the post had outlasted its usefulness and was vulnerable to a devastating attack if the Confederates seized the high ground nearby. Rather than await an inevitable defeat, Hooker wanted the post abandoned and its garrison added to their army. It was common knowledge that Lincoln wanted Harpers Ferry held as long as possible. The two strong-willed men were at an impasse, and Thomas couldn't guess how they would resolve their differences.

Encamped in the green hills of Maryland, in more comfort and safety than they had known since Camp Curtin, the 49th waited, rested, and thought of home and loved ones far away. Thomas wrote to Dorothea, and sleeping, dreamed of her, her bright eyes, her warm smile, her gentle curves, her fragrance, her soft skin beneath his hands. When he returned home, he was resolved never to leave her again.

He saw no quick end to the war, and he knew he was not alone in this belief. The men of Company L would continue to fight, to do their duty to their country and one another, but experience had hardened them, given their patriotism a sharp, fatalistic edge as sure as any knife put to the whetstone. Their sacrifices might not be in vain, but they would not bring a swift end to the war either.

On the morning of June 29, the news sped through the federal camp like flames through tinder: Exasperated with his commander in chief's refusal to acquiesce in the Harpers Ferry matter, Hooker had submitted his resignation. Major General George Gordon Meade, commander of the V Corps, had been named his successor, awakened at three o'clock that morning by a courier who prefaced his announcement with a warning that he was the bearer of "trouble."

Thomas knew little of the new commander of the Army of the Potomac except that he was a regular army officer; his predilection for offensive action had won him the favor of Mr. Lincoln; he had led successful campaigns in the Seven Days' Battles, Antietam, Fredericksburg, and Chancellorsville; and bursts of temper interrupting his usual taciturn nature had earned him the nickname Old Snapping Turtle. Thomas did not envy him his promotion. The major general must have been surprised to be named the fourth commander of the federal army in eight months, and he could not have been pleased to take command in the midst of a campaign. He also had surely learned from his predecessors' fates that failure usually meant swift replacement.

Thomas figured Meade had not slept any more that night after learning of his promotion, for by sunrise he had devised a plan to send the Army of the Potomac into Pennsylvania on a broad front. To increase their speed and flexibility, Meade divided the army into three wings and sent them northward along different routes. The left wing, comprised of I, III, and XI Corps and commanded by the intelligent and greatly admired Major General John F. Reynolds of Lancaster, led the advance, with Reynolds's own I Corps forming the vanguard. Brigadier General John Buford's cavalry would screen their advance and attempt to determine the precise location of Lee's forces.

Thomas had no time to dash off a letter to Dorothea as they broke camp. Major General Sedgwick led the VI Corps through green hills and rolling farmland beneath hot summer skies, a ten-mile-long column stretching down the dusty roads linking the sleepy towns of New Market, Ridgeville, and Mount Airy Station. At nightfall they reached New Windsor, where Thomas immediately sought out Jonathan, hoping he might know what awaited them. Though the field hospitals were typically at the rear, as an officer, Jonathan occasionally caught wind of dispatches before word reached the ears of the infantry. After a fruitless search during which he had begun to worry that maybe Jonathan had been killed and no one had thought to tell him, Thomas learned from one of the musicians in the ambulance crew that when Meade's order to march north had come, Jonathan had been with the I Corps consulting with Dr. George New, the surgeon in chief of the 1st Division. He had moved out with them and was probably already somewhere around Uniontown.

Thomas absorbed the news, stunned. Jonathan wouldn't have willingly left the men of the 49th to face battle without their most trusted physician. "Has Dr. Granger been reassigned?" he asked. The last time they had spoken, Jonathan had complained angrily about surgeons prevented from returning to their regiments after accompanying their wounded patients to hospitals. Jonathan's skills would make him a prized addition to any corps or hospital, but he was devoted to the men of the Elm Creek

Valley and would have fought a transfer.

"We were told he'd rejoin us in Pennsylvania," said the musician.

Relieved, Thomas settled for leaving a hastily written note with the man, knowing that by the time Jonathan received it, his questions would have been answered one way or another.

The next day, the VI Corps trudged more than thirty-five miles to the northeast, encamping at Manchester. By then, speculation had traveled through the ranks that the Confederate troops were converging in south central Pennsylvania from the north and west. As far as Thomas could tell from the few plausible details he sifted from the rumors, Major General Meade intended first and foremost to protect Washington and Baltimore from a Rebel assault, which made perfect sense. If General Lee moved his army south, the Army of the Potomac could create a line of defense along the southern shore of Pipe Creek in northwestern Maryland — hence the need to send the VI Corps northeast to anchor the line. They surely would not linger long in Manchester but would march again in the morning, crossing the Mason-Dixon Line and pushing on to Hanover, Pennsylvania.

But the first day of July dawned hot and

sultry and brought an unsettling turn of events — Sedgwick had been ordered to redirect the VI Corps to Gettysburg with all speed. As the men made haste to break camp, rumors abounded; the most convincing ones claimed that John Buford's cavalry had arrived in Gettysburg on June 30 in search of Lee's army, only to be warned by frightened civilians that a Confederate division had marched eastward through town four days earlier, and that more enemy troops, perhaps numbering in the tens of thousands, were at that very moment approaching from the west. Buford's patrols had confirmed some of these alarming reports and received others from local farmers that a Confederate army twenty thousand strong had reached Cashtown, only nine miles to the west. At night their campfires could be seen dotting the foothills of South Mountain. The Rebels had cut telegraph lines and severed railways, cutting off communications and isolating the town. Buford's exhausted cavalry brigades stood alone where perhaps as many as fifty thousand Confederate infantrymen would soon converge.

Realizing he lacked sufficient numbers to hold the advantageous high ground controlling the roads along which Meade's army would approach Gettysburg, Buford had deployed his men north and west of the town, hoping to delay the Confederate advance long enough for reinforcements to arrive. He had sent couriers racing to General Meade as well as to Reynolds, six miles to the south with the I, II, and XI Corps, the nearest Union infantry, to urge them to hurry. Buford's cavalry, numbering fewer than three thousand, then engaged the enemy.

Fierce fighting carried on throughout the morning of July 1. By half past nine o'clock, Buford's men had taken up a final defensive position along McPherson's Ridge, when a lookout spotted horsemen galloping up Emmitsburg Road. One carried a flag, a white circle on a field of red — the I Corps had arrived, just in time, and there was Reynolds, leading his infantry column. He and Buford, old friends, had conferred, had planned the infantry's advance, and had sent couriers to warn the citizens to seek shelter in safer parts of the town, warnings that went mostly unheeded. Reynolds had deployed Cutler's brigade, and then the Iron Brigade, and then as the gallant Reynolds had urged his men forward to engage the enemy, he had been shot in the head, knocked from his horse, and killed.

Thomas went cold at the news of the shocking loss. He prayed the rumors were exaggerated — perhaps Reynolds had been merely wounded and was even now regaining his strength in a field hospital, perhaps with Jonathan attending him — but the tales rang with severe and solemn truth. He steeled himself and marched on with his fellows, backtracking through Manchester, making haste for Gettysburg. In northern Maryland they passed a few resolutely secesh folk, who shut themselves up in their houses and scowled out the windows as the men in Union blue went by, but others welcomed them with cheers and visible relief. One stoop-shouldered, white-haired woman stood at the gate of her small cottage, a basket on her arm, handing out chunks of bread still warm from the oven as the men passed by. From several yards away, Thomas heard her murmur, "God bless you, son," to each soldier, and the men's grateful replies. The sourdough aroma made his mouth water, and as he approached the gate, he gnawed the inside of his lip and estimated the diminishing supply in her basket. At last he reached the woman, and he thanked her even before the bread was in his hand. As he took the first welcome bite, their eyes met briefly before she glanced down the road to the scores of hungry men still coming after him. "Gracious me," he heard her exclaim in despair as he marched on. "There won't be enough by half!" Not by half, not by a small fraction of a half, he thought as he hungrily savored the last crumb. His stomach growled, a gruff plea he could not satisfy.

The Littleton Pike was crowded thickly with wagons, frightened people fleeing the scene of battle with horses and cattle and worldly goods they dared not leave behind for the Rebels. The corps crossed into Pennsylvania, and all around him Thomas could feel the men of the 49th quickening. These were not the hills of home, but they were on the soil of their home state, and the enemy preceded them. They passed through towns the Rebels had raided, saw the stark, stunned terror mixed with relief on the faces of the Northern civilians who had never expected the war to come to their fields and front doors and now thought they beheld their rescuers. In Union Mills they were greeted by cheering, weeping crowds, who shouted warnings of the Confederate forces they had witnessed, their numbers, their ferocity, their lean and hungry avarice. Several pretty young women scattered flowers in their path, declared the men their gallant liberators, and sang patriotic songs. One lovely, spirited girl threw an entire bouquet, and whether she intended it for Abner, no one could say, but he was the one to catch it. Some fellows teased him and joked about her evident good taste, but Abner never broke stride as he reminded them that he was happily married and handed the ribbon-tied flowers to a younger, single man.

Night fell. The cheers faded behind them as onward they marched on unfamiliar roads, not knowing what lay ahead of them, what they would find when they reached the rest of the army.

Then it was the morning of July 2, then noon, and then early afternoon. They had marched through the night, and seventeen hours and thirty-seven miles after they had set out, they reached the outskirts of Gettysburg. The evidence of heavy fighting lay all about them, battles past and ongoing, the crashing of artillery fire in their ears, smoke rising over a distant battlefield. "Glory be, hallelujah," Thomas heard a beleaguered corporal shout. "It's Uncle John and the Sixth."

Fatigued from the swift march through the night, Thomas nonetheless felt his blood surging, as he knew his fellows did. This was their land, their soil, and they would defend it. His heart pounded as the 1st Brigade, his brigade, was deployed. The rest of the corps would be held in reserve to the east of the city.

"Just our luck," grumbled Rufus Barrows as they set out. "I could use a rest."

"It could have been worse." Thomas didn't know why he bothered to reason with the older man, whose constant grumblings tried his patience. "We could have been among the first here, and in the thick of it."

Rufus grunted a response, but there was no time for anything else, for they were in the midst of it then, pressing forward, acrid smoke stinging their nostrils, the sound and fury of battle all around them. Thomas acted almost without conscious thought, on instinct honed with practice, driving forward, responding to calls to rally, to dangers seen and anticipated, shutting off the part of his rational mind that cried out that all was madness, utter insanity, the part that recoiled in horror at the blood and gore and broken bodies of his friends and the men in butternut and gray falling dead or worse yet, fatally and agonizingly wounded because of him, because of shots he fired, because he had taken their lives —

And then a pause, a respite, as the company was ordered to occupy a granite knob, an outcropping on the smaller of two hills to the west of the town. The Rebels had been run off for now, and though the skirmishing continued into evening, there was time to collect his thoughts, to reflect upon the battle. Thomas wanted nothing less. Exhaustion washed over him in waves. He wanted only to fill his empty stomach with a good, hot meal and sink into dreamless sleep.

He took up a position behind a large rock, not as secure as breastworks, but the best he could find. As he dug into his haversack for his rations, he heard a low groan from somewhere behind him, but a glance over his shoulder revealed nothing. "Did you hear that?" he asked Abner, who shook his head, his gaze fixed on the distant enemy lines. Thomas gave his head a shake to clear his ringing ears, but it was a poor remedy. Returning his attention to his haversack, searching for a piece of hard bread he was sure he had saved for later, he heard the sound again, quickly muffled. This time he traced it to a copse of trees about ten yards distant, up a slight slope.

"Are we missing anyone?" he asked Abner.

"You mean aside from the fellows killed on the way across the field?" Abner shrugged. "None that I know of."

Company L hadn't lost anyone that day as far as Thomas knew, but that didn't mean all were accounted for. Night was falling, and if anyone was lost and wounded, he might be impossible to find in the darkness. "I'll be right back," he told Abner, crouching as he crossed the granite outcropping and made his way to the trees, rifle in hand.

He heard raspy breathing from several paces away and stole forward quietly, raising his rifle when he glimpsed a mud-crusted boot extending out into a clearing from behind some low brush. "Who's there?" he said, his senses sharply alert. When there was no answer, he drew closer cautiously, ears tuned to the warning sound of the tearing open of a cartridge, the slide of a ramrod. The raspy breaths diminished as if the hidden man wanted desperately not to be found. Rounding the corner, pushing aside the low branches with the end of his rifle, Thomas discovered a young man in butternut and gray lying sprawled on his back, his boots loosened, his coat torn open to reveal a bayonet wound in the shoulder. His gear and haversack were gone, but Thomas barely noticed anything more, his gaze immediately drawn to the Rebel's face by tracks of blood down the front of his soiled shirt. Despite all Thomas had witnessed, one glance was enough to sicken him and force him to avert his gaze. A minié ball had struck the young man near the right temple and had emerged on the opposite side of his head. The left eye had been completely torn away, and blood and gore streamed from both sockets.

As Thomas came nearer, the youth dug his heels into the dusty earth and struggled to scramble backward. "Don't take my boots," he rasped. "Don't take 'em."

Thomas instinctively raised his palms, but the calming gesture was lost on the blinded youth. "I don't want your boots." The youth trembled, but Thomas sensed it was from shock and exhaustion, not fear. "Do you have water?"

"Yankees took all I carried." Defiantly, the youth added, "But not my boots. They tried, and stuck me in the shoulder when I kicked 'em for it, but they didn't get my boots."

"They're fine boots," said Thomas, taking his canteen and kneeling beside him. He raised it to the youth's lips and held it carefully while he drank deeply. "Are you hurt anywhere else?"

He shook his head, and as if he feared the answer, asked, "Tell me. Is it night?"

Thomas hesitated. "No. Not quite yet."

"I'd hoped it was night." He strangled a sob. "I can't see."

"I know."

"Is it bad? I mean, I know it's bad, but does it look bad?"

Thomas swallowed hard, unwilling to lie. The shoulder wound seemed superficial and had stopped bleeding before Thomas's arrival, but the head injury was something else again. "I've seen worse, but yes, I'm afraid it's . . . quite serious."

"I've got a girl back in Alabama," he rasped, shivering. "Prettiest girl in Dallas County. She said she'd marry me when I come home, when the war's over. But now . . ."

Thomas did not know what to say. "Rest easy." He dug into his pack and took out the Dove in the Window quilt, dusty and worn from months on the road, but still warm. He wrapped it around the youth and sat back on his heels, unsure what to do next. The granite outcropping was quiet for the moment, more or less, but he couldn't leave the boy there to be caught in the cross fire as the dueling armies advanced and retreated.

As he scanned the terrain, the popping of gunfire reminding him to keep low, the youth's trembling gradually subsided.

"Thank you," he murmured, drawing the quilt up to his chin and slipping his arms beneath it. "I'm mighty grateful."

"It's all right." There was no way around it; Thomas would have to carry the boy to safety. He had heard that the seminary on the ridge had been appropriated as a Union hospital, but it now lay behind enemy lines. If he could get the boy to an ambulance team, they would know where to deliver him. "I've got to get you out of here."

"You taking me prisoner?"

"I'm taking you to a doctor," Thomas replied. "Can you stand long enough to help me get you on my back?" The boy nodded, but when he tried to stand, he groaned in agony and slumped back against the ground. "Easy, now," said Thomas. "It's all right. I'll lift you."

"Wait," the boy gasped as Thomas shifted his gear and knelt beside him. "In my coat. In the inside pocket. There's a letter to my Malinda Jane —"

"You're going to a hospital. I'm going back to my company," Thomas reminded him. "You're better off sending it yourself."

"All right, then, but behind the letter, there's a pouch. I want you to have it. For your kindness."

Thomas refused, but the boy insisted, so

reluctantly, he obliged and found a tan leather pouch stuffed full of tobacco. "I don't smoke," the boy confessed. "My uncle keeps sending me the stuff and I have no use for it except in trade. You take it."

"I thank you," said Thomas, tucking the pouch into his haversack. He hadn't seen such fine tobacco nor such a generous portion of it in months. "Get set, now. This will hurt."

The boy clenched his teeth and grunted as Thomas clasped the youth's wrists together and hefted him onto his back, staggering forward until he regained his balance. He carried the boy along the granite outcropping and down the hill, praying soldiers on both sides would either not see them in the twilight or would recognize an act of mercy and hold their fire.

They reached level ground, the boy gasping in pain whenever Thomas lost his footing or started at the sound of a rifle shot or minié ball striking the ground nearby. In the shelter of a thicket, Thomas set the boy down for a few minutes' rest.

"Bless you," the boy mumbled after Thomas gave him the last of his water. "You're a true Christian and a gentleman."

Thomas let out a short, bitter laugh. If one excluded all the other men in butternut and gray he had shot instead of saved, perhaps he was. "It won't be much farther now."

"I changed my mind. Take my boots," the boy urged as Thomas stooped to lift him again. "I want you to have them."

"They aren't my size," Thomas said shortly, his voice straining as he shifted the boy's weight on his back, although he hadn't looked closely enough at the boots to be sure. He stumbled over something in the fading light and hoped it wasn't a man.

"Then listen. You ever get down to Dallas County, Alabama, you find Archibald Hammock. You tell him William sent you. He's kin to me, and I swear he'll make you the finest pair of boots you ever wore, free of charge when he hears what you done for me. He's with Captain Waddell's company now, but after the war he'll open up shop again, you wait and see."

"All right," said Thomas to quiet the boy so he would conserve the little strength remaining to him. He wondered if a day would ever come when he could travel peaceably to Alabama and seek out a boot maker without fearing he would be shot on sight as a hated enemy.

Jonathan would have preferred not to depart

with the I Corps, but Dr. New outranked him and he could not refuse his superior's urgent request. Nor could he deny that his services would be needed as soon as the fighting began, which it inevitably would, with Lee's men in Pennsylvania poised to attack Baltimore or Washington, and Meade determined to defend the capital. The VI Corps would soon follow, and he could rejoin his regiment then. Hoping that someone, perhaps his assistant surgeon or an orderly, would think to pack his personal belongings and bring them along, he hastily scrawled a message informing his assistant of his unexpected and unwitting change in plans. Then he quickly joined the surgeons of the I Corps as they prepared to move.

The surgeons followed behind the infantry along with the ammunition wagons and ambulances, General Meade having ordered that the medical and supply trains remain behind at Westminster in order not to slow their advance. Medicine wagons accompanying each division's ambulance trains carried a limited supply of medicines, dressings, and instruments, which Jonathan hoped would suffice.

The fighting was already well under way by the time he caught his first glimpse of Gettysburg, a pretty and prosperous town

213

of brick and whitewashed homes with neat gardens, broad streets, thriving businesses and churches, and several colleges. But structures on the outskirts of town bore scars from the battle, and broken fences and trampled wheat fields gave evidence of the Confederate raiders.

"There," said Dr. New, indicating a tall, stately building with a white cupola on top of a green ridge just west of the town, where the Chambersburg Pike met the Fairfield Road. "That will make a fine hospital."

Jonathan hesitated. The brick, four-story building seemed strong and spacious enough, and the ample windows would allow sufficient light to conduct operations by and fresh air to disperse unhealthy miasmas, but field hospitals usually were established one or two miles back from the front lines, to reduce the likelihood that they would come under fire. This building — a seminary, or so he gathered from the talk of the citizens who had imprudently remained to view the spectacle — was directly alongside the fight. Indeed, various Union forces had established themselves on the ridge, and Jonathan was as near to the artillery fire as he had ever been. "We'll be close," he cautioned the chief surgeon. "Perhaps too close."

"It will be all the easier for the wounded to reach us," said Dr. New. "In fact, the seminary appears so welcoming I suspect some wounded from yesterday and this morning have sought shelter there already. We'll hang a hospital flag from the cupola and we should fare well enough."

Jonathan nodded. There was no time to waste. He winced as a shell exploded nearby, and quickly arranged for the rest of the medical personnel to regroup at the seminary. Dr. New's prediction soon proved true; as they approached, they spotted victims of the first day's fighting awaiting them on the porch and in the entryway. Women — civilians from Gettysburg, as far as Jonathan could tell at first glance, neither trained nurses nor Sanitary Commission volunteers — tended to the maimed and suffering as best they could. Their relief at the sight of the surgeons and orderlies was greater than their eagerness to relinquish their duties, and while some hurried off to seek shelter with their families, others asked to remain, to offer whatever assistance or comfort they could.

Jonathan was grateful for any willing hands and quickly set the women to work heating water, soaking sponges, and preparing hot beverages. With practiced speed, the medical staff set out instruments and supplies — knives, forceps, scalpels, scissors, chloroform, brandy, ammonia spirits, bandages, plasters, tourniquets, needles, silk thread. The stretcher-bearers set out to canvass the fields to find the wounded and carry them back to the hospital while the surgeons attended to those already present. Some men were beyond saving; others would have to wait until the more seriously injured were treated. Swiftly, Jonathan went from soldier to soldier, staunching the flow of blood from severed arteries with tourniquets, probing wounds with a finger to remove minié balls and debris, dressing open wounds, administering liquor or sometimes morphine to lessen the pain and shock. The wounded kept coming, and before long the seminary building as well as the adjacent professors' homes and student dorms were occupied. Dr. New announced that he would ride into town and commandeer as many houses, barns, halls, or hotels that proved necessary. Jonathan barely had time to acknowledge his departure, barely had time to wipe the blood and pus from his scalpel on his apron between patients.

Explosions rattled the windows; the injured and the dying coughed up blood and cried out in pain. When a few wounded soldiers exclaimed that some of the artillery fire raining down upon them came from Union cannons, Jonathan remembered Dr. New's words as they had viewed the seminary from afar and shouted for someone to run upstairs and hang a hospital flag from the cupola. Preoccupied with a patient, he could only observe from the corner of his eye as an uninjured soldier dashed from the room carrying a coil of rope and something that for all the world resembled a woman's red flannel petticoat. It would do, he thought grimly as he went about his work. It would surely attract notice. Indeed, the firing upon the building soon subsided, although the threat of stray shells remained.

The afternoon wore on, and from time to time, someone would hastily step outside to watch the battle and return with confident assurances that the Union lines were certain to hold. Jonathan fervently hoped so, but the impressions he had pieced together from remarks of the wounded and the ambulance crews were far less sanguine. Major General Reynolds had been killed soon after the I Corps arrived on the scene. The untested and inexperienced Pennsylvania Emergency Militia had been largely ineffective in defending the state, having been scattered or captured almost upon first contact with the battle-scarred soldiers of Lee's army. In all that time, Jonathan treated no one from the 49th, or as far as he could determine even a single soldier from the entire VI Corps. Other field hospitals were scattered throughout Gettysburg and the surrounding countryside, so it was possible the men of the Elm Creek Valley were engaged in the fighting, their wounded directed elsewhere. But he did not know, and the not knowing troubled him.

Just then came an incredulous shout from the doorway that Stone's brigade and the 151st Pennsylvania had pulled back from McPherson's Ridge. Jonathan finished tying off a tourniquet and strode to the window, where the sight of what appeared to be entire blue-clad regiments making a strategic retreat to the seminary momentarily staggered him. It couldn't be, but the longer he watched, the more the movement of the lines confirmed his first unbelievable reckoning.

He raced to locate Dr. New. "We've got to evacuate," he said, describing what he had seen. "We're no longer safe here."

Frowning, Dr. New went to the window, peered outside, and quickly nodded. "Agreed. Any man stable enough to be moved must be moved now."

Jonathan returned to his patients as Dr. New led the evacuation, barking orders to the ambulance drivers to deliver the patients to the Christ Lutheran Church on Chambersburg Street and other secure locations in town that he had prepared earlier. Swiftly the ambulance wagons were made ready; men who could walk made their way on foot, and stretcher-bearers carried others. By mid-afternoon the seminary had been emptied of all but the most seriously wounded, but new bloodied and broken soldiers kept arriving, on foot or carried by friends, and Jonathan despaired of attending to all of them in time to save them. Most of the medical personnel and all of the civilian volunteers had evacuated, leaving a skeleton crew to care for the wounded who braved the increasingly hazardous journey up the ridge to the seminary.

Suddenly, beyond the seminary walls, the furious sounds of artillery fire and rifle shots surged. Jonathan spared a quick glance out the window only to see Union infantrymen regrouping on either side of the building, lining up along Seminary Ridge for one last defensive stand. He went cold, his heart in his throat, and he knew no hospital flag waving from a high cupola would protect them.

Transfixed, he watched nearly two thousand Confederates fall into ranks as they prepared to assault Seminary Ridge. "Doctor," someone shouted. He tore himself away from the window and raced to the side of a private from the Iron Brigade with a stomach wound so severe he surely would not survive the day; Jonathan administered morphine to ease his suffering, but there was nothing more he could do. Next he examined the mangled arm of a Wisconsin corporal who begged him not to amputate, but before Jonathan could reply, a terrible salvo burst from all sides of the seminary; the room dimmed as brown-gray smoke obscured the windows. Jonathan's ears rang from the noise; he clenched his teeth and flinched with each explosion as the corporal grasped the arm of his chair with his good hand, his legs twitching as if he fought the instinct to seize his rifle and join the fray or to dive for cover.

"I believe your hand can be saved," he shouted to the corporal just as the sounds of firing paused. He looked from the man's wound to the window and back, picking out debris with forceps, waiting for the sounds to resume. Instead he heard shouts and distant screams of agony. Gradually the smoke began to clear outside the west windows. He motioned for an orderly, who hurried over with a basin of red-tinged water and a sponge. "Rinse the wound," he instructed, drawn irresistibly to the window. As the smoke cleared, his stomach turned at the ghastly scene: The slopes of Seminary Ridge were thick and red with blood and the bodies of the dead and dying. The Union line had pinned down the few survivors a mere few hundred yards away in a shallow depression between the ridges, and as Jonathan watched, they concentrated the full force of their artillery fire upon them.

Yet even confronted by this massive assault, the Confederate troops pushed forward. Beside Jonathan, an Irishman from the 20th New York leaning on a makeshift crutch murmured a prayer and crossed himself. The Union breastworks erupted in the fire and smoke of gunfire, the seminary walls trembling with the thunder of artillery. "Look there," said an assistant surgeon, his voice shaking. An orderly called to Jonathan, but he was riveted with shock and alarm. As he watched, a regiment in tattered butternut and gray shifted around the Union breastworks until they flanked the defenders. Then they opened fire.

"Lord help the First Corps," the Irishman muttered. Someone grabbed Jonathan's arm and pleaded with him to come. He had time enough to see the Union line collapse from left to right and the surviving defenders flee for Cemetery Hill before he allowed himself to be pulled away from the window and led to the bedside of another wounded soldier. Frantically he worked to attend one man and then another, and yet another. Dr. Heard, the medical director, called out that all medical personnel who wished to evacuate could wait no longer. A few hesitated before fleeing for the door, but Jonathan, in the midst of tying a tourniquet before a screaming boy of eighteen bled to death before his eyes, could not leave. And then there was another reason not to go, and another. Sparing one glance for the window as he hastened from one bedside to the next, he saw Confederate soldiers swarming the ridge. A minié ball shattered a window, showering a patient with glass.

It was late afternoon, and the last of the Union defenders had gone. A chill went down the back of Jonathan's neck as the Rebels' exultant yells filled the air — shrill, unearthly, and piercing, more animal than human. Beyond the window, a sea of butternut and gray swept past, and suddenly soldiers burst into the room, rifles leveled, shouting for them to surrender, to put their hands in the air. Jonathan instinctively complied, forgetting that he held a scalpel until a gaunt private screamed at him to put it down. He opened his hand, and the scalpel fell to the floor with a sharp metallic ping. He stumbled backward against a bed as more Rebels came into the room, shouting with triumphant glee as they discovered the wealth of medicine and morphine and instruments. Before Jonathan knew what was happening, they had swept the shelves clean of supplies and had carried them off, leaving nothing essential behind, not a bandage, not a bottle of laudanum, not even the scalpel Jonathan had dropped on the floor.

From shouts and footfalls and crashes coming from other rooms, Jonathan knew the same scene was unfolding elsewhere in the seminary. A Rebel sergeant appeared in the doorway and informed them in a drawl that they were all prisoners of the Army of Northern Virginia, patients and surgeons alike.

Dry-mouthed, ignoring the rifle pointed at his chest, Jonathan kept his arms raised and found his voice. "We have patients who need our attention."

The sergeant glanced around the room, in its way more filled with blood and horror than the battlefield. "Well, get to it, then."

"Your men have taken all our instruments."

"Our surgeons have been deprived of instruments as well as medicines, thanks to your Yankee embargoes," the sergeant replied in the same steady drawl, resting his rifle in the crook of his elbow. "Put some of that vaunted ingenuity to work and make due with what you got. That's what we've been doing going on two years now."

"We have Confederate wounded here too." Catching sight of blood seeping through his patient's trousers, Jonathan forgot himself and lowered his hands to part the shredded wool and expose the wound. Seizing a corner of the bedsheet, he tore off a long strip and packed it into the injury. "We've treated them throughout the battle. In addition to the international laws protecting medical personnel, laws of basic human decency oblige —"

The sergeant waved him to silence. "I'll check with our medical director. In the meantime, make do."

He strode off, and after a moment of stunned silence, the medical team sprang back into action, working frantically, helplessly, to save lives. They could perform no amputations, could relieve no pain. The Rebel sergeant did not return. Once Jonathan stepped outside, trembling from exhaustion, he sank down upon the wooden steps now riddled with bullet holes. He was a prisoner, powerless to help the men in his care. Repeated entreaties to any Confederate soldier who entered the hospital were ignored or met with empty promises. He rested his elbows on his knees and buried his face in his hands. He had not eaten since suppertime the previous day; his apron and shirtsleeves were stiff and encrusted with dried blood.

Not far away, the battle continued on Cemetery Hill as the Union troops retreated in utter disarray. Confederate troops milled about the seminary, sparing Jonathan the occasional glance but otherwise leaving him to his exhaustion. Suddenly a stir went through the troops, and Jonathan looked up to see a white-bearded gentleman approaching on horseback. An aide-de-camp hastened to his side, and as they conferred, Jonathan overheard a few phrases not drowned out by artillery fire: The man on horseback wanted the hills occupied by the Union to be taken if practicable, but if not, the Confederates were to await the arrival of reinforcements. As the gentleman rode off, a debate broke out between two officers with different interpretations of the orders. Only then did Jonathan recognize the bearded gentleman as General Robert E. Lee himself.

At that moment, he spotted a Confederate ambulance wagon and staggered to his feet. "You there," he called out, hurrying over before they could ride off. "This is a hospital. Your soldiers have taken our supplies. We cannot tend to our wounded." He jumped as a stray minié ball struck a nearby tree, spraying him with splinters of bark.

The ambulance drivers exchanged a look, and the one holding the reins shook his head. "Our surgeons have only enough supplies for ourselves, and barely that. We'll hang a hospital flag from your cupola, but more than that we can't provide."

Clenching his teeth in frustration, Jonathan nodded his thanks and returned inside, where the soldiers' needs had only increased in his absence. Later he overheard that at some time during the early evening, a Rebel soldier had replaced the red flannel pantaloons with a yellow Confederate hospital flag. It was little comfort.

Night fell, and in the scant light provided by a lantern improvised from a jar of lard with a handkerchief wick, Jonathan tended his patients in vain, or so it seemed. Sometime before dawn, he stumbled, eyes half closed, down the hallway to a small office lined with bookshelves. Papers had been strewn about the floor amidst broken glass from the shot-out windows, and most of the leather-bound volumes had been knocked to the floor by Rebels searching for valuables. One shelf was bare except for a Bible, which had likely been cast down by one careless soldier and carefully replaced by a more reverent companion. Pushing aside the chair, curling up beneath the sturdy oak desk, Jonathan drifted off to sleep, often dragged back into wakefulness by the groans and coughs and cries of the wounded.

The first shafts of morning light woke him. He crawled out from beneath the desk, rubbed his face vigorously, and tried to ignore his growling stomach. As he made his way back to his patients, he passed two slightly injured soldiers removing the body of another from the foot of the stairs. Recovering from an amputation in an upstairs room, the man had cried out all night for water, but those who had heard his pleas had been in no condition to help him. Desperate, he had crawled from bed and made his way downstairs, where he had bled to death without satisfying his thirst.

Swallowing back his bile, Jonathan nodded and continued past. If he had not slept so soundly, if he had stayed in the room with his patients — but nothing could be done for the man now. All Jonathan could do was try to help those who yet lived.

But without supplies, without instruments, there was little he could offer them except water and encouragement. He thought of his black leather physician's satchel, left behind with his personal belongings in Frederick, Maryland, with the VI Corps. It was just as well he had been unable to retrieve it before moving out with Dr. New and the I Corps, for it surely would have been confiscated too.

"I beg your pardon, Doctor," a woman's voice interrupted his reverie.

He looked up from a patient — an Indiana youth whose future was uncertain — to discover a dark-haired young woman standing just inside the doorway, trembling and pale, a basket on her arm. "Yes, miss?" He wondered what horrors she had witnessed on her way to the seminary from the town. He had a sudden vision of the Confederate forces moving on from Gettysburg to Harrisburg and into the Elm Creek Valley, and his own dear Charlotte recoiling tearfully from the sights and sounds and smells of a ruined battleground. He prayed she would never witness such grievous things.

"I've brought bread and candles and liquor," the young woman said, taking a brave step nearer, her eyes darting around the room and lingering on bandaged stumps and blood-soaked wrappings. Involuntarily she raised the back of her hand to her mouth and nose, not yet aware that such gestures were futile, that nothing could block out the stench. "I — I'm not a nurse, but I've come to help if I can be useful."

"Yes, of course," said Jonathan. "I will gladly accept the liquor. These men need water — here, and upstairs, in every room and hallway. There's a pump outside, and some pails may still remain. You'll find sponges on the table there — we were able to salvage a few."

The woman nodded, but then hesitated, glancing to the window and the open doorway. "I have something more." She turned her back, set her basket on the floor, reached beneath her voluminous skirts, and when she turned back around she carried a small, worn leather case, the side split and one handle missing. "My father had a practice in town. This is his old set of instruments. He packed it away out of fondness when he replaced them with new. I thought you might have use for them."

Hardly daring to trust his good fortune, Jonathan quickly accepted the case. "Your father — he doesn't need this?"

She shook her head. "He was killed at Antietam. An assistant surgeon with the II Corps has his new case now. Or so I believe."

"I'm sorry for your loss, miss." Jonathan set the case on the floor and opened it out of sight of the Confederate soldiers who from time to time passed the windows. The instruments were older and well used, but the scalpel still carried a sharp edge, a pack of needles seemed like new, and a nearly full spool of silk thread remained wound without a single snarl. He could do much with this. Voice shaking, he thanked the young woman, who nodded, forced a quick smile, and hurried off to fetch water.

Immediately the medical personnel resumed their work, the bounty of the cracked leather case invigorating them. An orderly administered liquor to those in the greatest pain, but the bottle was soon emptied. Just as the last dropped was drained, a shadow crossed the doorway, and three armed soldiers entered the room. "Every sound or slightly wounded soldier, rise and come with us," one commanded.

A murmur of confusion went up from the staff and wounded alike. "Why?" asked Jonathan. "Where are you taking them?"

"We have orders to parole all able-bodied prisoners." The soldier motioned toward the doorway with his rifle. "Don't argue or you can join them."

Choking back his protests, Jonathan smoldered in fury as the Confederates culled the less seriously wounded soldiers from those who could not walk. From time to time the medical personnel argued the case of a particular soldier who should not and must not be moved, but more often than not, the Confederates ignored their pleas. Some of the wounded pretended to be worse off than they were rather than be dragged from the relative safety of the hospital, but their captors soon lost patience with "shirkers and shammers." Men who swooned and collapsed on the way to the door could remain behind only if spirits of ammonia failed to revive them. Seething as he helped one such man, pale from blood loss, back into bed, Jonathan imagined the scene enacted throughout the seminary and in all the buildings that had been appropriated as field hospitals. How many hundreds of men desperately needing rest and recovery were being taken away? Their only hope was to be swiftly paroled and returned to Union field hospitals. Many of them, he feared, would not endure the transport.

Evening fell, and despite the culling of prisoners, hundreds of seriously wounded men filled the seminary. Jonathan and his colleagues used the smuggled tools surreptitiously, improvising bandages and tourniquets from bedsheets and linens that were becoming ever more scarce. Confederate stretcher-bearers continued to bring wounded into the building, blue and gray in equal numbers. In the flickering light of the candles the young Gettysburg woman had brought, Jonathan worked until Dr. Haines of the 19th Indiana urged him to get a few hours' sleep, promising to wake him at first light.

Jonathan retired to the office where he had slept the previous night, but it seemed only minutes had passed before Dr. Haines shook him awake. They traded places, and as Jonathan made his way back to the staging room, he heard more explosions in the distance. He had no idea where the Rebel and Union lines were, but the battle apparently still carried on.

As Jonathan took stock of the room, an assistant surgeon informed him that only a few new patients had arrived overnight, all Confederate, but they were expecting a surge when the battle resumed in earnest that morning, which it surely would. Jonathan thanked him and began his rounds. He was scanning the room for the whereabouts of the smuggled instruments when a patch of dulled colors on the opposite side of the room caught his eye and tugged at his memory. It was a quilt draped over a sleeping patient whose head and eyes were bandaged, and as dread drew him closer, understanding swelled until it struck him with a force almost tangible.

He ran the last few paces to the man's bedside and seized the quilt. "How did you come by this?" There could be no mistaking it. The triangles of Prussian blue, Turkey red, unbleached muslin — he had seen this Dove in the Window quilt in his sister's home countless times, not merely that pattern but that same quilt, and had seen it in Thomas's bedroll a hundred times more. "Where did you get this quilt?" The wounded soldier stirred drowsily and mumbled a reply. Furious, Jonathan seized him by the shoulders, insensible to the man's injuries. "What became of the Union soldier you stole this quilt from, you Rebel bastard?"

He was barely aware of someone seizing him from behind and dragging him away as the wounded Rebel struggled to prop himself up on his elbows. The sight of the wounded man groping blindly at his bandages brought Jonathan to his senses. He shook himself free of the Rebel guard who restrained him and forced himself to take a deep breath before returning to the man's bedside. "How did you come by this quilt?" he asked roughly. "Did you find it on the battlefield? Did you take it off a dead man?"

The Rebel shook his head but winced in pain and sank back upon the bed. "It was given to me."

His voice betrayed his youth; he was scarcely past boyhood. "Given to you," Jonathan echoed. "That's a fine story, and perhaps you don't want to admit to disturbing the remains of the dead, but we all know it happens. I urge you to speak the truth. I know this quilt was not made for you."

An assistant surgeon studied him uncertainly. "You recognize this quilt?"

"I know it well."

"That ain't reason enough to assault this boy." The Confederate guard spat on the floor. "One quilt looks much like another."

"It was my brother-in-law's," Jonathan retorted, stricken with sudden grief. "He fought with the Forty-ninth Pennsylvania. My sister sewed this quilt with her own hands." Thomas never would have parted with the quilt his beloved wife had given him on their sixth anniversary. Thomas must surely be dead. "Did you kill the man who carried this quilt?" he asked the wounded Rebel. "If so, you must remember where it happened, and you must tell me where he lies." How could he tell Dorothea? How could he break her heart and tell her that the man she loved had died? He could not bring himself to do it. He would write to Gerda; Gerda would find the words to soften the blow. Nor could he leave Thomas's body to rot on the battlefield. "I appeal to you as one man to another to tell me what you know."

"I don't know where he is but I didn't kill him." The young soldier's voice shook from exhaustion and emotion. "As far as I know, he lives yet. He found me where I lay wounded on the smaller of the two round hills south of the town. He gave me water to drink, he wrapped this quilt around me, and he carried me here on his back."

"Not here," a Union patient spoke up weakly. Blood had soaked through the bandages around the stumps of his knees and had dried to a rust-brown crust. "Two

Rebs brought him in on a stretcher last night. He was unconscious."

Hardly daring to hope, Jonathan asked, "Do you think you would recognize the stretcher-bearers if you saw them again?"

The amputee shrugged and shook his head. "I might. It was dark, what with all the lanterns stolen."

The last was a jab at the Rebel guard, who muttered a retort under his breath but refused to take the bait. Another soldier appeared in the doorway then and called him away. He shot Jonathan a sharp look of warning as he left; Jonathan held up a hand and nodded to indicate that his fit of rage had subsided.

"Even if your brother-in-law didn't bring me all the way here, he did carry me two, maybe three miles on his back before I blacked out." The blinded Rebel let out a bitter laugh. "From the sound of it, he was hale and hearty until then, but I didn't get a good look at him and couldn't tell you what he looked like."

Jonathan inhaled deeply and raked a hand through his hair. Such an act of mercy identified Thomas more accurately than any description of his physiognomy. The young soldier's story rang true, but Jonathan's mind would not rest easy until the stretcher-bearers who had carried him to the seminary confirmed their part of it. And if it was true, what had become of Thomas after he had brought the wounded Rebel off the granite hill? Had he crossed enemy lines on a mission of mercy only to be shot or taken prisoner? Out of respect for his compassionate gesture, had he been allowed to return to his company unharmed? Had he even made it that far, or had he been killed while carrying the unconscious Rebel to safety? An ambulance crew could have found the Rebel soldier on the battlefield and brought him to the seminary, leaving Thomas to lie where he had fallen. Until Jonathan found them and asked, he could only speculate — and hope and pray for the best.

He thanked the blinded boy and offered to examine his wounds, thoughts racing as he tended his patients. The morning waned, and just as he had finished his rounds and was preparing to convince the guards to let him search for the stretcher-bearers, a party of three Confederate soldiers entered and informed them that, in light of the flood of new wounded that had come to the seminary, they would again round up all those soldiers well enough to be paroled. This time, the medical personnel would be included.

"You must be mistaken," said Jonathan, stunned. "Check with your superiors. There must have been some misunderstanding."

"There's no mistaking these orders." With the butt of his rifle, the Rebel soldier nudged Jonathan none too gently toward the door.

"We can't leave these men," protested Dr. New. "Who will care for them in our absence? Most of them can't even walk."

"After your parole, you can return as hospital nurses," a second Rebel said. He seized a private from the Iron Brigade by the shoulder and shoved him toward the door. "Step lively now."

"How long until we can return?" Jonathan demanded, but the soldiers made no reply. Reluctantly he allowed himself to be herded outside with his colleagues, where the walking wounded and other medical personnel from the professors' houses and student dormitories soon joined them. As they were escorted away from Seminary Ridge, Jonathan caught glimpses of the battle, which had resumed in earnest with the break of day. He could not tell how either side fared, but their captors' confident ease suggested that they expected another victory. As the distance between the prisoners and the seminary grew, Jonathan's apprehensions soared. How long would they march until they reached their destination? How many of the more than three hundred suffering men in the seminary alone would perish in the meantime? How many more languished in the hot sun on the battlefield? And what of Thomas? Each passing moment made it less likely that he would find the stretcher-bearers before their memories of one soldier out of thousands faded.

They marched deeper behind Confederate lines until they reached a fenced corral that had been converted to a holding camp of sorts for the prisoners. Their numbers staggered Jonathan; he estimated as many as five thousand Union men, some wounded, all fatigued, hungry, and thirsty. They were offered water and instructed to wait. Before long, soldiers set up a white tent just beyond the gate to their open-air prison. Shielding his eyes from the sun, Jonathan glimpsed a table and chair within. The breeze stirred the tent flaps, and Jonathan saw a Rebel lieutenant seating himself behind the table, while an aide prepared pen and ink and straightened a stack of white papers upon it. Soon the aide emerged from the tent, tied back the tent flaps, and announced in a loud, clear voice that the prisoners must form an orderly line and their parole would be arranged presently.

Determined to return to the seminary as quickly as possible, Jonathan wove through the throng to claim a spot near the front of the line, but he was still several hundred from the beginning. Many soldiers sat down on the ground, their backs against the fence, too tired to stand and willing to wait for their turns. Others bantered with their guards, demanding food and water. As time passed, word began to spread that the conditions of their parole were not unreasonable; after signing a paper acknowledging their release, they would be provided with provisions and marched to Carlisle, and from there, on to Harrisburg, where they would be exchanged for Rebel prisoners held by the Union. "What good will that do my patients back at the seminary?" Jonathan asked the Michigan private who told him the rumors. "They could all die in the meantime."

The private shrugged. "Maybe the Rebs will make an exception for surgeons."

Jonathan was counting on it. As the line moved forward and he approached the tent, he noticed that while most men emerging from the back were led under guard to the right, about one in three was instead directed to the left. Other men around him noticed the same, but none could offer any explanation. There seemed no pattern to the sorting, no separation of men by regiment or state or rank that they could discern.

At last, Jonathan was directed from the corral into the tent. When prompted, he offered his name and rank, and then quickly added, "When we were rounded up, the medical personnel were told that we could be paroled and then returned to care for our patients. How soon will that be accomplished?"

The lieutenant, a gray-eyed Virginian a few years younger than himself, with a face tanned red-brown, shook his head. "I'm afraid that won't be possible."

"What do you mean? Those men need care. There are international and humanitarian laws regarding the treatment of doctors captured while acting in our professional capacity —"

"I regret you were misinformed." The lieutenant passed Jonathan a sheet of paper from the top of the pile. "Please read this and sign your name on the line."

Jonathan snatched up the pen, dipped it in the inkwell, and skimmed the document, already preparing the argument he would unleash to this man's superiors. A phrase caught his attention; he read it a second time, then returned to the top of the page and reread every word, carefully. "I am to swear 'Not to bear arms against the Confederate government until I am released from the obligation I am about to assume.' It would be disingenuous for me to sign this, as I have never borne arms against the Confederate government. I am a surgeon."

The lieutenant looked weary. "Then you should have no trouble signing it."

"But if I were attacked, or if I were required to defend the lives of the patients in my care, I may be morally obligated to take up arms against the aggressor." He scanned the page, shaking his head at one foreboding phrase after another. "What assurances can you provide me that the United States government will recognize these arrangements?"

"Why wouldn't they?" returned the lieutenant. "Do your generals not care about the safety and comfort of their officers and men?"

"I can't sign this." Shaking his head, Jonathan held out the document to the lieutenant, who folded his hands on the table and regarded him steadily. When he did not take the paper, Jonathan returned it to the top of the pile and set the pen on the desk. "I cannot in good conscience sign a pledge that I cannot be sure I will follow in order to participate in a prisoner exchange I'm not sure you're authorized to offer."

"This pledge was good enough for many of your fellow surgeons," said the lieutenant. "I assure you, Dr. Granger, your stubbornness will not see you returned to your patients any sooner."

"From what you've said," Jonathan retorted, "if I sign or if I do *not* sign, I won't be permitted to return to my patients in any case. At least this way I will leave this tent with my loyalty and integrity intact."

The lieutenant sighed and motioned to the guards, and as Jonathan was escorted from the back of the tent under armed guard and led off to the left, he at last understood the method behind the sorting he had observed from within the corral. The Union men sorted themselves, each according to his conscience.

He was taken to a barn on a hillside where hundreds of other men waited without water or other provisions. Feeling dazed and slightly ill, he took stock of his surroundings, his heart gladdening when he spotted several colleagues from the hospital. A few others soon joined them, but some who should have been there did not appear, and

Jonathan could only assume that they had agreed to the conditions of parole.

There were a few injured but mobile men among the prisoners held in the barn, and Jonathan and the other medical personnel tended to their needs as best they could without instruments, medicine, or a drop of water. Later they were given a bit of food and drink, and as night fell, they were offered civilian blankets that Jonathan guessed had been taken from Gettysburg merchants, paid for in Confederate bills.

Restless, uncomfortable, with only the blanket and a thin layer of straw between himself and the hard earth floor, he thought of his patients. He hoped the more able-bodied wounded had managed, somehow, to tend to those worse off or that Confederate surgeons had taken over the hospital and treated the Union wounded as he had treated theirs, or that more brave citizens of Gettysburg like the dark-haired young woman who had smuggled her father's medical bag to the seminary had come to their aid. What he would not give to have that cracked leather case of instruments with him now. He thought of lovely Charlotte, his dear son, and the precious infant daughter he had never held. He thought of Gerda, and knew she would have told him he had made the right choice in refusing to sign away his conscience to win his parole. He thought of them both in the sewing circle at his sister's house, receiving word that he had been captured.

He must have drifted off to sleep thinking of the women he loved, for then he was being shaken awake. Bleary-eyed, he nonetheless recognized one of the musicians in the I Corps ambulance crew, who had somehow managed to retain his drumsticks and had tucked them into his belt, although his snare drum was nowhere to be seen.

"They're giving us a bit of bread and coffee. Not real coffee," the musician amended before Jonathan had even a moment to look forward to the unexpected delicacy. "Rumor is we'll be marching today."

Jonathan sat up and scrubbed the dust from his eyes with the back of his hand. His head throbbed and his back ached. "Marching where?"

The musician shrugged grimly. "A Confederate prison, I expect. Where that might be or how far . . ."

He shook his head and said nothing more. There was nothing else to say. Only God knew what would become of them now.

CHAPTER FIVE

Because her position with the *Register* frequently took her to the telegraph office, Mary Schultz Currier was the first of the Union Quilters to hear of Governor Curtin's call for emergency troops to defend the state as the Army of Northern Virginia approached the Potomac. She was also the first of them to learn of his appeal to all citizens to guard and maintain the free institutions of their country and to defend their homes, firesides, and property in that hour of imminent peril. A day later, Harrisburg was in uproar as residents burdened with luggage crowded aboard trains, desperate to flee the city. In the capital, staff frantically packed books, papers, artwork, and other valuables for the evacuation. Throughout south central Pennsylvania, farmers and bankers and businessmen loaded wagons and boxcars and raced to transport belongings and cash and livestock across the Susquehanna River, determined to preserve their lives and keep their worldly goods out of Rebel hands.

Throughout the Elm Creek Valley, men who had been too young, too old, too badly needed at home, too essential in their occupations, or too ambivalent about the war to enlist earlier now responded to the threat against their own homes and families. As they prepared to depart for Harrisburg, the Union Quilters hastened to supply them with all the necessary provisions. On an evening at the end of June, Anneke sat on the front porch, racing to sew a dozen haversacks in the last of the summer daylight, but she glanced up from her seat on the front porch when Hans came in from the stables. "I could make one for you as well," she offered, indicating the pile of sewing by her side.

Hans leaned against the porch post and scraped the mud from his boots with a stick. "I have no need of a haversack."

"You would if you answered the governor's call."

Hans sighed wearily. "Anneke, I'm tired of explaining my position to you over and over again."

"But this is different. This is an emergency," she persisted. "The enemy is at our front door."

"The enemy is on the other side of the Potomac River in Maryland," he corrected her. "That is hardly our front door. A few Rebel companies may cross to raid and skirmish in southern Pennsylvania before the Union Army drives them out, but I need claim no special insight into the mind of General Lee to say with all confidence that Water's Ford is not his target."

"You don't know that," snapped Anneke. "We have great resources in the valley — food, boots, horses, money in our banks. Those Rebels would love to seize all that we have, just as they did in Chambersburg last fall. And if they want horses, where do you think they'll come first? Why, to Bergstrom's horse farm, that's where."

He grinned, but his eyes were hard. "I don't flatter myself that I'm that famous. They'd probably stop by the livery stable in town first."

"That's not half as amusing as you seem to think it is."

"My love, if you believe any part of this conversation amuses me, then you are greatly mistaken. The Elm Creek Valley has no railroad running through it, no major cities. We are on no major supply routes, we mine no coal, and we have no heavy industry. Yes, we have food and goods and livestock, but even that is not reason enough to force an army through that difficult southern pass, not when other towns with the same blessings lie outside that natural defense."

"So you would have other towns raided and other men sent to defend them, just so long as *you* don't have to fight and *your* property lies safely protected by mountains and difficult roads."

A muscle worked in his jaw. "You profoundly misunderstand me. I would have no one raided. I would have every man lay down his weapons this minute and go home to his farm and family before another life is lost."

His voice carried a warning to say no more, so Anneke pursed her lips to hold back a sharp retort and returned her attention to her work. Hans sat on the second step, tugged off his boots, and made his way into the house, where Gerda was preparing supper. Not even Gerda could talk sense into her brother, not that she had tried. She didn't need to, Anneke thought bitterly. Perhaps Jonathan wasn't Gerda's, but he was serving his country instead of hiding behind optimistic predictions of the enemy's reach. Gerda could take pride in the man she loved in a way Anneke could not.

Soon Anneke learned that the same natural defenses Hans claimed would protect them from invasion beckoned citizens from Harrisburg and beyond to seek refuge within the valley. The Barrows Inn filled to capacity within two days of Governor Curtin's call for emergency militia, and soon every room in every boardinghouse was taken. As more and more frightened Pennsylvanians spilled into town, the Union Quilters called an emergency meeting at Two Bears Farm to discuss what to do. They quickly agreed to open Union Hall as temporary housing for these unfortunates until the crisis passed, and to urge local churches to do the same. They would need to prepare bedding, food, necessary items — the list went on and on, and Anneke promptly volunteered to direct the effort.

"Are you sure?" Dorothea asked. "You've already taken on so much, and you have three young children at home."

Anneke assured Dorothea she could do all she volunteered to do, and more. If that meant she would have less time to devote to Hans, and that she would be obliged to spend more of his money on the Union cause, it would be a small price to pay to redeem the Bergstrom family in the eyes of the community.

When their plans were in order, Mrs. Barrows read a letter that had recently arrived from her youngest and only remaining son, David. At the time he wrote it, the 49th had been in Virginia preparing to cross the Rappahannock River near Deep Run Ravine, although they had surely moved on in the meantime.

"If only the mail could come faster," sighed Mary. "Letters take so long to reach us, we never know where our men are, only where they've been."

"We must prepare ourselves for lengthier delays," cautioned Dorothea. "The Confederate invasion will surely disrupt mail service for however long the crisis endures."

It was a disquieting thought, and Mrs. Barrows sighed as she resumed reading her son's letter. " 'Mother I know you and the good ladies of your quilting bee are as patriotic as any Union soldier but I wonder about many people back home, for their support seems to have weakened of late. The newspapers ask why we have not thrashed Lee yet and to that I say if they would but come out here and fight with us they would understand soon enough. I shake my head Mother to read that the same people who cried out in horror when Negro soldiers

251

were talked of now exclaim, 'Why not send the Negroes to fight?' That would suit me fine. I would rather have an honest brave colored man at my side than a dozen Copperheads who will neither fight for their country nor openly stand against it. I can respect a good secesh soldier who dares fight for what he calls his state's rights but I scorn those cowardly traitors who will choose neither one side nor the other.' "

"From his mouth to Mr. Lincoln's ears," said Constance. As the Union Quilters chimed in their agreement, Anneke felt her face flush hot with shame. She held perfectly still, not daring to look up from a knothole on the floor and find her friends' eyes upon her. Though David's commentary on colored soldiers had drawn their attention, thanks to Constance, surely they had not missed the similarities between the Copperheads David so despised and Anneke's husband.

" 'Three of our officers have been ordered home to bring out conscripts and to recruit,' " Mrs. Barrows continued. " 'I fear they will bring us back few indeed as some will scrape together the three hundred dollars to buy their way out and still more will run away from the draft.' "

"I wonder which officers will be sent

home," said Mary. "Not my Abner. He's only a private."

"Nor my Thomas," said Dorothea ruefully.

"Jonathan is a captain," said Charlotte. "I pray they will send him."

"As do I," said Gerda fervently.

Anneke tore her gaze from the floor, dismayed by her sister-in-law's indiscretion. Charlotte was glaring darkly at Gerda, clutching the armrests of her chair and gathering herself as if preparing to unleash a torrent of vitriol upon her rival for Jonathan's affections. For that was what Gerda was. Even if none of them talked of it, they all knew it.

But before Charlotte could utter a word, Dorothea spoke. "As do I. I miss my brother terribly, and I know he longs to see his beautiful baby girl. He is also respected and admired throughout the valley. The Union Army needs recruits, and Jonathan can be very persuasive."

"Indeed," said Anneke quickly. "We shall all be glad to have our doctor home, even if only for a little while."

All at once, Charlotte's frisson of anger dissipated. "If he *is* one of the officers they send," she said. "If anyone will be able to come now that the Rebels are on our threshold."

"It's possible that the Rebels will do little more than raid and skirmish, as they did in Chambersburg," said Anneke, recalling Hans's prediction.

Mrs. Claverton's mouth pinched in worry. "I pray they do no more."

As the conversation turned to the likelihood that no officers would be sent home on recruiting missions until and unless the current crisis was resolved in favor of the Union, Anneke said a brief, silent, guilty prayer of thankfulness that Gerda's ongoing disgrace had diverted attention from Hans's. But she knew her husband had gained only a temporary reprieve in the judgment of his neighbors. His refusal to serve had not been forgotten, nor, she feared, would it be forgiven.

The refugees from the southern counties brought alarming reports that confirmed Constance's worst fears: The Army of Northern Virginia had crossed the Potomac and was surging into Pennsylvania. They occupied towns, terrifying the citizens, capturing prisoners, confiscating horses, tearing down fences and outbuildings for firewood, raiding chicken coops and pigpens, destroying railroads, severing telegraph lines, cleaning out shops and businesses and leaving worthless Confederate scrip behind in payment. The raw recruits of the Pennsylvania Emergency Militia had been no match for the battle-scarred veterans of Lee's army, and they had scattered or had been captured with little difficulty.

Constance's heart thudded in her chest as she hurried about Union Hall tending to the refugees, overhearing frightening tales of menacing Rebels and narrow escapes as she directed newcomers to cots, passed out quilts, and distributed bread. In Franklin County, she learned, Major General Jubal Early had burned the Caledonia Iron Works and the workers' homes despite General Lee's well-publicized order not to destroy private property. In York, an elderly veteran of the Mexican War had refused a Confederate sergeant's order to turn over his horses, and when the sergeant attempted to take them anyway, he seized a rifle and shot four Rebel soldiers before he himself was killed. In some regions the invaders had ordered residents to turn over their guns, demanded cash payments, and threatened to destroy the towns if the people did not comply. The refugees' vivid descriptions haunted Constance's thoughts until she could all too clearly imagine the terrifying events occurring on the streets of Water's Ford.

Intermingled with her apprehension was surprise and confusion, for Constance was astonished by how many of the refugees were men, and not elderly men, either. When Anneke had asked her to help run the Union Hall shelter, she had expected to care for women and children and the infirm, those who dared not stay behind to defend their homes. There were some women and children among the refugees, of course; entire families had evacuated the threatened regions together. But for the most part, those who sought shelter at Union Hall were men who had fled with their families' livestock and valuables. At first, Constance was appalled to discover that the men had left their wives and children to fend for themselves during the invasion, but as they talked among themselves, she learned that they had done so because they thought their higher duty resided in preserving what they would need to provide for their families after the crisis passed. Without horses, they could not farm crops; without crops, they would not be able to feed their families the next month and the next season and the next year. A temporary absence from their families even in a time of grave peril was preferable to permanent economic ruin. And, the refugees assured one another, their families were in no real danger because the Confederate soldiers were men like themselves and thus the natural protectors of women and children. Though they were traitors to their nation, the Rebels would be compelled by natural law to do the vulnerable no harm. The very enemy soldiers who would steal a man's horses, cattle, and property would surely be chivalrous enough to refrain from harming his dependents.

Constance, who knew firsthand all about the supposed chivalry of Southern men and their treatment of the most vulnerable, thought that any man who would put his trust in the goodwill and honor of an invading army was out of his mind. She prayed for the women and children whom she imagined cowering in root cellars as gunfire rained down upon their homes, and as she worked in Union Hall, she struggled to conceal her feelings from the men in her care. She did not want to think them cowards, for they seemed to believe they had made a difficult but prudent decision, and most of them were unmistakably anguished and worried as they queried her for news of the invasion. Still, she could not imagine Abel leaving her and their boys to face an enemy army without him even if it meant sacrificing every goat, cow, and horse to his name.

On the last day of June, Constance returned home after a weary day at Union Hall to find an unfamiliar wagon in front of the barn and several horses she did not recognize in the corral with their own. She saw children running through the fields as she rode up the drive, and as she slid down from the back of her mare and led it to the trough, she heard a shout of laughter. She spotted her sons climbing the cherry tree near the house, and a moment later she recognized the seven children with them as her nieces and nephews from Mercersburg. Quickly she finished tending to the mare and hurried into the house, where she found Abel sitting at the kitchen table with his brother, Joshua; Joshua's wife, Margaret; Abel's two sisters; and his younger sister's husband, Adam. They looked pensive and angry, and Abel's elder sister's face was streaked with tears. She clutched a teacup with a shaking hand and did not look up as Constance entered.

"The Rebels have reached Mercersburg?" she asked breathlessly, untying her bonnet and hanging it on a hook. She saw that Abel had set out bread and cheese for their guests, but she quickly went to the pantry and brought out blueberry preserves and corn relish also, to hold them over until she could prepare supper. "Are you all right? You were right to come to us, and you should stay as long as you need to. Were the children frightened? Where's Ephraim?"

Abel's elder sister, Louisa, choked out a sob and embraced her younger sister, burying her face on Frances's shoulder. Alarmed, Constance looked from one bleak face to another. "Where's Ephraim?" she repeated.

"Confederate troops have invaded Mercersburg," said Abel. "They rounded up dozens of colored folks and sent them south under guard."

"They're going to be sold into slavery," said Joshua, his voice brittle with anger. "A few of the people they rounded up were escaped slaves, but most of them were freeborn."

"Lord save them." Dizzy, Constance held on to the edge of the table and lowered herself into a chair as she guessed the rest. "Ephraim. They took Ephraim."

Abel nodded.

"We're not safe, none of us," Margaret cried, clutching her husband's hand. "We've got to flee north. Tell them, Joshua."

Joshua nodded. "We have no choice. Pack

only what you need. We'll leave at day-break."

"Yes, of course. We must." Constance took a deep breath and fought to steady herself. Ephraim. Sweet, funny Ephraim, the kindest and most generous of her brothers-in-law. He had never felt the lash, had never spent a day of his life as anything less than a free man. Slavery would crush him. They would have to find him, to purchase his freedom as Abel had purchased hers, but first — "We have friends north of the Four Brothers Mountains. We've known them since our Underground Railroad days. They'll surely help us. But first we should send word to the other colored families hereabouts. That can't wait until tomorrow."

"We're not going," said Abel. "We should send word, and let other families do as they must, but we are not going."

Joshua lifted his hands in frustration and shook his head as if he had already tried, and failed, to change his brother's mind.

Constance stared at Abel, disbelieving. "What do you mean, we're not going? There's an army on the way, an army of slavers. Do you want to risk having our boys taken from us and sold into slavery? I would die before I'd let that happen."

"As would I," said Abel firmly. "Listen. If

260

we make a run for it, we won't know what we're running to and we'll be leaving our homes and farms to be ransacked. The southern pass is the only route an army could take into the Elm Creek Valley from that direction. If we build defenses there and guard them fiercely, not one single Rebel soldier will set foot on our land or near any of our children. We know the terrain and we'll hold the high ground. I'm telling you, this is the best way. This is the only way."

Constance's thoughts raced. She pictured the southern pass high in the Appalachians, the narrow and treacherous road, and the thick forest where sharpshooters like Abel could hide and pick off any enemies who dared approach. She thought of her sons forced to flee their home, to seek refuge in strange towns like the poor souls she cared for at Union Hall. She had never wanted her boys to become runaways like so many of their people.

Abel was regarding her steadily, awaiting her answer.

"You must do what you think is best," she told him. "But as for me, I think you're right. Staying and defending the southern pass is our best hope."

Pleased, Abel slapped his palms on the

table and turned to the others. "What do you say?"

"Whatever they're doing with contraband down South, they still aren't ready to put colored men in the army up here in the North," Margaret said. "They'll turn you away as they've done twice before at Camp Curtin."

"We don't need to join the army to defend our families," said Adam. "I'm with you, Abel."

"I can't run anymore," said Louisa, the eldest sister, her voice thick with grief. "My children are frightened enough with their father taken from us. I trust you, brother. If you say you can hold the pass, I believe you."

"I do too," said Frances.

"This is madness," exclaimed Margaret. "Abel and Adam, you're both crack shots but the two of you can't hold off an army."

"It won't be just the two of us," said Abel. "There are men enough within ten miles of here to build fortifications and guard the pass."

"Then you'd better send word to them right away, because the three of us can't do it alone," said Joshua. Margaret pressed her hand to her lips, her eyes filling with tears. "Margaret, don't you weep. You and the children will be safe here on the farm. I swear to you, we won't let one single Rebel enter the Elm Creek Valley."

It was almost twilight when Anneke heard a horse's hooves pounding outside as a rider approached the house; before Hans could peer out the window, a knock sounded on the door. It was Abel Wright, in too much haste to accept their invitation to come inside. Catching his breath, he told them of his plans to construct defenses around the southern pass to forestall the Confederate army's advance into the Elm Creek Valley. "We need every willing and able man," he said. "With so many off with the Forty-ninth, our numbers will be few. Will you join us?"

Abel did not seem surprised when Hans offered to lend him whatever tools and supplies the defenders required but declined to join them. Anneke felt her cheeks flush with shame as the two men went outside to the barn. Abel Wright, twice rejected by the Union Army, a colored man denied many rights taken for granted by his white neighbors, was still patriotic enough to take up arms in response to the governor's call for emergency troops. And what would Hans do, an immigrant who owed all his good fortune and freedom to his adopted country? He would lend tools, nothing more. He would not even take the tools up to the pass himself but would deliver them to the Wright farm while Abel raced off on horseback to seek volunteers from other families.

Anneke put the baby and the twins to bed and returned to her rocking chair, where she lit a lamp and took up her sewing. Sensing her anger, Gerda stayed up with her for a while, reading aloud to her from *Harper's Weekly* and trying to amuse her into a better humor. Anneke scarcely heard a word her sister-in-law uttered, so outraged and bewildered was she by her husband's inexplicable behavior. When the war was far distant, it could be easy enough for a man to swear not to harm another, but when it was near, threatening his own wife and children, how could he then refuse to fight?

As the hours passed, Gerda gave up trying to soothe Anneke's temper, and yawning and stretching, bade her good night. Alone in the front room, the windows open to the still, humid summer air, Anneke brooded and waited for her husband's return, too angry to sleep. At last she heard the team and wagon on the road outside, heard the door to the stable open, heard Hans guide the horses inside. She put away her sewing and trimmed the lamp, and before long he came inside, tired and bleary-eyed from the hard moonlit drive after a long day in the fields and corral.

"The Wrights have family staying with them," said Hans as he washed his face and hands in the kitchen basin. He helped himself to a slice of bread and a wedge of cheese. "They were chased out of Mercersburg. Rebel soldiers were rounding up colored folks and sending them south into slavery. Abel's brother-in-law was one of the men seized."

For a moment, horror and dismay blotted out Anneke's anger. "Adam or Ephraim?"

"Ephraim."

"God help him." And his wife and his children. "Do they know where he'll be taken?"

Hans shook his head. "I don't suppose they'll be able to inquire after him until the threat passes."

"This threat won't pass on its own," she said, her anger returning. "Brave men like Abel will have to force it away."

Hans sat down and propped his elbows on the table, cutting himself another slice of bread. "I am truly very sorry that my determination to follow my conscience is such a difficult burden for you to bear."

"It wouldn't be a burden if it made sense," she exclaimed. "Violence is unpleasant, yes, and I can understand why you would not abandon your predilections when there are plenty of other men to fight and the war is far away. But now the war is coming here, and still you do nothing."

"Anneke, these are not mere predilections," he said. "You speak as if this is merely a matter of taste, as if deciding never to take another man's life is akin to choosing between tea or coffee with my breakfast. I cannot and will not kill, not to save the Union, which you know I love and respect, not to end slavery, which you know I abhor, not to prove my patriotism to the neighbors, not even to please you."

"But what about to save me?" she countered. "What if a Rebel soldier burst in here right this minute to shoot me and the children? What would you do?"

"There is no Rebel soldier standing on our front porch ready to burst in." Hans let his head fall against the back of the chair and closed his eyes. "I was just outside and can assure you of that."

Tears of fury sprang into her eyes. "Not tonight, perhaps."

"Or any other night. I'm still firmly convinced that General Lee will not cross the

Susquehanna. Even if he does, he has nothing to gain by sending his army into the Elm Creek Valley. Even if he did, Abel Wright will provide a formidable defense."

"And you will not even help him construct the fortifications," she retorted. "If you don't wish to take up arms, that's one matter, but you will not even help build the defenses that will protect your own family, your own farm and property."

"Those fortifications are the instruments of war. I can't build something that will help one man kill another or it would be as if I fired the rifle myself."

"But you helped build Union Hall! The sole purpose of Union Hall is to raise money to provide for the Forty-ninth!"

"That is not its sole purpose, and even if it were, there's a difference between firing a bullet into someone's chest and providing food, clothing, and necessities for men in need."

"How so? Those 'men in need' are soldiers, and soldiers are instruments of war."

Hans was silent for a long moment. "Very well, my love." He rose and pushed in his chair, leaving his second piece of bread untasted. "You win. I should not have helped build Union Hall."

"What precisely have I won?" Anneke

cried tearfully. She heard a floorboard creak overhead as Gerda stirred, but she was beyond caring who overheard their argument. "Tell me what you would do if a Rebel soldier entered this room intending to kill me. Would you do for love of your wife what you would not do for love of country, or would you stand there and let him shoot me?"

"I would try to take his gun away so he could not shoot you," said Hans. He seemed — not angry, not ashamed of himself, but disappointed, profoundly disappointed in her. "I would put myself between you and him, and he would have to get past me to get to you."

"But you would not kill him, not to save my life, not to save the children."

"I doubt very much that I will ever be put to such a test except in words, and except by you, but since you demand an answer — no, Anneke. I would not kill him."

"Then I cannot believe you love me or our children."

His locked his gaze on hers. She could not read the thoughts that lay behind his steely eyes, but she refused to back down and look away. "I do love you," Hans said, "and it is because I love you and believe you love me that I will not kill for you."

She took a deep, shaky breath. "If you will not look to the defense of your wife and children, then I will have to see to our safety myself."

"Do what you must, Anneke."

He left the room without looking back.

Men and boys from throughout the Elm Creek Valley responded to Abel's call, bringing tools and rifles to the southern pass. The crowd in Union Hall thinned as men who had fled Chambersburg and York and Gettysburg joined the locals in the defense of their refuge. While Louisa and Margaret remained back at the farm to watch the children, Frances accompanied Constance to Union Hall to care for the refugees. "I can't just sit and wait," Frances fretted as they rode into Water's Ford. "I must feel as if I am doing something to help, however small my contribution."

Dorothea must have felt the same, for when they arrived they found her already hard at work serving cornmeal mush to the children. Anneke was there too, but whereas Dorothea had left her daughter at home with the housekeeper, Anneke had brought her sons along. Constance had not expected to see Anneke until later and the children not at all; Anneke usually left the boys at home with Gerda and did not arrive until mid-morning, after she had breakfast with her family and took care of her morning chores. When Constance remarked about this in passing, Anneke said coolly that she and her sons had taken up residence in Union Hall for the duration of the crisis, for she felt safer amongst men she knew would take up arms in their defense. Startled, Constance looked to Dorothea for an explanation, but Dorothea merely shook her head and went about her work.

For a week, Constance and her sisters-in-law awaited word from the men defending the pass and prepared for the worst, packing clothing in satchels and food in barrels in case they had to flee. Occasionally, the defenders allowed refugees through the pass, and they brought news from the fortifications as well as from the towns they had fled. Small bands of armed and mounted Copperheads, invigorated by the Confederate approach, had picked their way through the forest and had approached the southern pass, but the men of the Elm Creek Valley had fought them off, engaging in three skirmishes before the attackers apparently abandoned their plans. The Army of Northern Virginia did not appear headed for Washington City or Baltimore after all but was gathering in Adams County. General Hooker had resigned and General Meade named his successor. A fierce battle raged in Gettysburg, not only in the surrounding heights but also in the very streets of the town. In response to the threat, a freeborn Philadelphian named Octavius V. Catto had raised a company of colored men and retained white officers under Captain William Babe, a white veteran with the Pennsylvania Volunteer Reserve Corps. Armed, uniformed, and equipped at the city arsenal, the company traveled by train to Harrisburg, where they were peremptorily rejected with the excuse that Negro troops had not been authorized. After three days of battle with horrific casualties on both sides, the Union Army emerged victorious at Gettysburg. General Lee's army was retreating from Pennsylvania with the Union's VI Corps leading the pursuit.

Little by little, as railroad and telegraph lines were repaired, news about the extent of the destruction in Gettysburg trickled in to Water's Ford. Only when the Confederate Army was well south of the Mason-Dixon Line did the refugees feel safe returning to their homes. As the families and men and women with children departed, Union Hall gradually emptied and was restored to its former appearance. Soon only Anneke remained, bewildering Constance, who recalled that Anneke had said that she had moved into Union Hall for her protection. Now that her defenders had departed, she and her sons would be safer and far more comfortable in their own home, but as Anneke arranged cots and quilts in one of the upstairs offices, it was evident that she was in no hurry to leave.

When reports of scores of wounded soldiers languishing in barns and in homes and on the battlefield reached them, the Union Quilters organized a drive for bandages, food, and medicine. They sent off a wagonload of supplies with a group of volunteer nurses, many of whom were anxious to go not only to care for the wounded but also to seek news about their husbands, sons, and brothers who had fought at Gettysburg. They carried with them bottles of peppermint and pennyroyal to ward off what they had been warned was the overpowering stench of thousands of rotting corpses, human and equine.

Other civilians were also eager to visit the battlefield. Tales spread of sightseers and souvenir hunters, insensible to the soldiers' distress and determined to take home relics and treasures from the conflict. They con-

272

stantly got in the way, arousing the ire of the doctors and nurses who had stayed behind to care for the wounded, who numbered in the thousands. But inconsiderate tourists were not the only ones who earned the enmity of the caregivers and soldiers. For every story of valiant Gettysburg women who provided food, shelter, and nursing to the suffering, rumors abounded of local men who levied fees upon wounded soldiers to transport them from the battlefield into town, citizens who charged the troops exorbitant prices for food and drink and other necessities, and farmers who demanded rent from exhausted Union regiments camping overnight on their land. Constance hoped that the tales were false, but they were just awful enough to carry the ring of truth.

Abel was one of the last men to leave the fortifications in the southern pass, but he soon returned as a member of the new local militia formed from the defenders he had called together. On the sixth of July, the town council resolved to provide for the militia to man the defenses in shifts until the war concluded, and Mayor Bauer personally asked Abel to lead the colored company. If the Confederates threatened them again, they would be prepared.

But for the moment, it seemed that the crisis had passed. Lee's army had withdrawn to Virginia. Normal life, for wartime, resumed in the Elm Creek Valley. Abel's family returned to Mercersburg and began inquiries into the fate of Ephraim and their other colored friends and neighbors who had been taken south into slavery. The Union Quilters resumed their usual efforts to provide for the men of the 49th, eagerly awaiting their first letters in the aftermath of Gettysburg, because until they knew how their loved ones fared, they would stand on a precipice of doubt and worry and fear. But there was pride too, for they had responded to the threat of danger with courage and resourcefulness.

Proudest of all was Constance, for her husband had at last served his country as he had so longed to do. He had been hailed by the town council and appointed the leader of the colored company of the local militia. His resourcefulness had saved the valley, and everyone who heard of it acknowledged him as the hero of Wright's Pass.

Dorothea pushed Abigail on the swing Thomas had made by boring holes through the ends of a sanded board, threading sturdy ropes through them, and knotting the ropes around a branch of a towering elm a few yards from their back door. The lowest branch was still fifteen feet off the ground, and Dorothea could not glance up at the tight knots high above without remembering how nervously she had watched as Jonathan climbed the tree to tie them.

"Abigail won't be able to use a swing for more than a year," she had said, trying to talk her brother out of it. She had thrown Thomas a beseeching look, but he was too busy watching Jonathan shinny up the tree with the swing slung over his shoulder to notice. "You can hang a swing for her when you return home."

"That could be years," Jonathan had replied, his voice strained from the effort of climbing. "I should do it now, while I'm thinking of it. You'll be glad to have a diversion for her when she's big enough."

"Let him do it," Thomas joked, "or I'll have to."

Now Abigail was almost two years old, and she loved the swing. "Your father and Uncle Jonathan made this for you," Dorothea reminded her each time they walked hand in hand to the elm tree. Abigail had been only a baby the last time she had seen her father, too young to remember him except from Dorothea's stories. How would she respond when he finally came home? Would she smile and run to him, or would she hide her face in Dorothea's skirts, since she would not truly know him?

Thomas seemed to think Dorothea would not know him either. His last letter, sent from Virginia before the Battle of Gettysburg, had consisted of a single sentence: "My love, I fear you will not recognize me when I return, I have changed so much and done such wretched things." Distressed, she had written back immediately, two pages expressing her undying love and devotion and assuring him that nothing he could have done was unforgivable. He had not yet replied. She had not heard from him in weeks. The most recent letter any of the Union Quilters had received had come to Mary from her husband, Abner, while encamped in Frederick, Maryland, but that letter too had been written before Gettysburg. Dorothea and her friends were so anxious for news that they could hardly think of anything else.

When Abigail tired of the swing, Dorothea led her back to the house, taking their time, picking wildflowers, wistfully enjoying the simple pleasures of Abigail's happy prattle. She was a contented child, beloved and bright, but often quiet and contemplative, her father's daughter. Thomas would be so proud of her.

After lunch on the porch, Dorothea left Abigail in Mrs. Hennessey's care, saddled her bay mare, and rode into Water's Ford, with her sewing kit and letters to mail in the saddlebag. She stopped first at the post office, her heart leaping with joy to behold a letter from Thomas. Thanking the postmaster, she blinked back tears and traced her name written in her husband's familiar, elegant script. Opening the letter, she walked outside and nearly bumped into Gerda on her way in. "A letter from Thomas," Gerda exclaimed happily. "What a relief. I hope it was sent after Gettysburg and not merely delayed all this time."

Dorothea fervently hoped so too. "Hurry back and we can read it together."

"Perhaps I'll have one of my own to read, and not merely these to send," said Gerda, a note of longing in her voice. Dorothea could not resist glancing in her basket and glimpsed three letters — one to Gerda's parents in Germany, one to Josiah Chester in Virginia that was unlikely to be delivered any time soon, thanks to the war, and one to Jonathan. Dorothea had not heard from her brother in so long that she almost would not care if he had sent Gerda a love sonnet just as long as he had sent some word to assure her of his safety.

Dorothea seated herself on a bench and decided to skim Thomas's letter while she waited for Gerda, in case Thomas had penned a few passionate lines of his own that she would not want to share with her friend — or, more private yet, expressions of the deep melancholy that had colored his last few letters. The date at the top of the page, July 7, sent her spirits soaring, for it meant that Thomas had survived Gettysburg. She ached to think that he had been so near to home but had been unable to close the distance that separated them even when it was at its smallest since the 49th had departed Camp Curtin. He told of the battle, of the VI Corps's pursuit of the Army of Northern Virginia, and then, just as Gerda emerged from the post office, he broke such terrible news that she cried out.

"What is it?" Gerda exclaimed, hurrying to her side. "Is Thomas all right?"

"He's — Thomas — Thomas is fine." Shaking, Dorothea grasped Gerda's hand and pulled her down beside her on the bench. "Gerda, prepare yourself. I have something terrible to tell you."

Soon afterward at Union Hall, as her

friends arrived and gathered upstairs in the east gallery, Dorothea drew Charlotte, Lorena, and Mrs. Claverton aside and privately told them of Jonathan's disappearance. Lorena grew pale and sank into a chair; Charlotte collapsed sobbing into her mother's arms. Through the doorway, Dorothea glimpsed Gerda watching them pensively as she arranged chairs in a circle in the gallery, surely wishing she could share in their grief but rightly suspecting she would not be welcome.

When Charlotte had composed herself, they joined the others, who had already guessed something terrible had happened. Dorothea could not bear to prolong their anxious worry a moment longer. "Jonathan is missing," she said, unfolding Thomas's letter and smoothing out the creases as she prepared herself to read.

July 7, 1863

My beloved wife,

We have made camp for the night and I improve a miserable day greatly by taking pen in hand and writing to you.

By now you have surely heard about the tremendous campaign that concluded in Gettysburg a few days ago.

Although the VI Corps did not reach the battlefield until the afternoon of July 2, the First Division was promptly deployed and was soon engaged in the fight. I hope you will forgive me, my love, but in the aftermath of the day's fighting, I parted with the beautiful quilt you made for me. If you had seen the poor wounded soldier to whom I gave it, you would have agreed that his need was greater than mine. Perhaps in your compassion for the suffering you would have taken the quilt from my bedroll yourself and draped it over the young man with your own gentle hands.

As terrible as that day was, worse was yet to come. May heaven save you from ever witnessing anything akin to the gruesome scenes we beheld on the battlefield that Independence Day morn. Everywhere the ground was trodden into mud and strewn with the blackened and mangled remains of men and horses. All around lay broken caissons and cannon, abandoned packs and gear, the litter of cartridges and spent bullets, watches and field glasses and buttons and torn cloth. Trees were hewn and splintered, fences demolished, and the horrific smell of death and decay permeated the air.

Throughout the morning we dug shallow trenches to cover the remains of the thousands of poor souls who had lost their lives since the battle begun. For those who yet clung to life, doctors set up field hospitals in barns and tents, attending to patients moaning in anguish on doors suspended by chairs in lieu of beds. I cannot describe for you the piles of amputated arms and legs that accumulated within these crude hospitals, nor the stoic expressions on the wounded men awaiting their turns beneath the bone saw. The images will haunt my nightmares as long as I live.

That same morning, General Lee sent a messenger under flag of truce to General Meade proposing an exchange of prisoners. Our Meade, perhaps reluctant to return several thousand seasoned veterans to the Confederate ranks, or to relieve Lee of the burden of the thousands of Union troops who would clog the roads, require the reassignment of Rebel troops to guard duty, and generally slow the Confederate army's movements, declined his offer. I understand General Meade's decision and cannot fault him for it, but I wish with all my heart he had chosen otherwise, as I will soon explain.

In the afternoon a gentle rain began to fall, but it soon became a steady downpour. From our "fishhook" defensive position, we observed a Confederate wagon train loaded with the wounded and dying begin a slow and steady journey west along the Chambersburg Pike, escorted by several artillery batteries and at least two cavalry brigades. It was evident that Lee's army was on the move, but we could not determine their intentions. It was late afternoon before Meade was able to confirm that Lee was indeed retreating and not planning a strategic maneuver, by which time the rain had turned into a thunderstorm. Knowing the weather would slow the infantry to a crawl, Meade sent the cavalry in pursuit immediately but ordered the rest of us to hold until morning.

Since the VI Corps was the freshest, as all but two of our brigades had been held mostly in reserve throughout the battle, we were sent in direct pursuit of the Rebels along Fairfield Road, conducting reconnaissance in force. Meanwhile the rest of the army was sent south on a course parallel to Lee's through the eastern foothills of South Mountain, and then to turn west across the mountains to the Potomac River to cut off Lee's escape.

Two days ago, still in Pennsylvania, we caught up with Lee's army just beyond Fairfield, but Gordon's Rebel brigade held the pass and possessed every advantage the terrain afforded. I have heard rumors that Meade commanded Sedgwick to send the VI Corps forward despite the odds, but Sedgwick declined, abandoned the pursuit, and marched us back to Emmitsburg. Today we retraced our steps, for Meade has ordered all seven corps south on parallel roads, and tomorrow we will climb South Mountain at Turner's Gap and Crampton's Gap. Though we face long and harrowing marches in the days ahead, a not insignificant portion of the corps believes that if we catch up to the Rebels in retreat, we may be able to finish them off once and for all and bring the war to a close. Most of us, however, are less hopeful that the war will end so soon. We are exhausted from long and difficult marches as well as from the arduous fighting that preceded the pursuit. The rain and heat too are taking their toll. If we could have but a day of clear, sunny weather to rest and recover, I believe it would make quite a difference in our strength and morale, but Washington City favors speed and pursuit, and so it must be.

My darling Dorothea, I'm sure you will have already seen the casualty lists from the battle by the time you receive this letter, but there is one whose name you will not read there, whose fate is nonetheless a matter of grave concern. Your brother Jonathan had been consulting with another surgeon in the I Corps at the time the order was given to march from Maryland into Pennsylvania. He was separated from the VI Corps throughout the battle, and by all accounts his efforts tending to the wounded in a field hospital established at the Lutheran Seminary on the heights west of the town were nothing short of heroic. On the first day of battle, the Confederates advanced beyond Seminary Ridge and took prisoners of all the wounded within the hospital and the medical personnel who attended them. Jonathan, like many others, was offered parole, but as best as I can determine, the terms were contrary to the dictates of his conscience and he refused to sign. He was last seen marching south amongst a column of more than a thousand other patriotic Union men who had declined to accept the Confederates' terms.

My love, your brother is greatly admired and respected by the army medical establishment and I have been assured that every effort will be made to determine his whereabouts and to secure his release. You must take courage, and help Charlotte to do the same. You should take comfort in one another at this time of your mutual need. Pray, and do not lose hope. . . .

I will write again as soon as I can. Kiss Abigail and remember that no matter how many miles separate us, I remain

Your loving husband,
Thomas

Dorothea had omitted reading aloud several lines following Thomas's entreaty that she and Charlotte comfort each other: "You are strong and good, and I know you will not forget Gerda. Though she possesses greater fortitude than Charlotte, her suffering will be all the more acute for she cannot seem to care too much for Jonathan. You and I know what she feels for him, and with you alone Gerda will not need to conceal her anguish. Offer her solace, for although her devotion to Jonathan is misguided, it is real."

As the Union Quilters embraced Charlotte, Lorena, and herself, Dorothea reflected upon Thomas's prescience, for the friends had compassion and condolences in abundance for Jonathan's wife, mother, and sister, but none for Gerda, who loved him just as dearly, though unwisely.

When Gerda wrote, she could forget the pain of separation from her beloved, her anguish at not knowing what had become of him. She wrote to exhaust herself, so that at the end of the day she would sink into a dreamless sleep and not lie awake imagining Jonathan's arms around her, or worse yet, his eyes staring at the night sky above some Southern prison camp or sightlessly at the dirt covering a shallow grave.

She drowned the pain in her heart with words, filling page after page with an account of the recent Rebel incursion into Pennsylvania and its dreadful aftermath. When the women volunteers returned to Water's Ford from Gettysburg, having been replaced by professional doctors and nurses from the United States Sanitary Commission, Gerda interviewed them and compiled their reflections into a compelling report that filled the entire front page of the *Register*. Heart aching for Jonathan, she wrote of his capture and disappearance, but reluctant to seem to care too much for him alone, she wrote pieces of equal length for each soldier of the Elm Creek Valley who had sacrificed his life in the battle. To stoke her own faltering courage, she composed a summary of the defense of Water's Ford, praising its citizens for their response to the crisis and singling out Abel Wright for his foresight and valor.

On the day that story was scheduled to run, Gerda quickly cleaned up the kitchen after breakfast and prepared a cold lunch for Hans to eat later so that she could go into town and claim the first copies as they came off the printing press. Hans saddled a coal-black stallion for her and asked her if she planned to stop by Union Hall afterward.

"I shall," she said. "Do you want me to carry a message to Anneke?"

"Tell her I want her to stop this foolishness and return home with the children at once."

"Oh, that will certainly persuade her."

Gerda shook her head and, with her brother's help, climbed into the saddle. "You should go see her yourself. She and the boys miss you, and the boys are anxious and unhappy in Union Hall."

Hans frowned. "You said they were all right."

"I meant that they're safe and comfortable, but it's obvious they'd rather be in their own home with their father." And their loving aunt, she added silently. She missed the boys terribly and, from the way they ran to her when she visited the hall, she knew they missed her too. As rambunctious and exhausting as they were, she had not realized how much joy and laughter they had added to her days until they were no longer underfoot. "Go to Anneke, beg her forgiveness, and ask her to return. Her heart will melt and she will come home."

Hans shook his head. "That I cannot do. I've done nothing that requires forgiveness. I won't apologize for following my conscience."

"Very well, don't apologize," said Gerda, exasperated. "You could still tell her you love her and want her and the boys to come home."

"If she doesn't know that I love her yet,

telling her today won't make any difference."

On the verge of a caustic retort, Gerda nodded in farewell and chirruped to the horse. Hans had been a willful boy and had grown to be an even more stubborn man, but his standoff with Anneke frustrated Gerda beyond measure. How a husband and wife who adored each other could allow a philosophical disagreement to divide them confounded her. She and Jonathan didn't agree on every point of politics or religion or literature or countless other topics, but they explored and debated their differences, never failing to learn something new about the opposing point of view that either strengthened their own convictions or prompted them to reconsider. Surely, Hans and Anneke could do the same, if Hans would only listen tenderly to Anneke's complaints and hear them for what they truly were, confusion about his beliefs and concerns for her and the children's safety. For her part, Anneke ought to respect Hans's commitment to obey his conscience and not misinterpret his eschewal of violence as an absence of love for his family or a disavowal of his role as their protector. What they could not do was continue to live apart and not speak to each other. When so many husbands and wives and lovers were separated by the war, Hans and Anneke's wasteful squandering of the blessing of time together provoked both Gerda's impatience and her sorrow. What she would not do for one more Saturday evening discussing ethics or politics over the supper table with Jonathan. What she would not give to once more see his smile or hear his laughter, to smell his own unique scent of tobacco smoke and wool and soap, to dream of the day they would finally be together in a home of their own. Did Hans and Anneke believe they had all the time in the world to reconcile? Gerda and Jonathan had waited years for the chance to be together and had been willing to wait many more, but now Gerda feared that blessed day would never come. Hans and Anneke risked more than they suspected, postponing their reconciliation while waiting for the other to capitulate.

At Schultz's Printers, Mary had several copies of the latest edition of the *Water's Ford Register* ready for her. As Gerda admired the headline, Mary teased, "Although you say not a single word against him this time, I'm sure Mr. Meek will nonetheless find something to complain about."

"Of course he will." Gerda carefully folded

the papers and tucked them into her basket. "He wouldn't approve of Abel Wright's defenses. That Copperhead would have been dissatisfied with anything short of a hero's welcome for General Lee, and as Rebel troops stormed the Elm Creek Valley, he would have had us invite them home for tea and cakes."

Mary laughed. "Somewhere in Bellefonte, he's telling his wife, 'That blasted G. A. Bergstrom. At least when the Confederacy finally does take over, they'll burn his home first.' "

Gerda laughed, but then abruptly stopped. "Do you really believe my writing has made me a target?"

"No more so than Schultz's Printers is." Mary folded her arms and regarded Gerda curiously. "You mean to say you haven't considered the consequence of boldly proclaiming your political views for all the world to read?"

"All the world? No indeed. I had no idea the *Register* boasted that sort of circulation."

"Perhaps you should have chosen a more obscure nom de plume." Mary tapped her chin with her finger thoughtfully, leaving a smudge of ink. "Wasn't the Caledonia Iron Works burned — against General Lee's strict orders that private property was not to be harmed, even — because Jubal Early was furious at the owner for the anti-Confederate remarks he made as a member of Congress?"

"Indeed," said Gerda faintly. "I hadn't considered that my words would outrage anyone but Mr. Meek and a handful of Pennsylvania Copperheads." But she couldn't discount Mary's warnings, even though she had made them in jest. One of the people she had interviewed after Gettysburg had referred her to Dr. Samuel Schmucker, a professor at the same Lutheran Seminary that had been turned into a field hospital. The Confederates had vowed to arrest him because of his abolitionist statements, but thanks to a timely warning from a loyal former student, he had fled Gettysburg before the Rebel army had arrived. If not for that, he might have shared Jonathan's fate — whatever that was.

"I wouldn't worry," Mary hastened to reassure her, sensing her dismay but only partially understanding the cause. "Once they discover that G. A. Bergstrom is a woman, they'll likely decide you're perfectly harmless and leave you alone."

If not for the potential jeopardy to her brother, Anneke, and the children, Gerda might almost prefer to have her home burned to the ground than to have her writing dismissed merely because she was a woman. "They'll have to invade the valley to get to me," she said with false bravado. "I'm in no danger, not with the hero of Wright's Gap manning the defenses."

She bade Mary good-bye and carried the papers to Union Hall, where she found Anneke weeding the garden while the boys played ball nearby, the twins romping happily while their younger brother toddled after them. The boys ran to meet her, and as Anneke rose, smiling and brushing the soil from her hands, Gerda could not miss the pained look in her eyes that appeared when Stephen and David demanded, as they always did, why Aunt Gerda had not brought their father with her.

"You should come home," Gerda said in an undertone when the boys ran off to play. "Hans misses you terribly."

"He can't miss me too badly or he would have come himself instead of sending you."

"He didn't send me. I came of my own accord. I'm worried about you." Then, inspired, she resorted to the one argument she knew would strike home. "People are beginning to talk."

Anneke's brow furrowed. "What are they

saying?"

"What do you expect? Nothing this scandalous has happened in the Elm Creek Valley since — well, since I gave birth to a bastard child. You've deserted your husband and you're living alone in a public building with three small children. I've heard that the regulars at the High Street Tavern have placed bets upon when Hans will sue you for divorce."

Anneke's cheeks flushed pink. "He would never do such a thing."

"How do you know?"

"I just do. He loves me."

"And you love him, so for heaven's sake, go home. Don't stay here alone and become grist for the gossip mill. Believe me as someone who has been ground upon that millstone for many a year. It is not a pleasant experience."

"I can't go home," said Anneke, although Gerda doubted very much that, if pressed, she would have been able to offer a single plausible reason why not. "Dorothea has invited us to stay with her. Perhaps I should accept."

"But Dorothea is as much a pacifist as Hans," protested Gerda. "How are you safer under her protection than your own husband's?"

"We might not be, but at least it wouldn't be as scandalous as living here on my own." Anneke nodded, resolved. "I'll move today. Did you bring the wagon?"

"I rode horseback."

"Would you return with the wagon this afternoon, please?"

"Hans would never allow me to carry you and the boys and your baggage anywhere but home."

"Then on your way home, would you be so kind as to stop and ask Dorothea to send her hired man?"

Exasperated, Gerda threw her hands in the air and agreed. At least Two Bears Farm was a few miles closer to home than Union Hall.

She hugged the children, made one last plea on Hans's behalf, and departed, but before returning home, she stopped by the post office to mail a letter to Josiah Chester. She had a letter to Jonathan in progress at home, but she had no idea where to send it. There were no letters waiting for her, but the sympathetic postmaster confided that Charlotte Granger had received a letter from Virginia. "Isn't that where Dr. Granger studied?" Mr. Reinhart asked.

"No," she said, wondering. "He studied in Baltimore and Massachusetts."

"Perhaps the Clavertons have family there? How strange that would be, for such loyal Unionists to have Confederate relatives."

"Mrs. Granger has a cousin in North Carolina," Gerda recalled. "I suppose it's possible that a distant relative wrote to her. Not all families have allowed the war to divide them, and the state of one's residence doesn't necessarily determine one's politics. There are loyalists in the South just as there are Southern sympathizers here."

"True enough, Miss Bergstrom," the gray-haired postmaster said admiringly. "You should have been a schoolteacher, you're so clever."

Gerda managed a smile as she departed, but the thought of Charlotte's letter unsettled her. She hurried to her horse and set off quickly down the south road along Elm Creek, but as she approached Two Bears Farm, her heart grew heavy with dread. Dorothea might know who had sent the letter and what news it brought, but suddenly Gerda was afraid to ask. It was probably nothing of consequence, she told herself, merely a letter from a cousin full of family gossip and lamentations about the war. She could not avoid calling on Dorothea before the end of the day lest she break her promise to Anneke, but she could postpone her visit a little while longer, to give her nerves time to settle.

She passed the entrance to the winding road that led through the forest to Elm Creek Farm and continued another mile to the Wrights' land. From a distance the dairy farm was the perfect image of pastoral splendor — a stout red barn, a spacious and sturdy milk house, a two-story whitewashed residence, chickens in the yard, golden grain in the fields, cows and goats grazing in their separate pastures.

Two dogs ran barking to greet her, tails wagging, and escorted her up to the barn. She tied up the horse and pumped water into the trough, then carried her basket around the side of the house to the kitchen garden, where she found Constance harvesting green beans. "We made the front page," she declared, unfolding a copy of the *Register* with a triumphant flourish. "Where's the Hero of Wright's Pass? I confess I came dangerously close to panegyric in my description of his construction of the defenses and the skirmishes with those Copperheads. Let's read this aloud in front of him and embarrass him tremendously."

"He isn't here," said Constance shortly. "He's gone."

"Gone? Gone where?" Disappointed, Gerda folded the newspaper. She had wanted to give it to him herself. "Up to the pass?"

"To Philadelphia." Deftly, Constance combed through the foliage, searching out ripe beans, and plucked them with one hand, dropping them into the basket she carried with the other. "They're organizing colored regiments at long last. Abel, his brother, and their sister's husband have gone off to Camp William Penn to enlist."

"But this is good news, isn't it?" Abel had wanted to enlist for years, and now it seemed his wishes would be fulfilled.

"I want what he wants." Constance looked up from her work, and Gerda saw then that her eyes were red-rimmed as if she had spent hours crying alone. "I had hoped that he would be satisfied leading the colored company of the Valley Emergency Militia."

"Not Abel."

"No." Constance snapped another bean off the vine. "Not Abel."

"Are George and Joseph upset?"

"On the contrary, they're delighted. They couldn't be prouder." Constance pressed the back of her hand to her brow. "George hopes the war lasts long enough so that he'll be able to enlist when he's old enough."

"God forbid." Gerda couldn't imagine the war lasting another year, much less six. "Is there anything I can do to help you, Constance?"

Constance hesitated. "One of our heifers will calf soon. May I call on Hans when the time comes?"

"Of course," said Gerda, certain her brother would be happy to help. "If there's anything else —"

"Only one thing." Constance wiped soil from her hands onto her apron. "I don't know how the other Union Quilters will feel about this, but I'd like us to send a share of our fund-raising money to Abel's regiment too."

"I can't imagine any of our circle would object," said Gerda, but Constance frowned as if she could imagine it all too well.

Gerda offered to leave the newspaper inside so Constance could mail it to Abel. Constance seemed cheered by the idea, and she managed a smile when Gerda said that she was on her way to Dorothea's house and she would be sure to propose that the Union Quilters support Abel's regiment. Now she had double reason to call on Dorothea, and she could not allow jittery nerves to keep her from it any longer.

She backtracked north along the Elm

Creek road and returned to Two Bears Farm. From a distance she spotted a wagon near the barn that had not been there when she passed earlier. As she drew closer she recognized the team belonging to Dorothea's parents, Lorena and Robert, and her heart began to pound faster. Their presence on the same day Jonathan's wife had received a letter from Virginia was very likely pure coincidence, she reminded herself as she halted near the trough, watered her horse, and tied him to a fence post near a patch of green grass. The elder Grangers visited their daughter and granddaughter often, all the more so since Thomas had marched off to war. And yet Gerda needed to steel herself before knocking on the kitchen door and letting herself in.

The family had gathered in the kitchen — Dorothea sitting in her usual chair, face pale and drawn; Lorena seated at her right with little Abigail on her lap; Robert stiffly pacing, the skin of his face and hands leathery brown from decades of farming; and Charlotte, cradling baby Jeannette while her son played with a wooden boat on the floor nearby.

Dorothea saw her first and rose to meet her. "Gerda, my dear friend," she said, as if to remind her parents and sister-in-law to be civil.

"What is she doing here?" asked Charlotte flatly. Her eyes glistened with tears.

"Perhaps she's heard from Jonathan too," Dorothea reminded her, before taking Gerda's hands in hers. "Have you? Have you had any word from my brother?"

"No," said Gerda, her heart sinking. In their expressions she saw shock, worry, disbelief, fear. "What's happened? Where's Jonathan?"

They all looked to Charlotte, who pressed her lips together and shook her head, holding her daughter close.

"This morning Charlotte received a letter from Jonathan," Lorena answered for her, voice trembling.

"Thank God he's alive," said Gerda, faint with relief. "Is he well? Is he coming home?"

Lorena shook her head, grief-stricken. "He's being held at Libby Prison in Richmond as a prisoner of war."

CHAPTER SIX

Upon his arrival at Libby Prison, Jonathan had been permitted to send only one letter of no more than six lines. "My dear wife," he had written in the margins of a piece of newspaper. "Imprisoned in Libby at Richmond, Virginia. No chance of exchange. Send food, socks, no money. Uninjured but want nourishment and clean water. Filthy and overcrowded, many sick here. Kiss the children. God bless you." The hasty scrawl was nothing like Jonathan's usual elegant flourishes, the abrupt phrases lacking all his poetry. Though she had read the letter only once, every word and pen stroke was seared into Gerda's memory. She reminded herself that she was fortunate Charlotte had allowed her to see the letter at all; a more jealous wife would have forbidden the woman her husband loved to see his precious words. Only later, when Gerda's shock subsided enough for her to reflect, did she consider that perhaps Charlotte had permitted her to read the letter out of spite rather than compassion. Gerda could not forget that, allowed only one letter, Jonathan had chosen to write to Charlotte. Likely, Charlotte wanted her to take note of that.

Upon hearing the terrible news, Dorothea had immediately written to Thomas's family back east, beseeching them to ask their influential political acquaintances to obtain more information about Jonathan's circumstances and to do all they could to secure his release. They were able to confirm that Jonathan was quartered with other officers at Libby Prison, a three-story brick warehouse on Tobacco Row that had held a ship's chandlery and grocery business before the war, and to obtain permission for him to receive packages as the sporadic mail service permitted. From a sympathetic friend in Richmond, Thomas's uncle received two newspaper clippings that he sent on to Dorothea, who shared them with Gerda. An article from the July 30 edition of the *Richmond Sentinel* listed several Yankee officers who had recently arrived at the prison and alluded to Jonathan, although it did not mention him by name: "Five hundred and twelve commissioned officers are now in our hands, exclusive of 21 surgeons and 9 chaplains." Dorothea and Gerda agreed that the brief story's frustrating lack of detail did little more than assure them that Jonathan was in good company. A second article, which ran in the *Richmond Enquirer* two weeks later, reported that three new officers and 110 men captured at Union City, Tennessee, had been incarcerated at the prison. "There are now 4,868 prisoners registered at the Libby," the article concluded. The number seemed astonishingly high. Gerda, who knew how easily typesetting errors could occur, thought it must surely be a mistake, but Dorothea worried that unless the warehouse was enormous, the prison must be dangerously overcrowded, which would inevitably lead to discomfort and disease.

Weeks passed. Twice, arrangements for Jonathan's parole fell through mere days before he was to be released. Finally, in September, Gerda received a letter of her own, though she was surprised to discover he had addressed it to G. A. Bergstrom rather than Gerda. "My dearest friend," he had written in a shaky hand. "Serving in prison hospital. Mr. Pocken, Mr. Skorbut, Mr. Diarrhoe, & Mr. Verhungern my constant companions. Socks and pickles most welcome, thank you. Forgive my silence.

Remember my heart. God bless you."

It was only thirty-five words, and yet she cherished none of his letters more. She knew he was permitted only one letter a week, and each of the six abrupt lines was rich with significance for her alone. He knew how much it had hurt her that he had written to Charlotte several times and never, until now, to her. At last she understood why: His messages had to pass scrutiny by his Confederate wardens, and a letter to an unmarried woman not related to him would provoke unpleasant questions. Moreover, the German words he had used to name his "companions" — smallpox, scurvy, diarrhea, and starvation — revealed ugly truths about Libby Prison that the Confederates would not want decent people of conscience in the North and South alike to know. Jonathan risked much by trusting her with this cruel secret. What other horrors accompanied the afflictions he had named?

She must learn more. She must discover all she could about the inhumane conditions the Union prisoners endured at Libby Prison, and then she must expose the truth in the *Water's Ford Register*. The public outcry would compel the Lincoln administration to arrange for the men's release, or, if that proved impossible, to redouble their

305

efforts to seize Richmond and free the suffering prisoners themselves.

Dorothea supported her plan and gave Gerda the address of the sympathetic friend of Thomas's uncle, a certain Miss Elizabeth Van Lew, in hopes that she would be able to provide more articles from Richmond newspapers. "I confess I hope you discover the prison is not as inhospitable as we fear," Dorothea told her as she copied out the address, "although that will make a dull story for the *Register*."

"I suspect we will discover it is worse than we can imagine," Gerda cautioned her friend, with a pang of guilt, for she had not told Dorothea about her first letter from Jonathan. How could she, with its entreaty to remember his heart? Both Dorothea and Charlotte had read between the lines of his subsequent letters, but only Gerda knew for certain that the prison was rife with disease and hunger.

Gerda wrote to Miss Van Lew, explaining her purpose and asking her to send any Richmond newspaper reports of Libby Prison she could collect, as well as her own personal observations as a resident of the city. Mindful of the hardships Miss Van Lew likely faced in the besieged Southern city, she also included a few federal silver dollars to defray the costs of postage. "How long until this letter reaches Richmond?" she asked Mr. Reinhart anxiously when she posted it.

His brow furrowed in sympathy. "It's difficult to say. It depends on how amenable the armies are to letting postal carriers cross the lines. Sometimes they're agreeable on both sides, sometimes battle makes travel impossible, and sometimes the Rebels accuse our carriers of using our deliveries as a pretext to spy."

"In the latter cases," Gerda said dryly, "I assume they smile and cheerfully allow the postal carriers to pass through the pickets at will."

Mr. Reinhart chuckled. "I only wish it were so, Miss Bergstrom."

Gerda sighed. It could be weeks until her letter reached Richmond, another week for Miss Van Lew to collect relevant newspaper clippings, and weeks more for her reply to reach Water's Ford. "How about the silver dollars I've enclosed?" she asked. "Do you think they'll be safe? Should I have wrapped them in a handkerchief to conceal them?"

"Your money will be safe as long as the United States Postal Service carries it," Mr. Reinhart replied proudly, lifting his gray-bearded chin. "As for what happens after it crosses into enemy territory, I couldn't rightly say. Miss Bergstrom, if I may be so forward, what business does a loyal young lady like yourself have sending Union silver into the Confederate capital?"

Despite everything, Gerda almost laughed. Only a kind gentleman twenty years her senior would consider her a "young lady" rather than a tired old spinster. "She's a friend of the Nelson family and a good Union woman despite her city of residence," Gerda explained. "She's helped Mrs. Nelson and the Granger family stay informed about Dr. Granger during his imprisonment, and I'm going to ask her to help me learn more about the conditions at Libby Prison."

"Ah, yes. Dr. Granger." The postmaster frowned. "That's a bad business."

"Indeed, but precisely how bad, I won't know until and unless I receive a reply from Miss Van Lew."

"Miss Bergstrom, if I might offer a suggestion . . ." Mr. Reinhart hesitated. "Your correspondence to Miss Van Lew sounds urgent. Those silver dollars may tempt thieves. You might do well to send a second letter, a duplicate of the first, but without the temptation of silver. It may be more likely to reach its destination, and if the lady is as kind as she seems to be, she won't require payment to help you."

Gerda immediately agreed that sending a second letter would be a prudent measure. When she told Mr. Reinhart that she would return as soon as possible with a duplicate but that she would like to post the original immediately, he offered her paper, pen, and ink so she could make a copy without leaving the post office. He even invited her to sit at his own desk in the small office in back, where she could work in much greater comfort than if she stood at the counter. Then, when she finished and gave him both letters to send, he refused to accept payment. "Consider it a token of my admiration for your commitment to the Union cause," he said, stamping and marking the envelopes.

She thanked him profusely and left the post office for Schultz's Printers to inquire if Mary had any news of the 49th. Mary had not heard from Abner in more than a week, nor had the most recent casualty lists come in yet. Disappointed, Gerda picked up the latest copy of the *Register,* discussed a new assignment with Mr. Schultz, and returned home.

Then, she waited. She did not wait idly; all the housekeeping had fallen to her since Anneke had moved into Union Hall and then to Two Bears Farm, and her writing for the *Register* occupied her spare moments. She met weekly with the Union Quilters for their ongoing work to raise money for the 49th Pennsylvania and the 6th Regiment of the United States Colored Infantry, which, Abel Wright reported, had moved from Camp William Penn to Fort Monroe and from thence to Yorktown. Twice weekly, Dorothea brought the boys to Elm Creek Farm to visit Hans, where she gently urged him to make peace with Anneke and welcome her home. Gerda doubted that any amount of coaxing would move her intractable brother, and she told Dorothea that if the two would ever reconcile, it would be because Anneke acquiesced first. Dorothea smiled and assured her that back at Two Bears Farm, she was plying Anneke with the same entreaties.

At the end of October, Anneke organized the annual Harvest Dance at Union Hall with a sure hand, raising more money for the 49th and the 6th than any of their previous fund-raisers. For the first time since his arrival in the Elm Creek Valley, Hans did not attend. Letters from Jonathan were brief and rare, though the Union Quilters continued to send him food and clothing, hoping that at least a small fraction of their packages would reach him. Almost daily, Gerda visited the post office but usually left with little more than Mr. Reinhart's encouragement not to abandon hope.

She could not give up, nor would she as long as Jonathan's release depended upon her discovering and revealing the inhumane conditions within Libby Prison. Surely if the truth were known, the Union would stop at nothing to see all the prisoners released, either through exchange or liberation by force. She also knew that she could not wait for Miss Van Lew to reply, for Gerda had no way to be certain that the Richmond patriot had received either of her two letters. She would have to seek information from other sources, obtain copies of Richmond newspapers by other means. Regrettably, her own contacts were limited to her friends and family back in Germany, who could not help her in this matter, and her acquaintances in rural central Pennsylvania. Of these, who better to put her in touch with a Southern newspaper than a newspaper editor who sympathized with the South?

Hans questioned the wisdom of appealing to the man who had castigated her time and time again in the pages of his newspaper, but when she pointed out that she would introduce herself as Miss Gerda Bergstrom and not the infamous G.A., he sighed, raked his fingers through his beard, and agreed to escort her. "He'll have to be a confounded fool not to discover that Gerda and G. A. Bergstrom are one and the same," he warned as he hitched the team to the phaeton he kept for energetic drives and for impressing customers who wished to put a horse through its paces before purchasing it.

"He believes G.A. to be a man," said Gerda, taking her seat and resting her basket on her lap. "I expect to be in and out of his offices before there is time to pique his curiosity."

"A strange woman's strange request will be enough to do that," said Hans, but he took the reins and drove them to Bellefonte, the county seat and a prosperous, bustling town for all that it was not yet connected to the railroad. Gerda had chosen a Thursday morning for her errand, thinking that, since the *Democratic Watchman* was published on Fridays, Peter Gray Meek was likely to be in, whipping up a fresh batch of vitriol before firing up the press.

They drove along Water Street and past the Diamond at the center of town, coming to a halt near the entrance to the newspaper office. Gerda remained seated, gathering her thoughts for so long that Hans eventually asked, "Would you like me to come in with you?"

"Heaven forefend," Gerda declared, clutching her basket and exiting the phaeton. "If I say I am Miss Bergstrom, Mr. Meek is likely to conclude that you are Mr. G. A. Bergstrom, and he may fly into a rage and strike you."

"Very well, I'll wait outside. If he gives you any trouble, shriek as loudly as you can."

"So you may come to my rescue?"

"No, so I can find a better vantage point to view the spectacle of you fleeing the building in a shower of pieces of type."

"A woman could not ask for a more dutiful brother." Gerda gave him a cheerful wave. "Wish me luck."

"Good luck, sister. You'll need it for this fool's errand."

She laughed to hide her nervousness, strolled to the front entrance with her basket on her arm, glanced at the proud declaration painted on the window — THE BELLEFONTE DEMOCRATIC WATCHMAN, THE INDEPENDENT VOICE OF PENNSYLVANIA — and entered through the front door. The smell of ink and paper reminded her of

Schultz's Printers, but the men bustling about were intent on their tasks, barking orders and jokes to one another, with none of Mr. Schultz's dignified reserve or Mary's friendliness.

A young man with his coat draped over a nearby chair and his shirtsleeves rolled up to the elbow spotted her and approached the counter. "May I help you, ma'am?"

"Yes, I do hope so." She managed a smile as she drew closer, although she felt that each step took her deeper into the lions' den. "I wondered if I might speak with your editor, Mr. Peter Gray Meek?"

The young man grinned, and she had the sudden impression that he was trying hard not to laugh and remind her that he knew the name of his own editor. "May I ask who wishes to speak with him and on what business?"

The young man had a high forehead, thinning hair, and a cleft chin, and he looked to be little more than twenty. A clerk, she decided, or an apprentice of some sort, and rather impertinent for his position. "My name is Miss Gerda Bergstrom," she said, carefully enunciating the first two words of her name and slurring the last a trifle. "I'm afraid my business with Mr. Meek is confidential."

"Really." He lowered his voice and leaned upon the counter, propping himself up on his elbows. "Do you have top secret information about another Confederate invasion? Or perhaps you wish to place an advertisement requesting correspondence with a soldier?" His eyes widened in feigned alarm. "Or perhaps you've come to warn me that the police are on the way and my arrest is imminent, in which case I will thank you and beg your pardon while I finish the latest edition before they take me away."

It took Gerda a moment to understand. "You're Peter Gray Meek?" This young man was her radical firebrand nemesis? "You're just a boy!"

He straightened and folded his arms across his chest. "I'm the proprietor of this establishment, I'll thank you to know."

"Yes, of course you are," she quickly replied. "That is indeed why I come to speak to you. The brother of my dearest friend has been detained in Libby Prison, and I'm afraid his correspondence with her and his wife has been quite limited. As you can imagine, we've been filled with the most unbearable dread not knowing what conditions he endures."

"Perhaps it's better not to know," he said. "Such details may be too gruesome for the

315

fairer sex to know, especially in regard to one's husband or brother."

"Which is precisely why I've come in their stead." Gerda silently rejoiced in his unwitting gift of a plausible explanation. "I shall discover the facts and share with them only what I believe they can bear to hear."

His wide brow furrowed. "And you've come to me because of my vast knowledge of Virginia military prisons?"

"No, indeed, unless you happen to boast such knowledge. I would consider myself excessively fortunate if you did."

"Alas, I don't."

"I believe, however, that editors of Richmond newspapers do, at least as far as a prison in their own city is concerned," Gerda replied. "I had hoped that you might be able to introduce me by letter to the editors of the *Richmond Sentinel* and *Gazette* and ask them to provide me with the information I need."

"You must believe that all newspaper editors belong to a secret society like the Masons and that our loyalty to our brethren surpasses that to our separate countries."

"Perhaps not for all newspaper editors, but you, Mr. Meek, given your sympathies to the Southern cause, surely they would accommodate you."

"I see." He studied her. "You said your name was Miss Gertrude —"

"Gerda."

"Miss Gerda — Bergstrom, I believe you said. Are you by any chance related to a Mr. G. A. Bergstrom of Water's Ford?"

Feigning puzzlement, she shook her head. "I can tell you in perfect honesty that I have never met a Mr. G. A. Bergstrom."

Peter Gray Meek rested his palms on the counter and leaned toward her, eyes narrowing. "Well, Miss Gerda Bergstrom, if that is truly your name, you may tell whoever sent you that he won't catch me incriminating myself. Does he think me fool enough to admit to a perfect stranger that I habitually commit treason by carrying on correspondence with Rebels and traitors?"

"I — I wasn't accusing you of any such thing, but your newspaper — you certainly do seem to support the Confederate cause —"

"I believe that totalitarian government and not seceding states are the real threat to our union," he thundered. "Be sure to tell your employer that. Good day, Miss Bergstrom. I'll thank you to leave and carry away whatever sordid tales you wish to invent. I have a newspaper to publish."

Gerda hastily left the shop and hurried

317

down the street to the phaeton. Hans stood nearby leaning against a tree, arms crossed over his chest, hat pulled down over his eyes. At the sound of Gerda's approach, he looked up. "That was a quick visit. Did you get what you came for?"

"No." Gerda didn't wait for his assistance but gathered her skirts and climbed into the phaeton. "He thought it was a trap. Apparently assisting me would be akin to admitting treason."

Hans climbed in beside her and took up the reins. "I guess he has reason to be suspicious. He's been arrested for his writings before, and he has a lot of enemies who'd like to see him behind bars."

"Or at least silenced." Gerda frowned and leaned back in her seat as Hans chirruped to the horses and sent them on their way. The entire trip had been a waste. The only good to come of it was that she had kept her identity secret, although she could only imagine how Mr. Meek would describe Mr. G. A. Bergstrom's latest provocation in the pages of the *Watchman.*

Two days later, just when she began to despair of ever learning enough to hasten Jonathan's release, Mr. Reinhart greeted her at the post office by declaring, "Miss Bergstrom, I do believe your patience has been at last rewarded."

"I make no pretense to patience," she said, hurrying to the counter, where the postmaster beamed and handed her a thick envelope. The postmark had smeared, but she could make out the words *Richmond, Va.* Miss Van Lew had at last responded.

She clasped the envelope to her chest and cried, "Thank you, thank you, dear Mr. Reinhart!" She didn't wait for a reply but flew from the post office and hurried down the street to Union Hall, dodging puddles and mud, to read her letter in private out of the chilly drizzle.

She let herself in through the back door with a key she carried with her whenever she came into town, lit a lamp in the kitchen, and murmured a prayer before breaking the seal. As much as she needed grim details for her report, she would much rather discover that her worries had been unfounded and that the prisoners of war were comfortable, healthy, well-fed, and as content as could be expected under the circumstances.

November 4, 1863

My Dear Miss Bergstrom
Please accept my heartfelt condolences

regarding the misfortune of your friend Dr. Jonathan Granger and his incarceration at Libby Prison. I am happy to send you what newspaper clippings I have at my disposal, but I daresay my own personal observances will be far more honest and factual, as I call regularly on the prison to nurse ill prisoners and provide them with various clothes, bedding, foodstuffs, and medicines.

On one of these visits I made the acquaintance of your Dr. Granger, and I have spoken with him on several occasions since. He works in the prison hospital, a small room on the eastern side of the first floor, and although medicines and instruments are scarce, he is nonetheless a great comfort to his patients. I hope it will not distress you too much to hear that you would find him greatly changed, as the prison diet is inadequate and he is often troubled by an affliction of the chest. Despite his own suffering, he is devoted to his fellow officers and is a tireless advocate for them, risking reprimands and retaliation by demanding better food for the soldiers and informing on guards who cruelly abuse their charges both with demeaning language and their fists.

Righteous anger compels me to be blunt: These Union officers, captured in honorable warfare, daily experience conditions and circumstances unauthorized by all civilized military precedent and the proscriptions of humanity. At present, more than five hundred and seventy officers occupy the six rooms on the top two stories of the building; each room is twenty-nine feet square, allotting only six square feet of space to each man. These rooms are used for all living purposes — sleeping, cooking, eating, etc. — and although there are four small, barred windows at either end, prisoners are ordered never to come closer to them than three feet, or they are shot by guards watching from outside. In the summer the rooms are so unbearably stifling that the men have broken the glass in the vain hope of catching a fresh draught of air, but in the wintertime the broken windows allow frigid air within. The men are never permitted outside and thus never benefit from fresh air, sunshine, or exercise.

One room alone is furnished with bunks, and that is the only furniture. The rooms are so overcrowded that the men are forced to sleep spoon-fashion, lying head to foot in alternating rows upon the floor. So tightly packed are they that the highest-ranking man in each room is in charge of calling out, "Spoon over!" at regular intervals throughout the night so that all will roll over in unison. All prisoners are supposed to be allowed one blanket each, but not every man has received one, and often the sick and weak find themselves robbed of even this poor comfort by the stronger and more desperate among them.

Rations, as you can imagine, are scant and of poor quality. Some of the men have been permitted to use their own funds to send out into the markets of the city for vegetables, etc., but the scarcity of food in the city has sent prices soaring and the prisoners have no ready source of money, since any money sent by friends in the North is confiscated and held by the wardens. As Dr. Granger has passionately argued to the authorities here, poor nutrition allows disease to flourish. Vermin too thrive in these conditions, and thus Dr. Granger and the other imprisoned surgeons wage a constant battle against the flux, scurvy, typhoid, fits of the nerves, and other afflictions too numerous to list here. When the infirm perish, their remains are placed in the west cellar. Three or more deaths each day are not uncommon. The bodies are allowed to accumulate until a full wagonload is obtained, and only then are they hauled to Oakwood Cemetery for an ignominious burial.

In addition to these deplorable conditions which they endure day to day, the prisoners are forced to suffer indignities and punishments prohibited by the rules of civilized warfare. They are routinely addressed in coarse, insulting language unbefitting the tongue of a gentleman, and some have suffered strong blows of the open palm or closed fist. Such cruelties are not limited to uncouth enlisted men serving as guards; the second in command himself has been known to kick prisoners merely for lying on the floor in the daytime. The basement has been divided into dungeons for the confinement and punishment of unruly prisoners, but often assignment to these cold, dark, oppressive cells seems entirely arbitrary, as some men have been ordered to them for the most minor of offenses.

Miss Bergstrom, I regret the pain my blunt words must surely have caused

you, but you seem a sensible and patriotic woman intent on discovering the
truth, and I would not insult you by
providing you with anything less. You
must not believe the newspaper accounts
that praise the cleanliness of the hospital
ward or the stacks of books and games
provided to divert the prisoners in their
long and lonely hours. The commandant
knows how to put on a pretty show for
inspectors who are there for a few hours
and walk away satisfied without ever
engaging in a single free and open conversation with a prisoner, for the men
are obliged to choose their words carefully when under the watchful eye of a
warden. I trust that your newspaper account will be of a different sort altogether, and if you are able to speed
the exchange of even a handful of these
poor officers, I will be proud to know
that I have played a small part in your
mission.

Please assure Dr. Granger's family that
I will do all that I can for him. I pray
that the Union will soon triumph and
our nation will once more be at peace.

Until then I remain your friend and
fellow loyal Unionist,
Miss Elizabeth Van Lew

Stunned by the horrific revelations, Gerda set the letter aside with trembling hands and read the three newspaper clippings Miss Van Lew had enclosed — a description of a Catholic service offered for the prisoners by the Right Reverend Bishop Magill, an account of more than six dray loads of provisions, clothing, and reading material for the prisoners "brought from Yankeeland, by the last truce boat," a report of three Confederate guards arrested for trading with Yankee prisoners — and understood immediately why Miss Van Lew urged her not to rely upon newspaper accounts alone. Northern writers could not visit the prison to make their own observations, and Confederate writers would be reluctant to reveal their fellow Rebels' inhumane crimes.

Miss Van Lew's righteous anger made every line ring with eloquent truth. So powerful did Gerda find her words that her first inclination was to ask Mr. Schultz to print the letter verbatim. Upon further reflection, it occurred to her that she did not have Miss Van Lew's permission to do so, and in fact, having her name attached to such a condemning report might put the Richmond resident in grave danger. Rebel troops stationed in the city might arrest her or set fire to her house in retaliation — or at the very least, the commandant of Libby Prison would refuse to admit her ever again, and the prisoners would suffer for it.

Resolved, Gerda poured her anger and grief and outrage onto the page, drawing heavily upon Miss Van Lew's letter but identifying her only as "A Richmond Correspondent" and concealing all incriminating details. No one would expect the author of such a strong indictment to be a woman, Gerda thought with satisfaction. Miss Van Lew would remain anonymous and safe, as safe as any loyal Union woman could be in the Confederate capital, and free to continue her essential work. And as long as she did, she would keep untangled the fragile thread of hope joining Gerda to her beloved Jonathan.

When she delivered the final draft to Schultz's Printers, Mr. Schultz called her back into his office and asked her to sit while he read. Line by line, his face grew ever more grave, and when he finished, he set down the copy on his desk with a sigh and massaged his brow. "You believe your 'Richmond Correspondent' to be a credible source?"

"I do," she replied. "My correspondent is

a loyal Unionist with firsthand knowledge of Libby Prison."

"A guard or a warden, I presume." He did not ask, so Gerda did not correct him. "The language encourages me to believe he writes the truth. Liars tend to embellish. I see very little to change in your piece. You have, I presume, warned Dr. Granger's family?"

"Warned them?"

"Prepared them for the distressing details. Surely it would be better for them to learn from a caring friend about the appalling circumstances Dr. Granger is forced to endure. It would be quite a blow to discover them first in the newspaper with no fore-knowledge."

"Of course," said Gerda, abashed. "I'll tell them right away."

"See that you do." Mr. Schultz rose, so she did as well. "I'll run your story in our next edition. Fine work, Miss Bergstrom. Fine work indeed."

The glow of his praise quickly faded as she left Schultz's Printers. Later that after-noon, she carried an earlier draft of her report to Two Bears Farm, where Dorothea and Anneke listened in horrified silence as she read it aloud. "I'll share it with my parents and Charlotte," Dorothea said when she finished, holding out her hand for the page. Gerda gratefully agreed, relieved to be spared the ordeal, well aware that her presence would only augment the Grangers' pain.

When the next edition of the *Register* was published, the people of the Elm Creek Valley responded to G. A. Bergstrom's report with shock and outrage. Mayor Bauer and the town council quickly passed a resolution calling for condemnation of the "criminals in charge of Libby Prison" and urging Secretary of War Edwin M. Stanton to do all in his power to secure the prisoners' release. Dorothea and Anneke assisted Gerda as she mailed copies to Secretary Stanton, General Meade, Governor Curtin, and President Lincoln, for good measure. When Gerda took the letters to the post office, Mr. Reinhart read the address for Mr. Lincoln's copy and remarked, "You could perhaps deliver this to him yourself, you know."

Gerda smiled. During her frequent visits to the post office through the years, she had become rather fond of the kind gentleman. "Perhaps I should. I've always wanted to see Washington City."

"You wouldn't need to travel so far. Mr. Lincoln is coming to Pennsylvania next week to dedicate the Soldiers' National

Cemetery at Gettysburg." His smiled, hopeful. "My eldest daughter and I were planning to attend the ceremony. You're most welcome to join us. I'm sure Mr. Schultz would be grateful for your firsthand account of the ceremony too."

Overwhelmed by the fortunate stroke of serendipity, Gerda gratefully accepted. Hans needed some persuading; Gerda assured him that they would be gone only one night, Mr. Reinhart's nineteen-year-old daughter would accompany them, and she and Harriet would share a bedroom in the private home of the Gettysburg postmaster and his wife. "We will be completely safe, and there's nothing untoward about my traveling with a father and his grown daughter," she told him, laughing at his sudden interest in propriety. "Besides, Mr. Reinhart is an elderly gentleman and entirely trustworthy."

"Trustworthy he may be, but elderly he is not," said Hans. "He can't be more than four and fifty." But Hans's enthusiasm for the chance that she might meet the president was almost equal to her own, and he agreed that a personal delivery of her report to Mr. Lincoln would surely catch the president's attention.

Shortly after dawn on the morning of

November 19, Mr. Reinhart arrived at Elm Creek Farm, shook Hans's hand, and introduced the Bergstroms to his eldest daughter. Harriet was a sweet, slender girl with trusting brown eyes and golden hair parted in the middle and drawn back into a snood. "Father has told me so much about you," she said, smiling as she placed a hand on Gerda's arm. "And of course everyone in the valley is well aware of your good works with the Union Quilters. You do so inspire the rest of us to contribute the works of our hands, needles, and kitchens to the Union cause. I've looked forward to meeting you almost as much as Mr. Lincoln."

Gerda could not fail to be charmed by the younger woman's words, and as Mr. Reinhart drove the carriage south through the valley and over Wright's Pass, they became fast friends. Harriet had lost her beloved mother when she was but a girl, and since the age of twelve, the care of her younger siblings had fallen upon her. "They are such good, dear children that it's no bother at all," she confided, lowering her voice so her father wouldn't overhear, "although I do wish Father had remarried for his own sake, to assuage his grief. He loved our mother dearly, but I have heard that someone fortunate in marriage the first time is inclined to find wedded bliss again."

"I have heard the same," Gerda said. She had never thought of Mr. Reinhart as a father or grieving widower, and silently she chastised herself for thinking of him only as the town postmaster, there to post letters and sell stamps. In all their frequent meetings, she had never asked him anything about himself or his family.

"He is good and kind, and he never raises his voice to us," Harriet continued. "While I wish God had not seen fit to call my mother home so soon, I am grateful that he left me and my siblings in the care of the best of fathers, and the best of men."

"He must indeed be the best of men to have earned such praise from a beloved daughter," Gerda said, smiling. "We should ask Mr. Lincoln to put his face on a coin."

Harriet laughed, and when Mr. Reinhart turned around to glance curiously at them, she assumed an expression of surprised innocence that promptly told him that he was the subject of their conversation. He smiled wryly and shook his head, and as soon as he turned back around, Harriet and Gerda dissolved into laughter.

The company made it a pleasant drive despite the rough road, fog, and overcast skies. The day was unseasonably humid, with none of the crisp clarity that usually refreshed the waning of autumn. As they approached Gettysburg, the road became so crowded with riders and wagons that Gerda feared they would arrive too late to observe the ceremony. Mr. Reinhart assured her that even if they missed the opening procession from the center of town to the new cemetery on the ridge, they wouldn't miss the prayers and speeches that followed.

They reached Gettysburg by ten o'clock and left the carriage and horses at the home of Mr. Reinhart's fellow postmaster, who had left a note on the front door explaining that he and his family had gone to the ceremony and would greet them properly later. Linking their arms like old friends, Gerda and Harriet followed Mr. Reinhart through the crowded streets, turning this way and that, until suddenly Gerda found herself near the front of the throng where the people had halted to keep the parade route clear. "There," Mr. Reinhart said, touching her elbow and nodding down the block. Tall enough to see over nearly everyone else, Gerda spotted a tall man in a dark suit and top hat, who seemed rather oversize for the proud chestnut bay he rode. Two other dignified riders flanked him, but she scarcely noticed them, for after a disconcerting moment, she recognized the tall, melancholy man in the center as President Lincoln himself. She watched, awestruck and admiring, as he rode solemnly past. This was the man who had freed the slaves, the man who would save the Union if anyone could.

"It's he," Harriet murmured, clutching her arm in breathless excitement. "It's the president."

Gerda nodded and watched until he and his companions at the front of the procession went by, followed by other dignitaries, men she took to be prominent local citizens, and the black-clad widows of some of the fallen soldiers interred in the national cemetery. The procession was still ongoing when Mr. Reinhart offered one arm to his daughter and the other to Gerda, quietly explaining that if they departed at once, they would be able to find places much closer to the main stand. "All the better to hear the stirring speeches," he said as they quickly set out. "And to deliver your important report to the president."

As they made their way south of town, they spotted the lingering traces of battle — splintered and scarred trees, broken fences, rifle pits, pieces of artillery wagons and harness, scraps of blue and gray and butternut clothing, bent and abandoned gear. By the time they arrived, a crowd thousands strong had already gathered at the cemetery, seventeen acres of the former battlefield. The main stand was grandly adorned with flags and banners, with chairs arranged for the dignitaries and speakers processing through Gettysburg. A military escort comprised of a squadron of cavalry, two batteries of artillery, and a regiment of infantry formed a hollow square several ranks deep around the main stand, awaiting the arrival of their commander in chief. The mood was solemn and respectful, and despite the vast numbers of men, women, and children gathered before the stand, the noise of the crowd rarely rose above a murmur.

Gerda guessed it to be not long after eleven o'clock when the procession finally reached the grounds. Upon the president's arrival, the military escort saluted and stood at attention as he, the members of his Cabinet, and other dignitaries numbering perhaps as many as two hundred fifty took their places on the stand. In an undertone, Mr. Reinhart pointed out some of the eminent men — Mr. Curtin, governor of Pennsylvania, whom Gerda recognized from his portrait; the governors of Maryland, Indiana, New York, Ohio, and New Jersey;

and several esteemed generals of the Union Army. Mr. Lincoln seated himself beside his secretary of state and reserved the chair on his right for the renowned orator Mr. Edward Everett, who was to deliver the main address of the day, but perhaps due to his advanced years had not participated in the procession. Mr. Everett was not only an excellent speaker, Mr. Reinhart explained, but also a former secretary of state under Millard Fillmore, former senator, ten-year member of the House of Representatives, governor of Massachusetts, United States Minister to Great Britain, two-time vice presidential candidate, and president of Harvard University. He was also, Gerda guessed, sequestered in his tent, making some last-minute changes to his speech, for the chair at Mr. Lincoln's right remained empty for quite some time. Whenever the crowd grew restless, the Marine Band would strike up a jaunty march, alleviating their impatience for a time. At the back of the audience, a photographer set up a large, back-draped camera on a tripod, frowning at the young boys who stood in front of the lens, tipping their hats and doing their best to spoil his images.

Suddenly, there was a brief smattering of applause as Mr. Everett emerged from his tent. Mr. David Wills and Governor Seymour of New York descended from the platform to meet him and escort the white-haired orator to his place at Lincoln's right hand. The dignitaries on the platform rose as Mr. Everett slowly walked to the president, who greeted him respectfully as every man among the thousands removed his hat in nearly perfect, reverential silence.

The ceremony commenced with a funeral dirge composed by Mr. Birgfield and performed by his band. After the last notes faded away, the Reverend Mr. Stockton, chaplain of the House of Representatives, delivered an eloquent and impassioned prayer praising God, thanking Him for his infinite perfections, patience, and redeeming grace, and asking for His blessings upon the deceased, the bereaved, the Union, its leaders and people, and its efforts to suppress the rebellion. As he spoke, the heavy fog that had shrouded the procession suddenly cleared, shafts of sunlight illuminating the cemetery as if in divine benediction. Moved, Gerda cleared her throat, but she quickly composed herself, declining Mr. Reinhart's gracious offer of his handkerchief. She was there on behalf of Jonathan and the *Water's Ford Register,* she reminded herself. She was a correspondent, attending in a professional capacity. She must remain dispassionate and not allow herself to be swept away by the strong sentiments of the occasion.

Next the Marine Band performed the hymn "Old Hundred," and then Mr. Edward Everett rose, and without notes of any kind, commenced his oratory. "Standing beneath this serene sky," he began, his voice high, strong, and clear, "overlooking these broad fields now reposing from the labors of the waning year, the mighty Alleghenies dimly towering before us, the graves of our brethren beneath our feet, it is with hesitation that I raise my poor voice to break the eloquent silence of God and Nature."

Gerda did not sense any hesitation in his manner, nor did she believe he truly considered his voice poor — or if he did, he was very foolish indeed, for his fame as an orator offered sufficient evidence to the contrary.

She was about to whisper her observations to Harriet when Mr. Everett continued, "But the duty to which you have called me must be performed. Grant me, I pray you, your indulgence and your sympathy."

Gerda could hardly ignore the elderly man's humble request, and soon, like the thousands upon thousands of people gathered around her, she found herself spell-bound. For nearly two hours, Mr. Everett spoke, captivating his listeners with a detailed narrative of the origin of the conflict between North and South, the events leading up to the clash of armies at Gettysburg, and the battle itself, embellished with references to ancient Greece, its gods, poets, and funeral rites for fallen heroes. Despite her resolution to remain an objective observer, Gerda often forgot to take notes, caught up in the power of his speech. "Wheresoever throughout the civilized world the accounts of this great warfare are read," Mr. Everett concluded, "and down to the latest period of recorded time, in the glorious annals of our common country, there will be no brighter page than that which relates the Battle of Gettysburg."

As he returned to his seat, the audience broke into enthusiastic and sustained applause, which he acknowledged graciously. When the crowd fell silent once more, the band played another hymn. Gerda watched as President Lincoln, seated on the platform no more than six yards away, reached into the breast pocket of his suit coat, withdrew a few small pieces of paper, shuffled through them, and read over the one on top, his customary expression of sadness deepening.

After the hymn, the marshal rose and introduced the president, who tucked away the papers, rose, and slowly approached the front of the platform. The audience hushed and stilled, and so perfect was the silence that Gerda could hear the president's footfalls on the wooden boards of the stand. His eyes were brooding, his brow furrowed. "Four score and seven years ago," he began slowly, his voice as clear as a sunny Kentucky morning, "our fathers brought forth on this continent a new nation, conceived in Liberty, and dedicated to the proposition that all men are created equal."

"Amen," someone spoke up from amidst a group of colored men and women standing off to one side. Amen, Gerda silently echoed as President Lincoln's simple eloquence made her understand how, in a very real sense, their words and ceremonies that day could not consecrate the cemetery, for it had already been consecrated by the blood of the brave soldiers who had given their lives so that the United States of America might endure. What the soldiers had done on that battlefield in July was far more important than what anyone said and did there that day, and they must commit themselves to completing the work yet unfinished.

"We here highly resolve that these dead shall not have died in vain," continued Mr. Lincoln, "that this nation, under God, shall have a new birth of freedom — and that government of the people, by the people, for the people, shall not perish from the earth."

Tears in her eyes, Gerda stood as the rest of the gathered thousands did, motionless and silent and deeply moved. Suddenly, Mr. Lincoln turned and went back to his chair, but so transfixed were his listeners and so startled by the brevity of his remarks and their abrupt conclusion that they remained silent and still for a long moment after he had resumed his seat. Then, like a great exhalation of a breath, the audience burst into thunderous applause. "Yes, yes!" someone cried out. "Government for the people!"

Mr. Reinhart dabbed at his eyes with his handkerchief and cleared his throat. "Father, you're weeping," exclaimed Harriet.

"The poor unfortunate photographer," Mr. Reinhart said, indicating the man at the back of the audience who, too late, had ducked beneath the black drape of his camera. "The president concluded so early, he missed his chance to take an image."

Harriet and Gerda exchanged a knowing look. Gerda found it charming that the postmaster had been deeply moved by the president's words, just as she had been.

When the cheers and applause faded, the Gettysburg Choir sang a dirge and the Reverend Henry Lewis Baugher, the president of Gettysburg College and an alumnus of the Lutheran Seminary, where Jonathan had been taken prisoner, offered the benediction. Then the ceremony ended. Remembering her mission, Gerda watched in dismay as the marshals formed an honor guard around the president and escorted him down from the platform.

"I'll have no chance to meet him now," she lamented.

Harriet squeezed her arm in sympathy, but Mr. Reinhart said, "We've come too far to give up so soon. Let's follow Mr. Lincoln and see if we can't catch up to him."

Where the president went was to the home of Mr. David Wills, the cemetery organizer and Mr. Lincoln's host during his stay. A crowd had gathered outside the three-story residence in the center of town, called the Diamond, not far from where the procession had begun earlier that day.

"He'll have to come out sometime," Mr. Reinhart remarked. "He's scheduled to attend an address by the lieutenant governor of Ohio at the Presbyterian church later this afternoon, and his train leaves for Washington City at half past six. If we look sharp, we should be able to catch him coming or going."

Mr. Reinhart escorted Gerda and Harriet to a comfortable spot on the lawn of the town square, as every bench and chair was already occupied by other visitors, and hurried off to fetch their picnic basket from the carriage. By the time he returned, the women had good news to report: They had overheard that Mr. Lincoln was presently dining in the Wills home with a very large company, but between dinner and the Ohio address, he would receive callers in Mr. Wills's front hall.

Quickly they ate their simple meal of bread, cheese, sausage, apples, and cider and returned to the Wills residence, where already hundreds of admirers milled about the entire block of York Street awaiting the opportunity to meet the president. At last the door opened and a queue formed. Gerda's heart pounded with anticipation as she waited her turn, and as she climbed the stairs and entered the Wills home, she could scarcely breathe as she silently rehearsed what she would say.

Mr. Lincoln sat in an armchair with his legs crossed, shaking hands and smiling modestly as he accepted good wishes from one and all. When only three people stood before her in line, Gerda took out the carefully folded newspaper and quickly smoothed out a few wrinkles.

Then it was their turn. Mr. Reinhart introduced himself as the postmaster of Water's Ford, and then introduced his daughter and Gerda. "Miss Bergstrom writes for our local newspaper, the *Water's Ford Register*," he said, beaming as proudly as if Gerda were his daughter too. "She's written a compelling report about the unfortunate circumstances of Union prisoners of war that I'm sure you will want to read."

"Tell me, Miss Bergstrom," said Mr. Lincoln, glancing at the paper she carried. "As a fellow toiler in the literary vineyard, what did you make of my remarks today?"

Gerda swallowed and found her voice. "I believe, sir, that you offered the most clear and eloquent summary of the nature of liberty, dedication, sacrifice, and the ideal of democracy that I have ever heard."

His dark eyebrows rose, and with a trace of dry humor, he said, "The silence that greeted my conclusion suggested that my remarks had fallen upon my listeners like a wet blanket."

"Indeed not, Mr. President," she said. "The silence was reverential and contemplative, not disappointed. With all due respect to Mr. Everett, I believe you captured more perfectly in two and a half minutes what he attempted to do in two hours."

Mr. Lincoln's mouth quirked as if he were suppressing a smile. "I thank you, madam, but the august Mr. Everett was much better received."

"Your report," Harriet reminded her in an undertone.

Gerda held out the paper. "Mr. President, in the spirit of this solemn occasion, I wish to remind you of the many unfortunate Union officers who are, even at this moment, enduring inhumane conditions at Libby Prison in Richmond. I hope that my humble attempt to illuminate their circumstances will move you to obtain their release before they too are obliged to give 'that last full measure of devotion.' "

He thanked her and accepted the paper, and then their interview was at an end. They were directed from the hall not the way they had entered but through a door facing the Diamond, where Governor Curtin stood shaking guests' hands as they departed.

"You did it," exclaimed Harriet when they were on the street again. "I'm certain Mr.

Lincoln will read your article on the train ride home and take action as soon as he reaches Washington."

"I do hope so," said Gerda fervently. To think, she had pled her case personally to the president of the United States. If that didn't hasten Jonathan's release, she could not imagine what would.

Mr. Reinhart led them back through the town to the home of his fellow postmaster, Mr. David Beuhler, where they were warmly welcomed and shown to their rooms to rest from their long journey and the day's excitement. Later, over supper, Mr. Buehler told them of his own experiences of the Battle of Gettysburg, which he had spent far from home. "We postmasters had heard General Ewell's Second Corps were targeting post offices and other federal installations," he explained, as Mr. Reinhart nodded his concurrence. "The postmasters of Fairfield and Greencastle were captured and are even now languishing in Confederate jails as prisoners of war. So, although I was greatly displeased to leave my family, I packed the most valuable government property in my valise and took the next train to Hanover."

When Mrs. Wills asked how the Elm Creek Valley had fared during the invasion, Mr. Reinhart described the defense of

Wright's Pass but quickly turned to the subject of Gerda's plea to Mr. Lincoln. "How the president could fail to be moved by such sincerity and devotion to the Union solider, I do not know," he declared. "I have no doubt that Miss Bergstrom's report will accomplish its noble purpose and become the greatest symbol of the Elm Creek Valley's patriotism to come out of this terrible war, second only to the Forty-ninth Regiment's service itself."

"Perhaps third, if you include the Loyal Union Sampler," teased Mrs. Wills. "After all, it has a head start in the race for fame."

"You've heard of our quilt?" asked Gerda, surprised.

"I should say nearly every lady in the North has by now, and a great many in the South besides." Mrs. Wills regarded Gerda curiously. "You mean you haven't seen the article?"

Gerda shook her head, utterly bewildered. Immediately, Mrs. Wills sent a servant to her drawing room to retrieve the latest issue of *Harper's Weekly.* The maid quickly returned, and a glance at the cover told Gerda that it was a more recent edition than the last she had seen. "It came out only a few days ago," said Mrs. Wills, leafing through the pages. "Ah. There we are. 'Pennsylvania

Ladies Wield Their Needles for the Union,' " she read aloud, and passed the magazine across the table to Gerda.

There, above an article describing the Union Quilters' triumphant fund-raiser and the subsequent success of the events they had hosted in Union Hall, was a meticulous black-and-white engraving of the Loyal Union Sampler.

CHAPTER SEVEN

The engraving was identical in nearly every detail to the photograph displayed in the foyer of Union Hall, so it was a simple matter to determine how the editors of *Harper's Weekly* had learned about the sampler. Within days of the magazine's publication, letters began arriving at the Water's Ford post office addressed to the Union Quilters of Union Hall. Many letters simply offered praise and congratulations, but many more requested enlarged drawings of some or all of the blocks, and others requested patterns. Several ladies wrote to explain that the Union Quilters had inspired them to create their own versions of the sampler to raise money to support their own local regiments.

At first, Anneke responded to each letter courteously, providing a sketch of a quilt block if but a single drawing had been requested, and otherwise offering apologies. "I wish we could grant every one of these requests," she fretted one evening as she and Dorothea sat by the fire at Two Bears Farm. The children had all been put to bed, and as much as Anneke wanted nothing more than to sit and rest before summoning up the energy to climb the stairs to bed, a dozen letters awaited a response.

"I do too," said Dorothea, glancing up from her knitting. "Especially those from quilters who want to make their own fund-raising samplers. Wouldn't it be wonderful if women all across the country organized as we have done, built their own Union Halls, and became stewards of important community assets in town after town?"

Anneke preferred to think of their group, their hall, and their quilt as unique. "There is only one Union Hall, and one Loyal Union Sampler."

"Oh, of course these other groups would need to call their quilts and halls something else, but think of it: Not only would a great deal of money be raised for the Union cause, but hundreds or perhaps even thousands of women would find their public voices. Think of all we have learned to do as we've run Union Hall. We've managed a thriving enterprise, we've faced down political opponents in the form of Mayor Bauer and the town council, we've learned negotiation and debate and discussion and how to achieve consensus —"

"Every Ladies' Aid Society activity can help women acquire those skills," argued Anneke, realizing even as she spoke that she was helping to prove Dorothea's claim. "It's not essential to build a hall."

"You make a valid point." Dorothea smiled as she put the last stitch into a warm woolen sock, the first of a pair she intended to send to Jonathan in Libby Prison. "Even if other groups want only to reproduce the sampler as an opportunity quilt and have no plans to build a hall, I wish we could help them do it, as long as the money raised from ticket sales will help the Union cause."

Anneke could not disagree with that, nor was she content to reply to the ladies' flattering letters with apologies that the Union Quilters could not provide the patterns. Indeed, why couldn't they? "Faith Morlan won drawings and templates for all of the blocks as well as the Union Sampler itself," she said, thinking aloud. "Perhaps she would let us borrow them and make copies — except I believe my hand would fall off if I tried to please every quilter who has written to us."

"If we begin providing drawings and templates upon request, we can expect more inquiries as word spreads." Dorothea gestured to the paper and ink bottles Anneke had spread out upon her desk. "Making a single sketch for an occasional quilter is one matter —"

"But making all one hundred twenty-one blocks for even a single quilter is something else entirely. The war would be over before I finished."

"One can only hope," said Dorothea with a sigh, casting on stitches for the second sock in the pair.

Anneke wrung her hands and flexed her fingers as if they already ached from the effort. "It's a pity I can't turn out these drawings as easily as Mr. Schultz does copies of the *Register*."

Dorothea laughed sympathetically, but then the clicking of her knitting needles suddenly fell silent. "Couldn't we?"

A few days later, they approached Mary with their idea to sell the patterns for the Loyal Union Sampler by subscription through Schultz's Printers. For a fee, subscribers would have a new pattern mailed to them each week, with the last installment offering instructions for arranging and sashing the blocks. Thus they could begin offering the patterns immediately instead of waiting until all one hundred twenty-one patterns were designed. Quilters who discovered the sampler later, after all of the patterns were available, would have the option to purchase them by weekly subscription or pay the total amount and receive them all at once. All the profits minus Mr. Schultz's production costs would be contributed to the 49th Pennsylvania, the 6th United States Colored Troops, and the Veterans' Relief Fund for the infirm soldiers of the Elm Creek Valley and their families.

Mary thought it was a wonderful idea and assured them that Schultz's Printers could handle the work. "We'll raise money for the Union by selling the patterns, and the quilters who subscribe will raise even more by making their own opportunity quilts," she said, promising to speak with her father at once. At the next meeting of the Union Quilters, Mary announced that her father supported the plan and had offered to donate advertising space in the *Water's Ford Register* so they could reach as many potential subscribers as possible. He would also ask other newspaper editors he was acquainted with across the North to do the same.

"I'll ask Peter Gray Meek," Gerda volunteered, and her friends dissolved in laughter.

Anneke realized that all their excitement

and planning could be for naught if Faith were unwilling to lend them the templates and instructions she had won. Anneke prepared a list of persuasive arguments and rehearsed what she would say when she and Dorothea called on the Morlan farm in the foothills of Four Brothers Mountains in the north of the valley, fearing Faith might be reluctant to have her once unique quilt become merely the first of many duplicates. To her delight and enormous relief, they had barely finished describing their subscription service and all the good it would accomplish before Faith heartily agreed. So pleased were they by Faith's eager generosity that Anneke and Dorothea held a quick, whispered conference in the front room while Faith hurried off for the bundle of instructions and templates; when their hostess returned, they invited her to join the Union Quilters, taking the place that Eliza Stokey had left empty when she had moved away so many months before.

Faith happily accepted and promised to join them at their next meeting. While Dorothea drove them home, Anneke sorted through the envelopes of templates and instructions, sighing with perfect contentment. She had long wished to have them for herself, imagining the infinite variety of quilts she could make from just those one hundred twenty-one blocks, and now she could, for she intended to purchase the first subscription.

She was so lost in reverie that when Dorothea turned the wagon from the main road up the hill to Two Bears Farm, she exclaimed, "Aren't you going to take me home?"

She realized her mistake even before Dorothea replied. "I'd be happy to take you home whenever you like," she said, pulling on the reins to bring the horses to a halt. "Would you like to pick up the boys and your things and go right away?"

"No. No, thank you." Anneke felt foolish. "I was lost in thought. I forgot."

"You forgot that you took your children and left your husband?"

"I haven't left my husband."

"You haven't spoken to Hans in weeks except in messages passed through me or Gerda," Dorothea pointed out. "Rather abrupt and cold messages at that. By most reasonable measures, that's leaving your husband."

"I haven't left him." Anneke clarified. "We're having a difference of opinion, but we'll reconcile eventually. I never intended this separation to be a permanent arrangement."

"How and when will you reconcile if you never speak to him?"

Anneke frowned. She had no good answer for her friend, so she said nothing. All she wanted was for Hans to come to her and assure her he would protect her and the children, that he would not sacrifice their safety to some amorphous, idealistic principle. If she went home without those reassurances, Hans would interpret her return as an apology, an admission of fault, and an acceptance of his beliefs. Anneke did not accept them; she couldn't accept what she could not understand. Instead she had hoped he could make one exception in the event his wife and children were endangered. She knew Hans was not the sort of man to jettison his convictions to please someone else, but she had not realized he was so inflexible, nor could she have ever imagined that he placed his commitment to his principles above his duty to his family. With each passing day, Anneke also feared a little more that he did not love her as much as she had believed.

"The longer you wait, the wider the breach will become," Dorothea said. "Why don't you come with me the next time I take the boys to visit him? You don't have to stay if you don't like what he says, but you should at least prompt the conversation."

"Hans knows where I am," said Anneke, resigned. "If he has anything to say to me, he could come to me and say it."

"But you're the one who left. It would be quite reasonable for him to interpret that as a sign that you don't want to speak to him."

"Then the next time you see him," Anneke replied, "you may imply I would be willing to hear what he has to say for himself."

"Imply? Why don't I simply tell him?"

"Because then he'll think that I told you to tell him."

"Which is what you did."

"I don't want him to know that. I don't want him to think he can sail into the room with that — that charming, overconfident grin and say a few words and all will be well."

"No, indeed. You want him to suffer first." Dorothea shook the reins, and the horses pulled the wagon the rest of the way up the road to their own barn, although Anneke knew Dorothea wished she could turn the wagon toward Elm Creek Farm instead. Anneke did too, but she would not go crawling humbly back to Hans, not when he was the one who had disappointed her.

In the weeks that followed, Anneke, Dorothea, and Mary collaborated to transform the templates and handwritten notes into printed patterns while Mr. Schultz advertised the program in his paper and enlisted six other editors from Wisconsin to Vermont to do the same. Gerda, who already visited the post office almost daily in hopes of a letter from President Lincoln, collected and organized the subscription requests. By the first week of the New Year they were ready to send out their first issue, the pattern for Faith's contribution to the Loyal Union Sampler, Charley Stokey's Star. Just before they went to press, Gerda was inspired to add to the page a brief tribute to Charley Stokey so that all their subscribers would understand the inspiration for the block. Anneke thought Eliza would be comforted to know that quilters across the North would learn about her husband's courageous sacrifice and remember him as a fallen hero as long as the quilt block endured — which, considering how quilt patterns were passed down from generation to generation, could be a very long time indeed.

Anneke wished she could be certain that although she had begun the patterns at Two Bears Farm, she would finish them safely and happily back at her own home.

Without her two dutiful sons, Constance could not imagine how she would have endured Abel's absence. It was not only the determined, industrious way George and Joseph went about their chores, taking pride in the knowledge that they were the men of the house with their father away. Nor was it only their unspoken resolve to tend the livestock so well that upon his return, Abel would find the farm running as smoothly as the day he had departed. Nor even was it the pride in their voices when she overheard them speculating about what their father and the 6th USCT might be doing at that very moment, or the pride in their words when they wrote school compositions about freedom and liberty. It was all of those things, and Abel's certainty that the war would end slavery in the United States forever, that enabled Constance to persevere through the long, lonely, apprehensive days without her beloved husband. Upon waking on those bleak winter mornings, her first thought was that this might be the day a messenger would come with the dreaded news that Abel had been killed in battle. Her second thought was that her boys needed her, so instead of pulling the quilt over her head and sinking deeper into melancholy, she would climb out of bed, wash and dress, and face the day.

She could not have managed without her sons, nor without the Union Quilters, especially Dorothea, Gerda, Anneke, and Prudence, who had become a good friend in the time since they had worked together on the Loyal Union Sampler. Prudence's younger brother was in the 49th, but he was a poor letter writer and the few letters he did send went to his wife in Grangerville. Prudence lived in a small flat above her dressmaker's shop and had no horse of her own, so every few weeks, Constance had George drive Prudence to her sister-in-law's home so she could visit and catch up on the news. To thank them, Prudence had sewn George a fine new suit, pleasing him greatly and delighting Constance, who had been putting off the task of sewing him a new best suit to replace the one he had recently outgrown.

Sometimes, Prudence picked up crumbs of information about her brother from other men's letters if the writer happened to mention him, but since Abel served in an entirely different regiment from the other men of the Elm Creek Valley, Constance never benefited in this way when the Union

Quilters read letters aloud at their meetings. Thankfully, Abel wrote often, and Constance shared his letters with the circle of quilters as proudly as anyone. Some of the women, those she was not close to, seemed only to listen politely without any real interest, and she assumed this was because they knew Constance would not mention any of their beloved soldiers. A few others hung on every word, fascinated to hear that colored soldiers were marching, fighting — and dying for their country, Constance was tempted to remind them — just like white soldiers. Constance had read the editorials in the Eastern newspapers and knew that many white officers had doubted the colored men's will to fight and had reckoned that they would turn and run the first time a Rebel fired upon them. Even so, she had not expected members of her own sewing circle, women who knew Abel as the hero of Wright's Pass, to have such low expectations, and it displeased her to see them so pleasantly surprised by news of the 6th's accomplishments with the Army of the James. Hadn't colored soldiers bravely advanced over open ground in the face of deadly artillery fire at the Battle of Port Hudson, Louisiana? Hadn't the 1st Kansas Colored Volunteers fought off a fierce

Confederate attack at Honey Springs in Indian Territory after a brutal two-hour engagement? Hadn't the 54th Massachusetts led the assault on the well-fortified Fort Wagner in South Carolina, sacrificing many brave men on the beach before the rest were able to scale the fort's parapet, retreating only after fierce hand-to-hand combat and suffering terrible casualties? How many more times would the colored soldiers have to prove their valor before their critics fell silent?

But the women in her sewing circle surprised by the colored soldiers' courage were not critics, Constance reminded herself while Prudence read her brother's latest letter to his wife, which she had lent to Prudence to share with the Union Quilters since it mentioned Thomas Nelson and Rufus Barrows. It would be unkind to call them ignorant; perhaps it would be better to say they lacked experience and were not well informed. They knew few colored folks and believed what they read about them, and all their lives they had heard that the colored race was inferior. Even some abolitionists believed that; they just didn't believe it justified slavery. Their hearts were in the right place, and time and exposure to the truth and a willingness to amend long-held beliefs could eventually lead them to the conclusion that white folks and colored were indeed created equal.

"I have a letter from Abel," Constance spoke up when Prudence finished reading her brother's.

"Oh, do read it," said Dorothea. Prudence, Gerda, and a few others nodded eagerly, while the ladies she knew less well assumed expressions of vague interest and patience. They would come around, Constance told herself firmly as she unfolded the page.

February 8, 1864

Dear Wife,
    I write to you from quarters to which we recently returned after an excursion near Richmond. I cannot travel through the state of Virginia without reflecting that it was the birthplace of my Beloved Wife and yet it was never a kind home to you. It had natural beauties that I once admired, but the war and winter have diminished them and I believe it will take the citizens many years to recover after the present national difficulties have passed.
    I do not believe it will be long now

362

until this ungodly rebellion shall be put down and the sin of slavery that has too long afflicted our great nation will be trampled beneath our boots. If you could but see the brave men of color I am honored to fight alongside, you would marvel at the great outpouring of our strength and courage. Our people know that this is our war and from far and near we are rallying with the hearts of lions. If the Lord favors valor and righteousness then the Union shall prevail, and we may look forward to a brighter day when all our people shall have the full enjoyment of freedom.

But now on to our most recent excursion: Having ascertained that Richmond was poorly defended, General Butler at Fortress Monroe conceived of a plan to send Brigadier General Wistar, commander of the garrison at Yorktown, on a lightning raid to surprise the garrison at Belle Isle, where a considerable number of Union prisoners are confined. It was thought that a powerful and sudden surge from our lines might free them —

"Free prisoners, at Richmond?" gasped Charlotte, white-faced. "Does he mean Libby Prison?"

"He wrote Belle Isle," said Dorothea, taking her hand. Her face, when she regarded Constance, was full of hope and apprehension. "It is a different prison."

"It is a deplorable place," said Gerda darkly. "An island in the James River west of the city with a handful of shacks and tents meant to house thousands. Most of the men have not even a blanket to sleep upon, and they are constantly at the mercy of the sun, wind, and rain."

"Constance said Richmond; I heard her quite clearly." Charlotte shot Gerda a fierce glare before turning a pleading look upon Constance. "You did say Richmond, didn't you?"

"Abel did say the attack was to be upon Richmond," said Constance carefully, "but I've read the letter through and he doesn't mention Libby Prison. If you let me finish—"

"Richmond has more than one prisoner of war camp," Gerda explained. "Officers are sent to Libby Prison. Enlisted men remain on Belle Isle."

Charlotte would not look at Gerda or even acknowledge that she had spoken. "But why would they attempt to free one prison and not another in the same city? Why would they rescue the enlisted men and leave the officers behind?"

"Perhaps Abel will explain," said Dorothea. "Go on, Constance. Please continue."

Constance nodded and read on.

It was thought that a powerful and sudden surge from our lines might free them. The Sixth formed part of the force detailed for this endeavor which advanced on the Confederate capital four thousand strong. But our excursion was doomed from the beginning by a snake in our midst in the form of a Union soldier held by another regiment under sentence of death for serious crimes. The night before we set out, this soldier escaped and fled to the Rebel lines and as you might expect of a traitor, he promptly spilled all he knew about the planned raid. Unaware of this betrayal, the Sixth marched forty-two miles in twenty-four hours, which was a severe test of our endurance, let me tell you. At last we reached Bottom's Bridge twelve miles from Richmond only to find the road blocked by felled trees and the enemy prepared and waiting for us. Though we carried out our orders with great alacrity and swiftness, the Rebels repulsed our assault, and since the element of surprise had obviously been lost, General Wistar broke off the attack and withdrew.

As you can imagine upon our return to quarters we were sorely aggrieved to learn the reason why our mission was doomed before it began. It is a hundred-fold times worse to be betrayed by one of our own than by a Rebel scout.

I believe we will remain here in York-town for the present although I would not refuse a second chance to assault the Confederate capital. Until that city is taken I do not believe the war will end so it is there we must strike. I will be sure to tell the general this at our next meeting, for he is always eager to hear a private's opinion on such matters.

I thank you and the good ladies of your sewing circle for their attentive generosity in supplying us with the scarves, quilts, and reading materials. We have a library but it is poorly supplied, and those of us who read are eager to teach those who do not. These men are as hungry for knowledge as they are for freedom, and they are avid students. Thinking of our poor brethren still in bondage, I am reminded of the passage in Frederick Douglass's book wherein he notes that teaching a colored man to read is to forever unfit him to be a slave. He will become discontent with his station and endeavor to become more than his master wants him to be. Education is the pathway from slavery to freedom, and if I may be so bold as to add to that great man's words, soldiering is the path from freedom to full citizenship. As Mr. Douglass himself wrote last summer, "Once let the black man get upon his person the brass letters US, let him get an eagle on his button, and a musket on his shoulder, and bullets in his pocket, and there is no power on earth or under the earth which can deny that he has earned the right of citizenship in the United States." I carry that clipping from the Monthly pressed between the pages of my Bible and I reflect upon it each night before my prayers. To see this promise fulfilled, I will risk my life in battle. To see slavery ended forever, I will risk my life in battle. God grant that I may live through this war to enjoy the fruits of the colored soldiers' labors in this terrible conflict.

I am called to fatigue duty upon the fortifications, so I must close. Tell George and Joseph I am proud of them.

They are good and dutiful sons and it puts my mind at ease to know that they are with you while I must be away. I wonder if they will learn to run the farm so well that when I return they might not want to obey their old father anymore. If they discover a better way to do things in my absence, then so be it, I will work for them instead.

I remain always your loving husband
until death,
Abel

Constance folded the letter to a silence so complete she heard the whisper of her fingers upon the paper as she slipped it into the envelope. "So you see, in the end they liberated neither prison," she said, watching Mrs. Barrows and Mrs. Claverton exchange a significant look and Mary shift uncomfortably in her chair.

"But this still gives us reason to hope," said Dorothea stoutly, her gaze darting to Gerda before resting upon Charlotte. "Though this raid failed, it proves that the Union Army has neither forgotten its prisoners nor abandoned them. They will surely make another attempt."

"They would have no excuse for forgetting their prisoners," said Gerda, "not with my report submitted to the commander in chief himself."

"Oh, honestly," exclaimed Charlotte. "You would take credit for the raid in addition to everything else."

"I claim nothing of the sort," said Gerda, surprised. "I brought the terrible circumstances to Mr. Lincoln's attention, nothing more and nothing less."

Charlotte waved a hand dismissively. "I'm sure you didn't tell Mr. Lincoln anything he hadn't already heard through more official channels, but if the raid had succeeded, all we would have heard from you for the next three months would have been how your brilliant report inspired the liberation of Jonathan and scores of other officers."

Gerda's eyes narrowed, and for a moment Constance was sure she would impale the younger woman on a spear of invective, but then Gerda took a deep breath and sank back into her chair. "Well. We'll never know now, will we?"

Subdued, Charlotte blinked back angry tears and took up her quilt hoop, lowering her head until her ebony curls concealed her face.

"We all wish Jonathan had been freed," said Mrs. Claverton quietly. "It doesn't matter how or who is responsible."

"But how astonishing it would have been if Abel had been the one to free Jonathan," said Lorena. "I can imagine the look on my son's face to see his neighbor there, opening the door to the prison."

"Can you imagine what Abel would have expected for the Negro soldiers in that case?" asked Mrs. Barrows, shaking her head in amusement. "Perhaps the right to be a general, or to run for president."

Mrs. Claverton laughed, but Constance was unsettled. "What do you mean?" she asked.

"Well, your husband seems to believe the Negro soldiers will be greatly rewarded for their service, more so than regular soldiers," Mrs. Barrows explained. "Why should Negroes benefit more than whites?"

"I don't think he believes anything of the sort," said Constance stiffly. "Already the colored regiments receive lower pay than white regiments. And that's for those who accept their pay. Some refuse it rather than agree to take less than whites get for the same duty."

"Mrs. Barrows, don't you agree that by serving their country, the colored soldiers have earned all the rights and privileges of citizenship?" asked Dorothea. "Rights that they never should have been obliged to earn, but have been already granted to them by the Constitution?"

"I'm no Copperhead, and I've been an abolitionist since before either of you were born," Mrs. Barrows quickly replied, looking from Dorothea to Constance and back. "But I confess I never thought Negro men would be permitted to vote and such things."

"But that's a privilege denied you as a woman," said Gerda, "and you've argued for that right as a woman as fiercely as any of us."

Constance noticed that while several of the Union Quilters nodded, and others were regarding Mrs. Barrows with puzzlement equal to her own, others held perfectly still and were careful not to meet anyone's eye, telling her as clearly as if they had shouted that they agreed with Mrs. Barrows.

Flustered, Mrs. Barrows set her quilting in her lap. "I know. I realize I contradict myself. But I'm not the only one who feels that way. You see —" She gestured helplessly. "We just don't know what to do with you, all you free Negros."

"Do with us?" echoed Constance, letting out an incredulous laugh. "Why, do nothing with us. White folks 'doing' with us has 'done' us nothing but injury. Give us the rights granted to all in the Constitution and then leave us be to abide by the same laws and rights and privileges as you. We don't want your charity or pity or anxious worrying over us. We want justice. We have the right to equal liberty with you — white with colored, women with men. If we can't stand on our own two legs, then let us fall, but at least give us the chance to stand. That's what you say to the men who don't think you have brains enough in your head to vote, isn't it? Well, it's the same with us. You ladies here, every one of you, have more in common with colored folks than with white men sometimes. You just don't know it."

"We know it now," said Dorothea, and Constance could have laughed had she not been so frustrated, because out of all of the women present, only Dorothea had known it all along.

The winter of 1864 brought bitter cold to North and South alike, slowing the pace of battle but inflicting a different and no less dangerous suffering upon the soldiers. Thomas wrote of deep snowfalls and friends who had lost toes to frostbite. Abel thanked the Union Quilters for the warm woolen socks and scarves and asked for more for his fellow soldiers in the 6th, for many of the men were former slaves whose women-folk were still in bondage and unable to provide them with necessities. Dorothea took a very small comfort in knowing that as deplorable as Libby Prison was, at least Jonathan was indoors, out of the elements, unlike the poor souls held on Belle Isle. Although Gerda had heard nothing to indicate that Mr. Lincoln had read her report about Libby Prison and had resolved to take action, she did receive occasional letters from her new acquaintance, Miss Van Lew in Richmond, which she read aloud at the meetings of the Union Quilters just as the wives and mothers of soldiers did. Miss Van Lew wrote frankly of the hardships the prisoners endured, but her tone seemed more guarded when she mentioned Jonathan in particular. Dorothea gathered that he suffered from a persistent illness of the chest and had lost weight, but she trusted that if his condition worsened, Miss Van Lew would inform Gerda, and if she could do anything to ease his suffering, she would.

As grateful as Charlotte was to have any news of her husband, it upset her that Miss Van Lew wrote to Gerda instead of her. "Those letters should come to me," she told Dorothea privately, her pretty features hardening in anger. "I am his wife. I should not have to hear about my husband through his lover."

It was the first time Dorothea had heard Charlotte refer to Gerda in that manner, and her sister-in-law's grief pained her. "I agree it would be more appropriate for Miss Van Lew to write to you," she said, "but what can we do? Gerda cultivated the friendship. If we ask Gerda to end the correspondence out of respect for you, she may not agree, although she may simply stop sharing her letters with the rest of us rather than offend you. If she does stop writing to Miss Van Lew, we don't know that Miss Van Lew will trust you or me as a confidante as she trusts Gerda. Gerda does not always act as I wish she would, but she is my friend. I would rather have news of my brother through her than hear nothing save what Jonathan can fit into his rare, six-line letters."

Her anger subsiding, Charlotte reluctantly agreed that she had little choice but to endure the insult of that particular messenger if she wished to continue receiving the precious messages. Dorothea's heart went out to her sister-in-law. She had no doubt that Charlotte loved Jonathan dearly, and longed to have him love her alone in return. Charlotte had done nothing to deserve the scandal and shame she had tolerated for so many years for Jonathan's sake. Dorothea wished Gerda would recognize the folly of her enduring desire for Jonathan and tell him firmly that he must devote himself to his wife, as he had vowed to do when he married her. If only Gerda would say the words, Jonathan would respect her wishes, but this Gerda would never do. Despite all evidence to the contrary, she clung to the hope that she and Jonathan would be married one day, a hope as stubborn and unfounded as her persistent belief that she would eventually obtain Joanna's freedom after years of fruitless striving.

The Union Quilters doggedly endured the cold, bleak days, longing for their husbands and fathers and sons, working from dawn until dusk to hold farm and home and family together, contriving new fund-raisers and persisting with the tried and true to earn more money for their adopted regiments. The Loyal Union Sampler pattern sales exceeded their most optimistic predictions, with new subscription requests keeping pace with their pattern publications. Knowing that the people of the Elm Creek Valley needed their spirits lifted almost as much as the men at the front did, Dorothea organized entertainments at Union Hall, collecting silver and greenbacks from grateful neighbors eager for diversions from the frigid winter and the war, which seemed similarly frozen in stalemate. And yet, it seemed to Dorothea that Northern confidence was rising by almost imperceptible degrees, even as it declined in the South. The Union blockade was holding, the core Southern territory shrinking. Perhaps it would not be tempting fate to hope that the war would be over before the presidential elections in the fall.

On a snowy Monday in mid-February, Dorothea was in the kitchen kneading bread dough while Abigail played with her favorite rag doll on the floor nearby, when she heard the merry jingling of bells. She glanced out the window above the sink and spotted an unfamiliar cutter pulled by a black horse coming up the road, the driver unrecognizable in a heavy coat and scarf. "Mrs. Hennessey?" she called. They were not expecting company as far as she could recall.

"She's in the washhouse doing laundry," said Anneke, returning downstairs after putting baby Albert down for his nap and, after encountering some resistance, putting the twins to bed as well. "I daresay a housekeeper is a luxury I could grow accustomed to. Shall I summon her for you?"

"No, it's all right," said Dorothea, indicating the scene outside with a nod. "Someone's paying us a call."

"In this weather?" Anneke joined Dorothea at the window and peered outside. "I know that horse. It's one of Hans's. He sold it to Mr. Schultz."

They watched the horse and cutter continue up the road until a corner of the house blocked them from sight. Suddenly anxious, Dorothea put the dough in a bowl and set it near the stove to rise, wiping flour from her hands with her apron. She scooped up Abigail and carried her to the front room window where the view of the road was better, Anneke close behind. As the cutter approached, she suddenly recognized Mary's fifteen-year-old brother at the reins, and her heart went into her throat. Her thoughts flew to the casualty lists that Mr. Schultz collected daily from the telegraph office — but if Thomas's name was on it, the Schultzes surely would not have sent young Peter to tell her. Unless — Mary had mentioned that Peter had hoped to get a job as a messenger since he was still too young to enlist in the army —

"Mama?" said Abigail worriedly, placing her hands on her mother's face.

Dorothea realized she had been clutching her daughter too tightly and immediately relaxed her grip. "Sorry, darling," she said, forcing a reassuring smile.

"Do you want me to speak to him?" asked Anneke.

Dorothea took a deep breath, shook her head, and opened the front door just as Peter reached the top step.

"Mrs. Nelson, Mrs. Bergstrom," he said, his dark eyes snapping with excitement, his cheeks and the tip of his nose red with cold. "There's been an escape from Libby Prison."

"An attempted rescue," Dorothea corrected. "Yes, I know. Mr. Wright wrote to his wife about it."

"No, no, not that, ma'am," he said. "A group of prisoners tunneled out. The story was in *The New York Times* this morning." He tugged off a mitten, reached into his coat, and pulled out a folded newspaper from the inside breast pocket. "Your friend Miss Bergstrom asked me to bring you this."

Heart pounding, Dorothea handed Abigail to Anneke, took the newspaper from the eager young man, and began to read.

INTERESTING NEWS FROM
RICHMOND.

378

Reported Escape of One Hundred and Nine Union Officers.

WASHINGTON, Sunday, February 14.

A gentleman who, to-night, arrived from the Army of the Potomac, saw, before he left there, a Richmond paper of Thursday, found on the person of a deserter who came into our lines, in which appears an article stating that one hundred and nine officers have escaped from the Libby Prison, by digging a tunnel under the street for that purpose. It is supposed the prisoners had been engaged upon the work for at least a month. They were missed at roll-call, and forthwith troops were dispatched in various directions to capture them. Four were overtaken on the Williamsburg and Hanover Court-House road. The others, it is suspected, were secreted in the neighborhood in Richmond. The guards were arrested on the belief that they were in collusion with the prisoners, but were afterward released, the subterranean mode of escape having become known. The paper says that NEAL DOW was not among the runaways, but was probably waiting to accompany the next batch.

ANOTHER REPORT.

Capt. John F. Porter, of the Fourteenth New York Cavalry, arrived here to-day overland from Richmond, having escaped two weeks ago from Libby Prison. He left the prison in a Rebel uniform, having secured an abandoned one, and remained nine days in Richmond without exciting suspicion. Among the officers recently escaped from Libby Prison are Colonel STREIGHT, Colonel TIPPEN, Major JOHN HENRY and Colonel RODGERS; but it is not known yet whether they have succeeded in getting clear of the Rebel dominions. The rations issued to the officers in the prison consisted of a quart of rice to sixteen men every eight days, a small piece of corn bread every day to each, about four ounces of very poor fresh meat once a day, and salt and vinegar very rarely.

Dorothea read the article a second time, breath catching in her throat. "One hundred and nine men escaped," she said in wonder. "Is anything more known about the identity of these men?"

"My father and Miss Bergstrom are trying to get more details by telegraph. My sister sent me to fetch you in case you want to join them."

"I'll mind Abigail," said Anneke, kissing the little girl's cheek until she squealed in delight. "You go."

Dorothea nodded, snatched off her apron, and tossed it on the kitchen table in passing on her way upstairs for her wraps. In a few minutes she was bundled up and tucked beneath a pile of quilts in the cutter beside Mary's brother. Anneke and Abigail waved from the window as they sped off, the horse's harness bells jingling merrily as the cutter's runners swiftly glided over the snow.

Dorothea plied Mary's brother with questions, but he had already told her all he knew, so she was obliged to wait and wonder and silently urge the horse to hurry. It seemed hours until they pulled up to Schultz's Printers, where Dorothea breathlessly thanked the young man, scrambled out from beneath the quilts, and hurried inside. There, in the warmth of the print shop, she found Mary, Mr. Schultz, and Gerda poring over a newspaper spread upon the counter. They glanced up as she unwound her scarf and tugged off her mittens. "What news?" she asked breathlessly. "Do you have word of my brother?"

"Nothing that mentions him by name,"

said Mr. Schultz. "We've heard that of the one hundred nine men who escaped, at least twenty have been recaptured, and several drowned in the James River attempting to leave the city."

"Jonathan would not be among them," Gerda hastened to reassure her.

"No, of course not," said Dorothea. Jonathan must have told Gerda he could not swim, and perhaps he had also confided that he had feared the water since that childhood day he and Dorothea had taken the rowboat upon the floodwaters not long after Elm Creek had shifted its banks and drowned Thrift Farm. Just as they had spied the foundation of their former home through the cloudy waters, the swift current had overturned their boat. Swept downstream, they had clung desperately to the boat until it caught upon a partially submerged log, which they had used to drag themselves to shore. From that day forward, Jonathan had dreaded the water and would wade in the creek only up to his ankles. Dorothea was certain Jonathan would have submitted to recapture before he would have attempted to escape Richmond by swimming across a river.

"The telegraph clerk promised to bring us news if any news comes," said Mary, and she offered to make them coffee while they waited. They passed the afternoon drinking coffee, discussing newspaper business and the news of the war, and jumping every time the door opened. Only once did a boy from the telegraph clerk's office burst in and declare that the *Richmond Examiner* reported that nearly fifty escaped prisoners had been recaptured in the countryside between the city and the Union lines. Those retaken included prominent officers Colonel Ely of the 18th Connecticut and Colonel Thomas E. Rose of the 77th Pennsylvania. Impatient, Gerda queried the boy about whether he had any news of any escaped Union surgeons but had forgotten to mention it, but the boy indignantly straightened to his fullest height and assured her that he never forgot a word of a message. Frustrated, Gerda waved him off and settled in a chair, resting her chin in her hands and staring off into space gloomily.

Eventually they ran out of speculation and fell silent except to occasionally note the easing of the snowstorm outside. Mary and Mr. Schultz had resumed their work, and Gerda had picked up a pencil and paper and was writing furiously. Dorothea watched the snow falling outside and thought of her brother. He would not have braved the James River, and the longer Dorothea pondered the escape, the more she wondered whether Jonathan would have run at all, or whether he would have remained behind to care for the ailing prisoners. Had he not stayed at the Lutheran Seminary to protect the wounded rather than evacuating when he had the chance? That decision had led to his capture, so perhaps later, when faced with another opportunity to flee, he would have chosen differently. But if he believed duty compelled him to remain with his patients, he would not have escaped even if the front door to the prison had been left unlocked and unguarded.

The afternoon light began to wane, and still there was no news. Reluctantly, Dorothea asked the Schultzes if Mary's younger brother could take her home. "It's just as well Charlotte didn't join us," she said, pulling on her wraps as Mary left to summon her brother. Gerda made no reply, and Dorothea knew at once that no one had sent word to Charlotte. "Oh, Gerda, honestly."

"I truly didn't think of her," said Gerda. "You said yourself it's just as well."

"That she didn't come into town only to wait and learn so little," Dorothea replied sharply. "She has the right to know."

"She wouldn't want to hear it from me,"

Gerda pointed out. "I see her face when I read Miss Van Lew's letters. Besides, as you've said, there's little to tell."

Dorothea studied her friend and decided that Gerda was telling the truth: She had indeed not thought of Charlotte. It was impulse and thoughtlessness, not spite, that had compelled her to send Mary's brother to Jonathan's sister rather than his wife. That distinction would matter very little to Charlotte.

Mary returned then and said that her brother was waiting outside in the cutter. Dorothea asked if it would be all right if they stopped at the Granger farm first so she could give *The New York Times* article to Charlotte. Mary assured her that would be fine, and so they set out.

February passed with no word from or about Jonathan. As time went by, Dorothea concluded that if Jonathan had been among the escapees or the deceased, they would have heard something. March brought melting snows and gusty winds, longer days and the return of songbirds, thoughts of spring planting, and at long last, a letter from Miss Van Lew, battered and creased as if it had been smuggled out of Richmond.

February 20, 1864

My Dear Miss Bergstrom,

Such extraordinary events have occurred at Libby Prison that I am confident the story of the grand escape has
already appeared in Yankee newspapers;
however, since news does travel slowly
in times of war, I must assume that you
are as yet unaware of the daring escape
more than one hundred Union officers
made not two weeks ago. Lest I give you
false hope, I hasten to add that the good
Dr. Granger was not among those who
fled. Whether he was unaware of the plan
or was unwilling to leave the patients in
his care, he will not say, but he remains
devoted to his men and is himself as well
as one could expect, given his circumstances.

I have enclosed two newspaper articles,
one from the *Examiner* and a second
from the *Enquirer,* which will give you as
accurate a description of the escape as I
could offer. To help your understanding
of their descriptions, I should explain
that the prison takes up an entire block,
with Carey Street and the city to the
north and the James River to the south.
The basement is exposed on the river

side, and whitewashed so that any prisoners passing in front of it would stand out in stark relief. The eastern section of the basement contains an abandoned kitchen that was once used by the prisoners, but was closed off long ago due to persistent flooding and an infestation of rats. The stairway to this area, appropriately dubbed "Rat Hell," was boarded up, but a group of prisoners contrived to move a stove and dig their way into an adjoining chimney to gain admittance to the eastern basement. From there they dug a tunnel three feet in diameter and fifty feet long, working over a span of seventeen days with no tools save a stolen chisel and a few wooden cuspidors. This I have heard from the men; the newspaper reports will give you the particulars.

There are, however, significant aspects of the escape omitted from these reports. The first will amuse you. It was rumored that the tunnel led not from the dank, rat-infested basement of the prison to a tobacco shed at the rear of an adjacent warehouse, but to my own home! Imagine if you will one hundred nine starving, exhausted prisoners tunneling six additional blocks just so they might enjoy the hospitality of my front parlor. I pride myself on being a gracious hostess but I do not flatter myself that I am worth that effort.

The second factor of note is the effect the grand escape has had on the prison and on the city of Richmond. One must not evaluate the success of the breakout solely upon the number of men who managed to reach Union lines. No one here believed escape from Libby Prison was even remotely possible. The Confederate capital was greatly upset by the failure of its prison to retain its prisoners, and their confidence has been strongly shaken. Compare this to the immense satisfaction and soaring morale of the prisoners who remained behind! It was they who replaced the stones to disguise the opening to the tunnel that had led their comrades to freedom; it was they who slipped in and out of the counting lines at roll call the next morning to confound the guards, whose counts kept coming up short by variable amounts. All of this kept the escape secret until the last possible moment, so that more than twelve hours passed before the Confederates realized that a mass jailbreak had indeed occurred.

Those precious hours made the difference for the men who remained free, I am certain.

Oh, the frenzy that erupted when at last the truth came out! Unaware of the tunnel, Major Turner assumed the sentinels on watch that night had been bribed — a misapprehension the remaining prisoners encouraged with false reports — and placed them under arrest. Messages and dispatches fairly flew from the prison, and cavalry and infantry alike were sent in hot pursuit, scouring the city for fugitive Yankees. One officer was spotted within the city by a newsboy, whose shouts alerted Rebels to immediately apprehend the poor man. Another fugitive was captured crossing a field outside the city by a hoe-wielding slave whose misguided loyalty compelled him to march the unfortunate man to his master's farmhouse, where a Confederate patrol soon collected him. These men were given heroes' welcomes by their fellow inmates upon their return to the prison, which I can only hope lessened their disappointment somewhat. Interestingly, the recaptured officers report that they were treated courteously by civilians and Rebels alike in Richmond and its outskirts; it was only upon returning to prison that the ill treatment resumed.

Of course our newspapers do not report on escapees who reached the Union lines safely, so if you have any news of them, I would be grateful for it. I know it will hearten the prisoners left behind to learn that their friends have thwarted Major Turner and his guards and, after regaining their health, may once again rejoin their regiments and fight the rebellion with a new sense of urgency.

Until then I remain your faithful correspondent in Richmond,

Miss Elizabeth Van Lew

P.S.: I believe my mail is being opened and read by Confederate agents. If, in the future, you write me any letters that contain incriminating information, rather than sending them to my home, please send them to me in care of the friend whose name and address appear below. I will have my servants retrieve them from her.

Silence greeted the end of the letter, broken only by Gerda's sigh as she folded it and passed it to Dorothea, knowing her friend would want to study it thoroughly. "It's a relief to know Jonathan is well," said Dorothea, setting the letter aside for later. "I don't believe he attempted to escape."

"Nor do I," said Gerda. "He always does put duty first, thinking of others' needs before his own."

"That is how you see him. That is how you've always seen him," said Charlotte scathingly. "There is so much that you don't know about what he needs, about what makes him truly happy."

Dorothea watched in dismay as Charlotte began gathering up her sewing. "Charlotte, dear —"

"No. Please." Charlotte shook her head and continued packing her sewing basket. "I can't bear another word."

Charlotte swept from the gallery, the sound of her footfalls fading as she descended the stairs to the front foyer. Within moments, Mrs. Claverton murmured an apology, collected her things, and hurried after her daughter. Watching them go, Dorothea's heart sank and she could not help wondering whether their circle had been irreparably broken. It had endured hardship and loss, scandal and betrayal, but it could not withstand the theft of a husband's affection.

Charlotte and her mother skipped the next meeting, but Mrs. Claverton returned the next week, and Charlotte too rejoined their circle the week after that, although she resolutely ignored Gerda and snubbed her awkward attempts to make peace. Dorothea understood that Charlotte's need for news and companionship transcended her dislike of Gerda, and privately she asked Gerda to be more mindful of Charlotte's feelings.

"What shall I do?" asked Gerda. "Stop reading Miss Van Lew's letters? Stop reading Jonathan's?"

Jonathan was permitted only one letter a week, and of these perhaps one out of ten went to Gerda. The pain and humiliation inflicted upon Charlotte when Gerda read aloud Jonathan's letters overwhelmed any reassuring benefit his words might have offered. "Don't read Jonathan's letters to the circle anymore," Dorothea said. "Each one sent to you is one not sent to Charlotte. Don't you understand how that makes her feel?"

The set of Gerda's jaw told Dorothea that she wished everyone would give more thought to how *she* felt, but she agreed to do as Dorothea asked.

As spring warmed the Elm Creek Valley, a fragile harmony settled over the circle, but

Dorothea knew one discordant note could spoil it again. Fair weather heralded the resumption of heavy fighting even as it called laborers to the fields and women to their kitchen gardens. Before the hard work of summer began in earnest, Dorothea was determined to finish a quilt for Thomas, to replace the one he had given away. At first she had thought to make another Dove in the Window quilt identical to the first, but then one of the Loyal Union Sampler blocks caught her fancy. It was Farm in the Valley, a simple but lovely pattern, and it had seemed an inspired choice for Thomas's new quilt after she reread one of his letters, her favorite of the many he had sent her.

My Beloved Dorothea,
    Dusk approaches, and finding myself with a few idle moments to spare, I improve them in writing to you. Forgive the shaking of my hand. We fought hard today, against as cunning and dangerous an enemy as I ever thought to face in my lifetime. They have entrenched themselves for the night, to wait and rest in expectation of our charge at dawn, but if I am to believe the rumors flying about our camp, we march at dusk. Since I do not know if I will live to see the sun rise,

I must imagine the bright warmth of day, which always seems to surround me when I remember your smile and the fondness in your eyes.

I miss you and Abigail with all my heart. Kiss her for me, and tell her Daddy will be home soon. I tell myself the war will surely end by Christmas, but then doubt steals over me, and I fear I will never see you again in this world. But as you have often said, my dearest, I must not dwell on such thoughts, but rather pray for a swift, just conclusion to this conflict.

So instead, I will imagine you are here with me, or rather, that I am there with you, for though I know you to be a woman of remarkable fortitude, I would not wish you to look upon the scene that lies before me.

When I close my eyes and think of home, it is springtime, with the smell of freshly tilled soil in the air. It is evening, our day's work is done, and I am pushing you and little Abby on the swing your brother hung for us from the oak tree near the pasture. The sun is setting, and the baby shrieks with delight, and you look over your shoulder at me and smile, and I know that I am still alive.

I pause in my reverie to tell you I have, at last, received word from Jonathan. He wrote little about his activities, saying, in summary, that wartime medicine is like nothing he learned at university. When I reflect on the broken bodies we send him, I cannot imagine any education that could have prepared him sufficiently.

Jonathan said he had heard from you, and that your letters gladden his heart. He also mentioned receiving word from our friend Gerda Bergstrom. Apparently Gerda has quite taken to your knitting lessons, for she sent him three pair of thick wool socks, which, he said, he was quite glad to receive. She also sent him a book of poetry, which he confessed he has not yet opened, for at the end of the day, he is too exhausted from his labors to do anything more than remove his boots and drop off to sleep.

He did not mention hearing from Charlotte. I hope this was an oversight on his part and not an indication that Charlotte is unwell. I suspect, dear wife, that your brother had indeed heard from her, but his thoughts were so full of Gerda that Charlotte was crowded out of his letter.

When I reflect upon our friends, I cannot help but pity Jonathan and pray for his heart to find peace. I know what it is like to find one's great love, and having been married to her for so many delightful years, I cannot imagine living without her, or being married to another. I know Jonathan respects and admires Charlotte, and I am certain he is a dutiful husband to her, but it is a pity he cannot spend his life with the one to whom he has given his heart.

I need not tell you to say nothing to your brother or to Gerda of my opinions. These are simply the ramblings of a weary mind, but I know you will indulge me and not chasten me for dallying in idle gossip. Indeed, any talk of those I hold dear, however trivial it may seem, carries great significance in each and every word when I am far from the warmth of their affection.

Now I am told I must douse my light, so I must end my letter in haste. I know you will forgive me for not sending Jonathan's letter on to you. He wrote that he sent you a letter of your own, and the tidings of loved ones are a comfort to me in this wretched place, and I would like to keep Jonathan's to read again at my leisure.

I miss you, my sweet wife, and once more I vow that when I return to the shelter of our little farm in the valley, I will never leave it again.

Kiss Abby again for me, and know that
I remain,
Your Loving Husband,
Thomas

Never was their own farm in the valley as full of hope and promise as in springtime, and as she sat on the front porch one mild afternoon in May, putting the last stitches into Thomas's quilt, watching the hired men in the fields and inhaling the rich scent of freshly tilled soil and the metallic scent of approaching rain, she wished with all her heart that although Thomas would not witness the sowing of the seed, he would be with her at harvest to enjoy the bounty of their farm, the comforts of their home, and the joys of their loving family.

Dorothea was so lost in wistful reverie that she did not notice the horseman coming up the road until he had nearly reached the barn. Then she saw he was a messenger, and her first thought was that there had been another grand escape from Libby Prison, and that this time Jonathan had joined in it. Then the messenger greeted her with respectful sorrow and handed her a telegram that told her of Thomas's death on the battlefield at the Spotsylvania Court House, and then all hope was gone.

CHAPTER EIGHT

Just after sundown, when men of the 6th stirred with the relief that followed the lessening of the broiling heat, the Rebels fired a barrage of artillery upon their trenches. Abel and his companions crouched low in their trenches and kept their heads down, not daring to peer over the parapet as they waited it out. As twilight descended and the enemy mortar battery sent shells raining down above them, the pickets sent word down the line that the Rebs were preparing to charge. The lieutenant ordered them to make ready, so Abel checked his weapon and took his place on the line. When the command came, they opened fire, and the enemy breastworks erupted in a sheet of flame. Abel guessed the firing went on for a good half hour before it died down and all was quiet again. The Rebs never did make their charge; it was a false alarm triggered by movement along their picket pits as they reinforced their breastworks.

Abel had just settled down to an uncomfortable rest on the rough ground of the trench bottom when another order came down that the regiment would be shifted to the left and placed at an angle to the earthworks that held a six-piece battery. The new position placed them near the front, with a better position for defense and an excellent view of the pickets and Rebel line. Once in place, the men were given spades and empty sacks, which they filled with sand and clay as they dug out the trenches and placed upon the parapet about three inches apart. The carpenter in Abel always regretted that they were forbidden to reinforce the parapets with head logs, but he understood why. The Rebel artillery was so close that a well-placed shell could knock the logs free and send them tumbling down, crushing the men they were intended to protect.

As the men of the 6th strengthened their position, a company from the 30th USCT was sent to place abatis outside the breastworks. This was dangerous work, and the shroud of night offered little protection from Rebel fire. As Abel filled sandbags and hefted them up to the rim of the trench, he glimpsed the pickets laying down cover fire in the direction of the red flashes from the Confederate muskets. Meanwhile, the men assigned to construct the abatis each carried a tree, sharpened on the end and stripped of branches, to the outer line. Singly and in pairs, each stole over the breastworks, set his sharpened log in place, drove stakes across it to hold it fast, and darted back to the safety of the trenches, dodging minié balls and bullets all the while.

When the work was done, Abel, exhausted, settled down on the earth floor of the trench to try to grab a few hours of rest in the blessed cool of night. He fell asleep to the call of whip-poor-wills.

He woke a few hours past dawn to the smell of wood smoke and coffee boiling. "What I wouldn't do for a fine breakfast," grumbled Joshua, moving his tin cup closer to the hottest part of the fire. "Flapjacks and sausage, some of Margaret's good bread and butter, and coffee without ashes floating on the top."

"Ashes bring out the flavor of the coffee," said Abel, sitting up and stretching. Somewhere on the other side of the trenches came the sound of rifle fire. He reached for his canteen and took a gulp, wincing at the stagnant taste, warm and disagreeable. He took a piece of hardtack pork from his haversack, stuck it on the end of a ramrod, and held it over the fire to toast it. While he waited, he boiled himself some coffee, but when he dug around in his haversack for the sugar he had tied up in a rag, he discovered that rain had soaked through the bag and dissolved it. The rest of his rations seemed none the worse, but he longed for fresh potatoes, fresh bread, fresh cheese and milk from his own herd.

As he ate, he heard the town clock in Petersburg strike the nine o'clock hour. Already that morning, Joshua told him, a number of men in the trenches to their right had been picked off.

"Lieutenant figures it's a sharpshooter with a long-range rifle," said Marcus, a Philadelphian not twenty years old. He jerked his head to the northeast, but wisely did not stand to point out the location. "There's a chimney standing about a mile away. They think he's up there."

Abel remembered spotting the ruins of a grand house from their previous position the day before. "That's where I'd've gone if I wanted to get a line on our fellows."

He had just finished breakfast when two Indians from the 1st Michigan Sharpshooters came through the trench from the rear, each carrying a Sharps NM 1859 breechloader with a telescopic sight. Abel let out a low, admiring whistle as the hawk-nosed, dark-eyed men passed, working their way forward to the front picket pits. His fingers itched to hold such a marvel of engineering. The long, heavy, eight-square barreled rifles were said to allow a man to fire ten shots a minute without changing position. He had seen some in action and he believed it.

He wished he could join the sharpshooters, not only for the chance to see how he fared with a telescopic sight but also to fend off the boredom. The previous night's movement and fortifying had provided a break in the monotony of the trenches, but now it seemed they were obliged to settle in to the tedium of waiting and keeping low and dodging the occasional shell. Gone was the excitement of their earlier triumph in mid-June, when the 6th, joined by the 4th, 5th, and 22nd United States Colored Troops, had attacked the Confederate earthworks south of the City Point Railroad, routing the defenders, overtaking their position, and pushing them as far back as the Jordan Point Road. Within two hours of fighting, the XVIII Corps had crushed more than three miles of Petersburg's eastern shield. Exultant in victory, they had spent the night in the Rebel fortifications, relieved the next morning by soldiers from General Birney's division. It was the first time the colored soldiers of the Army of the James had hailed the Army of the Potomac, and as the veterans of the Wilderness campaign relieved them, Abel sensed their grudging respect. Many white men had expected colored troops to cower in fear the first time a Johnnie shot at them. Until they saw for themselves how courageously colored men could fight, they couldn't believe it.

Why the Union forces had not pushed forward and attempted to overtake Petersburg then, when it seemed they had the advantage, Abel did not know. Instead they had settled into the trenches for a siege. General Grant's ultimate target was surely the Confederate capital, but Petersburg lay just south of Richmond on the Appomattox River. Not only was it an important supply center for General Lee's army and the city of Richmond, it also offered navigable access to the James River and was the junction for five railroads. Because of its strategic importance, Abel did not suppose General Grant would order the siege lifted until the city fell, although it seemed to him little ground had been gained or lost since that day in mid-June.

The trenches where the 6th now found themselves were stronger and better than most Abel had seen, especially with the improvements they had made the night before. Thanks to the new sandbags they had set in place, the parapets rose eight feet above the bottom of the trench, called the traverse, which was wide enough for four men to walk abreast. Along the outside wall, a bench of clay had been constructed for the men to stand upon when they fired at the Confederate works about one hundred yards away. All along the parapet, forked stakes were stuck firmly into the ground to serve as rests for the barrels of their rifles and muskets, allowing them to sight their guns just right for sweeping the top of the Rebel defenses. Holes for sleeping, about eight feet wide and five feet deep, lay behind the traverse, and cook holes lay farther back still. All these holes and trenches stretching back to the rear were connected by alleys, some covered and some not. Anytime the men dug out more, they threw the earth up the side facing the enemy, increasing their fortifications.

By midday the sun was blistering hot. One of the 6th spread a piece of shelter tent overhead to provide a bit of shade, but it also blocked the cooling breeze, so Abel wasn't sure if much advantage had been gained. He found time to write a letter to Constance, though he doubted he'd be able to mail it until the regiment was sent back to the rear. As suppertime approached, Joshua spoke dreamily about Margaret's roast chicken and creamed peas and apple pie until Abel's growling stomach drove him to ask his brother to quiet down or talk about something else. Joshua obliged, and as the sun began to set, smoke rose from the cook holes, and Abel contemplated another meal of hardtack. He had a small sack of beans in his ration, but no way to cook them. A decent meal would have to wait until the 6th was rotated to the rear.

Twilight deepened, and all around him Abel could hear his fellows taking deep breaths and sighing with relief as the heat relented a trifle. Suddenly, Abel heard the crack of a rifle, followed by a faint cheer from the picket pits ahead.

"What happened?" he asked. Marcus risked a peek over the parapet but quickly ducked back down, shaking his head. It wasn't until later that they learned that throughout the long, oppressively hot day, the Indian sharpshooters had stood in the picket pits with their rifles trained on the distant chimney. All day they had watched without firing a single shot. Then, as darkness descended, one of the Indians fired, and several pickets reported seeing a man plummet to the ground. The Rebel sharpshooter had been entirely concealed from view at the top of the chimney, but with the coming of night he had begun to descend. Though he had exposed only a small part of his body during the climb, that had been enough for the Indian, who immediately picked him off.

Another night in the trenches was followed by another day much like the one before, only hotter. Before noon, the Union heavy artillery took out the chimney so that it could not become the perch for another Rebel sharpshooter.

"Those Vermonters are going for ice again," Abel heard someone remark farther down the line, and he climbed up on the clay transom to take a look.

A dilapidated icehouse, battered by shelling, stood near the Norfolk and Petersburg Railroad on a small hill about fifty yards beyond the Union breastworks. The door facing their side stood open, offering a tempting welcome, but to reach it, a man would be obliged to sprint across an open field in full view of the Rebel line. Once inside the icehouse, the man would be more or less protected while he gathered all the ice he could carry, but he would face the same hazards as he ran back to the trenches with his frozen burden. Sometimes the daring soldier would make it back with his rubber blanket wrapped like a sack around the ice, but other times he was cut down and fell sprawling to the dusty ground, dead or writhing in agony until he died.

The men of the 6th were too far away to hazard the journey themselves, but from time to time, thirsty men on the side of the line closer to the icehouse took their chances. Abel wished he had a few slivers of ice to refresh his canteen. He could imagine the cool, fresh water quenching his thirst, holding back the heavy, sultry air for just a moment. But it would be suicide for him to make the run, so he could only watch whenever the Vermonters made a go of it, shaking his head in pity when they were cut down, and watching enviously when they made it back to the trenches and divided the ice among their fellows.

"Someone's heading out," said Marcus, watching through a narrow space between the sandbags on the parapet.

Abel climbed up on the transom and slowly, cautiously peered through a crevice just as a volley of cover fire erupted from the Vermonters' trench. Slight and swift, a soldier leapt from the hole and flew toward the icehouse, his rubber blanket folded in a tight bundle under his arm. Immediately the Rebels returned fire, some aiming for the trench, others for the runner, who darted this way and that as plumes of dirt rose and fell while bullets struck the ground all around him. Abel urgently muttered, "Go, go, go," under his breath and joined in the cheers as the soldier reached the shelter of the icehouse.

"He ain't made it back yet, Yank," one of the Confederate pickets shouted across the field.

"If I's him I'd wait till dark to come back," said a soldier standing on the transom, taking turns with Marcus peering through the narrow space between sandbags. Abel agreed; in the Vermonter's place he would enjoy the coolness of the icehouse until nightfall, and then return to the trenches under the greater if imperfect cover of darkness. But not twenty minutes later, the slight man appeared in the doorway, concealed from the Rebel lines though perfectly visible to his comrades, his rubber blanket slung heavily over his left shoulder. He signaled to his company, and as they set down cover fire he lit out, bent over from his burden and moving more slowly than before.

"He got to move faster than that," a soldier muttered on Abel's right just as the Vermonter's hat was struck off. Chunks of ice slipped from the blanket as he picked up speed. Then a ball struck his left leg and he pulled up lame. Someone on the line swore, and more balls struck the Vermonter in the chest and shoulder as he hobbled toward the trench. His company shouted for him to run, run, but another ball hit home and he fell flat on the ground, the blanket sack bursting upon impact and sending forth a shower of glistening wet crystals. The Vermonter never moved again.

"God bless him," said Marcus, resigned, drawing back from the parapet.

"All that ice," lamented the other soldier. "Look at it. Just look at it, there in the sun, melting away!"

"You can go fetch yourself some," said Owen, the oldest man in their company, a runaway from Georgia fifteen years free. A few men chuckled grimly, but the unhappy soldier shook his head and climbed down from the transom, seating himself in the relative cool of the traverse. An hour later, all that remained of the ice was a dark wet stain on the earth beside the cooling body of the unfortunate Vermonter. By suppertime, only the body remained.

At twilight, the pickets on both sides shouted insults back and forth for a few minutes before agreeing to a momentary truce to allow the Vermonters to remove their comrade's body from the field. The pickets on both sides took advantage of the ceasefire to meet in front of the 5th Corps line to exchange newspapers and trade coffee and sugar for tobacco. None of the colored troops ventured out, truce or no truce. The Confederates seemed to bear a particular hatred for colored men in Union blue.

"All right, you Yanks" came a shout from the Confederate fortifications after the body was removed from the field. "Hunt your holes right smart quick!"

Like that, the truce was over. The field cleared as men in blue and gray alike scrambled for their trenches, carrying the goods they had acquired in trade. Moments later the firing resumed. Such fraternization was officially discouraged by commanders on both sides, but some officers on the front lines were willing to look the other way from time to time. Abel wondered why no one had thought to visit the icehouse during the lull in the battle. It's what he would have done.

■ ■ ■ ■

The next day, Joshua told Abel that he was determined to have a decent meal for them all before the day was out. He said the same thing upon rising the next morning, and while frying up hardtack the following afternoon at supper. Finally he persuaded the lieutenant to allow him to make his way to the rear and buy supplies from the sutlers' wagons. It would be a three-mile journey there and three miles back, with plenty of opportunities to get himself shot coming and going.

"Don't risk it," Abel urged his brother. "It won't be much longer till we're sent to the rear, and you can buy all you want and eat your fill then."

But Joshua had fixed his mind upon serving up flapjacks with sugar for the entire company at their next breakfast, with fried chicken and biscuits to follow for supper, and pudding for dessert. The men pooled their money, and with misgivings, Abel contributed his share too. Joshua grinned and promised he would keep his head down, and then he was off, making his way through the traverses and down the alleys from trench to trench.

Abel tried to tell himself his younger brother was moving away from danger, at least for the first part of the trip, but the hours passed with agonizing slowness as he imagined every danger Joshua could encounter on the way. He was almost as angry as he was relieved when Joshua reappeared at mid-afternoon loaded down with a sack stuffed full of cans of condensed milk, white sugar, yellow cheese, flour, two chickens, cornmeal, carrots, potatoes, and other delicacies, as well as a shiny tin cook pot that reflected the setting sun and had likely drawn the attention of every Rebel sharpshooter on that side of Petersburg when the sun was high.

"Next time, wear this target over your fool head, why don't you," growled Abel, thumping the cook pot with the flat of his hand. Sheepishly, Joshua shrugged, but he was too delighted by thoughts of the coming feast to mind his brother's admonitions.

The chicken would spoil if he waited until the next day to cook it, so Joshua set himself to work in the cook hole while the ravenous men waited. As he heated oil in the cook pot, he mixed cornmeal and flour and a shaving of the cheese into a breading and dipped the chicken pieces into it. As the smell of sizzling oil and frying meat wafted from the cook hole, Joshua frequently had to order the men not to crowd him, and to appease them he passed around a loaf of soft white bread, the first they had tasted in weeks. Each man tore off a chunk and passed it on, saving the largest piece for the lieutenant, without whom the feast would not have been permitted. The bread all but melted in Abel's mouth, and his stomach growled in anticipation. Fried chicken. He had not enjoyed fried chicken since he could not recall when.

"Five minutes," Joshua called out. "Ready your plates, gentlemen."

The men were so eager that the lieutenant had to remind them that the war had not paused for their feast, and their positions must be covered. Abel was fairly confident his brother would think to set aside a portion for him, so he offered to man the parapet while Marcus and Owen made their way to the cook hole. "Look at that pudding," he heard a man exclaim. "Looks almost as good as my mama's."

"Hands off," Joshua warned. "That's for dessert and it's still cooling."

Any reply the hungry soldier might have made was lost in the sudden whoosh of a shell hurtling through the air and warning shouts from the other trenches. Instinctively,

414

Abel flung himself to the floor of the trench and covered his head just as a deafening explosion shook the earthworks. Sand and pulverized clay rained down all around him. Over the ringing in his ears, Abel heard shouted orders and the rapid popping of return fire. Gingerly he pushed himself to his feet, brushing dirt from his hair and clothes, shaking his head to clear it. Suddenly he heard a cry of despair, and his heart leapt into his throat as he recognized his brother's voice. "Joshua," he yelled, threading his way through the alleys connecting the trench to the cook hole. "Joshua, where are you?"

"Over here," his brother called, anguished.

Abel rounded the corner and spotted his brother. "Are you wounded?"

"Wounded? No, no, much worse than wounded," Joshua nearly sobbed. "Look!"

He gestured to the floor of the cook hole, where dirt and debris from the explosion had smothered the fire — and every savory morsel of their feast. "What a dirty trick," Joshua lamented, tears in his eyes. "That was a dirty Rebel trick!"

His cries drew Marcus, who easily ascertained what had happened and went away muttering in disappointment. Word quickly spread, and although a few of the company came to see for themselves, and to poke at the pile of dirt and cinders to see if any part of the meal had been spared, everyone went away disappointed. Not even the faint aroma of cooking remained.

"Good thing we didn't save the bread for supper," remarked Owen.

Joshua snorted, kicking at the pile with the toe of his boot. A thin wisp of smoke rose and faded. Angry, he kicked again, harder, and his boot struck something metal. Joshua quickly uncovered the cook pot, which was no longer shiny and sported a long dent down one side, but he found a rag and began wiping it clean.

"How about the rest of the supplies?" asked Abel.

Joshua looked up from the debris, suddenly remembering that he had left the sack in one of the alleys. Together the brothers found it beneath a thin layer of earth. The bag was soiled, but the remaining supplies inside it were undamaged.

"Tomorrow we are having flapjacks for breakfast," Joshua declared later as he fried himself a piece of hardtack for supper. "I aim to stuff myself with flapjacks if it kills me."

A week later, the 6th was relieved and sent

back to the rear for fatigue duty, none too soon, for in the trenches they had lost men to shells and bullets every day. They were ordered to set up camp in a strip of piney woods next to an open field, and almost immediately afterward they were put to work constructing breastworks. The command puzzled Abel, who wondered why the defense fortifications were necessary so far behind the trenches separating their new position from Petersburg. But for the first time in weeks, the sound of rifle fire did not constantly harass them, and although a stray shell sometimes sent them diving for cover, they were glad to be out of the trenches for a while. Abel suspected they would soon return.

The labor was hard, but except for the occasional low boom of artillery fire, the setting was almost serene. Pine boughs offered a soft, fragrant padding for their bedrolls. Blackberries grew in abundance, and a few days after setting up camp, Marcus and Joshua rounded up a few stray milch cows, one of which was assigned to their mess. They received their first mail in weeks, and could purchase food and necessities from the sutlers' wagons whenever they were off duty, and they swapped reading material with the men of the 30th USCT and other regiments.

One morning shortly after roll call, Owen, who had gone forty years without reading a word but had taken to Abel's lessons like a bright schoolboy, brought Abel a battered copy of *Harper's Weekly.* "Ain't you from Water's Ford, Pennsylvania?" he asked, holding out the magazine, dog-eared and torn from hard use and many readings, his calloused forefinger marking a particular page.

"That's right." Curious, Abel took the magazine and what did he behold but an engraving of the ladies' sampler quilt hanging proudly from the portico of Union Hall. He had to laugh. "Why, look here, boys," he called to his friends. "Come see what I used to build before I discovered breastworks as my true calling."

The men alternately praised and teased him, and all agreed that he had been holding back, because nothing they had seen him build in the past year had been half as fine as Union Hall. "After the war, I want you to build me a big house just like that one," said Owen.

"After the war?" said Marcus with mock astonishment. "I ain't waiting that long and neither should you. Enough of these tents. This here Union Hall's what our next winter camp should look like."

Everyone laughed, and for the remainder of their fatigue duty, the men of the company would ask Abel's opinion about where they should place the portico or the Greek columns for their breastworks. A former shop clerk from Philadelphia took to calling him the Renowned Architect, but the name was too cumbersome to stick.

No one in the 6th, not even the lieutenant, knew where they would be assigned next. "Picket duty or the trenches again, I reckon," said Owen when he and Abel discussed it. Abel wasn't so sure. While their regiment labored, another colored battalion drilled on the open field — long, hard, tedious drills for hours on end. The separate regiments deployed into lines of battle from double column at half distance, first in quick time, and later, as the men grew accustomed to the maneuver, on the double quick, and then on the run, each time ending with a vigorous bayonet charge at an imaginary foe. After several days, the brigades united and ran through the same drills as before, only as a larger force.

Abel did not know what they were preparing for — he would hazard a guess the men themselves did not know — but no officer drilled his men so intensely for nothing.

419

They were not seasoned troops, but he doubted these drills were merely to compensate for that lack of experience, since nothing could. It seemed to him that they were preparing to make an audacious charge, but where and when, he did not know.

After a day of rest, the 6th was sent back into the trenches near the front line of the breastworks west of the Norfolk Railroad. To their right lay a deep ravine. White troops were deployed there, but when the lieutenant and a few other white officers ventured down that way to pay the usual social courtesies, they were turned back without explanation. Frowning, the lieutenant said only that the sentries were under strict orders to forbid passage along that traverse to anyone, white or colored, officer or enlisted. The lieutenant was not obliged to explain even that much to Abel, and the fact that he said so much underscored the strangeness of it all.

Now and then, Abel and the other men of the 6th would see white soldiers moving out of the ravine with their uniforms encrusted with red clay of a peculiar shade that did not match the dirt of the earthworks or the trenches. When Abel heard that the men belonged to a Pennsylvania regiment, his interest was immediately piqued, but after asking around, he learned that they were from the 48th.

"Them's your neighbors, ain't they?" one of Abel's company asked him.

Abel shook his head. "No. Men from the Elm Creek Valley belong to the Forty-ninth. These men of the Forty-eighth —" He hesitated. "They're from Schuylkill County, east of home."

That was coal mining country, and the presence of men from the 48th Pennsylvania in the ravine, their uniforms strangely soiled, suddenly lent credence to the rumors that had circulated in the trenches throughout July that a mining operation was in the works somewhere along the line. The area near the ravine would be a likely place for it. There the Union earthworks arced forward, forming a redoubt the men had nicknamed the Horseshoe, which was only about 130 yards from a four-gun Confederate fort called Elliot's Salient. Half a mile beyond the fort lay a gradual, gentle slope with long, broad valleys on either side. If the Union could seize those heights, called Cemetery Hill for the graveyard upon the crest, they could easily attack the interior of the Rebel breastworks for a mile in each direction. If that could be done, Abel figured Petersburg would be theirs for the taking, and after that, Richmond.

Rumors flew thick and fast through the trenches. As best Abel could piece together, an officer from the 48th Pennsylvania had proposed digging a tunnel from the Union lines beneath the Rebel defenses to the fort, packing the excavation beneath it with explosives, and blowing it up. The army engineers thought it would never work, but the men of the 48th had mined more difficult terrain than what they now faced, and they were given orders to proceed.

Abel knew better than to pin his hopes on a bold scheme to take out the fort, especially since the only evidence he had that it truly existed was rumor, red clay on uniforms, the secrecy surrounding the ravine, and the intense drills practiced by the 30th and 19th USCT and the others. But with men of the 6th dying in the trenches every day, taken out by sharpshooters' bullets and bursting shells, he fervently hoped it was true. Something had to be done to push them through the current stalemate.

Then, on the afternoon of July 29, the lieutenant and other officers were summoned to a meeting at regimental headquarters. When the lieutenant returned, he told them that the XVIII Corps would be relieved in the trenches at nightfall by Mott's division of the II Corps and would move south.

"This is it," said Joshua as the men dispersed. "They're going to blow the mine tonight. We're lining up to attack the fort."

"Maybe so," Abel said, thinking of the other colored troops they had observed drilling vigorously while the 6th built breastworks. If anyone were going to lead a charge, he'd put his money on them.

After the sun had set, Mott's division relieved the XVIII Corps, and Abel and his men were issued rations and cartridges and told to be ready to march at a moment's notice. When the order finally came, they did not need anyone to tell them they must move quietly. The Confederates were so close that they would hear the shuffling of feet and the clanking of tin cups on belt buckles, drawing their fire or, worse yet, exposing their preparations for the attack.

It was after midnight when the corps reached an open wood near the railroad behind the trenches. They were ordered to halt, but while the other divisions were told to make themselves comfortable, the second division along with Turner's division of the Tenth Corps were sent on to the rear of General Burnside's troops as reserve supports. There they were told to await instructions as to where and when they would be required.

They had time to rest, to wait, and to speculate. The explosion of the mine was imminent, they heard. After the Confederate fort was destroyed, the IX would sweep forward and take Cemetery Hill. Once they were established, the XVIII would move in to reinforce them.

Abel knew he should rest, but excitement and dread and eager apprehension surged through him. He checked his gear and his rifle; he talked with the other men, trying to glean new information, but no one knew any more than he. Around two o'clock in the morning, a few gunshots cracked in the trenches, which within moments erupted into fierce fighting. Owen speculated that other Union troops moving into position had attracted the Rebs' notice, but if their luck held out, the Rebels would not catch on that something big was in the works. Abel could only nod and listen to the battle, taking a drink from his canteen to relieve his dry mouth.

After about a half hour the firing subsided and all was quiet again. All around him, Abel heard the quiet shuffling of feet, but it was so dark he could see little beyond the men closest to him. The minutes passed and stretched into hours. The sky grayed with the approach of morning, and Abel thought he could see the line of the Confederate defenses through the mist. Still nothing happened, no orders came.

Dawn began to pink the sky. Men who had slept roused themselves; others gathered in clusters to speculate about the cause of the delay, what might have gone wrong or whether anything more than elaborate troop movements had been intended in the first place. Suddenly, Abel felt the ground tremble beneath his feet, and felt rather than heard a low, dull roar in the distance.

"That's it, boys," someone shouted, and as one the men strained for a glimpse of the Rebel fort. Just then, a burst of red flame shot from the earth, and billowing clouds of black smoke, and a terrible rumbling that grew into a roar, with smoke and soil and dust rising and huge masses of clay and cannon and the bodies of the slain flung into the sky only to rain down heavily upon the earth. There was a moment of horrified, shocked silence before the guns on both sides erupted in noise and flame. Five minutes, ten, fifteen, the crashing of artillery went on, and to Abel it seemed as if the Confederate entrenchments were collapsing. Then came the yells of the charging columns, and as he peered through the rising clouds of smoke, Abel watched, bewildered, for leading the advance were white Union regiments, not the colored troops he had seen drilling again and again in preparation for this moment. The white Union troops plunged forward into the crater left behind by the explosion, a massive wound torn into the earth, a chasm at least 160 feet long, 60 wide, and 30 deep. Forward the men hurtled into the chaos and confusion, scrambling over the half-buried bodies of men in blue and men in gray, massing in the pit where a Confederate battery on Cemetery Hill hurled fire upon them.

For three hours, Abel watched with sickening dread as the white divisions struggled to capture Cemetery Hill, but they were pinned down, too late discovering that the crater was no safe rifle pit but a trap. Horrified, Abel watched as the colored forces were sent in after them. They fared no better. The Rebels had overcome their initial shock from the explosion and had massed a terrible counterattack. The IX Corps was being slaughtered. Through the smoke and confusion, Abel sometimes glimpsed the desperate flutter of white cloth, a handkerchief tied to a ramrod, a rag waved in a bloody fist. Sometimes the attempts to surrender were heeded, but sometimes they were not, and eventually awareness stole over Abel that the Confederates were ignoring appeals from colored men. Even as the colored soldiers waved the white flag and yielded their weapons, they were shot, bayoneted, slaughtered — white soldiers taken captive, colored men killed.

"They are soldiers," Abel heard himself mutter. "They are soldiers." There were rules even within the misrule of war. But the Rebels did not see soldiers at the other end of their rifles; they did not see men. They saw rebellious slaves. They saw unruly animals.

As if in a daze, Abel slipped away from the lines. There was no wrong to it. He knew now his division would not be deployed to support the IX Corps because the IX Corps would never take Cemetery Hill. No one called him back to the line and he saw he was not the only one compelled forward. White and colored alike had left the ranks and come to the front to do something, anything, to stop the slaughter and, if it could not be stopped, to mitigate the savagery.

He fell in with a stretcher-bearer and carried men from the edge of the crater to the wagons that would take them to the field hospitals. He hauled men out of the trenches where they had fallen and broken bones in the rush to escape the pit of death. With his bare hands he dug men half buried from the explosion out of the red clay and sand.

He was shaking the last drops from his canteen into the mouth of a boy cradling his entrails in his own arms when he felt a tug on his right shoulder. At first there was so little pain that he did not realize he had been hit until he felt the damp of his own blood seeping through his shirt. Clumsily, he knotted his handkerchief around the wound as his right arm went numb from shoulder to fingertips. He waited until the boy died before struggling to his feet and making his way to the rear, faint from lack of sleep and loss of blood. By mid-afternoon he had reached a field hospital where he sat with his back against a tree, dazed, exhausted, picking wool from his uniform out of the wound and listening as the sounds of battle went on and on while he waited for a surgeon to examine him.

He did not see how the disastrous battle ended. He did not need to see the retreat and count the wounded to know that it had been an utter failure.

It was late in the day before he was allowed into one of the tents serving as a field hospital.

"Got it," said the young assistant surgeon, holding up the minié ball he had dug from Abel's shoulder with his forceps. When Abel declined his offer to take it as a souvenir, the surgeon shrugged and let it fall to the ground with a soft thud. He wiped the forceps and scalpel on his apron, already wet with the puss and blood of a hundred other wounded soldiers, and called a nurse to pack the wound with lint and bandage it.

Abel took fever that night. Days later when the wound festered and putreficd, he swore at the surgeon who told him the arm would have to come off or it would mean his life, for he was a carpenter and a farmer, and if he lost his arm, it would indeed mean his life, but he was weak from fever and sick and could not put up much of a fight when the orderlies held him down and the surgeon took out his bone saw and someone came up behind him with the ether. When he woke up, his arm was gone and he never did find out which of the piles behind the field hospital it had been flung into, if there were separate piles for colored limbs and white limbs or if they were all heaped up together until they were buried in the same pit or burned on the same fire, as ash unlike as living flesh, colored skin and white skin intermingled and indistinguishable one from the other.

CHAPTER NINE

"Dorothea."

Dorothea started and turned away from the window. "Yes, Anneke?"

The younger woman, clad in her dress of Balmoral plaid and carrying her sewing basket, regarded her pensively. "Gerda is here to take us to Union Hall for the meeting. Won't you come?"

Dorothea knew she should go. Though Thomas had perished, the war went on. The surviving men of the 49th needed her as much as ever. But she could not overcome the dull lethargy that had settled upon her in the wake of Thomas's death. She could not bear to hear again how her husband was a hero, that he had died for a noble cause, and that her own sacrifice had ennobled her as his black-clad widow. He had died a hero's death, and for that reason her loss was a public one; it belonged to the town, to the nation. Other women might have found strength and solace in that, but Dorothea did not want to share her private grief with anyone. She wanted to be left alone to mourn.

"I don't think so." Her voice sounded distant and rusty from little use. "Not this time."

"You need to get out of this house. It's been four months since Thomas passed on. You can't stay shut up here in your room forever."

"Can't I?"

Anneke hesitated. "I suppose you could, but you shouldn't. We need you, Dorothea."

Another day and Dorothea might have smiled at her friend's transparent attempt to appeal to her sense of duty. "You don't need me. The Union Quilters are thriving under your leadership."

"Constance needs you," said Anneke. "Abel is despondent and she's at her wit's end."

Why should he be despondent? He had lost an arm, not his life. Not like Thomas. Abel should count his blessings. But Dorothea could not entertain such selfish, bitter thoughts for long, and she pushed them away. "What do you think I could do?"

"Goodness, I don't know." For the first time since the messenger had brought Dorothea the devastating news of Thomas's death, Anneke sounded impatient. "You always know what to say and do in such circumstances. If I knew what you would say or do, I could do it myself instead of nagging you to do and say it. Furthermore, unlike Abel, you still have two good hands. If you're going to sit up here and brood with the curtains drawn, at least piece some quilts for the soldiers while you're doing it. Be useful alone if not in our company."

For a moment, Dorothea could only stare at her, and then, despite everything, she laughed. "You certainly have an interesting way of comforting the grieving widow."

Anneke seemed completely dumbfounded by Dorothea's laughter. "Well, all my other efforts have obviously failed, and your way doesn't seem to be making you feel any better."

The idea that anything could possibly make her feel better, ever again, struck Dorothea as a curious puzzle. "I'll come," she said, though she did not stir from her chair. "Give me a moment to dress."

Anneke nodded and left the room.

Soon they were on their way. When they arrived at Union Hall and entered the upstairs gallery, Dorothea's friends hurried to meet her, surprised and delighted to see her again, sympathetic and solicitous, full of questions about how she felt and whether there was anything they could do for her. She smiled and thanked them, for there was no point in replying with the truth, that she needed Thomas and there was nothing they could do. Their concern and attentiveness should have brought her comfort, but their oppressive consolations threatened to suffocate her.

As Anneke led the meeting, Dorothea pieced Nine-Patch blocks and half listened to reports of fund-raisers and soaring Loyal Union Sampler subscriptions and new literature drives for the 49th and the 6th. Suddenly a particular name caught her attention, and she interrupted Anneke to ask, "Who sent us a letter?"

"Two ladies representing the Woman's National Loyal League," said Anneke. "A Mrs. Elizabeth Cady Stanton and a Miss Susan B. Anthony. They read about us in *Harper's Weekly,* and apparently the creation of Union Hall and our success at maintaining control of it impressed them. As I was saying, they'd like us to help them obtain one million signatures on a petition they intend to submit to Congress calling for them to free all the slaves at the earliest practicable day."

"And as *I* was saying," Mrs. Claverton broke in, "I don't see why this petition is necessary. Hasn't Mr. Lincoln already freed the slaves?"

"Indeed not," said Mary. "The Emancipation Proclamation frees the slaves in the Confederacy only in principle and not in fact, because presently the Union has no control over those states."

"And it does nothing for the slaves in loyal border states," said Constance. "I hate to say this about Mr. Lincoln, but his proclamation's less than it should be."

"How will this petition fare any better?" asked Mrs. Claverton. "It seems to me that it would carry even less authority in the Confederacy than Mr. Lincoln's proclamation did."

"True, but it may convince Congress that the people support the complete and immediate abolition of slavery everywhere," said Anneke. "That might embolden them to abolish slavery in the border states or make other laws to promote the cause of freedom."

Mrs. Barrows shook her head. "I don't know if this petition is any business of ours. Isn't our purpose to support our men at the front? If we're out collecting signatures for a petition that might not accomplish any practical good, then we aren't collecting food or making quilts or doing any number of other useful things that will increase the men's comfort."

"Our purpose isn't only to provide for these individual men but also to support the greater cause," Dorothea heard herself say, and all eyes shifted to her. "This war is as much about ending the great evil of slavery as it is about preserving the Union. The Union cannot be preserved half slave and half free. To save one, we must end the other."

"Hear, hear," said Lorena.

Dorothea thanked her mother with a smile. "I believe that supporting this petition as a group is well within our mission as established in our charter. However, if we aren't unanimous in our support, those of us willing to sign the petition and collect other signatures may do so as individuals."

"Let's take a vote," said Gerda. "Secret ballot or show of hands?"

"A show of hands should do," said Mrs. Claverton. "If we haven't learned by now to speak our minds and own up to our opinions without worrying about offending one another, I have very little hope for us."

A ripple of laughter went around the circle, and all agreed that a show of hands would suffice. The Union Quilters unanimously agreed to support the Woman's National Loyal League petition and to seek additional signatures from friends and neighbors throughout the valley.

"Dorothea, dear," said Lorena, "since you were the one to convince us that this measure deserves our support, I believe you should take charge of it."

Her friends promptly chimed in their agreement, and they were so loud and profuse in their praise that if Dorothea didn't know them better, she might have feared they would riot if she refused. She understood the impetus for their enthusiasm and was faintly, fondly amused that they thought she wouldn't realize why they wanted her to take on a new cause. They were relieved to see her out of the house, determined not to let her shut herself away again, and willing to try anything to restore her to her old self again. She knew what they could never imagine about strong, courageous Dorothea — that their efforts would be in vain. Her heart had died with Thomas, and if not for Abigail, she would have willingly followed him into the dark. However — to ease their worries, and because she admired Miss Anthony and Mrs. Stanton, and because the cause was indeed worthwhile, she would accept the role.

She asked her mother, Gerda, Mary, Prudence, and Constance to assist her, and as Anneke moved on to the next item on the agenda, Dorothea's thoughts lingered on her new task. She would surely come up with more and better ideas later, but to start, she thought they could divide the valley into regions, pair up, assign a region to each pair, and over the course of a few weeks, take copies of the petition around to all the households in each region. They could also set up a table in the foyer of Union Hall and solicit signatures as guests arrived for events. Perhaps the famous G. A. Bergstrom could write a piece for the *Water's Ford Register* explaining why the petition was necessary and how it compensated for weaknesses in the Emancipation Proclamation. Perhaps Thomas would be willing to —

She took a deep, shaky breath and blinked the tears from her eyes.

After the meeting, while waiting for Anneke to finish discussing the group's finances with Prudence, the acting treasurer, Dorothea caught Constance by the arm as she was leaving the gallery. "Constance, how is Abel?" She had seen him only once since his return from the military hospital, and suddenly her absence seemed neglectful.

Constance managed a smile. "He's all right, I suppose. His . . . stump is healing all right, but sometimes he wakes up in the night complaining of pain shooting up his right arm. It's gone and yet it still torments him."

Dorothea nodded. She had heard of such things from other returning veterans, and she was sorry Abel was afflicted with those inexplicable pains. "I understand Abel is in great distress, spiritual as well as physical," she said. "I hope in time his suffering will ease."

"Thank you," said Constance, her smile faltering. "It's good for you to think of him, when your loss is so much greater."

Dorothea pressed her lips together and nodded her thanks. She could not think of her loss or she would break down completely. "You're very kind. I — I wondered, how has Abel been managing around the farm? Perhaps we could ask some of the other returned veterans who have suffered a similar injury to visit him. They've had time to learn how to work around a farm with only one arm. Abel could benefit from their experience."

"That's a fine idea," said Constance. "He

tries do to his chores like always, but at the moment, he relies on our sons for the most difficult work. I'm sure he'd like to be more independent."

"I'll ask Mr. Goodwin to call on Abel tomorrow," Dorothea promised. "When Abel can resume his normal work, I think his spirits will rise accordingly. I also hope he'll find some comfort in the pride that surely must come from sacrificing so much in service of his country."

"Oh, yes, he's proud, all right," said Constance. "For all the good it does him. For all his grateful nation cares."

Her friend's sudden bitterness startled Dorothea. "What do you mean?"

"Abel's always cared more for his country than it's cared for him," said Constance scathingly. "He was willing to lay down his life for his country, and he lost an arm to this war, and still he wants to do more. He would, but his country don't need him now."

Dorothea didn't understand. "He was honorably discharged because of his injury. He surely didn't expect to be returned to his regiment."

Constance shook her head. "No, no, not that. You've heard of the Veteran Reserve Corps?"

"Of course." Several men from the Elm Creek Valley who had been wounded so severely that they could no longer serve on the front lines with the 49th had been appointed to the corps. Though no longer able to fight, they could perform other necessary duties, freeing up more able-bodied men for field duty. A few of the men from Water's Ford had been assigned to the 1st Battalion, which meant they could still hold a rifle and withstand the rigors of guard duty. From their letters home, Dorothea knew that these men often served as guards at prison camps or railroads, or as details for provost marshals escorting new recruits and prisoners to and from the front. The 2nd Battalion was comprised of men who had been more seriously injured, like Abel, and they generally served as cooks, orderlies, or nurses. It was honorable service, benefiting both the country and the patriotic men who remained eager to serve the Union despite their disabilities. "Does Abel wish to join the Veteran Reserve Corps?"

"He wanted to, but he was refused."

"Because his wound has not sufficiently healed?"

Constance looked as if she couldn't believe Dorothea needed it explained. "Because he's colored."

"That doesn't make any sense. He served on the front lines, he and thousands of other colored troops. Why not in the reserves?"

"You tell me," retorted Constance. "These good, brave men of color, they spill their blood on the battlefield, in trenches, in craters, on beaches, and it's still not enough. They prove themselves again and again, and their country still considers them less fit than a white soldier. Abel wanted to serve his country; he *still* wants to serve. And what does his country say? 'No thank you, boy, go back to your farm.' "

Appalled, Dorothea embraced her friend. "I'm so sorry, Constance, I had no idea."

Constance shook with anger, but she would not let a single tear fall. "I'm glad my husband is home. I don't want him to leave again. But if he wants to stir a pot of stew or mop floors at a military hospital in Washington City for his country's sake, I would let him go. He's the hero of Wright's Pass. He faced down enemy shells and bullets and the Lord knows what else with the sixth. He dragged a half-dozen men out of that Petersburg crater to safety before taking that bullet. I think he can handle a mop. I know he earned the right to try!"

Dorothea shook her head, dismayed and sickened. She had no words to offer in her country's defense, not a single word.

Anneke spread a quilt in the shade of the tall oaks and let the children take turns on the swing. Her arms tired out before their enthusiasm did, so she promised them more rides later after she rested. Abigail wandered about picking wildflowers, her golden hair in two neat braids down her back, while Stephen and David played tag and wrestled, sturdy and quick, as alike as any two brothers ever were. Albert stayed close by, resting his head in her lap, drowsy and overdue for his nap.

Two Bears Farm was at the peak of its mid-October beauty, the fields ripe and golden, the trees alive with birdsong and the humming of insects. A wistful sadness lingered upon the house, though, and Anneke longed for her own home. She missed her rocking chair by the fireplace, the musical burbling of Elm Creek as it wound through the leafy wood, the proud beauty of the horses in the corral and stable, her own quilts spread over her own bed, and Hans. She missed him most of all. Thomas was dead, Abel was terribly injured, Jonathan was languishing in prison, and many more husbands and sweethearts were lost and mourned throughout the Elm Creek

Valley. Anneke knew her dearest friends would do anything to have the men they loved restored to them whole and sound. When Anneke thought of how bravely her friends persevered in their grief and worry, she was ashamed that she had willingly left the husband who loved her so dearly. The disagreement that had filled her with such anger and compelled her to leave home seemed inconsequential now. How childishly she had behaved, storming off with the children and refusing to return until Hans vowed to protect them. Foolishly, she had expected him to come after her within a day, but now, after much time for reflection and remorse, she understood why he had not. He was not going to change, and he would not pretend otherwise. He would not make promises to her that he could not keep, and he had too much integrity to persuade her with lies. If she could not love and accept him as he was, she should not return home.

She understood at last, but she still could not return — not because she feared for her safety or resented that he would put principle before her, but because she was ashamed and embarrassed, and no longer certain that he wanted her back. The reassurances that Gerda and Dorothea offered were secondhand, and therefore doubtful. If only Hans would come and tell her himself — but since he had not yet, he probably never would.

A wave of loneliness and remorse swept over her. Sitting on the quilt, she buried her face in her hands and struggled to compose herself, the children's playful laughter throwing her grief into sharp contrast. She inhaled deeply, fighting back tears, and suddenly she heard horses' hooves on the road. She looked up sharply — somehow, despite everything, expecting Hans — but it was Dorothea, returning from an outing with her mother to collect signatures for the Woman's National Loyal League petition.

"Success," Dorothea proclaimed after she took care of the horses and joined Anneke on the quilt, setting her basket of papers aside. "We collected twenty-six more signatures today, for a total of two hundred forty-seven. If our other friends have equally good fortune this week, the total for the Union Quilters may surpass four thousand."

"That's wonderful," said Anneke, but something in Dorothea's expression conveyed worry. "Did you have another incident with a Copperhead?"

"Oh, no, not this time. After Mr. Beck threatened to set his dogs loose on us, we became more selective in the houses we visit." Dorothea shuddered, remembering. "Your records from the opportunity quilt ticket sales helped us tremendously. We knew where we were likely to receive a friendly welcome and where we were likely to be turned away — or threatened."

"If your day went well, what's troubling you?"

Dorothea sighed and frowned, her gaze on the children as they played on the grass. "I just came from Elm Creek Farm, where I delivered bad news to Gerda."

Anneke's heart thumped. "Is Jonathan —"

"Oh, no, it has nothing to do with Jonathan." Dorothea managed a wan smile as if to say that if she had lost another person dear to her, there would have been no mistaking her grief. "I'm afraid G. A. Bergstrom's secret is out."

She took a folded newspaper from her basket and handed it to Anneke. "The latest *Democratic Watchman?*" Anneke noted, reading the masthead. "Oh, dear. What has that dreadful Mr. Meek written now?"

Dorothea lay back upon the quilt and flung an arm over her eyes. "No summary I could offer would do it justice."

Thus forewarned, Anneke steeled herself and began to read.

THE MEDUSA REVEALED!
Mendacity, Thy Name Is Woman!

Faithful readers of the *Watchman* have seen within these pages many an insightful refutation of the infamous G. A. Bergstrom, who has for the past two years been stirring men's minds to blood and carnage, and who has desired nothing less than to convince the decent people of Pennsylvania that Abraham Lincoln is the chosen instrument of the Almighty, substituting extreme abolitionist ambitions, perceptions, and bigotry for the gospel of peace. No lover of truth can forget G. A. Bergstrom's notorious report about Libby Prison, which created consternation in the halls of local government and brought forth new and unnecessary proclamations, all without containing more than a smattering of factual details and the rest pure fiction. This editor knows this for a certainty, because as constant and loyal readers will recall, last year a spinster lady strolled into the *Watchman* offices seeking information about that very prison and undoubtedly also desiring to deceive the editor into betraying illicit communications with an editorial counterpart in the Confederate capital. Since no information was furnished to the spinster lady, who at the time was suspected to be in the employ of G. A. Bergstrom, that hapless scribe would have been obliged to invent such fantastical details as would most incite outrage and dismay. This was indeed what transpired, more to the shame of the newspaper that printed the report.

But as in the words of Shakespeare, "in the end truth will out," no matter how devious the weaver of lies may be, and "the devil hath power to assume a pleasing shape." In an act both foolish and rash, the spinster lady identified herself as Miss Gerda Bergstrom before fleeing the *Watchman* offices, her mission thwarted. Once in possession of that information, it was a small matter to discover the suspected agent of G. A. Bergstrom was none other than the "man himself." As contemptible as *Mr.* Bergstrom was in his love for slander and deception, his female incarnation is nothing less than an unwomanly monstrosity, the Lady Macbeth of Union Hall, responsible for the cancellation of the lecture by prominent Ohio congressman Clement Vallandigham and the manipulative force behind the suppression of free speech in our beloved state. Beating the drum of war, knowing that as a childless spinster she need not fear sacrificing any of her loved ones to the cannons and grapeshot, her hands have become indelibly stained with the blood of the flower of Pennsylvania manhood. Brazen readers will consider the rumors that suggest the attribution "childless spinster" is correct only by half, but the editor will leave it to *Watchman* readers to ruminate upon this fragment of public opinion and decide which half is which.

Sadly, this Medusa whose pen drips with the ink of lies and feminine hysteria brings shame upon her brother, Hans Bergstrom, a known good Democrat who declined citizenship rather than participate in Mr. Lincoln's abolitionist war, and who has contributed none of his prosperity to the Lincoln demagoguery beyond a few quilts sewn by his wife and given to Union soldiers with the guileless compassion of a true woman's heart. If the editor were to fault Mr. Bergstrom in any way, it would be to question why he permitted such untruths to be composed beneath his own roof, or, if his spinster sister scribbled her hawkish drivel without his knowledge, why he was unaware of the clandestine activities carried out within his household. However, such blame is disingenuous, for "G. A.

Bergstrom" fooled many people for many months, including this editor. One can only hope that once he is aware of his favorite author's identity, the editor of the *Register* will take away Miss Bergstrom's pen and urge her to follow her dutiful sister-in-law's example and take up a needle instead.

"Oh, my heavens." Feeling faint, Anneke closed her eyes and cast the paper aside. To think those vile, ugly, repulsive words had been written about someone she dearly loved. "What did Gerda think of this?"

"She was disappointed to have her identity exposed, and she's concerned that Mr. Schultz won't publish her writing anymore now that his readers know she's a woman. I'm worried too, but I'm hopeful that Mr. Schultz would rather offend a few readers than take Mr. Meek's advice."

"I think at least half of the Elm Creek Valley already knew she was G. A. Bergstrom," said Anneke dismissively, but she felt sick to her stomach. "There aren't enough Bergstroms in the Elm Creek Valley to make it much of a mystery. Gerda said nothing else?"

Dorothea allowed a small smile. "She commended Mr. Meek on his deft use of Shakespeare to give his claptrap an erudite gloss, and found his needless repetition of 'childless spinster' amusing. She wondered why, if it was but a 'small matter' to discover her identity, it took him nearly a year after meeting her to do so. She was also indignant that you were so maligned."

"Me? How was I maligned?"

"By the suggestion that you've done little more for the Union cause than stitch a few quilts. Without you, there would have been no Loyal Union Sampler, and therefore no Union Hall, and you've led countless other fund-raisers and projects and drives. Mr. Meek greatly underestimated your contributions."

Anneke was rather relieved that he had, for she would be crushed to read such terrible things about herself as he had written about Gerda. "What about Hans?" she asked hesitantly. "How does he feel about what Mr. Meek wrote about him?"

Dorothea sighed and sat up, and absently stroked Albert's tousled hair while he slept on the quilt. "He made a joke about how Mr. Meek damned him with faint praise. He wondered how he could be called a good, loyal Democrat on so little evidence that he was any more Democratic than Republican." She paused. "He was also relieved that Mr. Meek was apparently

451

unaware that you had left him and why, because Mr. Meek surely would have written terrible things about you had he known, and Hans could not have borne that."

With a moan of dismay, Anneke drew her knees up to her chest and lowered her head. She had not considered that word of her estrangement from Hans would leave the circle of her friends and family. To think of the shame she might have brought upon Hans and her sons — might still bring upon them, if the war of words between Gerda and Peter Gray Meek escalated. But even that was not as troubling as Mr. Meek's praise, which unwittingly painted Hans as a disloyal Copperhead. "Mr. Meek says Hans declined citizenship rather than enlist, and that he has done nothing to support the Union cause," said Anneke anxiously. "That's not true, or at least, it's not the whole truth, but people will believe it, and I fear that doesn't bode well for my husband, surrounded as we are by loyal Unionists."

Dorothea squeezed her hand. "Those who know Hans know the truth, and you shouldn't care about the opinions of the ill-informed."

"It's not their opinions that worry me."

Dorothea made no reply, but the look of stark concern in her eyes told Anneke that

452

her friend shared her unease.

Gerda stood at the kitchen table, paring apples with such force that it was a wonder she left any of the fruit unbruised. Hawkish drivel, indeed. She flung the peels and cores into the slop pail for the pigs and vigorously sliced the juicy, white fruit, tossing the pieces into a bowl. Hapless scribe. She seized her knife and thrust it at an imaginary foe. "I'll show you some feminine hysteria, you — you — shrill little mountebank."

"Sheathe your sword, unfeminine monstrosity!"

She whirled around to find Hans grinning at her from the doorway. When her heart stopped racing, she said, "You shouldn't sneak up on me when I'm contemplating blood and carnage."

Hans eyed her paring knife. "I see that. Tell me, is that apple juice on your blade or the ink of lies?"

She touched her finger to the knife, then to her lips, tasting. "Apple juice, this time." She set down the knife on the cutting board and leaned upon the table, suddenly weary. "Oh, Hans, this isn't funny."

"No?" He mulled that over. "I think it is, from a certain point of view."

"What skewed point of view is that?"

Gerda sighed and brushed a strand of loose hair off her forehead with the back of her hand. "How will I ever show my face in town again?"

"How will you not?" Her brother looked genuinely bewildered. "Nothing Meek wrote is worse than what's been whispered about you for five years."

"That's different. I started those rumors myself to protect an innocent child, and the people closest to me know the truth."

"The people closest to you know the truth this time too. What are you making?"

"Pork roast with apples, and your clumsy attempt to change the subject has not gone unnoticed."

"Alas, I don't have your gift for subtle words." He kissed her on the cheek. "Have I told you recently that you're my favorite sister within a hundred miles?"

"I'm your only sister on the entire continent. You are incorrigible. You do realize that, don't you?"

He grinned naughtily and was about to retort when they heard horses' hooves pounding on the road. They went to the window, and through the autumn foliage Gerda glimpsed four, perhaps five, men on horseback milling about near the upper entrance to the banked barn on the other side of Elm Creek. A man bellowed something Gerda couldn't discern, and a second man shouted something that might have been Hans's name, and then another dismounted and entered the barn.

"Something's wrong," said Hans, immediately somber.

Gerda quickly wiped her hands on her apron and followed him to the door. "Who is it?"

"I couldn't tell, but they must have news from town. Bad news, from the sound of it." He hesitated. "Maybe you should wait here."

"Don't be ridiculous." Gerda snatched off her apron, tossed it on the table, and hurried after him.

Not finding Hans in the barn, the four riders had already crossed the bridge over Elm Creek and were approaching the house, each armed with a rifle. Gerda recognized one of the men from the construction crew that had built Union Hall and the eldest as a farmer whose land lay adjacent to the Morlan farm in the foothills of the Four Brothers Mountains in the north end of the valley. The other two she did not recognize.

As the men approached the house, Gerda braced herself for terrible news from the war, wondering what it could be. Surely not

455

a Union surrender, surely not that. A terrible loss in battle, perhaps, but even that could be overcome. Anything short of losing the war could be overcome. Except for losing Jonathan — She took a deep, steadying breath. No, if Jonathan had died in Libby Prison, the news would not come to her by four men on horseback.

The eldest of the four men, his face lined and sunburned, squinted at Hans as the men brought their horses to a halt in front of the house. "You're Hans Bergstrom?"

Hans nodded. "That's right."

"We read about you in the papers and figured it was only fair to let you speak your piece."

"What piece would that be?"

"Your defense against the charges," said the man from the construction crew.

"What charges?" asked Gerda, looking from one stern, smoldering face to another. "My brother's done nothing wrong."

"Begging your pardon, ma'am," said the youngest man, who looked to be barely eighteen and rode a black stallion with white fetlocks Gerda recognized as one raised in Hans's stables. "Maybe you should go back inside."

Apprehension seized her. "What do you intend to do that you don't want me to see?"

"You're accused of being a Copperhead," said the eldest man to Hans, "of sympathizing with the Confederate Rebels, of refusing to become a naturalized citizen in order to avoid the draft, of neglecting to pay the three hundred dollar fee to pay for a substitute, and of failing to support the Union cause."

"I'm no Copperhead," said Hans evenly, "nor am I a Republican."

"You must be one or the other," the fourth man spat.

"On the contrary, I don't, because I'm not, and yet here I stand," said Hans, seeming indifferent to the men's scowls at his brash tone. "As for neglecting to pay for a substitute, it was never required of me, since I was never drafted. As for failing to support the Union cause, well, I pay my taxes, amply and on time, and although I don't know what specific use my share was put to, I'm sure it was enough to purchase a cannon or two."

"My brother helped build Union Hall," said Gerda, directing her remark to the man who had served on his crew and knew she spoke the truth. "He has supported the work of the Union Quilters throughout the war, and each one of you knows what we've done to provide for the men of the Forty-ninth and the Sixth Colored. Mr. Gilbert, your wife made ten blocks for the Loyal Union Sampler. Ask her what we've done."

Mr. Gilbert regarded her grimly without replying, but the fourth man, who wore his strawberry-blond beard cut in a Vandyke reminiscent of the illustrations Gerda had seen of General Custer, glared at Hans. "More shame on you, that you leave your family's share of the work to your women-folk."

"I support the Union, but I don't support war," said Hans. "My wife and sister are capable of making their own decisions and may support whatever cause they choose."

"How can you say you support the Union but not the Union's war?" said the man with the Vandyke, incredulous. "You're just going to stand there and tell us you're no Rebel sympathizer and expect us to believe it?"

Hans removed his hat, studied the brim, ran a hand through his hair, and tugged the hat back on his head. "I don't expect you to listen to or believe a word I say, but the truth is, I have very little sympathy for any man who would hold another in bondage, or anyone else who would kill him for it."

"How short are your memories?" Gerda exclaimed. "Not five years ago, this farm was a station on the Underground Railroad. My brother and I went to prison for protecting runaway slaves. And now you believe our family supports the Confederacy?"

"Not your family, ma'am, just your brother," said the eldest. "Like I said, we read the papers. We know who you are and what you believe. If you tell us your brother shares your opinions but is just too fool stubborn to admit it, we'll leave you in peace."

Gerda threw her brother a desperate look, but he merely regarded her stoically. "My brother and I don't share every opinion, but I challenge you to find any two siblings who do," said Gerda defiantly. "I swear to you that he is no Copperhead and that he wants the Union to thrive and democracy to prosper as much as any of you."

"That's not good enough," the Vandyke rider snapped, moving his horse closer to Hans. "Defend yourself or face judgment."

Hans looked up at him, squinting into the sun. "Who are you to judge me?"

In response, the man lashed out with the butt of his rifle, striking Hans on the head. As Hans reeled from the blow, the horseman kicked, the toe of his boot connecting with Hans's ribs.

Gerda cried out and dashed to her brother's side. "Why would you do such a thing?" she demanded, shaken. "My brother has done nothing wrong. He's told you he's no Copperhead."

"He's no loyal Union man, that's for certain," said the eldest rider. "If he's not with us, he's against us." He nodded to the man with the Vandyke, who kicked Hans a second time, harder. Gerda tried to hold him up but his legs gave out and he collapsed to the ground.

"If you won't support the Union one way, you'll support it another," the eldest rider declared. Turning to his men, he added, "Round up the livestock. Fire the barn."

"Don't you dare," Gerda exclaimed, holding Hans as he groaned through clenched teeth.

The youngest man glanced at Gerda, and then to the eldest rider. "What about the house?"

"Leave the house." The eldest man turned his horse toward the barn. "The women are loyal. Let the house stand for their sake."

As the men rode off, Hans struggled to his feet. "We've got to stop them," said Gerda, desperate. Fighting to catch his breath, Hans shot her a grim look, and she knew there was nothing they could do, no way to summon help in time, no way to hold

460

off four armed, angry men determined to do wrong.

Hans leaned upon Gerda as they made their way from the house toward the barn. They watched from the bridge over Elm Creek as the men rounded up the horses from the stables and the corral, herded the cows from the pasture, and chased squealing pigs around the sty until the men gave up in frustration. The man with the Vandyke disappeared into the barn. Soon after he emerged, thick plumes of gray-black smoke began to billow from the doors and windows, red sparks rising and falling to earth, the cracking of burning hay eventually drowned out by the roaring of the blaze. Another man lit the end of a long tree branch in the flames and carried his makeshift torch to the stables, while another set fire to the smokehouse. Instinctively, Gerda rushed forward, but Hans caught her arm and held her back, and only then did she become aware of the other men's guns leveled at them so they dared not attempt to put out the fire. Brother and sister stood watching silently as one by one the outbuildings went up in flames. Only when the barn was fully engulfed did the four men ride off with the livestock.

Gerda and Hans ran across the bridge,

ashes whirling about them in the windstorm created by the heat of the fire and settling upon the ground like snowflakes. Hans sprinted ahead and made for the barn door, where he hesitated. Gerda screamed at him not to go in, for nothing he might salvage was worth his life, but he darted inside. Moments later he emerged dragging the plow, with harnesses and tack flung over his shoulder, but just as he turned to make another attempt, the roof fell in with a terrible groan of timber and iron.

"There's nothing more you can do," Gerda shouted, flinging herself between her brother and the barn. His gaze darted to the stables and he tore himself free. There too he was driven back by smoke and heat, though the blaze was less intense than in the barn.

"Fetch buckets and sacks," he shouted. Reluctant to leave him lest he plunge into one of the outbuildings, Gerda nevertheless picked up her skirts and fled to the house. She filled a washbasin with smaller vessels and old gunnysacks and hauled them back to the burning buildings, balancing the basin on her hip, stumbling all the way. Hans met her on the bridge, and as they filled basins in the creek and flung the water upon the stable, Gerda saw that he had saved a half-dozen saddles, a pile of blankets and pads, and a long coil of rope from the stables.

Suddenly a wagon emerged from the forest; Gerda feared the riders had returned, until she recognized the Wrights, Constance at the reins, Abel in the back with the boys. They halted at a safe distance and within moments were hauling buckets of water from the creek and soaking gunnysacks in the cold water, beating out fires that caught when embers fell upon the dry grass. Gerda's nostrils stung from the smell of wood smoke and burnt tar.

"What happened?" Constance shouted over the roar of the fire as she and Gerda hauled the washbasin full of water to the smokehouse. "Lightning? A lantern?"

"Men," Gerda choked out, heaving the water onto the flames. As they fled back to the creek, she glimpsed more horses coming from the north; after a moment of fear, she saw that they were Dorothea's hired men. Soon another wagon brought Mr. Craigmile and his son, and in due course other neighbors, alerted by the plume of rising smoke, came from far and near to help.

For hours they worked to save what they could of the stables and the other outbuildings, knowing an attempt to extinguish the barn would prove futile. By evening, only smoldering ruins above charred stone foundations remained of the barn, but half of the stable survived, and the smokehouse and other outbuildings showed minimal damage. Exhausted and heartbroken, Gerda brought water to her weary friends and neighbors, coughing and barely able to see for her smoke-stung eyes. Hans's voice broke as he thanked them for their help and told them, at last, what had happened. Mr. Craigmile vowed to go to the authorities at once, and the other men promised to help the Bergstroms regain their livestock. Hans coughed, cleared his throat, and thanked them again, adding, "If I don't get the horses back, I'll be ruined."

The neighbors fell into somber silence. Gerda knew they were thinking of their own farms and business, and how everything they earned above what they used to feed and clothe their families went right back into the farm in the form of new tools, new outbuildings, new livestock. Gerda felt faint when she thought of how many years and seasons her brother had put into breeding his horses, all that they had planned to do with the money he would earn selling the foals, and all they would have to do without if they could not get the horses back.

"Let's round them up now," said Abel, eyes narrowed in anger. "The men as well as the livestock."

"I say we string 'em up," declared one of Dorothea's hired men.

As a few others chimed in their assent, Hans waved them to silence. "I'm all for restraining them until the police arrive or escorting them to prison ourselves, but we're rational men, not a crazed mob, and I want no one lynched on my behalf."

The men agreed, some of them reluctantly. Mr. Craigmile mounted his horse and rode off to the courthouse with the names of the two men the Bergstroms had recognized and descriptions of the others. Dazed, Gerda sat on a smooth, flat stone beneath a willow tree and let the sound of the water rushing over the creek bed lull her into a numb calm as she watched wisps of smoke rise from the ruins. Later, when the embers cooled, they could comb through the debris and search for anything salvageable. Until then, there was little else their neighbors could do to help, so they left for their own homes. The Wrights departed last of all, after Hans and Abel conversed in hushed tones that Gerda didn't think she was meant to overhear, debating whether Abel ought to spend the night in case the raiders returned. Not until Gerda returned to the house and found the pork and apples on the stove, the table set, fresh tomatoes and cucumbers tossed with vinegar for a salad, bread and butter sliced, coffee brewing, did Gerda realize that Constance had not been among the neighbors working in the rubble. Now she knew why she had not seen Constance toiling with the others, and her heart was full to overflowing with grief and gratitude.

She and Hans were ravenous. They scrubbed their faces and hands clean at the pump and changed out of their sooty clothes, but the odor of burning had infused their skin and hair, and Gerda could imagine never being rid of it.

"If any good will come of this," Gerda said, as they finished the last of their supper, "it is that we now know who our true friends are."

"And our enemies," said Hans, taking the last slice of pork from the platter.

Gerda pushed her plate aside and rested her head on her arms. "This is all my fault. If I had not been so outspoken in the newspaper, if I had not antagonized Mr. Meek —"

"No, Gerda, I won't have you talk that

way," said Hans firmly. "You spoke the truth as you know it. You wrote what you believe in, but you never encouraged anyone to do wrong. Mr. Meek, on the other hand —" He took a bite of baked apple and shook his head. "His closing words in his denunciation of you were calculated to incite men to violence. To hear his account of it, you'd think I was offered citizenship and turned it down because of the war, when the truth is I never sought citizenship."

"Why didn't you?" asked Gerda. "In your heart, are you still loyal to King Wilhelm?"

Hans snorted, then winced and clutched his side where the Vandyke rider had kicked him. "No. I admire Mr. Lincoln very much, and if I could choose my leader, he'd do as well as any. I just didn't like the idea of renouncing the land of my birth. Can't a man be loyal to both countries that made him who he is?"

"Some people would say no."

"Well, I don't like someone else telling me I have to choose."

"I see." Gerda managed a smile. "Principle and stubbornness, yet again."

"My tragic flaws." Hans sighed and ran a hand through his hair, wincing again when his fingers brushed over the lump left behind from the blow he had taken from the rifle butt. He did not seem to notice the ashes that drifted to the tabletop. "All I lack is hubris and I could be a hero from a Greek tragedy."

Alarmed by her brother's wincing and stiff, painful movements, Gerda asked, "Shall we call a doctor to look at your injuries?"

Hans waved her off. "It's nothing. It'll pass. With Jonathan gone, the nearest doctor is in Grangerville. Hardly worth the ride."

"Hubris," Gerda declared. "You weren't lacking it after all."

Hans smiled wryly. "My point was that you did nothing wrong. Meek all but told those men to rob us since we'd given nothing to the Union cause —"

"Nothing, indeed," scoffed Gerda bitterly.

Hans held up a hand. "But even then I can't place the blame on Meek. He probably won't lose any sleep when he hears about our losses, and I'm confident he'll persuade himself that he bears no responsibility whatsoever, but in the end, whether Meek influenced them or not, those men chose to come here and do what they did. In the end, the blame lies with them, not with you and not with Mr. Meek."

Gerda inhaled deeply, instinctively coughing from the lingering wood smoke. "I reserve the right to be a trifle angry at Mr. Meek."

"Do what you must, sister," said Hans. "Just don't burn down his barn."

They lingered at the table a moment longer, finishing the coffee Constance had brewed for them. Then, while Hans went outside to tend to the pigs and chickens, which the raiders had not taken, Gerda cleared the table and washed the dishes. When Hans returned, they dragged themselves upstairs to bed. "I will miss my horses," said Hans just before he closed his bedroom door. "They were fine horses, the best I've bred. I hate to think of some Rebel shooting at them."

Only then, as she climbed into her own bed, did Gerda realize that he never expected to see his beloved horses again. He expected the raiders to turn the livestock over to the Union Army; Gerda had assumed that was mere talk and that all along they meant to keep their stolen goods for themselves. Mr. Craigmile had promised to return in the morning to report on his meeting with the sheriff. She supposed they would learn the fate of their livestock — and consequently, the fate of Elm Creek Farm — when he came.

Gerda was accustomed to waking before dawn to the sound of her brother's footfalls on the steps as he left to do his morning chores, but the next morning she slept past sunrise and lingered in bed, staring up at the ceiling, dreading the work that awaited her that day. She wondered if she had not heard Hans that morning because he too still lay abed, his usual morning chores gone off with the livestock. Perhaps he had risen and was even now digging through the embers. Yes, that was far more likely. She threw off the quilt and forced herself to her feet, made a quick toilet and dressed, steeling herself for the day. Hans would not linger in bed feeling sorry for himself. He was probably even at that moment salvaging tools or door hinges from the ruins and awaiting Mr. Craigmile's visit. He would want his breakfast.

As she left her room, she heard the clatter of a coal scuttle in the kitchen and smelled coffee brewing. She quickened her pace; Hans had enough to do without fetching his own breakfast. Hurrying into the kitchen, she snatched an apron off the hook beside the door — and stopped short at the sight of Dorothea at the cookstove, frying eggs and ham.

"Dorothea," she said, tears springing into

her eyes. "How kind of you to come."

Dorothea set down her spatula and rounded the table to embrace her. "I'm so sorry," she said, her own eyes shining with unshed tears. "Such monstrous deeds — I can hardly believe it."

"I know." Gerda clung to her. "When I woke this morning, I hoped it had been a terrible nightmare, but it's real. The barn, the stables, the livestock — all of it gone."

Dorothea nodded, and Gerda realized that Dorothea, of all her friends, would understand her loss completely.

"It'll be all right. Somehow." Dorothea hugged her firmly and returned to the cookstove. "Mr. Craigmile is here," she continued, turning the eggs so they wouldn't burn. "He and Hans are talking out by the ruins."

Gerda nodded. "Mr. Craigmile reported the fire to the sheriff last night. Hans had no horse to ride or he would have gone himself. Mr. Craigmile promised to tell us what came of it."

"Well," a familiar voice declared from the doorway, "I for one hope he's come to tell us that those horrid men are behind bars and someone's driving our horses and cows back home where they belong even as we speak."

Gerda looked over her shoulder, hardly

471

daring to believe that Anneke had returned, but there she was, red-eyed from weeping, chin raised in determination, Albert on her hip, and David tugging on her skirt and asking if he and Stephen could go out to play.

With a cry of relief and joy, Gerda hurried to embrace them all.

When Hans came in to breakfast, his hands and face scrubbed clean of the ash and soot that lingered on his clothes, he kissed his wife tenderly, took his place at the head of the table, looked around at the faces of his family — and one dear neighbor — and seemed for all the world to be a man who considered himself richly blessed. As they ate, he told them that when Mr. Craigmile had described the two unfamiliar men, the sheriff had recognized them immediately and had dispatched deputies to the four men's homes. The man with the Vandyke beard had come as a refugee from Gettysburg and had remained in Water's Ford ever since, taking a job at the livery stable. He did not answer the deputy's knock, and the woman who kept his boardinghouse said she had not seen him since the previous afternoon, but he had paid his rent through the end of the month and his belongings remained in his room. Mrs. Gilbert, the wife of the man Gerda recognized from the construction crew, reported that her husband had left the previous morning to go hunting and she expected him back within a week. The wife of the eldest raider said that her husband had been hired to collect horses for the Union Army and was driving a small herd to Camp Curtin; he had promised to return in a few days. As for the youngest of the men, his weeping mother reported that he had taken his late father's prize stallion, one of the best of Mr. Bergstrom's famous stables, and had ridden off to join the cavalry, having recently come of age.

Upon receiving his deputies' reports, the sheriff had immediately dispatched a rider to Wright's Pass, where the militia guard confirmed that four men meeting the riders' description had left the valley shortly after noon, leading about a dozen fine horses that they claimed had been confiscated for the United States Cavalry.

"So it would seem our horses have been drafted," said Hans, smiling ruefully at Anneke as she cut him a second thick slice of bread and buttered it.

"What about our cows and the calf?" said Gerda. "The guards at Wright's Pass made no mention of them."

"Perhaps the riders kept them as a commission," said Anneke. "As a reward for their selfless service to the nation."

"They're branded. If they're still in the valley, we'll find them, and we know where to start looking." Hans sighed and rubbed at his beard. "I fear we will not see those horses again."

"But when the raiders return home — as it seems they soon will, except for the one who intends to enlist — the sheriff will arrest them," said Dorothea, but she seemed uncertain. "Surely they'll be obliged to pay for the damages to your property, and for the theft of your livestock if it can't be restored to you."

"I'm sure the sheriff will do all he can," said Hans, resigned. "I confess the loss of my best sires and brood mares grieves me. I have to start over. It's as if I just got off the boat from Germany, only I'm older than I was then and not quite so daring."

"You're not starting over completely," said Anneke. "We have this lovely home. You have me and the children."

"You have friends," added Dorothea. "You're not alone on the western frontier. We will all do what we can to help you get back on your feet again."

Hans smiled wanly. "Will the Union Quilters make an opportunity quilt to rescue me from ruin?"

"You are not even close to the edge of ruin," said Dorothea, "but if it would keep you from tumbling in, of course we would make you a quilt. Our first task, however, should be a barn raising. By the time the barn is finished, we might have something for you to put in it."

When Hans laughed, it was as if a dark cloud blocking the sun had drifted aside, illuminating them in diffuse light, a promise of better days to come. Their world had been shattered, but Anneke had come home, and the children were smiling and happy to see their family reunited. Dorothea's words gave Gerda hope that with the help of their friends, they would be able to gather the scattered pieces and stitch them back together.

A knock sounded on the front door. Anneke had Albert on her lap, so Gerda excused herself and went to answer it. To her astonishment, she discovered the kindly postmaster standing on the front porch. He had never visited them at the farm before. "Mr. Reinhart," she said, opening the door wider. "What a surprise. Do come in. You must have heard about the fire."

"I did," he said, removing his postmaster's cap and coming inside. "My daughter, Harriet, sends you her sympathies. She's put together a basket for you — some preserves and bread and a cake, I think. I planned to bring her to call on you this afternoon, but there was news, sorrowful news, and I had to come right away. I am so terribly sorry, Miss Bergstrom. The army messenger went to Mrs. Granger, and Mr. Schultz sent his son to Two Bears Farm, but, I thought, who would come to you?"

Cold, ominous dread stole over her. "What's happened?"

His kind face was shadowed with sorrow — but not for himself. For her. "Perhaps you should sit down, Miss Bergstrom."

She stared at him, disbelieving. Before she could reach for a chair, Dorothea was at her side. "Why would Mr. Schultz send his son to my home?"

"Mrs. Nelson." Surprised and dismayed, Mr. Reinhart guided them to the sofa and gently eased them down upon it. "I am terribly grieved to bring you unhappy news."

Gerda could not bear not knowing for a moment longer. "What is it? Please, Mr. Reinhart. Tell us."

"A casualty list came this morning by telegraph," he said. "It included a list of men lost at Libby Prison."

Gerda felt the room spinning. She heard

Dorothea gasp.

"It grieves me to tell you this, my dear ladies, but Dr. Granger's name was on it."

CHAPTER TEN

When Charlotte received the news, Gerda later learned, she fainted.

There had been a prisoner exchange. Jonathan was supposed to have been included, but when the prisoners lined up to march under armed guard to the train station, Jonathan was not among them. Upon arriving in Washington City, a captain from the 5th New York Cavalry reported that the surgeon had perished from typhoid two weeks before he would have been released.

After Mr. Schultz ran a lengthy, laudatory obituary in the *Register,* the entire Elm Creek Valley mourned the loss of its beloved physician. Somehow, despite his earlier proximity to the front lines and his later imprisonment, few people, it seemed, had considered Jonathan to be in any real danger. He did not engage in battle; he tended the sick and wounded. Of all the men of the 49th, he had been expected to survive.

Reeling from grief, Gerda paid little attention to the calls for a public funeral. Her beloved was gone. What did it matter how the town honored him, how they paid tribute to his honorable sacrifice? He was gone, and the world seemed drained of color and light.

It was a shock, a few days later, when she answered a knock on the door and discovered Charlotte standing there, clad from head to toe in mourning black, her eyes shadowed and skin pale as if she had not slept since receiving the terrible news. "Charlotte," Gerda greeted her numbly. The young woman had not set foot on Elm Creek Farm since before her marriage. "I — I —" She opened the door wider, glancing beyond Charlotte to the buggy where her younger brother waited, still holding the reins. Apparently the young widow did not intend to stay long. "Please, do come in."

Charlotte entered without a word and accepted Gerda's invitation to sit in the front room while she made tea. With shaking hands she carried the tray from the kitchen to the front room, wishing Anneke were there, but she and the boys were off playing near the creek.

"I . . . should have called on you to express my condolences," Gerda said haltingly as she poured. "I thought, perhaps, it would be better if I stayed away."

"Indeed it was." Charlotte added sugar to her cup, but left it steaming on the table. "I would not have wished to see you."

Gerda sat down and knotted her fingers together in her lap. "I understand."

"I don't believe you do." Charlotte regarded her squarely. "Even so, I would not have come to you except that I need your help, and I can think of no one who would understand my desires more than you, nor anyone more indebted to me and obliged to help me."

"Indebted to you?"

"For all the grief and sorrow you have caused me through the years."

Heat rising in her face, Gerda cleared her throat and took a deep, steadying breath. "I never meant to cause you any distress."

"And yet you did all the same, carelessly, without thinking." Charlotte pursed her lips and inhaled deeply. "My husband deserves a proper Christian burial in his family plot on Granger land. I cannot bear to think of him coldly disposed of in some pit with dozens of others hundreds of miles from home."

Gerda closed her eyes and shook her head, a futile gesture that failed to block the dreadful image from her imagination. "I cannot either."

"He should be put to rest where his loved ones can visit him and tend his grave."

Gerda wished it could be so. It would be a cold comfort to lay flowers upon his grave, but it would offer him the dignity he had earned in life. She nodded and sipped her tea, unwilling to speak lest she break down in sobs in front of her longtime adversary.

"I intend to go to Libby Prison to retrieve his body, and as I cannot go alone, I want you to accompany me."

Gerda stared at her. "You cannot mean it."

"I do."

"Richmond is the capital of the Confederacy. It is surrounded by the Rebel army."

"Yes, so I've heard."

Gerda uttered an incredulous laugh. "General Grant and General Meade and the entire Union Army haven't been able to enter Richmond, and yet you believe you could?"

"No," said Charlotte. "I believe *you* could, with the help of your friend Miss Van Lew. You've said that she regularly sends her servants from her home into her gardens outside the city. Surely if her servants are permitted through the lines, they would be able to escort us back in."

Gerda shook her head. "This is madness. The Rebels would never let us pass."

"I disagree. We are two women in mourning, not soldiers or scouts. Why should we not be allowed into the city? We won't be smuggling anything in, and we will take only my husband's remains out."

"You don't need me for this," said Gerda. "Dorothea will accompany you. As Jonathan's sister she is a far more appropriate companion for you, and she's clever enough to outwit any Rebel who might attempt to interfere. I'll write you a letter of introduction to Miss Van Lew. That should suffice."

Charlotte shook her head, the black ribbon of her black silk bonnet tied so firmly that the bonnet barely moved. "Dorothea couldn't leave Abigail."

"Then take your mother."

"My mother will be caring for my children in my absence."

"Your mother can go with you, and I will look after your children."

"Absolutely not," said Charlotte. "Jonathan always respected my wishes to keep you as far from our children as possible, and my resolve in that regard has not altered one bit. Don't think his death has softened my heart toward you. Don't mistake my presence here as an overture of friendship. I need you for this one duty, that is all."

Gerda looked away, her heart wrenching in pain as she imagined the conversation between husband and wife. She had not realized that Jonathan had intentionally kept her away from his children. She had assumed that Charlotte had wanted to avoid her, and since Charlotte was always with her children except when the Union Quilters met — under such circumstances, of course Gerda rarely saw the children except at large public gatherings. She had thought nothing of it, until now. But perhaps there had been nothing to think of. For all she knew, there had been no such agreement, and Charlotte was merely trying to wound her.

Suddenly, Charlotte stood, leaving her tea untasted. "Time is of the essence. Think of what my husband would have wanted before you make up your mind. Send word to me by the end of the day."

Gerda was so shocked, she forgot to rise and see Charlotte to the door. The sound of Charlotte's younger brother chirruping to the horses and the carriage driving off roused her. She rose and hurried to the window, her thoughts churning as she watched the carriage cross the bridge over Elm Creek and disappear behind the charred ruins of the barn.

Gerda went outside and paced on the front porch, pondering Charlotte's request. What would Jonathan have wanted her to do? In their many conversations about the meaning of life and the divine purpose of mortality, Jonathan had often said that he believed the body should be respected as part of God's creation and as the earthly vessel of the immortal soul, but after death, it was an empty shell. She did not believe that his spirit would remain restless for all eternity if his body were not buried beneath his home soil and the proper ceremonies performed. Jonathan would have scoffed at such a notion, just as he would have urged Charlotte and Gerda not to endanger themselves for his sake.

And yet, he would have wanted Charlotte, Dorothea, and his parents to be comforted. He would want his children to remember him. He would not want the people he loved most dearly to be distressed over his ignominious burial, even if it meant nothing to him. And, Gerda was forced to admit, if Charlotte needed Gerda's help to make her grief easier to bear, Jonathan would want Gerda to help her.

She had little choice — but not because of any debt she owed Charlotte. She would help Charlotte out of love for Jonathan, as her own private memorial to her lost beloved.

When she told Hans what she intended to do, Hans tried to persuade her to reconsider, and when that failed, he offered to accompany them. Gerda would have preferred to have him along, but as a healthy Northern man of enlistment age, he was likely to be forbidden passage at the border or apprehended as a prisoner of war. When the Wrights heard of their plan, Abel too offered to escort them, but a veteran of the United States Colored Troops would fare even worse in the hands of Confederate soldiers than a civilian. Even Mr. Reinhart, who seemed to blame himself for their sorrow since he had delivered the heartbreaking news, wanted to help. "I would consider it an honor to accompany you and Mrs. Granger to Richmond," he said after Gerda explained the reason for her most recent, most urgent letter to Miss Van Lew. "You may assure your brother that you will be safe under my protection."

Gerda had never been fonder of the postmaster than at that moment. "You are kindness itself, but it is too great a risk for you. I couldn't bear it if you were taken prisoner as other postmasters have been."

Reluctantly, but graciously, he accepted her refusal, adding that he took it as the highest compliment that she cared so much for his safety. He also urged her to send Miss Van Lew a telegram in addition to the letter informing her of their imminent arrival and requesting her help; whether a telegram was any more likely to reach Miss Van Lew than a letter was impossible to say, but it would be a prudent measure.

Gerda thanked him for his advice, which was sound as always, and went to the telegraph office straightaway, where she sent messages to Miss Van Lew as well as Mrs. Philippa Whitehall, the friend living outside Richmond who acted as their intermediary, passing along letters they dared not risk to the Confederate mails. She prayed that Miss Van Lew would receive at least one of her messages and prepare for their arrival. Without the Richmond woman's assistance, Gerda could not imagine how they could enter the city, much less Libby Prison.

They could not wait for Miss Van Lew's reply but had to depart immediately. Gerda thought it cruel to remind Charlotte that they might already be too late. In her first letter to Gerda, Miss Van Lew had explained that bodies were stored in the prison basement until enough had accumulated for a full wagonload, and only then were the corpses hauled away for burial. As offensive as it was to imagine Jonathan's body treated with such disrespect and disinterest, their only hope was that he had not yet been taken away. If he had already been buried, Gerda could not imagine how they would find his location in a mass grave or arrange for his disinterment.

She packed a satchel and, at the last moment, included the velvet purse containing her life savings, all the money she had earned selling preserves at the market and writing for the *Water's Ford Register.* At one time she had thought she would use the money to buy Joanna's freedom, but Josiah Chester had never responded to a single one of her letters and probably never would. Perhaps he had died, a casualty of the war. Perhaps Joanna had perished as well. Gerda and Charlotte would need cash to purchase railroad tickets, a coffin, and transportation home. Perhaps they would need bribes for the prison guards; Miss Van Lew would know. It would be foolhardy to save the money for the increasingly unlikely occasion of purchasing Joanna's freedom, when she and Charlotte were likely to face urgent, immediate needs in the days ahead.

On the morning five days after receiving word of Jonathan's death, Gerda bade Anneke and the children farewell and climbed onto the wagon seat beside her brother. First they drove north, to fetch Charlotte from the Granger farm. Once, it had belonged to Dorothea and Jonathan's uncle, with whom their family had lived after losing their utopian community to the floodwaters of Elm Creek. The Claverton farm was adjacent to the north, and many years before, both families had noted that if their children were to wed, the properties likewise would make a prosperous union. Thus Jonathan and Charlotte had been intended for each other long before they were old enough to choose for themselves.

Gerda, a recent immigrant unaware of the families' long-standing ties, had learned of their engagement in the cruelest of ways — Anneke had encountered Charlotte at the dressmaker's shop being fitted for her wedding gown. Stunned by the revelation, Gerda's instinct was not to believe it. In the two years she and Jonathan had known each other, their friendship had deepened into affection enriched with respect and mutual understanding. Though Jonathan had never professed his love for her, he had given every indication of it in their many conversations and long walks, their lingering glances and accidental touches, his words, his actions, the smile that lit up his face whenever he saw her — no, she had not imagined love where only friendship resided. Nor in all their many conversations had Jonathan mentioned an engagement, the surest sign of all that it did not exist. Gerda prayed Anneke had simply misunderstood what she had seen at the dressmaker's shop.

But the next time Jonathan called on her, he had confessed the truth: He and Charlotte were to be married in six weeks. All his life he had understood that one day they would wed, and when he had come of age, he had dutifully proposed, believing that it was what he wanted, never thinking that he would find any greater happiness than satisfying his parents' expectations. He had never imagined that one day he would meet Gerda, that he would discover a soul mate and know the meeting of true minds. Gerda was devastated. At last he had confessed that he loved her, but although she begged him to break off the engagement — for their sake as well as Charlotte's, for it was deceptive and wrong to marry her when he loved someone else — he refused. Charlotte loved him, and he had promised to marry her. He could not put his own desires before honor and duty.

Thus Jonathan and Charlotte married, and thus Gerda was forsaken. So great was her anger and grief and confusion that for a long time, she could not bear to see him. They grew estranged, but those qualities they had admired in each other from the start did not alter with time, nor did their feelings fade, and so gradually they resumed their old friendship. Jonathan called on her, came for supper every Saturday, discussed with her literature and politics and religion and philosophy and many other subjects that, Gerda guessed, did not interest Charlotte. It was almost as it had been before his marriage, except that Gerda no longer entertained fanciful notions that one day she and Jonathan would marry. That they would love each other for the rest of their lives, she was certain. That she continued to nurture a small, wistful hope that someday they would be together, she could not deny. But although she had indulged in foolish dreams through the years, she had always known that the same sense of duty that had compelled Jonathan to marry Charlotte would prevent him from leaving her, nor could Gerda wish any misfortune to befall Charlotte, even if it meant that Jonathan would be free. She also knew that she could not forget how he had deceived her, how he had hurt her, though she tried her best to forgive. So Gerda had contented herself with the knowledge that Jonathan loved her, that he was as unhappy with their separation as she, and that he at last recognized his mistake in marrying Charlotte.

Or so she had told herself, until the war. The war had utterly separated them, especially after his imprisonment, when from conversations lasting hours they had been curtailed to one six-line letter every six weeks. He married Charlotte, lived with her, slept with her, fathered her children, and built a life with her, but always, always, Gerda had had his words. Her hours and days and thoughts and heart had been filled with his words, and then the war had stolen even that from her. The loss of that one small part of Jonathan she had retained, that one vital intimacy they had not sacrificed to his marriage, suddenly rekindled every longing she had sublimated into benign friendship. Suddenly she longed to share his life with the same intensity of passion she had felt before that fatal day she had learned of his engagement, as if none of the disappointment and betrayal of the intervening years had ever happened.

In the long, anxious months of his imprisonment, she had wondered if his thoughts followed the same path. They always had thought alike, and perhaps this time too they had reached the same conclusion. For Gerda had come to believe that if Jonathan found their separation as unbearable as she did, upon his release, he would be unable to let it continue. Confronted with the dreadful possibility of losing her forever, he would find the will to leave Charlotte and follow his heart. If he did, Gerda knew his heart would lead him to her.

But now Jonathan was dead, and her dreams of a life by his side were turned to ashes as surely as the barn and stables.

At the Granger farm, Hans hefted Charlotte's satchel into the wagon and helped her onto the seat, clothed in mourning black and veiled. They said little as they traveled south through the valley and climbed the rolling Appalachians to Wright's Pass. The militia guards recognized them but would not have hindered them even if had they not; they were concerned with Rebels entering, not a man and two women leaving.

The road to Harrisburg took them on a

scenic route along the Susquehanna River. When they passed Camp Curtin on the outskirts of the city, Gerda could not help recalling that fateful day when the men of the Elm Creek Valley had gone off to join the 49th Pennsylvania. If only Jonathan had not been compelled to serve — but for Jonathan, there had never been any other choice but to put his skills to use for the Union cause. How sad it was that he would not see the end of the war, and the end of slavery in their reunified nation. Her heart welled up with grief when she thought of everything he would miss — the inevitable though distant Union victory and the peace that would follow, his postwar homecoming, his children's first birthdays, all the wonderful books yet to be written that he would have loved, years and years by Gerda's side. The earth would turn and days would pass without him, seasons would come and go, but Gerda wished to live forever in any day she had spent with him.

When they reached the Harrisburg train station, Hans queried them — whether they had enough money, their letters of introduction, food for the trip, the name and address of Thomas Nelson's friend who would meet them in Washington City, second thoughts — and eventually seemed satisfied that they had done all they could to assure a safe journey. Still, his misgivings as he helped them board the train were apparent. "If you run into trouble, send a telegram at once, and I will come as quickly as I can," he told Gerda as the train whistle blew. "Don't hesitate to call on the Nelsons' friends if you need them."

She assured him they would be fine, and as the train started up, her brother stepped back upon the platform and watched, frowning worriedly beneath a furrowed brow, as the train pulled away from the station. Sighing and settling back into her seat, Gerda considered striking up a conversation with Charlotte, but the young woman had already opened a book and was reading, or pretending to read to avoid speaking with her. Gerda had brought a book of her own, but instead she gazed out the window at the passing scenery. The city soon gave way to rolling countryside, and she lost herself in memories of Jonathan from happier days.

They changed trains in Baltimore and continued on to Washington City. Gerda had often imagined traveling to the nation's capital, but never under such circumstances. The sun shone as if it were midsummer, and unlike back home, little autumn color had touched the lush green trees. Soldiers guarded every train station, giving Gerda the unsettling sensation that they were hurtling into the thick of the fight.

It was early evening when they arrived. As they gathered their belongings and disembarked, they overheard other passengers discussing the places they planned to visit and the upcoming presidential election. "Perhaps we should stop by the Executive Mansion so you may advise Mr. Lincoln on his campaign," said Charlotte. "Since you are such intimate friends."

"He likely does not remember me," said Gerda shortly, carrying her satchel to the exit without bothering to see if Charlotte followed. "It was more than a year ago that we met in Gettysburg, and it was an eventful day."

"Surely the sheer brilliance of your report fixed you in his memory. You do recall your report, which was going to inspire Mr. Lincoln and the Union Army to liberate Libby Prison?"

Stung, Gerda turned to face her. "You will never know how truly sorry I am that I failed."

In reply, Charlotte pursed her lips and pushed past Gerda to disembark. After a disorienting moment on the platform, surrounded by other passengers and waiting friends and noise and confusion, they spotted a gray-haired man with thick gray muttonchops, standing near the ticket window. He wore a black wool coat with a white rose in the lapel, just as his telegram had promised. The gentleman saw them at the same moment, nodded in greeting, and worked his way through the crowd toward them.

"Mrs. Granger?" he said to Charlotte, and to Gerda added, "Miss Bergstrom?"

They confirmed his guess, and he introduced himself as William Bastwick, a long-time friend of Thomas Nelson's father. He escorted them to his waiting carriage, and within moments they were on their way to his home, where, he promised, his wife would have a hot supper waiting for them. Gently and graciously, he offered them his condolences for their recent losses. "I've known Thomas Nelson since he was a boy, and a more brilliant scholar I never hope to meet," he said. "I never had the pleasure of making Dr. Granger's acquaintance, but I understand he was a remarkable man, a gifted surgeon as well as a true patriot."

"Thank you," Gerda and Charlotte said in unison. When Charlotte frowned, Gerda realized, too late, that Mr. Bastwick had been speaking mostly to Charlotte. And why not? As far as Mr. Bastwick knew, Gerda

496

was no more than a friend of the family.

They drove past the new capitol on the way. Construction had begun before the war, and the dome had been only recently completed. Earlier that day, Mr. Bastwick remarked, Mr. Lincoln had issued a proclamation setting aside the last Thursday in November "as a day of Thanksgiving and Praise to Almighty God the beneficent Creator and Ruler of the Universe." Mr. Bastwick approved, noting that even in troubled times, perhaps especially in troubled times, it was necessary and good to remember to give thanks to God.

"I confess I'm not feeling very thankful these days," said Charlotte. "I doubt even a presidential proclamation could inspire me."

"You're in mourning, my dear," said Mr. Bastwick as the driver pulled to a stop in the porte cochere of a stately three-story, whitewashed brick residence overlooking a park. "In time you will remember your blessings. You have two young children, if I recall correctly."

"Yes." Thinking of them, Charlotte's mouth turned in a small, wistful smile. "They are a blessing to me, especially now that my husband is gone. I see all that was best about him reflected in our son and daughter."

Her eyes darted to Gerda as they climbed out of the carriage, her expression inscrutable. Gerda wondered if she was thinking of her vow to keep Gerda away from her children. Weary, Gerda contemplated telling her that she had nothing to fear, that she had no intention of poisoning them with her corrupt presence, but she didn't have the stomach for a bitter argument, especially in front of their kindhearted host. She preferred the silence they had shared on the train.

Mrs. Bastwick welcomed them warmly at the door and showed them to a guest room, where they freshened up for dinner, which was served in a formal dining room with dark cherry wainscoting and elegant floral wallpaper. Pale and visibly exhausted, Charlotte only picked at her food, but Gerda savored every morsel of the roast duck and acorn squash. Afterward, Charlotte declined a cup of coffee, excused herself, and retired, but Gerda remained to discuss the next day's plans with the Bastwicks. In the morning, Mr. Bastwick would accompany Gerda and Charlotte as far south as the train would carry them, which varied according to the movement of the armies. They would disembark as close to Richmond as they could, then hire a driver to carry them to the Whitehall residence in the outskirts of the city. That evening or the following morning, depending upon the arrival of Miss Van Lew's servant, Gerda and Charlotte would enter Richmond, where they would stay with Miss Van Lew until the commandant of Libby Prison agreed to meet with them. Then Miss Van Lew would take them to the prison, where Charlotte would beseech Major Turner to release Jonathan's body to them. Gerda would purchase a coffin and hire a driver to carry them back to Mrs. Whitehall's home, where Mr. Bastwick would be waiting to take them to the train station. From there, they would make the long journey home.

"You've had no word from Miss Van Lew?" asked Mr. Bastwick.

"No, but we had to leave soon after I sent the telegrams," Gerda explained. "It's possible her reply arrived after our departure."

"Of course," said Mr. Bastwick, but Gerda knew he was thinking that it was possible neither Miss Van Lew nor Mrs. Whitehall had received their urgent messages. Their entire journey might be thwarted if the women were not expecting them.

Suddenly exhausted, Gerda thanked the Bastwicks for their generosity and bade them good night. She slept uncomfortably in the bed beside Charlotte, waking frequently throughout the night, disoriented by the unfamiliar beams and shadows on the ceiling until she remembered where she was. Despite her restless night, she woke at dawn feeling alert and clearheaded. Charlotte stirred when Gerda slipped from beneath the quilt and climbed out of bed, and as Gerda poured water into the washbasin and made her toilet, she watched in the mirror as behind her, Charlotte sat up, stared bleary-eyed at Gerda's back, then shook her head, muttered something disparaging and unintelligible, and fell back against the pillow.

"I'm no happier about our close quarters than you," said Gerda, drying her face and replacing the towel on the hook.

Charlotte threw back the quilts and rose. "Yes, I'm sure I'm not the Granger you prefer to share a bed with."

"Stop it," snapped Gerda. "You disgrace his memory."

"*I* disgrace him?" said Charlotte, incredulous. "You're a fine one to accuse me of that."

Vigorously, Gerda unbraided her hair, brushed it out, and braided it neatly again. "Hate me if you must. If it helps you to grieve, go on and hate me."

"Do you really believe that hating you has ever helped me?"

Gerda did not know what to say. She packed her satchel and went downstairs to breakfast. The Bastwicks were already at the table, conversing in low, urgent tones, and Charlotte soon joined them. Gerda's stomach was a knot of apprehension, and though Mrs. Bastwick urged her to eat, she could only swallow a few mouthfuls of porridge and buttered bread. It was a warm, sunny morning, the garden still misty with dew, but her hands were cold. She tried to warm them around her coffee cup.

Mrs. Bastwick had the cook pack them a lunch for the train and a cold dinner for later. Her chin quivered as she bade them good-bye and cautioned them to take care. At the station, Mr. Bastwick insisted upon paying for their tickets and purchased a private compartment so that they could travel in comfort and speak freely. He carried a letter of introduction from a member of the Virginia legislature, a longtime friend with whom he had served in Congress for eight years. If Confederate patrols confronted them along the way, Mr. Bastwick hoped the letter would ensure their safe passage.

The farther south they journeyed, the

more visible the scars of war were upon the landscape — abandoned breastworks, overturned earth, splintered and charred trees. "It will take a generation for the land to heal," said Mr. Bastwick, watching from the window as they passed through the hills of northeastern Virginia. Gerda nodded, noting that the gentleman had turned his thoughts to a time after the war as if it might be soon upon them. It did seem generally understood that the war was approaching its conclusion. If only men on both sides would not insist upon fighting to the last but would bow to the inevitability of a Union victory and lay down their arms to prevent the additional loss of life. The end of the war would come too late for Jonathan and Thomas, but not for many others. Her heart went out to the women who would lose the men they loved on the last day of the war.

The conductor passed through the train, announcing that the next station would be the end of the line, for it was the last before the front where they could turn the engine. After disembarking, Charlotte and Gerda waited on the platform while Mr. Bastwick hired a livery wagon. Charlotte's face was drawn and pale beneath her veil.

"You should eat something," said Gerda,

though she knew her advice would be unwelcome. "You need to keep up your strength for what lies ahead of us."

"Are you referring to our travels," said Charlotte hollowly, "or to life without Jonathan?"

An ache in Charlotte's voice gave Gerda pause. "I was referring to our travels, but you may take it as you wish." Through the window of the ticket office, she spotted a coffeepot brewing on the stove. Leaving Charlotte seated on a bench, she went inside and persuaded the clerk to let her buy a steaming cupful, which she carried back to Charlotte. "Drink this," she urged briskly. "And you really should have a bite to eat."

"I'm not hungry," said Charlotte, but she drank the coffee, sipping slowly, staring off into space. Gerda muffled a sigh and glanced at the clock hanging near the ticket window, wondering what was keeping Mr. Bastwick and fearing that the army's demands for fresh horses to replace those killed in battle meant that none remained in the town for Mr. Bastwick to hire.

"I've often wondered what my husband saw in you," Charlotte said distantly, her small, pale hands cradling the steaming cup. "I know he considered you the cleverest woman he had ever met, but why he would continue to admire you after the passage of time, I could never understand."

Gerda hardly knew what to say to that. "He loved me."

"He loved *me*," said Charlotte. "He was fond of you, that I will admit, but he *loved* me."

Gerda could not imagine any subject she wanted to debate less. "As you wish."

"Even now you won't allow yourself to see the truth." Charlotte took a deep drink and straightened on the bench. "Why did you cling to your devotion after he had made his choice? Was it because of your son?"

For a moment, Gerda forgot the old lie and had no idea what Charlotte was talking about. Even when she remembered an instant later, she still replied, "I don't know what you mean."

"Oh, drop the pretense. You've fooled most of the Elm Creek Valley, but I know those boys aren't twins. I know it even though Jonathan would never tell me whether he indeed fathered your child."

"He said he had not?"

"He would not say either way." Charlotte brushed aside her veil and fixed Gerda with a piercing look. "I've seen you with those children, and you behave as a fond aunt should, but never once have I detected in your manner the longing of a mother denied her child."

"I don't wish to discuss this."

"Jonathan was not that child's father, was he?" pressed Charlotte. "Nor are you his mother, nor are those children twins."

Considering the number of years Charlotte had brooded over her husband's attachment to his lost love, it was perhaps inevitable that she would one day discover the truth. "You must tell no one," Gerda said, instinctively lowering her voice. "You have no idea what damage you could cause."

"What of the damage your lie has caused to me and my children?"

"If I tell you the truth, some of the truth, will you promise never to reveal it to anyone?"

Charlotte paused, considering. "Yes, I will. If I believe you're being honest with me, I will take the secret to my grave."

Gerda could not tell her everything, but she would confess what Charlotte most wanted to know. "Jonathan never so much as kissed me."

Gerda quickly put her back to Charlotte so she would not have to see the grieving widow's expression change from surprise to relief to satisfaction, like the sunlight breaking through clouds. She should have been happy to offer Charlotte some small measure of comfort in her grief, but instead she felt as if she had conceded the last claim she had to Jonathan's love.

About two hours after they arrived at the station, Mr. Bastwick returned with a hired wagon and a single horse. They set out for Richmond, following the route recommended by the owner of the livery stable, who frequently delivered goods from the station to the front lines. When they reached the Union pickets, they were warned of the dangers lurking ahead and urged to turn back, but when they explained their purpose, the soldiers, perhaps thinking of what they would want for their own remains, did not impede them. Their hopes to avoid Rebel soldiers vanished within a few miles of Richmond when a northbound cavalry patrol encountered them on the road and ordered them to halt. Gerda fought to conceal her surprise at the men's gaunt faces and threadbare uniforms as Mr. Bastwick showed them the letter of introduction from his former congressional colleague and explained that he was escorting the young widow to collect her late hus-

506

band's body.

"Seems like a grim task for such a fair young creature," said the captain, looking from the letter to Charlotte's face, beautiful despite the veil and her sorrow.

"If you please, sir," Charlotte said, "I know my husband best, and after so much time, only I can identify him beyond any shadow of a doubt. I am sure your wife or sweetheart would insist upon doing the same for you."

"Alas, I have no wife," said the captain in a slow Virginia drawl, returning the letter to Mr. Bastwick, "and my sweetheart left me more than a year ago for a man who decided to sit out the war."

When Charlotte sniffed to show her disdain for such inconstancy, the captain smiled and told them they could proceed — after his men searched the wagon. The soldiers confiscated the food hamper but took nothing else as far as Gerda could see, although she was glad that she'd had the foresight to pin her purse to the inside of her skirts rather than leave her money in the satchel. Before long, the captain ordered his men to let them pass, warning Mr. Bastwick that they might not be permitted into the city proper. "You, sir, should take care to keep that letter close to hand," he added. "Another officer might have taken you prisoner and held you for ransom."

Mr. Bastwick assured him he would be cautious and shook the reins to start the horse.

"Those men looked as if they hadn't eaten a decent meal in weeks," said Gerda quietly as they drove off. "I suppose we should not be surprised that they took our food."

"I'm thankful they took only our dinner and left us the horse," said Mr. Bastwick grimly, gradually increasing their speed as they left the patrol behind.

Mr. Bastwick knew the region well from visits before the war, and thanks to the directions provided by the livery stable, they reached the Whitehall residence before six o'clock in the evening. For no reason whatsoever, Gerda had expected Mrs. Philippa Whitehall to be a plump dowager, and she was surprised to discover a slender, energetic woman close to her own age, becomingly clad in a subtly made-over dress of blue silk, her only obvious concession to the deprivations of war. Philippa came outside to the whitewashed portico to greet them and quickly ushered them inside the spacious, redbrick Georgian home while a colored servant took care of the horse.

Gerda's relief that her telegrams had apparently been delivered suddenly gave way to the realization that they were in a slave state. She wondered if the man leading the horse away was a slave.

Inside, they met Philippa's husband, a tall, thin man who looked to be ten years her senior, who leaned on a cane as he shook their hands. Two young daughters about three and five years of age were brought to the foyer to curtsy to the guests before being whisked away by a matronly colored woman for their dinner in the kitchen. Philippa noted the intensity of Gerda's look and said, "While some of our neighbors use the term 'servant' euphemistically, I assure you that ours are indeed servants, and not slaves." Gerda, embarrassed to have been caught judging her hostess, stammered an apology. Sympathetic, Philippa cut her short with an understanding laugh and invited them to the dining room.

The meal was sparer than the one they had enjoyed the previous night in Washington City — sweet potato pie, boiled greens, fresh bread, and custard — but was surely the best the Whitehalls could provide. Gerda was glad to know that Mr. Bastwick had two pounds of coffee beans for them and two more for Miss Van Lew hidden at the bottom of his satchel, gifts to thank them for their assistance. The Whitehalls asked about their travels, and although Charlotte said little during the meal, Gerda was relieved to see that she nearly cleared her plate, perhaps out of consideration for the Whitehalls' generosity in sharing the little they had.

Philippa had seemed on the edge of her seat throughout the meal, and as soon as the maid returned to clear away the dishes, she turned to Charlotte, seated at her right, and said, "My dear Mrs. Granger, I hope you will forgive me for waiting until now to tell you, but good news can be as shocking as bad. You seemed peaked when you arrived, and I thought it would be prudent to fortify you with a good meal first."

Charlotte stiffened. "Fortify me for what?"

"She said 'good news,' " Gerda reassured her, then turned back to her hostess. "Has Miss Van Lew already spoken to the commandant? Has he agreed to release Jonathan's remains to us — to Mrs. Granger?"

"Oh, no," exclaimed Mrs. Whitehall. "That is to say, Miss Van Lew has spoken to Major Turner, but he will not give you your husband's remains, Mrs. Granger, because your husband is not dead."

Charlotte went very still. "What do you mean?"

Philippa clasped her hands and beamed. "Your husband is alive. Miss Van Lew spoke to him only yesterday. He is the worse for his ill treatment, as all the prisoners are, but he is alive and working in the prison hospital. He sends you his love."

A scarlet flush rose in Charlotte's cheeks. "Are you certain?"

"Miss Van Lew says it is so, and I trust her."

"But —" Gerda hardly dared hope it could be true. "How can this be? We saw the casualty list. His name was on it."

"A dreadful mistake," said Mr. Whitehall. "The list was composed from the released prisoners' reports, but of course the men had no documents, only their memories. Someone erred and counted Dr. Granger among the deceased."

Charlotte pressed her hand to her heart, her breath coming in small gasps. "He lives," she said faintly. "My husband lives."

Mr. Whitehall looked around the table, regarding each of his guests with solemn intensity. "Miss Van Lew believes that due to the doctor's poor health and your fortuitous arrival, you should appeal to Major Turner to release him on humanitarian grounds, due to his illness and his profession. You may have no other opportunity. Back in March, Richmond's provost marshal ordered the evacuation of most of the city's prisoners to Georgia."

"Georgia," Gerda exclaimed. "So far away."

Mr. Whitehall nodded. "Indeed. Most of the enlisted men have since been sent to a prison in Andersonville, but the transfer of the officers from Libby was delayed while the Rebels constructed a new prison in Macon. Transfers began as soon as the building was completed, but fortunately, Dr. Granger has not yet been sent south, perhaps because he is useful in the Libby Prison hospital. However, as you can see, if he cannot obtain his freedom now, it is unlikely he will do so before the end of the war. I should warn you, this will be a far more difficult undertaking than seeking the release of his remains."

"But far preferable in every regard," exclaimed Gerda, overwhelmed. To soar from the depths of loneliness to the pinnacle of hope in a matter of minutes — her mind was reeling. She wanted to set out for the prison immediately, that moment, before she had time to take another breath.

Her beloved Jonathan was alive.

■ ■ ■ ■

They were obliged to wait until morning to make the trip into Richmond, but thankfully, Miss Van Lew sent her buggy for them early. Mr. Bastwick and the Whitehalls sent them off with good wishes and warnings to be careful and to follow Miss Van Lew's lead in all things. Charlotte was too excited and nervous to do more than nod, but Gerda assured them they would obey Miss Van Lew's instructions to the letter. She would have agreed to anything to see Jonathan again.

They left the countryside behind and entered the city. Although Gerda had seen the toll war had taken on Gettysburg, the scars of a three-day battle were slight compared to the wounds Richmond had suffered during its prolonged siege. Market stalls were bare, soldiers appeared on nearly every street corner, and buildings were pockmarked from shells or bore gaping, crumbling holes from heavy artillery. About an hour after they set out, they arrived at an elegant mansion on the south side of Grace Street on Church Hill, with six tall white columns supporting a high portico on the southern aspect, many windows framed by black shutters, and six chimneys. Lush trees and a thriving garden surrounded the house, and birds chirped and sang in the foliage.

Miss Van Lew and her mother greeted them in the front parlor. "My dear Miss Bergstrom," she said, taking Gerda's hands in hers. Her dark hair was pulled back into a French knot, with curly wisps framing her face. She had a strong nose and chin, and her gaze was steady, clear, and intelligent. "It is good to meet you at last, after such a lengthy and beneficial correspondence."

"The benefit has been all mine, I believe," said Gerda, smiling. "I cannot tell you how grateful I am — how grateful Mrs. Granger and I both are — that you're willing to help us."

"I'm sure you've put yourself at considerable risk for our sakes," Charlotte added. "Your letters have been such a comfort to me throughout these long months. I'm grateful to you beyond my ability to express."

Miss Van Lew smiled wryly. "We'll see if there's any need for gratitude later." She called for a servant to bring tea. Gerda, her memory prompted, offered her the sack of coffee beans Mr. Bastwick had provided, but insisted that she save it for another occasion for her and her mother to enjoy.

As they drank their tea, Miss Van Lew prepared them for their visit to the prison, warning that they had never witnessed such horrid conditions or seen men treated so brutally. They would avoid the worst of it, she believed, since they would meet Major Turner in his office and not enter the prisoners' rooms, as Miss Van Lew had on many occasions. The guards might be abrupt with them or impudent or indifferent, depending upon which were on duty. "You are a lovely little thing," Miss Van Lew remarked, scrutinizing Charlotte. "Your charms may soften the major's heart and encourage him to grant your request. If he refuses, a few pretty tears might win him over, if you could muster them up."

"That should not be a problem," said Charlotte, her voice trembling.

"Money also has persuasive charms," Miss Van Lew added. "Preferably Union dollars or silver."

"That will not be a problem either," said Gerda, earning her a puzzled glance from Charlotte, who was unaware of the purse she had hidden inside her skirts.

"Good," said Miss Van Lew briskly. "If Major Turner releases Dr. Granger, we should get him to the buggy and depart immediately, before the major has an opportunity to change his mind. I should warn you, ladies, you will find Dr. Granger much changed. The prison is harsh and unyielding, but please endeavor to conceal your distress when you see him."

"Then you are confident this Major Turner will grant our request?" asked Charlotte.

Miss Van Lew hesitated. "I am fairly confident he will let you see your husband. More than that, I do not know. Do you understand? Are you prepared to see him only to bid him farewell again?"

Charlotte was quiet for a moment. "No."

Gerda shot her a look of utter surprise. She had expected Charlotte to say that she would be thankful for even a moment with her husband. It was what Gerda would have said.

"No?" echoed Miss Van Lew.

"No." Charlotte straightened in her seat. "I am prepared to petition Major Turner relentlessly until he grants my request. I have no intention of leaving Libby Prison without my husband."

Gerda stared at her, dumbfounded, but Miss Van Lew smiled approvingly. "I admire your determination. Let us see if it bears fruit." She rose and sent her maid to tell the driver to prepare the buggy.

Soon they were on their way through the streets of Richmond, traveling south toward the James River and then west parallel to it. Gerda recognized the former warehouse at once from Miss Van Lew's descriptions — three stories of strong brick walls and barred windows surrounded by Confederate soldiers on guard.

They approached the front entrance until their way was barred and they were obliged to leave the buggy and proceed on foot. Miss Van Lew, a heavy basket on her arm, told Gerda and Charlotte to follow her and stay close. At the main gate, she spoke briefly with the sentinels, who recognized her from her frequent visits and knew she was allowed to enter. Gerda shuddered with foreboding as she passed through the gates and crossed the yard toward the front entrance. The prison gave off an air of palpable anguish and suffering, and she thought she heard men crying out in despair through the barred windows.

Inside, a lieutenant in gray stood in the foyer conversing with two guards, issuing them their orders for the day. He turned at the sound of the women's approach, his eyebrows rising in recognition. "Well, if it isn't the fair Miss Van Lew," he said in a Kentucky drawl. "What brings you here today? More misspent desire to comfort the Yankee rabble rather than our own boys?"

Miss Van Lew smiled. "Good morning, Lieutenant Todd. As you well know, our boys are not held captive here or I would surely do whatever I could for them too. I daresay this will surprise you, but I have nothing for the prisoners today, although I do have this good gingerbread." From her basket she took a loaf wrapped in cheese-cloth. "I seem to recall it is your favorite."

The lieutenant's face lit up as he accepted the loaf. "You recall correctly, miss."

"I have gifts for Major Turner as well. I wondered if you might take us to him."

"He's very busy."

"Yes, of course he is, which is why I've brought him some tasty delicacies to ease the burden of his labors." Miss Van Lew drew back the corner of the cloth covering the basket and nodded in satisfaction. "I can only imagine how disappointed he would be if he learned that someone had prevented me from delivering my gift. You know what a temper he has."

The lieutenant eyed Gerda and Charlotte for a moment before his gaze traveled to the basket, and then to his own gift of fragrant gingerbread, its warm and homey smell utterly incongruous with their stark surroundings. "I'm sure he'd be willing to make time for you and your friends," he said, placing one hand on the hilt of the sword strapped to his waist and gesturing down the hallway with the other. The women followed him to an office and waited outside while the lieutenant went to see if the major would receive them.

"You do know who that warden is, don't you?" Miss Van Lew murmured when they were alone. When Gerda and Charlotte shook their heads, she said, "That is Lieutenant David Humphreys Todd, half brother to Mary Todd Lincoln and brother-in-law to our dear president."

Astonished, Gerda had no time to reply, for Lieutenant Todd returned and announced that the commandant was willing to see them. They were escorted into an office that smelled strongly of cloves and tobacco smoke, with a window overlooking a high-fenced yard where the prisoners should have been allowed exercise. A young, clean-shaven man rose from his desk when the ladies entered, his spurred boot heels faintly jingling. He was not very tall, but he had an imperious manner no doubt cultivated by his authority over the lives and deaths of many far more superior men. Miss Van Lew introduced him as Major Thomas

Pratt Turner, he smiled and offered a slight bow, and they seated themselves.

Gerda could see at once that the commandant was wary of the Richmond socialite, and yet not immune to her charms. He welcomed the gifts of blackberry preserves, buttermilk biscuits, and cherry cordial, but after admiring the basket, he sat back with a small smile, knowing Miss Van Lew would ask a favor in return. Evidently he had not expected such an audacious request, however, for his smile gave way to an incredulous laugh. "My dear Miss Van Lew," he said, "you must know I cannot release prisoners simply on my own inclinations."

"Of course you could, if you wished," she replied, her charming smile never wavering. "Aren't you the commandant? What's one prisoner more or less to the Confederacy?"

"There are protocols of military order to follow. I don't have the authority to release a prisoner of war to his wife." He glanced at Charlotte. "No matter how impressed I might be by the great distance she has traveled to reach him."

"Well, if you aren't authorized to make such decisions, you should be," said Miss Van Lew staunchly. "Who would know better than you when it is prudent to release a prisoner or move him to another cell or transfer him to another prison? Dr. Granger is scheduled to be sent to Macon soon, isn't that right?"

Charlotte drew in a shaky breath, and the major, watching her, hesitated before replying. "Yes, that is so, although the exact date has not been set."

Miss Van Lew tapped her chin with a forefinger, thoughtfully. "When I consider the overcrowded conditions and the expense of feeding and transporting even a single soldier, it seems to me that the Confederate army would be glad to be relieved of the burden of Dr. Granger." She fixed her gaze on the major. "If you should benefit as well, what would be the harm?"

The major sat back in his chair and crossed his legs, resting his right ankle on his left knee. He studied Miss Van Lew, and then let his gaze rest upon Charlotte, whose tearful brown eyes were fixed on him beseechingly. His eyes flicked to Gerda for a moment, and Gerda felt herself summarily dismissed as he returned his attention to Miss Van Lew. "You make a fair point," he said evenly. "But the benefit must be great indeed, considering the significance of the favor and the risk to myself."

Charlotte clasped her hands so tightly that her knuckles whitened. She was trembling, and her voice shook as she said, "Major Turner, sir, I am prepared to offer you a token of my esteem and gratitude in exchange for my husband's freedom." She reached into her purse and placed a small sack on the desk before him. It hit the surface with a musical, metallic clinking.

The major did not examine it. "What is this, my dear?"

Charlotte sat ramrod straight, clutching her empty purse in her lap. "It is two hundred dollars in gold and silver coins."

The major looked genuinely regretful. "I'm very sorry, but that will not suffice. I'm sure you have no idea what consequences I might face if my superiors discover that I've released your husband without going through the proper channels or you would not have asked me to do so much for so little."

"That's not Confederate script in that bag," Miss Van Lew reminded him. "Come what may, gold and silver will remain valuable currency."

Major Turner's thick eyebrows rose. "Are you suggesting the Confederacy might not emerge victorious from this conflict?"

"I think we both know which way the wind blows. It may indeed be time to batten down one's own hatches."

The major frowned and stroked his beardless chin. For a moment, Gerda held her breath, praying that he would agree, but then he shook his head. "This will buy you two hours with your husband," he told Charlotte, and then indicated the basket with a nod. "I will arrange a private room, and you may enjoy Miss Van Lew's gift in the solace of each other's company. I will also offer you my assurances that I will see that your husband henceforth receives preferential treatment."

Charlotte's eyes brimmed with tears. "Is there nothing more you can do for me?"

The major rose, shaking his head. "I'm very sorry, my dear."

"Major Turner," said Miss Van Lew reprovingly. "Two hours with her husband, after risking such a long and hazardous journey and giving you her life savings, with nothing left over for herself and her children? You do realize, don't you, that by keeping her husband and sending him on to Georgia, you are both dooming her to widowhood and leaving her nothing to live on?"

Charlotte buried her face in her hands and shook with sobs. The major hesitated and sank back into his chair. Gerda smoldered with silent fury. How dare that little man barter for Jonathan's life and freedom? How dare he play God, that arrogant boy, deciding all of their fates based upon his own whims?

"How much?" Gerda snapped. "What's the price for Dr. Granger's freedom?"

The major regarded her as if he had forgotten she was there or had not realized she could speak. "Why, you truly are a Yankee woman. No social niceties from you, just straight to the point."

She knew that, not too far beneath the surface, he didn't want sweet manners; he wanted to fatten his purse. "You must have a price, so name it."

The major studied her. "I couldn't possibly release him for less that one thousand dollars."

Miss Van Lew drew in a breath sharply. "Major Turner, let us at least be reasonable —"

"Would you avert your eyes, sir?" interrupted Gerda, rising.

The major's brow furrowed as he looked up at her. "I beg your pardon?"

"Avert your eyes. Or turn around." She traced circles in the air to indicate the motion he should emulate. "Yes, turning around would be best, I think."

Hesitantly, he did as she bade him. The

moment his back was turned, Gerda reached under her skirts, unpinned the heavy purse, withdrew three hundred dollars, and slipped them into her pockets. Then she emptied the rest of the purse onto the major's desk in a shower of gold and silver coins and Union greenbacks. All the while she silently prayed for the Lord to deliver Joanna from slavery through some other means, because Gerda would no longer be able to purchase her freedom.

Startled, the major turned and stared for one brief moment of shock before hastily damming the flood of money with his arms to prevent it from spilling onto the floor.

"You may count it if you wish," said Gerda crisply.

"No," he said, glancing at the door as he swept coins and bills into a desk drawer. "I don't believe that will be necessary."

"We have a buggy waiting. Shall we fetch Dr. Granger ourselves?" inquired Miss Van Lew.

"I have to prepare his papers." The major stuffed the last bills into the drawer and quickly shut it. "He will be escorted to the main gate in fifteen minutes."

"We will be waiting." Miss Van Lew rose and gestured for Gerda and Charlotte to do the same. Charlotte breathlessly murmured her thanks, and then they quickly departed.

"What if they don't bring him?" asked Gerda as they hurried down the hall to the front door.

"Oh, they'll bring him, all right," said Miss Van Lew, smiling in satisfaction. She nodded to the guards as they crossed the yard, and soon they had passed through the gate and were hurrying down the street to the waiting buggy. As they climbed on board, she urged her driver to pull up to the front gate, explaining to the sentries that they were following Major Turner's express commands.

The minutes passed, each interminably long. Charlotte could not stop shaking. Without realizing she did it, Gerda reached for her hand and squeezed it. Charlotte squeezed back even harder, her eyes fixed on the front door of the prison.

And then it opened, and then two soldiers stepped out, a gaunt man in tattered Union blue stumbling between them, his beard unkempt, his head bowed, squinting in the sunlight. With a sob, Charlotte burst from the buggy and ran to meet him. Gerda and Miss Van Lew quickly followed, and together the three women supported him across the yard, through the gate, and into the buggy. The door was not yet closed when Miss Van Lew ordered her driver to hurry away with all haste. He nodded and cracked his whip, and the horse leapt away. Jonathan collapsed into Charlotte's embrace as the buggy sped six blocks to Miss Van Lew's home, where she disembarked and urged them not to stop until they reached the Whitehall residence outside the city.

"Thank you," Charlotte told her, reaching through the window to clasp her hand. "Thank you with all my heart."

"It was my great pleasure." Then Miss Van Lew turned to Gerda, her eyes twinkling. "When you reached beneath your skirts back there in the major's office, I thought you might produce a revolver."

"I hadn't thought of that," said Gerda. "Perhaps next time."

Miss Van Lew's laughter rang out until it was lost in the clattering of the horse's hooves as they raced off.

In the jolting carriage, Jonathan lay across Charlotte's lap, eyes closed, arms clasped about her slender waist. "My darling," he murmured hoarsely. "Oh, how I missed you, my love. This must be a dream."

Charlotte stroked his hair and bent to kiss him. "It's no dream, my darling. I'm here. We're going home."

Throat constricting, Gerda turned her

face to the window.

Jonathan had not spared one glance for her, not one. He clung to Charlotte as if he had feared he would never see her again and could not believe his good fortune to be in her arms again. He murmured her name as if to him her presence was all the evidence he needed to believe in the goodness and grace of God. There was no pretense or artifice in his love for her, or in her devotion to him. Perhaps it was something new, borne of his long months of suffering. Perhaps it had always been there, but Gerda had not allowed herself to see it.

But it was there, and having seen it in its most unadorned form, she could not deny its existence.

She watched through a veil of tears as the city gave way to countryside. Jonathan was safe, and restored to his beloved, just as she had prayed he would be, not knowing what that would mean for her.

Whatever happened between North and South in the days to come, her own long-standing war with the truth was over. She had lost, and she had won.

EPILOGUE

1868

Snow clung to the meadows, but already buds had appeared on the tall elms along the banks of Elm Creek and upon the slender branches of the young apple trees Gerda had planted west of the new barn. Anneke hoped they would thrive, and that someday David, Stephen, and Albert would climb in their branches, and Lydia would adorn herself with a crown of their fragrant blossoms. Gerda had often proclaimed that her delicious apple strudel would taste even better if made from fruit grown on their own soil. Hans always teased that she was welcome to make as many of the tender pastries as she needed to prove her theory, and he would do his part by eating them.

Balancing seven-month-old Lydia on her hip, Anneke peered out the window toward the corral, where the nine-year-old twins were holding ropes and harnesses for their father and listening intently to his instructions. Little Albert, all of six, had climbed the fence for a better view. Anneke could not see his scowl from that distance, but she knew he could not be happy, ordered to remain outside the corral for his own safety until Hans could closely watch him. Stubborn, sturdy Albert had too much of his father in him to bear even a brief exclusion well, but Hans had been obliged to lay down the law the previous autumn when he had gone to the barn at dawn to do his morning chores only to discover his youngest son happily trotting around the corral bareback on a colt that had not yet been broken to ride. Hans had been proud to discover his son's natural gift with horses but had also been alarmed enough to fix a bolt on the stable door out of the boys' reach.

"Poor Albert," said Anneke, shifting Lydia to her other hip. "Why don't we go outside and keep him company? What do you think, darling?"

The baby beamed, showing her two new bottom teeth, so Anneke took that as assent. She bundled them up in their warm wraps, because the day was chilly despite the thin sunshine of early spring. Singing nursery rhymes as they went, Anneke carried Lydia across the bridge over Elm Creek and past the barn. Hans and their neighbors had built it upon the foundation of the barn that had been destroyed three and a half years before, as soon as the scoundrels who had burned it had paid their court-ordered restitution. Rather, the three eldest had paid; the youngest had died within weeks of joining the cavalry, and the Bergstroms had asked the court not to seek payment of the debt from his grieving family. Restitution and six months in jail was a lighter sentence than Anneke thought the men deserved, but the judge had blamed their rash actions on an excess of loyalty to the Union and had been inclined to show mercy. The Bergstrom's stolen cows, discovered in the eldest raider's pasture, had been returned, but the horses had been swallowed up in the war, never to be found. Only the generosity of their friends, neighbors, and distant loyal customers had allowed Hans to save Bergstrom Thoroughbreds. Gifts of foals born of the horses Hans had sold them enabled him to fill his rebuilt stables, and after three difficult years, Hans's confidence that Bergstrom Thoroughbreds would recover had finally returned. Hans often declared that necessity had obliged him to breed the horses differently than he would have otherwise, resulting in better, faster, healthier offspring. The farm was stronger than ever after passing through the forge of adversity, he claimed. He said this about many things, including their nation, three years past the war but still struggling to rebuild. He said this about their marriage, which, Anneke believed, fared much better than the nation.

Albert spotted them as they approached, jumped down from the fence, and came to meet them, his boots crunching as they broke through the thin, icy crust on top of the snow. His lower lip was thrust out, and his fair hair tumbled over a furrowed brow. "Father won't let me ride unless he holds the bridle," he complained. "He says I have to wait until he's done with David and Stephen."

"I'm sure it won't be much longer," Anneke assured him.

"David and Stephen can ride by themselves. Why can't I?"

"They're older than you, darling."

Albert sighed heavily. In sympathy, Lydia reached out to him, and as he patiently held still so she could pat his face with her mittened hands, on a sudden impulse, she grabbed his knitted cap and threw it to the ground. Albert tried not to smile, but he grinned as he picked up the hat and tugged it back on his head. "Silly baby sister," he said.

"I'm sure Lydia sees you riding as your father holds the bridle and wishes she were old enough to do that," remarked Anneke.

Albert considered. "Maybe," he said, then turned and ran back to the corral, shouting, "Is it my turn yet?"

Be patient, Anneke wanted to call after him, but she smiled as she watched him run through the snow to his father and brother and beloved horses. She understood his eagerness. Like Albert and Hans, she too believed that the family's best days yet awaited them.

Constance stood on her front porch, wrapped in her shawl, listening to the welcome sound of the icicles dripping as they melted. At last, spring was coming. There was a hint of warmth in the air, and the daffodils she had planted around the house had poked their yellow heads through the last lingering patches of snow. Soon she could put in her kitchen garden. She smiled, thinking of the smell of rich, freshly turned soil and the taste of sweet snap peas and new potatoes. She was tired of turnips stored all winter long in the cellar. She had run out of ways to dress them up, and she wished she had something more appealing to put on the table, especially when company called, but turnips would have to do for a while longer.

Her eldest son, George, was the only member of the family who was sorry to see the winter end. He was smitten with a pretty girl from Grangerville he had met at the Harvest Dance the previous autumn at Union Hall, and every Sunday he had taken her riding in the cutter he and Abel had built. The Wrights had no buggy, and George could not take a young lady riding in their old wagon, so the coming of spring meant the end of George's courting for the duration of fair weather. Abel teased that he would be too busy on the farm to squire young ladies around the valley anyway, and George glumly agreed. He loved the farm, but he was surely thinking of other young men nearby whose parents did own buggies and who might begin calling on the girl in his absence. Constance figured if the girl in question couldn't wait for George one summer, she wasn't likely to stick with him for a lifetime, and it would be best to find out sooner rather than later.

Joseph didn't have time for courtship, nor did Constance believe he was old enough for it, although girls certainly caught his eye at school and at church. When he turned fourteen, he had begun an apprenticeship with Dr. Granger, accompanying him on his calls and assisting him on simple procedures. After two years, he was certain that he wanted to become a doctor, and Jonathan confirmed that he had the aptitude and the perseverance necessary for the profession. Jonathan had promised to write letters of recommendation and call on all his professional contacts to ensure Joseph's admittance to a prestigious medical school when he turned eighteen. When Constance expressed skepticism that a place like Harvard Medical School, Jonathan's alma mater, would allow a colored man to enroll, Jonathan assured her that a few colored men were studying there at that very moment, and that her only concern should be to encourage Joseph in his studies and begin saving for his tuition. It would not be easy, and Joseph was all but certain to encounter objections and hostility along the way, but if he wanted it badly enough, it would be possible.

Constance was not worried about either of her sons. The death of slavery had not brought about immediate equality and acceptance for people of color, but their time was coming. She knew it, and her sons knew it, and they had learned what good things came from faith, determination, and perseverance. They had their father's example to thank for everything they knew about persisting when almost all hope was gone and the obstacles seemed insurmountable.

The Wright family was truly blessed. Constance had lost neither husband nor sons to the war, and even Ephraim, Abel's brother-in-law captured during the Confederate invasion of Pennsylvania, had returned home safely after the war. His nearly two years in slavery had scarred him, but he had lived, just as Abel had survived his own more grievous, more visible wounds. With the help and advice of other wounded veterans, Abel had adapted tools and learned his chores anew so he could run the dairy farm almost as he always had. Thanks to George, the farm was more prosperous than ever, the herd healthy and prolific, the customers for their cheese, butter, and milk steadily increasing.

Another man might have been content with that, but Abel, always eager for a challenge, found inspiration in the pages of the *Soldier's Friend,* a magazine whose purpose was to help veterans adapt to civilian life. Even before the war ended, the editor, concerned with the plight of soldiers whose amputations prevented them from finding lucrative work, sponsored a penmanship contest for "the Left-Armed Soldiers of the Union." Members of this Left-Armed Corps were invited to submit a manuscript, either original compositions or copies of other authors' works such as poetry or political speeches. Cash prizes would be awarded for the finest penmanship, but the ultimate goal was for the winning manuscripts to attract the attention of potential employers.

Constance watched Abel as he mulled over the contest, and she was not at all surprised when, a few days later, he took out pen, ink, and paper and began practicing writing with his left hand, copying over proverbs and psalms. His first attempts were barely legible, but as the weeks passed, his shaky letters grew steadier, his spidery words more solid. Within a few months, his left-handed writing was as clear and precise as his right-handed penmanship had once been, but he would not be satisfied until it surpassed his right-handed writing to become as fluid and elegant as what he figured would be necessary to win the contest. When the time came to create his manuscript, he set the Bible verses aside and wrote a simple but eloquent account of his travails as he tried to enlist in the Union

Army. The final sentences, in which he proudly described his first days as a member of the 6th USCT, brought tears to Constance's eyes. She hoped the judges would be similarly moved.

She should have known better. Within two weeks, the manuscript was returned with a letter expressing the judges' regrets that Abel had been disqualified from the contest. As the purpose of the contest was to help veteran amputees obtain gainful employment, the organizers were obliged to limit it to veterans who could be hired for clerical positions, and as a man of color, Abel was unlikely to be considered for such work.

Abel had the farm and his carpentry. He had not entered the contest in hopes of finding clerical work but for the prize money, which he could certainly put to good use, and for the challenge of improving himself. Though disgusted by his exclusion, he took heart from another letter that arrived a day later, a personal note from one of the judges condemning the decision to disqualify him, which the judge declared was by no means unanimous. "Your penmanship was as fine as any of the submissions we received," he wrote, "but if the purpose of the contest was to discover the best example of Prose rather than Penmanship, your manuscript would have ranked among the very best. Your account of your patriotic determination to serve your country was powerful and inspiring, and I would greatly desire to read more of your work if you are inclined to put pen to paper again."

Abel chuckled and put the letter away, but when Constance mentioned it to Dorothea a few days later to amuse her bookish friend, Dorothea's eyes widened. The man who had written to Abel was a renowned editor and abolitionist, and if he said Abel's writing was good, it surely was. "If Abel has any inclination whatsoever to pen his memoirs," Dorothea said, "he should send the finished manuscript to this gentleman as soon as the ink dries."

Constance repeated Dorothea's message to her husband, who laughed and shook his head and said that he was a farmer, not a writer. So Constance enlisted the help of her sons, who urged their father to write down his memories of the war, if for no one else but his family and descendants. Constance reminded him of Frederick Douglass's narrative and how it had inspired countless thousands of people, white and colored alike, to fight for the abolitionist cause. She reminded him of the battles that remained to be won — not the least of which was securing the right to vote and all the other privileges soldiers like Abel had earned through their service to the country. "Your story could inspire change just as Mr. Douglass's did," she told him. "Think of what that would mean to people of color everywhere. Think of what it would mean for our sons."

Eventually, they won him over. Every evening after supper, and earlier in the afternoon if he finished his chores in good time, he could be found at the desk in the front room, writing, refreshing his memory by perusing letters he had sent home from the front, or staring off into space, lost in reflection. Six months after the war ended, he finished his manuscript and sent it off to the editor in New York. For weeks he heard nothing, and then on one fortuitous day, a telegram arrived with an offer to publish his book.

Recalling that blessed day, Constance watched from the front porch and smiled as she spotted Abel emerging from the barn, the three reporters from *Harper's Weekly* in his wake. It was his own private joke to show unsuspecting admirers from the cities how the Hero of Wright's Pass and the Sage of the 6th Colored really spent his days — not at his desk contemplating political and social theory but milking cows and making cheese. Too many white intellectuals emphasized how Abel differed from other colored men, how his newly discovered literary gifts set him apart, but Abel was wary of the dangers that could come from perceiving him as an anomaly among his race. He wanted everyone to know that he was like every other colored man — a husband, a father, a man desiring to use his God-given talents to support his family, improve himself, and contribute to his community — or rather, that every other colored man was like him. The rights and privileges he had earned, they too deserved.

A few months earlier, an article in *The New York Times* had lauded Abel's second book, an account of his Underground Railroad years, as "astonishing and riveting." These reporters looked rather astonished, Constance thought, as the celebrated writer introduced them to his favorite cows, and they seemed riveted by the desire to scrape the questionable muck from their fine shoes.

She smothered a laugh and waved to her husband, summoning him and their guests in for supper.

Gerda drove the chaise into Water's Ford

and stopped by Prudence's seamstress shop for a chat before making her customary visit to the post office. The postmaster smiled when he saw her enter, but she lingered near the front window until his other customers departed. Then she approached, took two jars of blackberry jam from her basket, and set them on the counter. "Good afternoon, Henry," she said. "Here's the delivery I promised, and right on time."

"Early, in fact," he said, holding up one of the jars to the light streaming in through the windows, and admiring the color. "My sons will be delighted. Thank you, Gerda."

"You're quite welcome." Gerda liked Henry's sons very much, and his daughter, Harriet, had become a dear friend, especially after she joined the Union Quilters. Gerda would be the first to admit that she was quite susceptible to flattery, and when his sons had proclaimed that her jam was the best they had ever tasted, they had won themselves a regular supply.

"I have something for you too," the postmaster said, reaching beneath the counter. "Something I think you've wanted for a long time."

"The vote for women?"

"No, I'm sorry. That's not within my power to provide." He set a letter on the counter before her. "This came from Virginia this morning."

"A letter from Miss Van Lew?" Gerda's longtime correspondent had fallen on difficult times since the end of the war. After it came out that she had not only cared for the Union prisoners at Libby but had also spied for General Grant throughout the war, the entire city of Richmond had ostracized her. Gerda hoped that if General Grant won the presidential election in the fall, he would find some way to help the brave woman. In Gerda's opinion, it was an outrage that a good, loyal woman like Miss Van Lew could suffer in the wake of a Union victory, and a cowardly Copperhead like Peter Gray Meek could be rewarded by being elected to the Pennsylvania state assembly even after being arrested five times during the war and accused of disloyalty, running the gamut from publishing improper political statements to high treason. Sometimes justice eluded the just.

Henry shook his head. "See for yourself, my dear. This letter didn't come from Richmond."

Gerda glanced at the postmark — and gasped to see that the letter had been sent from Wentworth County, Virginia. Astonished, she looked up at Henry, who seemed almost as eager to learn the letter's contents as she was. Quickly she opened the envelope, withdrew a single page, and read it aloud.

February 21, 1868

Dear Miss Bergstrom,

Please accept my sincere apologies for sending but a single letter in response to the great many you have sent to my family. It is unfortunate that your remarkable perseverance and prolificacy as a letter-writer will have been in vain, for I regret that I do not have the answers you seek. I cannot dispute that my husband once kept a servant named Joanna in his service, but I have no idea what became of her after she left us. My husband customarily brought chastened, wayward servants back to our plantation at Greenfields in order to impress upon our other negroes the sad fate of the runaway, but these unfortunate few would remain with us only a short while after that. Since servants proven faithless were useless to him, my husband would be obliged to sell them, usually to our relations in Georgia or South Carolina. I confess that I do not recall whether the servant named Joanna faced these consequences; my husband kept so many negroes that I did not know them all, and I doubt I would have recognized the one in question in any case.

I regret that I am unable to offer you more help in your search. It saddens me to chasten your enthusiasm, but every letter you may send us in the days to come, no matter how heartfelt or elegantly phrased, will meet with the same result. I have nothing to tell you about Joanna, nor shall I in the future. If I may say so, delicately, perhaps the time has come for you to abandon your fruitless quest before the perpetual disappointment takes its toll on your health.

I remain most cordially yours,
Mrs. Josiah Chester
Formerly of Greenfields Plantation
Wentworth County, Virginia

Gerda read the letter over again, silently. "How could she claim to be unable to recognize Joanna?" she asked. "Joanna was a house slave, her own seamstress."

"Mrs. Chester does seem rather disingenuous," said Henry. "Do you intend to take her advice?"

"You mean give up my search before it

takes its toll on my health?" scoffed Gerda. "Of course not. In fact, this new information might invigorate my quest. It should not be terribly difficult to determine who these Chester relations in Georgia or South Carolina might be. Now that war and slavery are no impediment, I might be able to find Joanna at last."

"I admire your determination." Henry gave her a slight bow. "As always, the resources of the United States Postal Service are at your disposal."

Gerda laughed. "Thank you, Henry."

"Incidentally, Dr. Granger received a parcel from Alabama yesterday. Do you know what it contained? Could there be a connection to your Joanna?"

Puzzled, Gerda shook her head. "I don't believe so. Joanna met Dr. Granger only once, and I doubt she caught his name." Then the full meaning of his words and tone sank in. "Henry. You of all people know that Dr. Granger and I rarely speak, and only when obliged to. How would I know what any parcel of his might contain?"

"Of course," he said, slightly abashed. "Forgive me a momentary loss of reason."

"There's nothing to forgive," she assured him. "But really now, is it proper for you to share information about your other postal customers in this way?"

"Only with you, my dear," he replied. "You know very well that secrets are safe with me."

"I know." He had earned her trust, and her trust was not lightly given. "Will we be seeing you and the children at Elm Creek Farm for supper Saturday afternoon?"

"As always. You know we wouldn't miss it for the world."

"I know," said Gerda again, and smiled as she left the post office, the long-awaited letter in her basket.

Dorothea sat on the quilt in the shade of the tall oaks, distracted from her writing by the pleasure of watching Abigail soar high into the air on the swing Thomas and Jonathan had hung for her when she was just a baby. She pumped her legs to propel herself forward and back, her long golden braids streaming out behind her, then falling lightly upon her shoulders, again and again.

How Thomas would have adored her.

With a wistful ache in her heart, she returned her attention to the papers on the writing case her brother had given her after the war, saying that she would make much better use of it. "My travels are over," he had declared as he presented it to her. "I intend to remain close to home for the rest of my life."

Dorothea indeed traveled more than her brother, far more than she had before the war, to attend rallies and conferences devoted to women's rights and woman suffrage, but she rarely carried the writing case with her, for she always found a suitable table to use when she wrote letters home. Instead, the writing case served her well on lovely spring days like that one, when warm breezes and sunshine and birdsong called her outside to work and enjoy her beloved daughter at play.

She dipped her pen in the inkwell, eager to finish the first draft of her speech before the next meeting of the Union Quilters. They indulged her by listening to her read her work and offering suggestions for revisions. Their advice never failed to improve her work.

Before she could touch pen to paper again, she heard a buggy coming up the road. "Uncle Jonathan! Aunt Charlotte," Abigail exclaimed, leaping from the swing in an act of heart-stopping daring. Before Dorothea could beg her to be more careful, the seven-year-old was off and running to meet the buggy. Dorothea tucked her papers into the writing case and followed, wondering what had brought Jonathan and Charlotte for an unexpected visit.

They greeted one another with hugs and kisses. "Where are the children?" asked Dorothea, seeing only the youngest baby in Charlotte's arms. A box rested on the backseat, where Dorothea had expected to see Abigail's cousins.

"Home with their grandma," said Charlotte as Dorothea took the baby so Jonathan could help her from the buggy.

"We won't be staying long," Jonathan explained, reaching into the backseat for the box. "We only came to deliver this."

"What is it?" asked Abigail eagerly. "Is it a present?"

"It's something that was sent to me but intended for your mother," her uncle explained, carrying the box to the shade of the front porch. Dorothea threw Charlotte a puzzled glance, but she merely smiled enigmatically and followed her husband to the house. Drawn by curiosity, Dorothea fell in step behind them.

When Jonathan urged her to sit, Dorothea tucked her skirts beneath her and seated herself on a rocking chair. The box was addressed to Jonathan and the seal had been broken. "Are you sure this is for me?" she asked.

"Read the letter first," said Charlotte, and Jonathan reached into his coat pocket and handed her an envelope. "It came with the parcel."

With a sudden stir of anxiety, Dorothea hesitated, then steeled herself and took out the letter.

February 10, 1868

Dear Dr Granger,

I write to you on behalf of my husband, Private Satterwhite Wilson, who you tended so kindly in the seminary hospital after the battle of Gettysburg. As you may recall he was terrible injured in the fighting and blinded and thus I take pen in hand as he cannot write so well. He has never forgotten your kindness and credits you with the saving of his life as well as the man married to your sister who carried him several miles off the hill they now call Little Round Top. Your brother in law gave my suffering husband the gift of his quilt upon which after laundering I discovered stitched into it the words, Made by Dorothea Granger Nelson for her beloved husband, Thomas Nelson, in our sixth year of marriage, 1858. Two Bears Farm,

Creek's Crossing, Pennsylvania. Now that there is peace between North and South my husband thought it proper to return it to Mr Nelson who is to us a hero and a true Christian. However our postmaster could not find the town of Creek's Crossing anywhere on any map so he thinks it must be a very small town. We despaired until my husband thought of you and got your name and town from a GAR post. He asks that you would do him one more kindness and return this quilt which was a great comfort to him in his hour of need to its rightful owner along with his sincere thanks.

Your brother in law may also recollect that my husband told him if he ever comes to Dallas County Alabama he must look up Mr Archibald Hammock who would make him a fine pair of boots. Mr Hammock has since moved to Texas but if Mr Nelson does come to Alabama he will find that my husband has become a fine boot maker in his own right despite his blindness and he would be very happy indeed to make him the best pair of boots he ever wore. He also would like to extend the invitation to you Dr Granger for without you both he surely would have perished in the war.

I add my thanks to you good men for your kindliness to my husband though he was Confederate and you Yankee.

I remain yours most sincerely,
Mrs Malinda Jane Holmes Wilson
Dallas County, Alabama

Stunned, Dorothea let the hand holding the letter fall to her lap. She looked up at Jonathan and Charlotte, her throat constricting.

"Go on," said Charlotte gently. "Open the box."

As if in a dream, Dorothea pulled back the lid and reached inside, tears filling her eyes when her fingers brushed soft cotton. She unfurled the folded bundle upon her lap, scarcely believing her eyes. The Dove in the Window quilt was not quite as she remembered it, worn and faded from hard use, but the triangles and squares of Turkey red and Prussian blue and sun-bleached muslin were the same. She knew it to be her own work, just as she knew that although Thomas had gone on before her, his love for her endured. He would live on in her heart and in their daughter until they met again in a better world, a world where

peace reigned and no war could ever part
them.

ABOUT THE AUTHOR

Jennifer Chiaverini is the author of the Elm Creek Quilts series as well as four collections of quilt projects inspired by her novels, and is the designer of the Elm Creek Quilts fabric lines from Red Rooster fabrics. She lives with her husband and sons in Madison, Wisconsin.